Grandpa's Legacy

By

Charles Tindell

Cut Above Books
Published by Second Wind Publishing, LLC.
Kernersville

Cut Above Books
Second Wind Publishing, LLC
931-B South Main Street, Box 145
Kernersville, NC 27284

This book is a work of fiction. Names, characters, locations and events are either a product of the author's imagination, fictitious or used fictitiously. Any resemblance to any event, locale or person, living or dead, is purely coincidental.

First Cut Above Books edition published February 2013.
Cut Above Books, Running Angel, and all production design are trademarks of Second Wind Publishing, used under license.

For information regarding bulk purchases of this book, digital purchase and special discounts, please contact the publisher at www.secondwindpublishing.com

Cover design by Tracy Beltran

Manufactured in the United States of America
ISBN 978-1-935171-88-1

From Second Wind Publishing
by Charles Tindell

Grandpa's Legacy

www.secondwindpublishing.com

Dedicated to my grandchildren

Julia, Alexander, Benjamin, and Joshua

ACKNOWLEDGEMENTS

I owe a debt of gratitude to the family who raised me: my mother, Virg; my Aunt, Wanda; and my grandfather, Paul.

While this is a work of fiction, it is fiction based on my experiences growing up on the North Side of Minneapolis. Many, but not all, of the depictions in this story come from real life experiences.

I thank Mike Simpson of Second Wind Publishers for having faith in my story and for his guidance and direction.

Much appreciation goes to my wife, Carol, for her support. Appreciation is also given to my sons, Scott, Andrew, and Robert for being loving and supportive.

Last, but not least, gratitude and appreciation to my readers. My hope is that the legacy you read about will be one that you will pass on to your loved ones and friends.

Prologue

Adam Trexler gnawed on his lip until it drew blood as he watched Danny Logan and his two pals use a baseball bat on Frank. Waiting in the night shadows near the rear entrance of Skelly's Liquor Store, he saw and heard everything in the adjacent gravel parking lot. Danny glanced over to where he waited, nodding as though to say, *Hey man, don't worry. We're kickin' his ass good.* He dreaded the moment when Danny would tell him that it was okay for him to come out.

The chilly November air caused Adam to shiver. He leaned against the brick wall of the liquor store. *How had it come to this?* A bus rumbled by on Broadway. He shut his eyes and pressed the back of his head into the hardness of the bricks. The sound and smell of buses always triggered the same memory.

It had been a little over thirteen years since he and his mother stepped off a Greyhound bus late one sultry summer evening in 1946 and were met by his mother's older sister, Wanda. The tall, gangly woman frightened him. Her dark eyes rested wearily on protruding cheekbones of a long, thin face. Although she was only twenty-nine, people often guessed Wanda to be in her forties. An irregularity in her spine prevented her from standing straight, causing her to hover over others. Her childhood had been filled with nicknames, the most descriptive being *the Vulture*.

Adam looked to his mother, waiting for her to tell Wanda to stand up straight. When Wanda went to give him a hug, he instinctively clung tighter to his mother, hiding his face in her skirt. "Remember, he's only four years old," his mother had said.

The depot had been crowded that night. Along with vivid memories of bus fumes causing him to cough and wrinkle his nose, he recalled his mother and Wanda laughing when he asked what the man on the loud speaker was saying.

Walking through the depot, he had hung tightly onto his mother's hand. Images, smells, and sounds came from every direction: a soldier playing a machine that made clanging noises; an old man sleeping on a wooden bench, his body twitching; a man and woman yelling at each other, using words that Adam's mother had told him never to say; the smell of cigarettes and sweet perfume, stale popcorn, and toilets that needed flushing; the sounds of moths and other night insects beating their wings against windows; and always the man on the loudspeaker sounding as though he was holding his nose shut while talking.

He was glad when they left the building and he was able to breathe in the night air. When they reached Wanda's car his mother put him in the back seat, telling him that he could lie down. As the car pulled away, however, he stood on the seat pinching his nose and talking quietly to himself while looking out the rear window.

After a long ride, they parked the car on a side street. He and his mother walked with Wanda a half block to a street where, to his puzzlement, there were no houses. When his mother tightened her grip, he wondered if it was because of all the traffic. A bus went by and he wrinkled his nose, covering it with the fingers of his free hand. He clamped his mouth shut and tried to hold his breath. Loud noises from across the street captured his attention. People stood laughing in front of a bar, loud music spilling from its open door.

A breeze swirled bits of paper and other debris along the sidewalk prompting him to ask his mother if the "Munchies" lived here. When Wanda asked what he was talking about, Adam's mother explained that where they used to live, the streets and sidewalks were always clean. Having taken Adam to see the movie, *The Wizard of Oz*, she had told him that those little people called the Munchkins came out at night and swept the sidewalks and streets. "He calls them 'Munchies'," she had explained. Wanda looked at Adam and shook her head. "You're not going to find any Munchies on Broadway."

The entrance to Wanda's apartment building stood midway in the block, tucked between a Woolworth's and a second-hand furniture store. When he asked if they were going to live in the stores, Wanda had laughed. "Oh no, we live in the apartments above them." They climbed two flights of creaky wooden stairs. Walking down a poorly lit hallway to the back apartment where Wanda lived, Adam grabbed hold of his mother's hand as monsters lurked at him from every shadow along the way.

After they entered the three-room apartment, the sound of the door being bolted had frightened him, but not as much as what happened next. When they turned on the kitchen light, he watched in horror as oval-shaped bugs scurried to find places to hide. "They're only cockroaches. They won't hurt you," his mother had said. That night, however, he didn't want to go to sleep. When he finally lost his battle to stay awake, he dreamt he was back at the bus depot.

He wanted to find the man on the loud speaker to ask him what he was saying. Moving past the old man sleeping on the bench, past the soldier playing the machine, past everybody, he found himself in a dimly lit corridor. Although afraid, he kept walking, drawn by the sound of the man's voice. Finally, he came to a door. On the other side of the door could be heard the man's voice. Turning the knob with both hands, he slowly opened the door. The room was dark, but enough light crept in from the corridor for him to see someone sitting on a stool, facing away from him. He took a step into the room, stopped, bit his lower lip, and inched toward the person. When he got to the man, he tapped him on the back. "Mister." The man turned, and to Adam's horror, it was not a man at all but a giant oval-shaped bug.

Adam woke up screaming. His mother had quickly come and turned on the light. She tried to calm him, saying that everything was okay. After turning off the light, she lay beside him. The next morning he begged his mother for them to get back on the bus to go home. He couldn't understand why she failed to see that Broadway wasn't a nice place to live. That day he made up his mind it would never be his home.

* * *

"Hey, Adam," Danny Logan shouted. "Ya can come out

now. He won't recognize ya. Hell, he won't recognize anyone."

Adam pressed the back of his head into the brick wall. He didn't want to be there. He didn't want to see Frank. All he wanted was to run and get as far away from Broadway as he could.

Chapter 1

Illuminated by moonlight, Adam's face appeared older than his seventeen years. From his bedroom apartment window he looked down at the orange neon sign across the street sputtering its message - *Hamm's Beer on Tap.* The sign hung lopsided in the window of the Broadway Bar. A brick propped open the bar's entrance door. Music from within competed for attention with Friday night traffic. Next to the bar, a print shop stood silent. On the other side of the bar sat Jack's Meat Market, its windows plastered with white wrapping paper announcing *Fresh Beef for Sale*. Only last month, the owner had been accused of selling horse meat.

"Business as usual, I suppose," Adam had quipped to his mother at the time.

"If they shut Jack's down, we'd have no other place to go," she had responded, adding with a twinkle in her hazel eyes, "Besides, horse meat never hurt anyone. You should see some of the stuff we serve at work."

She was kidding, of course. She often bragged that Andy's Sandwich Shop served the best grub on Broadway. When she first got the waitress job at Andy's, she joked that the place wasn't much bigger than a shoebox. With eleven stools lining an L-shaped counter, and a pinball machine squeezed into a corner, her analogy wasn't far off.

Adam leaned back against the headboard of his bed. His bedroom was a haven even though he had to share it with Oscar Johnson, a man who had moved in with them seven years before. He hated the idea of Oscar living with them and had argued about it with his mother again only two days ago. When he came home from school that day, his mother was sitting at the kitchen table working a crossword puzzle. Oscar was at work. The conversation started innocently enough.

"I'm going down to the Laundromat in a little while," his

mother had said. "Will you get together the stuff you want washed?"

Adam's dirty clothes were piled on a chair in one corner of the bedroom. He found a pair of Oscar's bib overalls mixed in, smelling of whiskey. "Why does Oscar have to live here?" he yelled as he stormed back into the kitchen. "The guy's nothing but a boozer."

"That's not true. He only drinks when he gets his paycheck."

His tone turned sarcastic. "So every couple of weeks I have to put up with a drunk for the weekend. Lots of fun."

His mother stuck her pencil through her dark-brown curly hair, nestling it just above her right ear. She got up, refilled her cup of coffee, and sat down, looking at him with pleading eyes. "I'm sorry, but at least Oscar's harmless. He doesn't get mean like some people we know."

"That's not the point. Why does he have to live here? People will think that you two…"

"That what? That something is going on between us? You know me better than that. If anyone thinks that, it's their problem. My gosh, Oscar is old enough to be my father."

Adam regretted what he had implied. Although his mother had been hurt by it, he couldn't bring himself to apologize.

"Like I've told you before, Oscar lives with us because he has no family."

"Yeah, but…"

Her eyes flashed with annoyance. "But what? There's nothing more to say. Oscar's a decent man even when he's drinking. The money he gives me for staying here comes in handy."

"If that's so, why can't we get a door for the bedroom closet?" He didn't know why he brought up the closet door; it was of no significance to him. He didn't care if what they had now, a bed sheet, cut and hemmed, was serving as a door.

"I've told you that I complained to the landlord when we first moved in. And do you remember what I told you he said?" She stared at him, waiting for an answer.

Adam shifted in his chair, regretting he had brought the subject up.

"He said that he'd have to raise our rent if he put in a door and did all the other things I've asked him to do. That's why there's no door on the closet. And that's why there's no door going into the bedroom."

He hated it when his mother made things a big deal. "If we're getting money from him, why can't we get a bigger apartment? Then I can have my own bedroom."

"Don't you realize that Oscar helps pay for our rent and groceries?" she asked, her voice sounding as tired as she looked. "Without that extra money things would be a lot tougher. I'm sorry that you don't have your own bedroom, but we couldn't even afford this apartment without his help."

As he lay in his bed, his mother's words floated through his mind. Although he hated to admit it, she had been right. The only consolation was that Oscar had a railroad job that often required him to be gone for several days at a stretch. That he had to share the bedroom with the man still angered him though.

Propping a pillow, he leaned back, and thought about the apartment he had lived in most of his life. Entering the three-and-a-half room apartment from the hallway, one walked directly into a half-kitchen, barely big enough for a small stove and some cupboards. The sink stood opposite the stove. Three quick steps through the half-kitchen brought one into a larger kitchen that had space for a table pushed against one wall, three chairs, a refrigerator, and a corner desk on which the telephone sat. Additional cupboards hung above the desk. The living room was the largest of the rooms and was connected to a bedroom off to the left.

The bedroom was okay for one person, but a tight squeeze for two. His bed was to the right, pushed next to the window. The window rattled whenever a bus or truck rumbled by below. To the left of the doorway was Oscar's bed, barely far enough away from the wall to have access to the only closet. Adam's dresser stood as a barrier between them. Oscar's dresser stood against the opposite wall next to the doorway.

Although his mother called the apartment "home," it wasn't a place he took pride in. He recalled the day Bradley Ross, a grade school classmate, came to visit. Bradley lived in a nice house four blocks away from Broadway. His father owned the jewelry store up the block from Andy's.

"Is this where your mom does the cooking?" Bradley had asked when he walked into the half-kitchen.

"Yeah." Adam was too embarrassed to tell his friend that was also where he, after heating water on the stove, took sponge baths.

He and Bradley had played several games of checkers on the coffee table in the living room. Adam made up some excuse about not going into the bedroom because of not wanting to answer any questions as to who slept in the other bed. When Bradley asked where the bathroom was, Adam told him it was down the hall, explaining that they had to share a bathroom with another apartment. The next day at school, the kids snickered when Bradley told them that Adam's home had no bathroom. Adam never talked to him again.

Adam pushed Bradley from his thoughts when his mother called from the living room.

"Butch, I'm going to play some bingo before I go to work. I'll see you in the morning. Okay?"

"Good luck," he answered, knowing she would play bingo for the next three hours. He liked the idea that the bingo parlor was only a block and a half from their apartment and right next door to where she worked. That meant that he could use her car, a '50 Buick, any night he wanted.

His mother, Virg (she preferred Virg over Virginia), had called him "Butch" from the first time the nurse brought him to her in the hospital. She told the nurses that although "Adam" would be on the birth certificate, he looked like a "Butch" to her. Adam had accepted the nickname when he was younger. As he grew older, that changed. His friends soon learned not to call him that if they wanted to keep his friendship. The only persons that he tolerated calling him Butch were his mother, Wanda, his grandfather, and—reluctantly—Oscar.

Laughter from across the street now caught Adam's attention. Looking out the window, he saw two kids race past a man leaning up against the street light. The man waved at them as he took a swig from a pint of whiskey. Disgusted, he lay back on his bed and stared at the string dangling from the ceiling light bulb. For the other people who lived here, this was Broadway. It was all they ever knew and cared to know. For them, it was a way of life they accepted. He, however, would never accept it. As soon as he graduated next spring, he planned to get as far away as he could.

Although he welcomed his private time, tonight, for some reason he couldn't explain, he didn't feel like being alone. Sitting on the edge of the bed, he brushed back a shock of dark-brown hair. Not having seen Wanda for a couple of days, he decided to drop in on her. His aunt enjoyed his visits. He was six weeks into his last year of high school and she would want to hear the latest report of what it felt like being a senior.

Ever since that evening at the bus depot years ago, Wanda's affection for him had grown.

Unable to bear children, she took him into her heart as though he were her own son.

When he was younger, she often brought him bags of chips from the Old Dutch Potato Chip factory where she worked. In addition, once a week she took him to Kass' Drugstore for an ice cream cone. Throughout the years, she always pictured him as a little boy whose dark brown eyes matched the color of his hair. She still occasionally referred to him as her little boy even though, at nearly six feet, he was three inches taller than she.

As he knocked on her door, he recalled how, over the years, she said that he and his mother were lucky to have an apartment with a view of Broadway. *Yeah, some view. Littered sidewalks. Drunks. Smelly, noisy buses.*

"Who is it?"

"Adam."

"Come on in!" another voice yelled.

He had no trouble recognizing Frank's voice. Wanda had married the jerk two years before.

Suddenly wishing he hadn't come, he opened the door and walked through the living room into the kitchen. His aunt, wearing a beige terry-cloth bathrobe, sat at the table holding a wet washcloth to her mouth. She glanced at him and looked away without saying a word. Her left eye, red and swollen. Her hair, disheveled. Frank sat across from her, grinning and sucking on a cigarette; ashes clinging to his sweat-stained tee shirt. A faucet dripped into a sink full of dirty dishes.

"We just had a little argument, Butchie. Nothin' much. Ain't that right, honey?" Frank reached across the table and took her hand.

"Is everything okay?" Adam asked, directing his words to his aunt.

Although she nodded, her eyes pleaded to stay out of it. When the beatings started shortly after she and Frank got married, he had asked her why she stayed with the guy. "Because I love him," she had said. He couldn't understand how she could say that. He had nothing but contempt for the man.

Frank seldom had a job for more than a few months and lost his last job after only a week.

When he wasn't working he drank and when he drank he became even more belligerent than when sober. Although she was a head taller than Frank, Wanda was no match for him. Short and stocky, Frank had a barrel chest and a stomach that flowed over the front of his pants. In his youth he had worked out with weights and, though the years had taken their toll, he bragged that he still could "kick the shit out of any of the young punks on Broadway." Always having some kind of get-rich scheme in the works, he constantly spent whatever money Wanda tried to save. His glory days had been the two years he served in the Marines after quitting high school at seventeen. A tattoo on his right forearm and a steel-gray crew cut were the only physical reminders of those days.

"Hey, Butchie, ya want a beer?"

"Would you like a Coke?" Wanda quickly asked, not looking at her husband.

Frank snickered. "Yeah, ya better get the kid some soda pop instead of beer. It'll go down easier."

Wanda shuffled slowly to the refrigerator and found a bottle of Coke amongst the bottles of beer.

"Hon, bring it here. I'll open it for ya."

Frank opened it, sending Wanda away, patting her rear with a fleshy hand. After she gave Adam his drink she sat back down at the table. Frank's hand crawled over and grabbed hold of hers. Sitting passively, her eyes avoided Adam's.

"How old are ya now, Butchie? Sixteen? Seventeen?" Frank's yellowed teeth reminded Adam of mules' teeth.

"Seventeen."

"When I was seventeen, I was pretty damn strong. Still am. Hell, I used to be able—" Frank sucked down a couple swigs of beer. "Ya want to arm wrestle an old fart like me?"

Wanda's face tensed. "Frank, leave him alone, please."

"Who the hell asked ya, goddamn it!" He tightened his grip on her hand until she winced.

"I was just—"

"Shut up! Your Butchie and me are havin' a discussion. When I want anythin' from ya, I'll tell ya." The grin disappeared from his face. "What do ya say, Butchie? Ya and me."

Adam dug his fingernails into his palm. His eyes shifted between Wanda and Frank. The dripping of the faucet pounded in his head. "I don't think so. You're too strong for me."

No one moved or said anything. Adam wondered if his aunt had picked up on the mockery in his answer to Frank. He felt as though the three of them were frozen within a photograph. The dripping of the faucet echoed off the walls.

Frank's eyes narrowed. He cocked his head and glared at Adam. His stomach rose and fell with every breath. His tongue wet his thick lips. Suddenly, his face broke into a grin. "Damn right I'm stronger." He patted Wanda's hand and scratched his belly. "Hon, get me another beer, and do somethin' about that goddamn faucet!"

Adam gulped down the rest of his Coke, said he had homework to do, and left. As soon as he got back to the apartment, he retreated to the bedroom. He plopped down on the bed and lay staring into the darkness.

Chapter 2

"Butch, wake up! Time for school."

"Okay, okay," Adam mumbled.

His mother bent over and brushed hair from his eyes. "Come on now. I've got water heating for you on the stove."

As soon as his mother left, he rolled out of bed and got partially dressed, waiting to put his shirt on after washing. When he walked into the living room, his mother had just finished fixing the couch into a makeshift bed.

"Won't take me long to fall asleep," she said.

"Sure wish you didn't have to sleep on that thing all the time."

"It's more comfortable than it looks," she said, patting the cushions. "Besides, I'm so use to this old couch that I couldn't sleep in a bed anymore."

In the half-kitchen, Adam took the pot of water off the stove and poured the steamy liquid into the washbasin sitting in the sink. After washing, he slipped on his shirt and combed his hair. Looking at his reflection in the mirror over the sink, he turned his head from side to side. Others thought of him as good looking. A couple of times when he had walked by a group of girls at school, he overheard one say to the others, "He's cute." His mother told him that his brown eyes and eyelashes came from his father.

On his way through the kitchen he stopped, dropped a slice of bread into the toaster, and stepped into the living room. His mother had settled on the couch, lying with a pillow behind her head, reading *True Confessions*.

"All ready for school?" she asked, putting her magazine down.

"I stopped at Wanda's Friday night," he said, his anger returning. "He beat her up again."

She immediately sat up, worry flooding her face. "How

bad?"

"Gave her a black eye. Face is all swollen." Adam finished buttoning his shirt.

"Oh, it sounds so much worse than last time," she said, wincing.

"I felt like ripping into him."

A look of concern flashed through her eyes. "You didn't, did you?"

"No."

Relief replaced her concern. "I'm so glad you didn't start anything. I—"

"He's the one that started it!" Adam snapped. "I would've finished it if I didn't think he'd take it out on her."

"Don't be angry with me," she said, looking hurt.

"I'm not. I…I just…feel tight inside."

Worried lines formed around her eyes. "How do you mean…tight?"

"I…I don't know. It's like…like when Grandpa talks about the spring inside a clock getting wound up too tight."

"Anything I can do to help?"

"Wanda's the one who needs help."

"I know," she said with a heavy sigh. "I better go check on her."

"I have to go. Mick's waiting for me."

"Aren't you going to eat anything?"

"I'll eat a piece of toast on the way."

Grabbing his jacket, he slipped it on, and scooped up his schoolbooks. After a couple bites of toast, he tossed it in the trash under the sink. Yelling good-bye, he opened the door, and flew down the steps. The cool morning air felt refreshing.

At the corner, Mick Brunner was waiting for him. They had made a pact that they would meet at Kass' Drug Store every morning to walk the ten blocks to school. He and Mick had become friends in a junior high woodworking class. They had teamed up on a project and hit it off right from the beginning. The first time Mick came up to his apartment, they had been watching television when Mick had to go the bathroom. With the old memory of having been ridiculed before, Adam explained that they shared the bathroom with another apartment. Mick had just smiled. “Hey, no big deal. If I have to wait in line, that’s what I’ll have to do.”

“Hi, big guy,” Adam said as he now walked up to Mick. Although he considered himself tall at nearly six feet, Mick still had a couple of inches on him. “How’re you doing?”

“Great. And do you know why? I finished that assignment for chemistry.”

“Man, I’m still working on that.” Adam envied Mick for finishing assignments ahead of time. Even though Mick always made the A honor roll, he never bragged about his grades, or his athletic ability. Starting at right tackle for the varsity football team, he was all-conference last year and honorable mention the year before.

“Will you give me some help if I get stuck on those last two questions?” Adam asked.

“Of course. What are friends for?”

They crossed to the next block. “Hey, check out those clouds,” Adam said. “They look like snow clouds, and it’s only the middle of October.”

“Don’t mention snow to me. We’ve still got three games left to play, and I sure hope it doesn’t snow.” Mick massaged the back of his neck.

“You’re not afraid of a little snow, are you?”

“Don’t get me wrong. Winter is my favorite time of the year. I love snow. I just don’t like playing football in the stuff.” He rubbed his neck again.

“What’s wrong with your neck?”

“Still sore from our last game.” Mick shifted his books from under one arm to his other. “And my right shoulder is bummed from the game before that. Got enough aches and pains without having to have the cold and snow affect them. Man, I feel like an old man sometimes.”

Adam reached for Mick’s books. “Do you want me to carry those for you, old man?”

“Get out of here!” Mick playfully swatted at him with his free hand.

“Can I ask you something?” Adam asked in a more serious tone.

“Sure.”

"When the weather changes, does your neck and shoulder feel it?"

"You better believe it. It's not so bad when I play because then the only thing on my mind is the game. But during practice all week long…then I can really feel it. And when my shoulder hurts, I know it's going to rain or something." Mick pointed to his nose. "Now, my honker is another story." He profiled it for him. Having a noticeable hump, it was the first thing that people noticed about him. His nose had been broken twice: once in a junior high fight when an older kid made the mistake of calling him ugly, and last year in the final game of the season.

"When you get banged up in football, how long does it take to heal?"

"That depends. My neck will probably take a couple of weeks. Coach tells me that the shoulder may be sore for a couple of months or longer."

"How long would it take for a black eye to heal?" Adam asked as casually as he could.

"What are you talking about? Who's got a black eye?"

They walked nearly a half block before Adam spoke. "Frank beat up my aunt Friday night."

"Oh, man. Not again. Didn't he just do that a couple of months ago?"

Adam nodded.

"How's she doing?"

"Not too hot." A knot formed in Adam's stomach.

"Does she go to work being beat up like that?"

"Knowing her, she will. The last time, she used makeup to cover up the bruises."

Mick shifted his books to the other arm. "Why doesn't she just leave the jerk? She doesn't have to put up with that stuff."

Adam kicked at a piece of paper swirling about on the sidewalk, wishing it was Frank's face. "She stays because she says she loves him. Now, can you figure that out?"

It wasn't until they had crossed to the next block that Mick replied. "I've got an uncle whose wife went out on him all the time. Did it for years. Everybody in the family told him nobody would blame him if he kicked her out."

"So did he?"

"Nope. All he says is that he loves her and could never kick her out. Family says he's crazy, but I'm not so sure."

"What do you mean you're not sure? He sounds as crazy as my aunt."

"Maybe. But the way I figure it, maybe your aunt and my uncle are married to a couple of losers, and it's better than nothing."

"Now, you're sounding crazy."

"Think of it this way. Maybe they're lonely people. Maybe what they got isn't the best, and you and me wouldn't put up with the stuff they put up with. Sure, they're kicked around, but a person will put up with a lot as long as they got someone. It sounds strange, but they need each other. That's the way it seems to me."

The stoplight turned red just as they reached the corner. They stood watching cars pass. When a break in the traffic came and without waiting for the light to change, they sprinted across as an oncoming driver honked at them. Adam reached the curbing two steps ahead of Mick.

"I told you, you should've come out for football," Mick said. "You're fast and got the moves of a receiver. There are a lot of guys who would give anything to have your quickness."

They walked for another block, stopping in front of a bakery to look in the window. The door opened and the aroma of freshly baked rolls floated out. They agreed they would stop for a cinnamon roll tomorrow morning.

"You know, your aunt and my uncle aren't that much different from the rest of us," Mick said as they continued their trek to school. "The way I figure it, everybody needs someone."

Adam shot a sideward glance toward his friend. "Who says?"

"I just know. People do. It's natural."

For Adam needing someone was a form of weakness. And if he was going get away from Broadway, he had to remain strong.

Mick stroked the bridge of his nose. "Stupid," he muttered.

"What's stupid?"

"Oh, I was thinking about the kid in junior high who broke my nose."

"I remember that," Adam said, relieved the subject had

changed. “That was Joey Breedman when we were in eighth grade, wasn’t it?”

“Yup. The two of us had it out, all right.”

“He broke your nose, but you cleaned his clock.”

“I know, but I shouldn’t have let him provoke me.” They walked for a quarter of a block before Mick continued. “Adam, we’ve been friends for a long time now. Remember right after ninth grade graduation, when we smoked a cigar on the school grounds?”

“Yeah. We were so sick we thought we’d never live to see high school.”

“You’ve got that right, and with all that we’ve been through, we’ve needed each other. Don’t you think so?”

Adam gnawed his lower lip. A bus went by, paper and dirt flying in its after-trail. Mick’s friendship was important to him, but he wasn’t sure that meant the same thing as needing it. Needing someone meant being weak.

“Hey, Mick! Adam!” The voice came from behind them. “Wait for me!”

Howie Cummins, lugging books and a bulging brown lunch bag, ran to catch up. Short and stocky, reddish blond hair, a winsome grin, and baby blue eyes gave him a cherub-like appearance. “Can you stop and let me rest for a minute?” he pleaded, leaning against a light pole, fanning his flushed face with an English book.

“What’s with you?” Mick asked.

“Man, I feel like I’ve just finished a four-minute mile.” Howie took a deep breath. “Guys, quick, tell me,” he sputtered. “What does a heart attack feel like?”

“You’re so out of shape, it’s pathetic,” Mick said. “Do some running. It’d do you good.”

Howie’s face registered a shocked expression. “Me? Run? You’ve got to be kidding.”

“Come on you two,” Adam said, smiling at the exchange between his friends. “Let’s get going or else we’ll be late.”

“And don’t forget,” Mick said. “It’s going to be a big day in Mattingale’s class. She’s assigning that special paper she’s been talking about since the first day of class.”

The rest of the way to school, the three joked and laughed

about the eccentric ways of Miss Mattingale, their English teacher. Adam couldn't forget about Frank, but he welcomed the chance to think about something else. He had a difficult time sharing his feelings, and wondered if he would ever experience that feeling of needing others.

"There it is," Howie announced as North High School came into view. "Isn't that tired, old building lovely? Doesn't it make you want to spend the rest of your life there, walking the hallways and sitting in the classrooms where beloved teachers—such as Miss Mattingale—fill our eager minds with the wisdom of the ages?"

North High School, a two-story brick structure located a block off Broadway, had been built in the late 1800s. The school stood like a bewildered dinosaur caught in a time warp. Together with a small parking lot and a magnificent football field, it spread out over an entire block.

"Hey, there's Danny Logan," Howie said as they crossed the street to the front entrance of the school. "That guy's been around just about every day since he was kicked out that first week. Look at him. He just stands and stares at the school. Can you figure that out?"

The tall, slender kid with the ducktail haircut was leaning up against one of the many large oak trees that lined the street.

"I guess everybody needs someone or something," Mick said, glancing over at Adam.

"Our school doesn't need Logan," Howie said. "I heard he knifed a guy the other night in a parking lot."

"We're all going to get the knife if we don't hustle to our homerooms," Adam said.

Adam had known Danny since junior high. They didn't hang out together, but Adam had once gotten him a pint of whiskey. He had taken it from Oscar one night when the older man had fallen asleep.

"Hey, man, I owe ya," Danny had said when Adam handed him the pint.

"Don't sweat it. I'll collect some day."

As Adam now headed into the school, he glanced back at Danny Logan. Danny just might be the answer he was looking for to settle the score with Frank.

Chapter 3

"I tell you, she doesn't," Howie said as he and Mick slid into their desks. Mick squeezed into the desk across the aisle from Adam while Howie sat in front of Mick.

"She doesn't what?" Adam asked. "And who is *she*?"

"Who else but Mattingale." Howie ducked a rubber band Mick shot at him. "You know how hot the weather was those first couple weeks of school? Even—" He ducked another shot. "Even with the windows open, this room was like an oven by mid-afternoon."

"So, what's your point?" Adam asked.

Howie shot a glance back toward Mick. "This clown doesn't believe me, but I say that Mattingale doesn't sweat."

"Wait a minute," Mick said. "Let's get this straight. I only asked how you know that. You don't have her at that time of day."

"I have this contact from Mattingale's sixth hour class."

"This place must be cooking by then," Adam said, thinking how their teacher always wore ankle-length, long-sleeved dresses buttoned to the top.

"You bet," Howie said. "It had to be a 150° in here that first week of school. Kids sweated like crazy, but old Mattingale looked as cool as a cucumber."

"So, she doesn't sweat," Mick said. "Big deal. That doesn't make her weird."

"Wait!" Howie said. "There's more. How about those white gloves? She wears them every day. Have you guys ever seen her without them?"

"I haven't," Adam said.

"Well, how about it?" Howie asked Mick.

"I guess I haven't either."

Howie smirked triumphantly. "What did I tell you? And you know what? She even wears them while she eats."

“Come on,” Mick said. “How do you know that?”

Howie’s face glowed with smugness. “I’ve a friend who went to her classroom during lunch.”

“During lunch?” Adam asked. “I’ve always heard her room is off limits then.”

“That’s right,” Mick added. “Even Principal Waite doesn’t dare to disturb her during lunch.”

“I wouldn’t know about that,” Howie said, dismissing Mick’s words with a wave of his hand. “Anyway, my friend went in and Mattingale was sitting at her desk. Her desk was covered by a white tablecloth. She was eating her lunch and listening to some long-haired music.”

“It’s called classical music,” Mick said.

“Same thing. Anyway, Mattingale was wearing her gloves while eating. I tell you she wears them all the time.”

“The other day she came into the lunchroom to get some milk,” Adam said.

Howie snatched a rubber band from Mick and aimed it at him. “And I bet she was wearing her gloves. Right?”

“Yeah, she was.” Adam watched the rubber band go flying over Mick’s head by at least a foot. “And she must be a pretty fussy lady.”

Mick opened his notebook and took a pencil out of his pocket. “What do you mean?”

“Because she rinsed and wiped the glass out before pouring her milk into it.”

“What about the gloves?” Howie’s eyes shined with anticipation.

“Oh, yeah,” Adam said. “All the time she was washing her glass, she was wearing them.”

Howie shook his finger at Mick. “See. What did I tell you?”

“Okay, okay, guys.” Mick put up his hands in mock surrender. “I’ll grant you that she’s got some different ways about her, but she’s a good teacher. You’ve got to admit to that.”

“I’d agree to that.” Howie turned to face forward, leaned back in his seat, and spoke out of the corner of his mouth. “I only say she’s got some weird habits.”

“Here she comes now,” Adam said.

The tall, thin woman with wiry gray hair set in a bun

entered, paused as she looked over her class, and silently glided to her desk. Her oval face, prominent cheekbones and a long, slender nose presented an air of royalty. Once seated, she took a key out of her purse and unlocked the top right-hand drawer of her desk.

"Wonder what she's got in there?" Howie whispered to his friends. "Bet it has something to do with those gloves."

Mattingale closed the drawer, locked it, and dropped the key back in her purse. She snapped her purse shut and placed it in the left-hand top drawer of her desk.

As soon as the bell rang, the murmuring in the room came to an abrupt halt. Adam had to give Mattingale credit because she commanded the respect and attention of her students.

Their teacher rose and looked around the room before moving around to the front of her desk. Her emerald green eyes gave her both a glow of radiance and an air of mystery. "Class, today I am thrilled to be able to finally assign the theme paper which I have kept you in suspense from the first day of school. I realize it had to have been difficult not knowing what this project was going to entail."

Her melodic voice came across as fresh and crisp as the powder-blue dress she wore. She enunciated her words, speaking them as an actress upon a stage.

"The assignment, I promise, will certainly be rewarding for you." She smiled as she gracefully moved from one side of the classroom to the other.

Adam looked out the window. Danny Logan still stood leaning against the tree, a curl of smoke rising from the cigarette in his mouth. Assured that Danny could be the answer to his problem, he settled back and turned his attention to his teacher.

Mattingale's eyes sparkled with excitement as she continued explaining the assignment. "I know this particular paper will be taxing, but it will also make you glow with the satisfaction of having put your literary skills to such a supreme test." She paused as though to signal her students to pay careful attention. "Yes, class, this paper will challenge you to mold a story using the clay from the very essence which you yourselves are made. Remember, as the brush is to the artist and the chisel is to the sculptor, so the pen is to the writer…"

She spent the rest of the hour expanding upon what the paper would mean for their personal growth. At one point, becoming so overcome with emotion, she told them to begin reading the chapter assigned for the following week. While her students read, she sat in her wooden swivel chair, rocking back and forth in an attempt to regain her composure.

"How long do you think it will be this time?" Howie whispered.

"Fifteen minutes," Mick whispered back.

"I say eight," Adam said.

Ten minutes later, Adam looked over at Mick and nodded toward their teacher as they watched Miss Mattingale rise from her chair. She walked to the front of her desk and resumed talking about the assignment. Her white-gloved hands moved gracefully as though she was conducting a symphony.

Adam caught Mick's attention again and pointed at Howie. Within moments, they could hear the faint sound of snoring. Only when the bell rang ending the class did the snoring stop.

The rest of the morning went well for Adam. He was feeling great when he walked into the school cafeteria at lunchtime. Howie and Mick, sitting at a table in the corner, waved him over.

"Hey, what did you think of Mattingale this morning?" Adam asked as he sat down and opened his carton of milk. "She really got carried away. I thought she was going to croak with emotion at one point."

"Speaking of croaking," Mick said. "Howie, did you know that you went to sleep and snored?"

Howie pointed to himself. "Me?"

"You better believe you were," Mick said.

"Can I help it? It was those gloves and the way she waved her arms around. They looked like white bouncing balls. Up and down. Back and forth." Howie's head began to move in sync with his words. "Man, I tell you, they had a hypnotic effect on me. I can feel it even now."

Mick chuckled. "Howie, ever since we've been friends—since third grade—you still come up with things that amaze me."

Adam took out a sandwich. "So, what are you going to write about?" he asked Mick.

"I'm not sure. Maybe something about football." Mick used

the eraser end of his pencil to scratch the back of his neck. "Not about the sport itself."

"What then?" Howie asked, opening his bag of potato chips.

Mick grabbed the bag from Howie, helped himself to a handful of chips before tossing it back. "Think I'll write about the character building stuff that comes from football. Maybe even write about the clay Mattingale talked about."

"What clay?" Howie asked.

Mick turned to Adam. "What about you?"

"What clay?" Howie asked again. "I didn't hear anything about clay."

Mick bit into an apple. "Mattingale talked about it while you were snoring and dreaming about those bouncing white balls. I'll tell you about it later." He took another bite of his apple. "Anyway, what are you guys writing about?"

Adam took a sip of milk. "I'm not sure."

"Me, either," Howie added as he emptied the rest of the contents of his lunch bag on the table. "Hey, guys. What do you suppose Mattingale's got in that drawer?"

"Why?" Mick asked. "What are you up to now?"

Howie glanced around the lunchroom and leaned over the table toward Mick and Adam.

"Look, you two. Wouldn't it be great if we could crack the secret of that locked drawer before we graduate? Just think, it might even hold the answer to why she keeps those white gloves on all the time. To crack both secrets at the same time. Wow! Wouldn't that be something to be remembered for?"

"Just how do you propose to do this?" Adam asked. "Mattingale always keeps that drawer locked and she puts the key in her purse."

"I'm not sure yet." Howie picked up his sandwich. "I need some time to figure this thing out."

Mick and Adam looked at each other and shrugged.

"I guess we'll back you," Mick replied hesitantly and then looked at Adam, giving him a halfhearted smile. "We will, won't we?"

"Sure, why not." Adam took another sip of milk. "What have we got to lose?"

"Plenty," Mick said. "You'll keep us informed, won't you?"

he asked Howie.

"You have my word on it, but just leave the master planning to me." He spent the rest of the lunch period without saying a word.

The whole day for Adam had been upbeat and, by the time he left school, he was in such high spirits he had forgotten about Frank. His spirits were elevated further when clear skies and the warmth of the sun greeted him outside. Since Mick had football practice and Howie decided to stick around the school to, as he worded it, "case out" Mattingale's room, Adam walked home alone, thinking about the time ahead. He would grab a snack, change clothes and then go to work. Even Broadway didn't seem so depressing at the moment. Everything changed, though, as soon as he stepped onto the block where he lived.

He walked ten to fifteen feet past the man, stopping to look at the display in the window of the clothing store. From the corner of his eye he could see that the old guy wasn't going to move. He knew it wouldn't be long before a customer would tell the storeowner that there was some drunk sitting on the sidewalk outside, using the storefront as a backrest. Sitting would be a polite but not an accurate description. The man, like a doomed ship at sea, was listing to one side.

Adam looked up and down the sidewalk, wanting to make sure no one was coming before walking up to the man. As he approached, the smell of urine mingled with the odor of dried vomit caked on the man's shirt. He was about to reach for the man when a heavy-set woman came out of a store several doors away and started his way. Quickly stepping aside, Adam backed up and then started to walk forward, making it appear that he was just passing by the old man.

The woman saw the slumped figure and hesitated, no doubt trying to decide whether to cross over to the other side of the street. Having made her decision, she continued to come ahead but changed the angle of her path so that when she did pass, she would be close to the curb. She would have stepped out into the street, Adam thought, if it hadn't been for the traffic.

Adam didn't know the woman. As she approached, she glanced at the old man, a look of disgust flooding her face. The only other acknowledgment she gave to the pitiful figure slumped against the storefront was a quickening of her pace as she walked by.

Pausing again in front of the clothing store window, taking notice of the well-dressed mannequins staring out at him, Adam waited until the woman was well on her way. Now, he would waste no time. He ran back to the old man.

“Get up, Grandpa!” he angrily shouted.

Chapter 4

Getting home from work on Saturday afternoon, Adam found his grandfather and mother at the kitchen table. His grandfather was sorting through the inner workings of an old chime clock while she watched. His mother enjoyed the opportunity of being with her father. “I can sit for hours and watch him tinker with his clocks,” she always said.

His grandfather peered over wire-rimmed bifocals that teetered at the edge of his nose. “Ah, Butch. Sit down. Sit down.”

Adam took off his jacket, tossed it over a chair and sat down opposite his mother. She offered to fix him a sandwich, but he declined.

“Not often anymore we spend time together.” His grandfather pushed his glasses back up. He reached over and patted his grandson on the shoulder.

When Adam was in grade school, the two of them had many outings walking to the city dump located across the railroad tracks, down by the Mississippi River. His grandfather told him that such a place was a history book of people. “Here you learn people’s lives…values. What used to be important to them.” Spending the better part of a day rummaging around, they always found a discarded clock to bring home.

“Pa, how’re you going to get all that back together?” Virg asked. “There are so many pieces.”

“I put together. Have patience.”

For Adam the moment was far different from the week before when he had picked his grandfather off the sidewalk. When he got him back to Wanda’s, Frank had answered the door.

“Well, if it ain’t Butchie and his wino grandpa. Where did ya pick him up this time?”

Adam headed for the couch as Frank walked away,

snickering.

"Oh, no, Pa!" Wanda said. "Not again."

After helping his aunt change his grandfather's clothes and giving him a sponge bath, Adam left.

Now, as he watched his grandfather sort through the intricate pieces of the clock, it was hard to believe it was the same person. When he was sober, he devoted his whole life to fixing clocks, taking great pride in restoring usefulness to what others saw as worthless junk. He once worked thirty straight hours on a wall pendulum clock he had found in a garbage can in a back alley. After he got it to work again, he wept. "Clocks like people," he announced. "Need understanding. Someone to care."

"Pa, how did you get to be so good at repairing clocks?"

Either he didn't hear the question or chose to ignore it. Adam guessed it was the latter. His mother had gotten the same response whenever she had asked about his grandfather's past. The family knew very little about his early years other than he had come to America at the age of fourteen with only a suitcase. The only thing left from those days was his name, Paul Kurtz. Though he learned the basics of English, he didn't embrace the language. He once mentioned that the area he came from was called Galicia. The next day at school Adam asked his geography teacher about it. "Galicia had once been part of Poland," his teacher said, adding, "There's a long history of sadness associated with that area of the world."

As Adam watched his grandfather examine one of the clock's flywheels, he wondered what kind of life he had growing up.

"Pa!" Virg shouted.

"What?" Paul scowled over his glasses.

"How did you learn to be so good at repairing watches?"

"Don't remember." Paul returned to his work. Either he didn't remember or he acted as though he didn't hear the question. Either way, the message was clear.

Virg had confided in Adam several years ago she had heard her father make a passing remark that something terrible happened to his family when he was young. When she had asked him about it, he had replied, "Don't remember. Too long ago."

Paul had lived alone for a few years before reluctantly

moving in with Frank and Wanda when he lost his job as a night watchman. He made no secret of it that he would have preferred to stay with Adam's mother, but there was no room. At least, at Wanda's, he had a couch to sleep on. He often came over to their apartment to work on his clocks, and to get away from Frank.

Virg got up and poured herself another cup of coffee. She sat back down, turning her attention to Adam. "How did work go today?"

Since the beginning of high school he had worked at Bloomberg's, a small clothing store on Broadway. "Okay. Next Saturday I'll have to work until closing time. Harry wants me to start working more hours."

"That's good. Harry's really showing you the ropes. What kind of things does he want you to do?"

"Some window dressing. I'll start next week. He wants me to decide what clothes to put on the mannequins."

Although Adam's job was okay, it held no future for him. His boss, Harry Bloomberg, had asked him to consider working full time after graduation. "If you worked hard and learned the business, you could be managing the store in four or five years." Adam, however, wanted no part of it, just as he wanted no part of Broadway.

"Butch, are you okay?" his mother asked.

"Yeah. Why?"

"Because you didn't seem to hear me."

Adam shifted in his seat. "I was thinking about something. What were you saying?"

"That I'm proud of you. You stay with Harry and I bet he'll even offer you a good job after you're done with school. Wouldn't that be something?"

Paul put down the magnifying glass. "Ah, Butch, no need that job. I teach. You work with hands. Learn about clocks."

"Pa, let him alone. He's got a good future there."

"What future? Put clothes on dummies? What kind job is that?"

"Don't talk like that, Pa. There's more to it than that."

"What? Sell clothes to other dummies," Paul said, chuckling at his own words.

"You're impossible," she replied, shaking her head in

disgust.

As his grandfather sorted through the pieces of the clock, Adam wondered how his aged hands could be so steady. Times like now, he felt such respect for him. At other times, he wanted to shake his grandfather and scream that, with his skills, he could make something of himself. He could open up a clock repair shop. Anything would be better than how he was living his life now. *Why is he wasting his life?* The more he asked it, the angrier he became.

"Butch, work with hands. Learn to take things apart. Put back together. Do that. You learn life." Paul scratched the thin tuft of hair that marked the spot of his widow's peak. "See clock here. Some dummy thinks useless. Throws away. I find in alley. Fix. No more useless."

His grandfather's face showed the markings of a hard life. "Like road map," he always said. His hazel eyes showed strength, but also a deep sadness.

"Pa, how are things with Wanda? Are she and Frank doing okay?"

"That damn Frank! No good. Throw him in dump." He pointed to the pieces of the clock. "This more use than him."

"Has he left her alone?" Adam asked, his body tensing.

"He better not try stuff when I around. I kick ass! He touch her and I—" A muffled explosion deep within him erupted, the coughing spell shaking his whole body. Already thin, his frail frame quivered as though it would shake off whatever flesh he had left.

The coughing, aggravated from his emphysema, grew worse whenever he got excited. Years ago a doctor told him that his lungs had been damaged from working in welding shops. The doctor advised him to stop smoking and to cut back on the drinking. When asked by his family if he would stop, his reply had been sharp. "I cut back. Cut back seeing doctors!" Whenever the subject came up, his reply never changed. "Ack, we live. We die. Enjoy life now."

"Are you okay?" Virg asked as he continued to cough.

He took out a handkerchief and wiped his mouth. "Okay." His eyes flashed with intensity. "Goddamn Frank!"

"Pa, you shouldn't use that kind of language in front of

Butch."

"Mom, don't worry about it."

Only when Frank's name came up, did he hear his grandfather swear. His grandfather didn't like living with Wanda and Frank and stayed away as much as possible. He would be gone for days, nobody knowing where he had gone. Sometimes he couldn't remember where he had been either. Eventually he would come back, or be found and brought back.

Paul picked up one of the gear wheels of the clock, examined it for a moment and laid it back down. He leaned back in the chair and rubbed his hand back and forth over the stubble of his chin. "Butch, listen. I teach. You learn fast. You no dummy." He motioned toward the pieces on the table. "After I clean up. Want put together? I show how."

"I don't think so." To work with him as though nothing had happened would be to deny that part of his grandfather that Adam detested. He tried to sort out his feelings for the man, but they were as confusing as the pieces of the clock that lay on the table.

"Why don't you let Pa show you?" his mother asked.

"Because I don't want to," Adam snapped. He stood and grabbed his jacket. "I'm going to use the car, okay?"

"Okay, but be careful."

Adam heard the disappointment in her voice. She would have loved for him and his grandfather to work together. "See you later," he said and walked out the door. Just as he got to the first landing, the entrance door opened and Frank came in.

Frank clutched a brown paper bag in one hand, molded to the shape of a bottle. He grunted with each step he took up the stairway. Adam was almost upon him before he looked up.

"Hi ya, Butchie."

Adam smelled the liquor on his breath.

"How's your grandpa doin' today? Puttin' together another one of his goddamn clocks?" He moved in front of Adam, blocking the way.

Adam shifted to one side to move past him, but Frank moved with him.

"I asked about that old man ya found passed out on the sidewalk last week. Ya remember that, don't ya?" Frank wiped saliva from the corner of his mouth. "I sure as hell remember ya bringin' that drunk to my apartment. Damn wino threw up all over my couch."

Adam's hands clenched into fists. "Get out of my way!"

"Wanda and ya had to wash the puke off his goddamn face. Made *me* want to puke. Damn no good—"

Adam shoved Frank against the railing.

Startled, Frank was momentarily stunned as Adam shot by him. "What the hell? Ya little punk! Goddamn it, I ought…"

Adam was out the door and onto the sidewalk. As the door swung shut, he heard Frank yelling. "Damn no good punk! I'll kick your ass!" He turned to go back in after Frank. He reached for the door, stopped, and walked away.

* * *

"Pa, did you hear that shouting in the hallway? Maybe I should go check to see what's happening."

"Ack, is nothing. Just usual stuff." He went back to pondering the parts of the clock, studying them as he would the pieces on a chessboard.

"But it could've been Butch."

He picked up the hour wheel and studied it. "Our Butch is man now. Take care of himself. Life itself be teacher. You baby too much."

"I don't and you know that," she replied, sounding hurt by the accusation.

He saw his daughter brush away a tear, but said nothing.

"I don't understand," she said. "In the past several years, Butch and I've been growing apart. We used to do so much together. We'd go to movies, out to the zoo, even fishing now and then. I remember the times we used to pack a lunch and a ride a bus as far as the money would take us. We'd eat our lunch at the end of the line and come…Pa, are you listening?"

Setting the magnifying glass aside, he looked at his daughter and pondered what he should say. Her sensitivity reminded him so much of his wife, Mary. She had been the strength of the family. That she died so young was something that he hadn't been able to reconcile and he often thought about where they would be now, as a family, if she had lived. Clocks he knew, but how to care for daughters, he didn't know. He was sorry he had said that she had babied Butch. If Mary were here, she would have been able to say the right things; she would have been able to comfort their daughter. Life may be a teacher all right, but for himself, it hadn't taught him enough.

"I tell Butch that I love him," Virg said. "I think he hears me, but it's like the words have no place to stick. There are times he seems so distant."

"What you mean?"

"I'm worried about him feeling that he can go through life not needing anyone. I'm afraid there'll come a day when he won't know how to ask for help."

He wanted to reach out and comfort her, to take her hand into his and reassure her that everything would turn out for the best. If only Mary could be here to tell him what to do. She would care for their daughter and make things right. He wanted to do all these things and more, but all he could do was to shrug his shoulders. His gesture, as it had done so often in the past, signaled that he didn't know how to carry on this line of conversation.

Several minutes went by before his daughter spoke. "What are you going to do with the clock once you're done with it?" It was a foolish question. Both of them already knew the answer. After fixing the clock he would sell it to the first person that came around, and then use the money to buy a pint of whiskey.

* * *

Adam had driven aimlessly around for nearly an hour. Although the thought of Frank still left him with a knot in the base of his stomach, he began to breathe easier.

Not wanting to go home just yet, he took a drive around Lake of the Isles, one of the more popular Minneapolis lakes. He noticed a family raking leaves at one of the homes as he drove. The parents and the two young kids were laughing as a playful collie ran through the piles of leaves. Glancing in his rearview mirror, he caught a final look at the family.

He rolled down the window, letting the wind splash against

his face. He turned onto Lake Shore Drive. A young boy squatted along the roadside about a block ahead. The youngster was watching something on the road. Adam slowed the car, afraid the youth might suddenly dash out to retrieve what looked like a squashed ball. "Tough luck, kid," he muttered.

Just as he got close enough to distinguish what the object might be, an oncoming car swerved slightly into his lane but quickly recovered. In that split instant, however, he drove past the young boy, missing the opportunity to see the object. Looking in the mirror, he saw the kid sitting by the road.

Adam went around the block. When he came back, the kid was still sitting on the curb. As he drove closer, however, the *squashed ball* turned out to be a turtle that had one side of its shell crushed. When he drove by, the kid had another turtle, turned over on its back, its feet kicking.

Chapter 5

Howie plopped down on a chair across from Mick and Adam, and stared at the tray in front of him. "I knew I should've brought my lunch. You guys were smart." He glanced around the school lunchroom. "I wonder how many other innocent students are being victimized by the cooks." He eyed his friend's lunch bags. "Wouldn't want to trade, would you?"

Mick and Adam shook their heads.

Howie prodded the food on his plate with his fork. "I can't believe it. Do they think we're guinea pigs?"

"What's the matter?" Mick asked. "I've never known you to turn down anything to eat. You're not sick are you?"

"Listen, you'd be sick, too." Howie pointed to his plate. "Look at this stuff. It's nothing but a pile of mop strings with ketchup and yellow dandruff. What is it?"

"They call it spaghetti." Mick turned to Adam. "Isn't that right?"

Adam nodded.

"Very funny, guys. That's only what they want us to think. Appearances can be deceiving." Howie looked toward the serving line. "You have to keep an eye on these cooks around here." He continued to poke around in his spaghetti. After several probes, he lifted a few strands with his fork. "If you ask me, this stuff looks like pieces of intestine from a frog I dissected in biology."

"Hey, watch it!" Mick said. "I'm eating my lunch." He eyed the spaghetti. "It can't be that bad. Look around. Others are eating it and not complaining."

"Yeah, I know, and they need to be saved."

"Come on, what are you up to this time?" Mick asked. "No. Wait a minute. I'm not sure I want to know."

"What do you mean?"

"I mean it's safer not knowing." Mick unwrapped one of his

sandwiches. "You're not going to get us into trouble with one of your harebrained schemes, are you?"

"Harebrained schemes?" A shocked expression swept across Howie's face. "Me? My ideas are great."

"What about last week when you proposed taking Mattingale's desk home over the weekend?" Adam asked.

"So big deal. You guys want to find out her secrets, don't you? You want to leave old North High with something to remember us by, don't you?"

"Sure, we do," Mick said. "But taking her desk? And don't tell me that you've forgotten the part about lowering it out the second story window with a block and tackle."

"It would've worked. It was a great plan. All I couldn't figure out was how to remove the window frame." He gestured to his spaghetti. "But this is different. This can be the beginning of a nation-wide protest against the junk they try to pass off as food. Are you guys with me on this?"

Mick leaned back in his chair. "Sorry, buddy. Count me out on this one."

"That goes for me, too," Adam said.

"Do I dare ask how you're going to do this?" Mick asked.

Howie grinned. "Just watch." He jumped to his feet with such quickness that his tan plastic chair tipped over backwards, clattering loudly on the tile floor. "Aaaagh!" he screamed. "There's a worm in my spaghetti!" He grabbed his tray, ran to the disposal can by the conveyor belt that led into the kitchen, and tossed the spaghetti—plate and all—into the can. When Alfred Sumstad, a pimply-faced skinny sophomore serving as a lunchroom monitor tried to tell him that he wasn't supposed to do that, Howie yelled, "I'm going to barf!" and ran out of the lunchroom.

The reaction from those in the lunchroom was at first a startled silence and then laughter. Adam and Mick waited for a few minutes but nothing happened. Within seconds after Mick had concluded that Howie's plan had fizzled, Charlotte Herman, a heavyset girl sitting behind them, shrieked, "It moved!" This time only a smattering of laughter could be heard. Mick and Adam looked at each other in disbelief. At the table across from them, Carl Benson, the starting left guard for the football team, stood up and picked up his plate of spaghetti.

"Hey, Carl!" Mick yelled. "What's the matter?"

"Man, I can't eat anymore. I'm stuffed."

Mick chuckled as he and Adam watched Carl dump his spaghetti into the disposal can while Alfred, the lunchroom monitor, looked on, trying not to gag.

The hysteria spread throughout the lunchroom as those who had school meals examined their spaghetti. It wasn't long before a traffic jam formed at the disposal cans. The conveyor belt became dangerously stacked with trays as Alfred stood motionless in a state of shock. Even the cooks checked their pans of spaghetti.

Mick and Adam sat quietly eating their lunches when Mr. Mueller, the gym teacher, walked up.

"You boys know anything about what was going on?" Mueller asked gruffly.

"No, sir," Mick said.

"We're just sitting here eating," Adam added.

Mr. Mueller eyed the two of them for several long moments. "Okay, but the wise guy who started this better know that I'm on his trail." He was about to say more when another student rushed up to inform him that a lunchroom monitor had just fainted.

It took a full twenty minutes to calm the lunchroom after a chubby kid by the name of Albert Goldstein threw up into his plateful of spaghetti, splattering the girl next to him. After that, even the sack lunches got tossed.

Chapter 6

On the way home from school under an overcast, chilly, drizzly day, Adam listened as Mick filled Howie in on what happened after Howie ran out of the lunchroom. "You sure did it this time," Mick said as he zipped up his jacket.

Howie's eyes lit up. "Do you really think so?"

"Oh, yeah. Even football practice was canceled, and it wasn't because of this crummy weather."

"It was? It was really canceled?"

"Supposedly, Coach Banks gave us the day off because it'd be an incentive for next week's homecoming game. Truth is, though, half the team members were sick to their stomachs, including the coach himself."

"Wow!" Howie snuck a look at his friend. "You're not angry, are you? I mean you being a football player and all that."

"Are you kidding? I think we should have a day off every week." Mick slapped Howie on the back. "You should be proud of yourself. They'll be talking about this for years to come."

"But I can't claim victory," Howie lamented as the three of them stopped at the corner and waited for the light to change.

"Why not?" Adam asked.

"Because Waite wants to suspend the person who started it." The light changed and they crossed onto the next block. "I hope nobody tells him. You know how tough of a principal he is."

"Don't sweat," Mick assured him. "No one is going to tell." He nudged Adam. "We'll back our buddy here up, won't we?"

"Sure."

"So don't sweat it," Mick said. "Tell you what. Get your mind on the homecoming dance next week. I went to a lot of trouble fixing you up with Cindy."

"Is she as nice as you say?" Howie asked. "I'm not too keen about a blind date. I always like to look over the merchandise first."

"Would I fix my buddy up with a dog? Trust me. She's a good looker. The two of you'll get along great." Mick turned to Adam. "Are you still going to take Sue?"

"Yeah." Adam didn't date much. He didn't want to get involved in a relationship and end up marrying someone from the area. The chances would be too great, then, that he'd have to stay on the North Side. He'd dated Sue off and on for the past year, but as far as he was concerned it wasn't serious and he wanted to make sure it stayed that way.

"The homecoming dance is going to be great," Mick said. "When we pull up in my dad's Impala, all eyes will be on us and we'll be strutting. Adam, I'll pick you up first, and then my Mary, and then we'll pick up Sue." He smiled at Howie. "After that, we'll swing by for you."

"How about my date?" Howie asked.

"We're saving the best for the last," Mick replied.

They walked several more blocks, the conversation jumping between the lunchroom riot, the upcoming triple date and, only briefly, the homecoming football game. Neither Howie nor Adam enjoyed sports very much and Mick simply didn't need to have football at the center of his life. When the talk did turn in that direction, it seldom came because Mick steered it that way. Adam recalled a conversation he and Mick had at the soda fountain of Kass' Drugstore one afternoon about his friend's plans after graduation.

"Just think," Adam had said. "A year from now and you'll be in college."

"I can hardly wait," Mick replied as he tore the paper off the end of his straw. "It's going to be great."

Adam sipped his cherry phosphate. "Are you going to get that football scholarship I heard your dad talking about?"

"Maybe. I'm really hoping for an academic scholarship."

"You'll probably get both. Won't you?"

"Possible, but I don't think I'll be using both." Mick slipped the straw into his drink. "I'm not sure I want to play football. I loved playing the game in grade school, but over the years, I've grown tired of it."

"Why are you playing now then?"

Mick fiddled with his straw. "My family. Dad played center

for North in the '30s, and my older brother was the starting quarterback for two years in the early '50s."

"So?"

"So, my family is all football. Even my mom's telling the relatives that I'll be first one from the family to play college ball."

"Why don't you just tell them you don't want to play?"

Mick laughed, but it sounded forced. "It's not as easy as it sounds. My dad would blow his top. He'd probably kick my butt out of the house."

"He wouldn't do that, would he?"

"He might." Mick took a deep breath. "I hate the thought of disappointing my family."

"What are you going to do?"

"Not sure…just not sure."

Adam was still thinking about that conversation when, at the next corner, Howie said he had to stop at the drugstore to pick up some medicine. He explained that his father had a heart ailment and had been warned recently by the doctor that he should take it easy. Howie might have worried about his dad, but he seldom talked about his own feelings concerning his father.

Mick waited until Howie was out of earshot. "I think he's hurting more than he lets on. I've been over to his house a couple of times in the past month. His dad doesn't look all that hot."

"That's too bad." Adam wondered if Howie's fun loving personality was his way of covering up his problems. "He's still pretty worried, then?"

"From what he tells me, his father barely has energy to do anything once he gets home from work. It's just lucky he's got a job that's not too strenuous."

"Where does he work?" Adam asked, realizing that he didn't know that much about Howie's family.

"Some place downtown. He does bookkeeping or something like that. I guess he's been at the same place over thirty years."

"Man, that's a long time."

"I know. According to Howie, the place would dry up and blow away without his dad. He's pretty proud of him. It'd be hard on him if anything happened. It was tough enough, his mother dying when she did."

The drizzle had stopped but the overcast sky gave the buildings on Broadway a gray, colorless look. Mick and Adam walked past a shoe store displaying a sign *Welfare Checks Accepted* in its window.

"Don't you ever get sick of this place?" Adam blurted out after he and Mick had walked past the store.

"What do you mean? What place?"

"Broadway. This whole area. At night I try to think what's good about it, and do you know what? I come up with nothing."

"It's not so bad around here."

"Says who?"

"You don't have to stay around. You can—"

"That's right! I don't have to!"

"Hey, man." Mick put up his hands like he was surrendering. "Cool it. I'm not hassling you on this."

Adam looked away for several seconds. "Sorry I blew up. It's just that it's a struggle."

A man walked by muttering something about kids taking up the middle of the sidewalk. Adam felt like going after the guy and punching him. They walked the next block in silence.

"I'm not planning on staying around here," Adam said. "I don't want to end up like everybody else. Who wants to be satisfied with a bottle of wine, or some lousy waitress job, or just trying not to get your ass kicked too often. What kind of life is that? You can try and fight it but it's…"

"I understand. I'm here to listen. Okay, buddy?"

Adam nodded, appreciating that Mick didn't press him. He had already shared more than he wanted.

They walked for another block, stopping to look at the movie billboard advertising coming attractions at the Empress Theater.

"Howie's always getting us involved with his scheming plots," Mick said as they crossed the street to Kass' Drugstore. "We should scheme something up just for him."

"Like what?" Adam asked, relieved the conversation had turned away from him.

"Don't know yet. He's always talking about doing something to be remembered for. So it's got to be something that he'll remember *us* by."

"Sounds good to me. We owe him for some of the stuff he's

pulled on us. Let me know. Okay?"

"Sure. If I come up with anything, I'll give you a call tonight. Take care." Mick turned and started walking away.

"Hey," Adam called out.

"Yeah?"

"Thanks for letting me spout off."

Mick nodded.

As Adam watched Mick walk away, he felt bad about blowing up at him, and angry with himself for doing so. When he thought about his friend going off to college next fall, he realized how much he would miss him.

Chapter 7

"You drink too much coffee," Wanda chided as Virg poured herself a third cup. The two sisters sat at the kitchen table. For the past half hour they had been waiting for Adam to come home from school. Wanda checked the clock. "What time will he be home?"

"Any minute now."

Wanda had come home early from work that afternoon and finding Frank gone, decided to take the opportunity to see Adam. She had been anxious to talk to him ever since Frank had come home mumbling about Butch shoving him on the stairway. Before she could get anything more out of him, Frank stumbled into the bedroom, flopped on the bed, and fell asleep.

"Was Frank really mad?" Virg asked.

"Not at all. Just a little upset. It was only the other day when I brought the subject up that he said something. I think it was all just a misunderstanding," she offered, afraid to tell her sister that Frank had said the very next day, "Your Butchie is lookin' to get his ass kicked."

A worried look crossed Virg's face. "What are we going to do?"

"It'll be okay." As Wanda watched Virg sip her coffee, she was reminded of another time she had said those words to her. Their mother had died of pneumonia. Virg was only three years old at the time. Wanda, at the age of ten, had assumed the role of mother for the household. How she managed to stay in school until she was sixteen and still run the household had been a testimony to her determination. During those years she also had to give her father support. He had become a broken man when his wife died. In the years following her death he started drinking, lost several jobs and finally had to sell their house. It was under those circumstances her motherly instinct had been shaped. Ironically, the more she took care of others, the more she desired to have someone take care of her.

"Butch just doesn't understand Frank," Wanda said. "He isn't as bad as he seems." Was she trying to convince her sister or herself? She didn't want to believe that she had made a mistake in marrying Frank. Her life had been lonely and she needed someone. After leaving school in the middle of her junior year, she had gotten a job at a bakery. She worked at the bakery for the next seven years. One evening she met a man in a local tavern, and within a month, they decided to get married. Since Virg had already quit school and had found a job, Wanda felt her sister could take care of herself and their father. She and her new husband moved to Minneapolis. Before they moved, she promised her father and sister that some day they would all live in a house together. After less than two years of marriage, her husband left home one morning for work and never returned. The following week she got a job at the Old Dutch Potato Chip factory.

"If Frank thinks that Butch pushed him, I'm afraid of what he might do," Virg said. "You know how mean he can get."

"Only when he's stressed out. Don't forget that the poor man is trying to get a job. Every time he gets one, the foreman seems to have it in for him. Frank doesn't have a chance."

"Are you sure that's the reason?"

"Of course," Wanda replied, irritated by her sister questioning her. "At his last job, he was accused of taking too much time for lunch. Frank tried to explain that he has a digestive problem and has to eat slowly, but his boss didn't believe him and the other workers made fun of him."

"Digestive problem? I don't believe that myself," Virg said. "When did he start having that?"

Wanda shifted uneasily at the lie she was about to offer. "He doesn't have a serious problem, but the strain of working affects his eating. That's why he has to take it easy in his jobs. The poor man has never had a break in his life."

"That doesn't give him the right to knock you around, does it?"

The question took Wanda by surprise. Virg had approached a subject they normally avoided. Stunned to hear the anger in her sister's voice, she sat there, unsure how to respond.

"Don't think that I'm angry with you," Virg offered, breaking the silence. "It's Frank that I'm mad at. We need to stick together as family. After all, it's only us two and Pa and Butch." She paused. When she spoke again, a compassionate plea replaced the anger. "I'm just concerned about you. You're the only sister I have. I just don't want anything happening to you."

"Don't worry. I'll be okay," Wanda said. "Look, I know Frank gets mean every now and then, but I love him. I wouldn't know what I'd do without him. After Joe left, I was so lonely. I don't want to feel that way again."

"But don't you see, we could have that house we've been talking about all these years. All we need is to get a down payment. We could manage that in two or three years." Virg reached across the table to take Wanda's hand. "Then we'd be together."

"That would be nice," Wanda replied as she held tightly onto her sister's hand.

"Sure wish Ma was around. I don't remember much about her, but I miss her. She made us a family, didn't she?"

Before Wanda could answer, the door opened and Adam walked in. As soon as he saw them, he stopped and stood in the half-kitchen as though trying to decide to stay or leave.

"You got a minute to talk?" Wanda made it sound more like a command than a question.

"Sure, I've got a little time." Adam sat down. "What is going on?"

"Butch—" his mother began.

"I'll handle this," Wanda said. She turned toward Adam. "Did you and Frank have some kind of problem the other day?"

Adam's eyes darted between the two of them. "No. Why? What did he say?"

"That you shoved him down the stairs. He thought that maybe you were angry at him for some reason." She wanted to ask Adam if he got hurt, if he was okay, but couldn't bring herself to do it. "You didn't push him, did you?"

"No!" Adam snapped. "I met him on the steps going out. I must've brushed up against him. He got knocked off balance a little but that was it. How would he know what happened, anyway? He was so drunk, he couldn't see straight."

"Are you sure that was all that happened?" Virg asked.

"As far as I'm concerned, it was." Adam got up, went to the refrigerator and got a bottle of milk. After pouring a glass for himself, he put the bottle back, and slammed the door. "Anything else now?"

"No, that's all." Satisfied, Wanda got up and walked to the door. She paused as she opened it, and looked back at them. "Start thinking about coming over for Thanksgiving."

"I can come later in the day," Virg replied. "I have to work the extra shift, but I know Oscar would like to come. Butch, you'll be there, won't you?"

"I don't know."

"Butch, it's a day you should be with family," Wanda said. She eyed her sister. "You should be at home that day."

"What can I do?" Virg asked, sounding reprimanded. "I have to work."

Wanda frowned and then turned to Adam. "One more thing, Butch. Be nice to Frank. He hasn't worked now for over a month and he's getting down, if you know what I mean."

"I'm going to work," Adam said.

* * *

When Adam got home from work that evening, his mother wasn't there. Oscar was watching television in the living room. He walked through the living room, hoping he could get to the bedroom without getting involved in a conversation. As unfriendly as he was to the man, he couldn't comprehend why Oscar continued to be so friendly toward him.

"Your mom's shopping," Oscar said as he looked up and smiled. "Said she wanted to get an early start on Christmas this year." He waited for a response but none came. "Did you get something to eat? I'll fix you something."

"I ate already," Adam lied. He didn't like Oscar doing any favors for him. "Did you wash?" he asked.

"Yah. Why?"

"Your face is dirty."

"By golly, bet you it's from working at the train yards." He picked up a small mirror from the coffee table. “Yah, you bet.” He chuckled as he held the mirror in front of his face. “Got train soot on my nose.”

For some reason, the fact that his nose was dirty struck Oscar funny that he laughed so hard he nearly choked on his snuff. “Phew,” he uttered as he spit a brown gob into a coffee can sitting next to his chair. “Good stuff, yah, but you don’t want to swallow it, by golly.”

Adam shook his head in disgust.

Oscar Johnson, in his late fifties, would never change. The Happy Swede, as he told Adam he was called down at the railroad yards, would always be - sober or drunk - good natured. Adam’s mother had told him Oscar’s story. Arriving from Sweden at the age of twenty-one, Oscar traveled to Minnesota and got a job working for the railroad. He lived alone in a boarding house until seven years ago when a fire destroyed it. He had known Adam’s mother from being a regular customer at Andy’s. When she heard about the fire, she felt so sorry for him that she invited the man to move in with them. It had proved to be a mutually beneficial arrangement. Oscar would have a place to live and an instant family. Adam’s mother, as she often reminded her son, would have extra money from the rent she charged Oscar.

The phone rang and Adam stepped into the kitchen to answer it. “Hello.”

“Hi there, buddy. It’s Mick. Have I hit on a scheme to get Howie! Wait until you hear it. It’s perfect.”

Adam listened with interest.

“This is going to be better than homecoming itself,” Mick proclaimed after sharing the details. “It’s going to be a date that Howie will long remember.”

Chapter 8

Adam stood outside his apartment building waiting for Mick. He had mixed feelings about the evening ahead. He looked forward to seeing Mick's scheme concerning Howie unfold, hoping it would get his mind off Frank for a while. He wasn't in the mood, however, for a date with Sue. It wasn't her. He just didn't feel very talkative tonight. After the confrontation with Frank on the stairs the other day, they were now on a collision course. Something had to be done to teach him a lesson, and the sooner the better.

The beige two-tone Impala, with Mick at the wheel, pulled up. Adam opened the door and paused for a moment. "Sharp!" he announced as he got in.

"Are you talking about me or the car?"

"Both."

Mick wore a light-brown crew-neck sweater and dark slacks. Howie had suggested that the three of them wear the same colored sweaters and slacks. Adam and Mick agreed to wear sweaters and slacks, but said no to the idea of having them be the same colors.

Adam settled in, gave the car's interior a quick once over, and ran his fingers over the top of the expansive dashboard. He rubbed his thumb across his fingers. "This baby's clean."

"It ought to be. I spent two hours yesterday giving it a wash and wax." Mick used his handkerchief to wipe a smudge off the windshield. He put the car in gear and pulled away.

Adam noted the pair of fuzzy pink dice swinging from the rearview mirror. "This car's clean, inside and out. I'm impressed."

Mick slowed down for the corner light that had just turned red. "You're impressed. You should've heard my father. He was so blown away that he said I should go out on triple dates more often."

"Does he still press you about football?"

"Oh, yes."

"But he let you have the car."

"Sure." Mick used the handkerchief to wipe another area on the windshield. "Of course, when he handed me the car keys, he said 'Anything for a future college football star.'"

"Haven't you talked to him yet?" Adam asked as the Impala moved swiftly through the intersection.

"You mean about me maybe not playing football?"

"Yeah. I thought you'd tell him."

"Are you kidding? If I would've even hinted about that, we wouldn't have this set of wheels tonight."

"Would he do that?"

Mick drove for another block before answering. "Your mom ever read you bedtime stories when you were a kid?"

"Not really."

"My father did. I remember sitting on his lap and him reading to me. I don't think I was more than 4 or 5 years old. And do you know what book he read from?"

Adam heard sarcasm in Mick's voice, but also something else. Anger or sadness. Maybe both.

"A book on the rules of football." Mick slapped the steering wheel with the palm of his hand. "Can you imagine that? I got to hate it, but I didn't say anything because I just enjoyed being with my father. And then after awhile I…"

"Has he always been that way about you and football?"

"Ever since I can remember." Mick slowed for a car turning a corner in front of him. "My mother told me that when I came home from the hospital, he put a football in the crib with me." He glanced over at Adam. "That's my father for you."

As the Impala moved down Broadway, Adam gazed out his window. The kaleidoscope of buildings and lights blurred as he thought about what Mick had shared concerning his father. What would it have been like for him to have a father when he was young? His own father had not contacted him in the sixteen years since the divorce between him and Adam's mother. His mother never talked about his father, and he never asked.

"Did you notice them?" Mick asked, pointing to the fuzzy pink dice.

"How could anyone miss those things?" He tapped them, causing them to swing back and forth. "They're not your dad's, are they?"

"Nope. He bought them for me to hang in the car tonight. Must've thought they'd impress the girls. Didn't want to tell him that they're not my style."

"So what are you going to do?"

"Figure I'll give them to Howie. He—" Mick honked at a man crossing the street without watching the traffic. "Howie likes stuff like that." He pulled up to a stoplight. While waiting for it to turn green, he rubbed the back of his neck.

"Neck bothering you?"

"A little. I did something to it in the game this afternoon."

"Too bad we lost. Washburn walked all over us."

"Walked?" Mick laughed. "36 to 6 is more like a stomp. Let's face it, they kicked our butts. The coach was so angry that he wouldn't talk to us afterwards. Man, I sure don't look forward to Monday's practice."

"You didn't play that bad."

"It sure wasn't my best game. You should've heard my father earlier this evening. He started giving me a lecture until my mother stepped in and convinced him to talk to me later. I can hardly wait for that. Man, I'd rather face my coach."

The light turned and Adam watched as the dice start swinging with the movement of the car. "You'll still make all-conference, won't you?"

"I don't know. Maybe. If I make it, I make it. If I don't, it's not the end of the world." He looked over at Adam. "Enough about football. We've got a big night ahead of us. Let's go get Mary and the others. I can hardly wait to spring our surprise on Howie. Do me a favor?"

"Sure. What?"

"Put the dice in the glove compartment, will you? If Mary sees them, she'll think I flipped or something."

"You got it. Anything else?"

"Yeah, don't let me forget to give them to Howie later."

The ride to Mary's didn't take more than ten minutes. Mick parked the car in front of her house. "Only five minutes late. Keep guard over this beauty. I'll be back in a minute."

Mick got out and started up the walk to the house. Just before he got there, the outside lights came on and the front door opened. Mary stepped out, and Adam watched as Mick gave her a hug. Mary looked toward the car and waved. She was wearing a long-sleeved light-colored sweater and a dark skirt. The light from inside the house reflected off her shoulder-length blond hair. He agreed with Mick that Mary was a beauty. She had been homecoming attendant last year but decided not to run this year. "Too much hoopla," she had told Adam. An honor student, she was interested in teaching English at a college level. Adam respected her from the first time he met her, and it grew after she told him she knew that a college teaching position wouldn't come simply on the basis of having been a homecoming queen.

Mick and Mary stepped inside the house for a moment. When they came back out, she was carrying a light coat. As they walked to the car, hand-in-hand, Adam got out and held the car door open for her.

"Why, thank you, you're the perfect gentleman tonight."

Adam got in after her. After Mick got in, Mary moved closer to him, leaning her head on his shoulder for a moment.

"I'm glad you and Sue are going tonight," Mary said once the three of them had settled. "How is she?" she asked.

"She's doing okay," Adam replied, wondering if Mary was probing to see when the last time he and Sue had dated. It irritated him a little. Since Mary and Sue often ate lunch together, she already knew that it had been over a month since they had dated. Maybe even two months. He wasn't sure.

On the way to get Sue, Adam sat quietly, listening to Mary and Mick talked about school. She asked if Mick had any ideas about Mattingale's writing assignment. As Mick shared his thoughts, Mary listened intently, making comments here and there, offering suggestions, and giving encouragement. She was already sounding like a teacher.

"Which house was it again that Sue lives in?" Mick asked Adam.

"It's that white one on the right. Just park right behind that Chevy. I'll jump out and be back in a minute." After Mick parked the car, Adam got out, walked up to the house and rang the doorbell.

Within moments, the door opened. “Hi,” Sue said. “Do you want to come in for a minute?”

Adam glanced back at the car. “I don’t think so. Mick’s got the car running.”

“Let me get my coat, then.” Sue was back within moments. “You look nice this evening,” she said as they walked to the car. “That brown sweater matches the color of your eyes.”

“Thanks.” He thought about repaying the compliment but didn’t, not because there was nothing to compliment. With long dark hair and bluish-green eyes, she looked attractive in her pleated skirt and long-sleeved beige blouse. Mary had told Mick that Sue had guys calling her all the time. As she got in the back seat with Adam, both Mick and Mary said hi, with Mary adding, “You look great tonight.”

Mick looked in the rearview mirror, grinned, and announced, “Okay, let’s go get Howie. This is going to be a night to remember.”

Chapter 9

"We'll be at Howie's in five minutes," Mick announced to his passengers, his voice crackling with anticipation.

Sue leaned forward and touched Mary upon the back of her shoulder. "What do you think of these two and what they have planned for Howie?"

Mary turned to face Sue and Adam in the back seat. "I wasn't too sure of it at first. Then I remembered all the things Howie has pulled."

"He sure has," Mick interjected, chuckling. "And he's got it coming."

Mary turned around, moving closer to Mick. "I hope Cindy doesn't get mad."

"I don't think she will. She's got a good sense of humor."

"Tell me just exactly how this is going to work?" Sue asked Mick.

"I've told Cindy that Howie is hard of hearing and that she's got to talk loud. And when we get Howie, I'll tell him that Cindy is hard of hearing and that he'll have to speak up." Mick drove around a car that had been doubled parked. "It's a good thing that Cindy's from a different school or else we could never have tried this."

"You can be so devious at times," Mary teased.

"Anyway, the four of us will talk loud to both Howie and Cindy. If this works the way it's supposed to, each of them will think we're doing it because the other one has a hearing problem."

Sue giggled. "This whole thing is great. I love it. It'll pay Howie back for what he did in the lunchroom. And to think, I used to like spaghetti."

Howie stood waiting for them at the curb in front of an older two-story duplex where he and his father lived. Mick had barely pulled up when Howie rushed up to the car and opened the door.

He looked in the back seat, gave a half smile to Adam and Sue, and climbed in the front next to Mary. "About time you showed up," he said.

Mick pointed to his watch. "Hey, buddy, we're right on time."

"Can I help it if I'm a little anxious? You've got to remember, I don't know too much about this chick."

"Hey, man, just trust me." Mick put the car in gear. "You and Cindy are made for each other. She's not only gorgeous but also has a great personality." He slowed the car as they approached a stop sign. "She's lots of fun and one of her school's best cheerleaders."

Mick drove as the girls chatted about who they might see at the dance and what the other girls would be wearing. After pulling up to a stoplight, he took advantage of a lull in the conversation. "Howie, there's one thing I forgot to mention about Cindy, but it shouldn't be a problem."

"What!" Howie cried. "Something you *forgot* to tell me? Let me out of this car now!" he demanded. "I'm going home and work on my stamp collection."

"I didn't know you collected stamps," Sue said.

"Tell her the truth, now," Mick said. "You don't have any stamp collection."

"So, I'll go home and start one."

"Come on," Mick said. "It's not that bad."

"Tell me then, what's wrong with her?" Howie kept anxiously glancing between Mick and Adam. "You guys aren't saying anything. That can only mean one thing. She's ugly, isn't she?"

"No," Mick said. "I told you she's gorgeous and I mean it. Now, I wouldn't lie to you about that. Just settle back, close your eyes, and relax. We'll be there in a few minutes."

Howie leaned his head back. "Oh, no!" he suddenly cried, straightening up. "I just figured it out. She's got a hairy chest, right?"

"Howie!" Mary scolded. "That's not even nice. Mick, tell him what you mean."

"Yeah, tell me!"

"All right, all right." Mick paused. "Cindy has a hearing

problem. You'll have to speak loud in order for her to hear you. That's all."

"A hearing problem? Great!" A puzzled looked came over Howie. "How are we going to dance with that white cane?"

"Howie, a white cane is for people who are blind," Sue said, giggling so hard that she barely got the words out.

"Cindy isn't blind," Mick said. "She's just hard of hearing," he explained as they turned onto a street lined with large oak trees. "Just trust me," he pleaded as the car slowed down.

"Why didn't you tell me ahead of time?" Howie groaned. "Just what I need. I'm going to the biggest dance of the year with a hairy-chest deaf girl who uses a white cane."

"Come on, Howie," Mick said. "I didn't tell you ahead of time because you wouldn't have come, would you?"

"You've got that right. Tell me how long before we get there. I want to know how much time I've got left."

"Another couple of blocks and we'll be there. I'll go up and get her, okay?" Mick didn't give his friend a chance to respond. "That way, you'll have a chance to check her out."

"You mean prepare myself." Howie looked out his window. "Mick, have you got any rope in the car?"

"No. Why?"

"In case I want to hang myself from one of those trees."

"Oh, Howie, don't be so dramatic," Sue said. "I'm sure it'll work out very nicely. Just wait and see."

"Eaten any spaghetti lately?"

"Howie, let's not get nasty," Mary chided.

"Yeah," Adam said. "Or else we *will* find some rope…to *tie* you up with."

"We're here," Mick announced. He parked the car and turned off the ignition. "I'll be back with your date in a second."

"Take your time," Howie said.

Mick walked up to the light-colored rambler, knocked on the door, and then looked back at the car. He waved and turned to knock again when the door opened and a girl, dressed in a poodle skirt and a short-sleeve blouse, stepped out.

"That must be Cindy," Mary said. "She's cute."

"I like her ponytail," Sue added. "She sure looks like a cheerleader."

"Do you think her cheerleading caused her to lose her hearing?" Howie asked.

Mick and Cindy stood and talked as he gestured in the direction of the car. Every now and then, she looked toward the car.

"Here they come," Sue announced. "She's *really* cute. Don't you think so, Howie?"

Before Howie could respond, Mick opened the car door. "Howie, this is Cindy!" he shouted. "Cindy, this is Howie!"

"Hi!" Howie shouted.

"That's Adam and Sue back there!" Mick yelled as he asked Adam to open the back door. "And this is Mary!"

"Hi!" Mary said.

Mick continued the charade. "Howie! You and Cindy sit in the back seat with Adam and Sue!"

Incredibly, as they rode to the dance, neither Howie nor Cindy caught on to the gag. When they arrived at the dance, Howie insisted they get a table close to the band, a rock and roll group called *Johnny O and the Swing Kats*.

It was during one of the intermissions that Mick's scheme was uncovered. Cindy, with her back to the others, had turned to read a banner on one of the walls. Howie whispered to his friends, "Guys, I can't hold it in any longer." Before Mick could stop him, Howie spoke to the back of his date in a normal speaking voice. "Cindy, you've got a great body and I love you. I want to marry you."

Cindy turned around, a startled look on her face. "What did you say?"

"I love your body and I want to marry you!" Howie shouted.

People sitting at other tables stopped in the middle of their conversations and stared at Howie who had turned a deep crimson. The drummer on the stage played a drum roll. "Yeah, man! Go for it!"

Mick laughed until tears came to his eyes. His outburst was contagious and before long, Mary and Sue had joined in. Even Adam chuckled.

Cindy lowered her voice. "Howie, can you hear me?"

"Yes!" he shouted and then gulped. "I mean, yes."

"I think we've been had." Cindy giggled. "What fun." She

wiped away tears of laughter. "This is one date I'll never forget."

"You won't?"

"Really, I won't." Cindy placed her hand on Howie's arm. "This is great. My friends at school won't believe this."

As the evening went on, it became increasingly evident just how much Cindy and Howie enjoyed each other's company. They danced and talked as though they had been together for months. During an intermission, the two of them decided to go for a walk.

"They're certainly hitting it off," Mary said.

"That's for sure." Mick turned to Adam. "Did you see the way she was looking at him?"

"Yeah, he's going to be hard to live with."

Mick took Mary's hand. "Let's go over and talk to Debbie and Tom."

Before they left, Mary turned to Adam and Sue. "You two want to come along?"

"I don't," Adam said. "Sue, if you want to, go ahead."

"Oh, no. I'll stay."

"You could've gone," Adam said after Mick and Mary left. "You're good friends with Debbie."

"Don't be silly. I want to stay with you. That's okay, isn't it?"

"Sure."

Nearly a minute went by before the silence was broken by Sue. "You've been quiet tonight. Is anything wrong?"

"No. Why do you ask?"

"I don't know. At times, it's just so hard to figure out what's going on with you."

"Nothing's going on. I've just been listening and watching people." Adam wished the others would come back. Sue had a way of probing that made him feel uneasy. "So, what do you want to talk about?"

"How's your aunt? Mick told me what happened."

Adam shot a glance across the room to where Mick and Mary sat visiting with the other couple. He hadn't told Mick to keep it to himself, but felt angry with him for telling Sue. She was the type of person who would want to be helpful. He didn't need her help. He didn't need anybody's help.

"I'm so sorry," Sue said. "You must feel bad about it."

"It's no problem now. She's doing better. How about yourself? I heard you talking earlier to Mary about some relative who's in the hospital."

Sue studied him. "Adam, why do you always change the subject when it comes to yourself and your feelings?"

"What are you talking about? I didn't deny that my aunt's going through some bad times, did I?"

"No."

"See? I'm just trying to be sensitive to your relatives. Didn't you say your aunt has cancer? That's a little more serious than what's going on with mine, isn't it?"

"Yes, but—"

"But what? When did she find out? And talking about feelings, how's your mother feeling about it? She's your mother's older sister, isn't she? I bet you…"

The rest of the conversation centered on Sue's aunt. Adam even managed to have her talk about how her mother was dealing with it.

"Hey, you two," Mick said as he and Mary came back. "It looked like you guys were engaged in something pretty serious."

Sue gave Adam a sideward glance. "Well, he certainly knows me and my family well."

Adam stood up. "I'll be right back. I see someone I need to talk to."

That *someone* was Danny Logan who had just come in with his girlfriend, Meg. The two of them stood at the door listening to the band. Adam had heard that Meg was close to dropping out of school.

"Hi, Danny," Adam said as he walked up to him.

"Hey, how ya doin'? Ya know Meg here, don't ya?"

"Sure. Hi."

"Hi." Meg paid more attention to the band than anything else. Her tight-fitting sweater and skirt drew the attention of guys walking by.

"Can we talk some time?" Adam asked Danny.

"How about now?"

"It's not a good time, now. How about tomorrow morning? I could meet you by Kass' Drugstore around eight."

"Naw, I won't be in any kind of shape in the mornin'." Danny stroked his chin, glanced sideways at Meg, and smirked.

"What are ya two talkin' about?" Meg snapped her gum and moved in closer to Danny, touching her hip against his. "I bet ya were talkin' about me, weren't ya? Tell me, Danny, what'd ya say?"

"I'll tell ya later, baby."

"Come on, Danny, tell me," she whined.

"Later, I said."

"How about Monday morning before school?" Adam asked. "We'll meet by the gate to the football field. Around seven-thirty."

"Sounds cool. See ya then." Danny put his arm around Meg's waist. "Come on, let's go have some fun."

Adam walked back to the table where his friends sat.

"Wasn't that Danny Logan you were talking to?" Mary asked.

"Yeah. I told him about Howie's lunchroom gag. I was curious what he thought about it."

"What did he say?" Sue asked.

"He would've put real worms in the spaghetti pots."

A frown crossed Mary's face. "That doesn't surprise me. No wonder he got kicked out of school."

"Here come Howie and Cindy," Sue announced. "They sure make a nice looking couple."

The six young people stayed for another round of dances and then left to eat. On the way to the *Hamburger Heaven Drive-in* they laughed about the evening. After they ate, Cindy was the first to be taken home. Howie walked her up to the door, the two of them disappearing into the shadows for a few minutes.

When Howie came back and climbed into the front seat, Mick glanced in the rearview mirror at Adam. "Don't you just want to kiss that innocent-looking face?"

"Not quite"

"Poor Howie," Sue said.

"What? Are you talking about me?"

Mick laughed. "Just stay in your own little lovesick world while I take Sue home."

By the time they arrived at Sue's, the boisterous laughter had been replaced by quiet conversation. Mick parked the car and Adam walked Sue to the door. At the door, he said good night and began to walk away.

"Adam?" When he turned, she asked, "Are you going to call me?"

"Ah…sure."

"I hope you won't wait too long to call this time."

"After the holidays, okay?" As Adam walked back and got into the car his thoughts weren't of Sue and their next date, but of Danny Logan and Frank.

"Why don't you drop me off next?" Mary said. "I'm tired."

Mick patted his shoulder, motioning to Mary to lean her head against it.

The drive to Mary's house didn't take long. Adam got out and climbed into the front seat with Howie while Mick took Mary up to her door. They didn't have to wait long for Mick to return.

Mick got in, started up the engine, and put the car in gear. "You're not mad at us for pulling that little joke on you, are you?" he asked Howie.

"Heck no. Cindy's great." Howie kept glancing back and forth between Mick and Adam. "You know what we did when we left the dance for awhile? We walked around the block a couple of times and talked about our families, school, my father, about all kinds of things. She's a good listener and a great talker."

"Sounds good to me," Mick said as he pulled away from the curb.

"And do you know what? We've got a date next week. She invited me to a dance at her school."

"Oh, oh. This sounds serious."

Mick and Adam listened as Howie talked about Cindy. Just as they got to Howie's house, Mick exclaimed, "Man, I almost forgot!"

"Forgot what?" Howie asked.

"Open up the glove compartment," Mick said. "We have a little gift for you. It's something to remember this evening."

"Cool," Howie said as soon as he saw the dice. "Thanks, guys. Do you know where I'm going to hang these?"

"Your school locker," Mick said.

"How do you know that?"

"Because we know you."

After they let Howie out, they drove several blocks before Mick glanced over at Adam. "You seemed a little distant tonight after you talked to Danny Logan."

Adam had expected Mick to say something ever since leaving the dance. "Guess I've just got some things on my mind."

"If Logan is part of those things, it means trouble."

"It's best you don't know. Just go with me on this, all right?"

"Okay, if you say so."

Adam gazed out the window during the rest of the ride home and thought about Monday morning.

Chapter 10

Danny Logan leaned against the chain-link fence, waiting for Adam. He reached for his smokes, rapping the pack against his palm. After plucking a slightly bent one out with his lips, he dug into his pocket for a lighter, and lit his cigarette. He took a long deep drag, slowly exhaling as he watched the smoke swirl away. Even though it was chilly out, he had zipped his jacket only partway.

"Hey, Danny."

Freddie Jagger, a guy Danny used to hang around with during lunch at school, strolled up.

"Hey, Freddie, my man. How're they hangin'?"

"Hangin' just fine." A puzzled look came over Freddie's face. "Man, what are ya doin' here? I thought Danny Logan was done with this dumb place."

"Gotta meet someone." Danny took another drag off his cigarette. "Goin' to do some business. Get some action. Know what I mean?"

Freddie grinned. "Same old Danny boy. Listen man, I'd like to stay and shoot the shit, but I gotta retake some stupid test. My old man is givin' me hell about failin' it."

"Tell your old man to take a hike." Danny grabbed Freddie's book, flipped through a couple of pages, and tossed it back. "Have some smokes with me and forget about all that shit."

"Man, I'd like to but the old man is pissed at me. If I fail this time, he's kickin' my ass out of the house." Freddie eyed Danny's cigarette. Glancing around, he reached for it, taking a couple of quick drags before giving it back. "Gotta go. Take care, man. And Danny?"

"Yeah?"

Freddie smirked. "I'll say hello to Briston for ya."

At the mention of Briston, Danny shot an angry look toward the school. "Yeah, say hello to that mother for me."

After Freddie left, Danny took another drag off his cigarette and flipped the ashes toward the school. He thought back to that day he was expelled for decking Mr. Briston, the typing teacher. Briston was already in the principal's office, sitting in a chair, when Danny was *escorted* in by two other teachers. Waite, the principal, sat behind his desk like some big shot.

"He shouldn't have yelled at me!" Danny said as he stood in front of Waite's desk.

"Keep your voice down, young man," Waite warned. "Now, tell me. What were you doing?"

"Nothin'."

"He was pounding on the typewriter keys with his fists trying to be a smart ass." Briston could only mumble the words as he held a cold compress to his mouth. His lip was badly swollen but the bleeding had stopped.

After calming Briston down, Waite turned his attention back to Danny. "And what have you got to say for your reprehensible behavior?"

Danny shot a sneering glance over at Briston. "I say nobody yells at Danny Logan."

"Young man, you're suspended for ten days." Waite's voice sounded controlled but Danny could see the veins in his temple pulsating. "You may come back after the ten days are up, but only after you have apologized to Mr. Briston."

As Danny now checked his watch, he shivered as the sun went behind some clouds. If Adam didn't come soon, he would split. Danny Logan doesn't wait for anyone. Rolling the cigarette between his thumb and forefinger, his thoughts went back to that morning in Waite's office. A crooked smile appeared on his lips as he recalled the shocked looks of Briston and Waite when he had given them the finger and walked out, announcing, "That's my apology!" He was still chuckling about that when Adam walked up.

"Hey, Adam, how're ya doin'?"

"Okay."

Danny cocked his head toward the school. "Man, I'm sure glad to be outta that crummy place. Don't have to put up with any more shit from teachers. So, man, what's happenin'?"

"Remember when I got you that whiskey in junior high?"

"Man, how could I forget that? Got a chick bombed on it. Had a good time with her. I owe ya for that."

"I'm here to collect."

Danny took a drag off his cigarette. "So, man, what do ya want?"

"To teach someone a lesson."

Danny flipped his cigarette away and stepped away from the fence. "Your talkin' some action, right?"

Adam nodded.

"You've come to the right man, then." Danny liked having a reputation as a tough guy. It kept him on the edge and he liked the excitement that came with it. "Sounds like some ass kickin' Anybody I know?"

"His name is Frank. He's married to my aunt. Thinks he's a tough guy."

Danny studied Adam for a moment. "Ya want in on it?"

"I...ah, would, but if Frank knew about me, he'd take it out on my aunt. That wouldn't be good. You know what I mean?"

"Yeah, sure. That's cool." Danny wondered how Adam would do in a rumble. "When do ya want this to go down?"

"Wednesday night."

"Why then?"

"Because every Wednesday he goes down to this bar."

"So, what time we talkin' about?"

"Around eleven-thirty. He always comes home at the same time. Walks past Skelly's Liquor Store and—"

"Hey, man, that's the spot to do it. In Skelly's parking lot. It's dark toward the back near the alley." Danny leaned back against the fence. "Do ya wanna watch? Ya can stand in the back by the alley. He'd never see ya."

Adam hesitated. "Sure. I'll watch."

"Okay, man! Now, we're cookin'." Danny took out his pack of cigarettes. "We'll meet ya around eleven."

"Who's with you on this?"

"What's it to ya?" Danny lit his cigarette while giving Adam a suspicious look.

"Frank's a big guy. Won't be easy to take him down."

"Don't sweat it. I'll take Pete and another guy." Danny didn't like Adam inferring that he couldn't handle this on his own.

"Who's that?"

"Johnny Tomaski. Do ya know him?"

"No, but didn't Pete just get out on probation?"

"Yeah, but it doesn't matter. He wouldn't mind goin' back." Danny flicked the ashes off his cigarette. "Man, they'd never get me in one of those joints. I'd die first. Ain't nobody goin' to lock Danny Logan up. Nobody." He picked a piece of tobacco off his tongue. "How far do ya want us to go with this guy?"

Adam's eyes narrowed. "Far enough so that he knows what it means to hurt."

"That's cool." Danny studied Adam for a moment. "Why don't ya come in with me? Got some things comin' up where I could use ya. What do ya say?"

"I'll give it some thought."

"Sure, ya do that. I'll catch ya Wednesday night around eleven. We'll meet in the parkin' lot."

* * *

Danny and Frank were still on his mind as Adam walked up the stairs and headed toward Mattingale's classroom to turn in an overdue book report. She had told him after class on Friday to be sure to have it on her desk the first thing Monday morning. When he opened the door to her classroom, he stopped in his tracks. Mick and Howie were on their knees examining the right-hand drawer of her desk.

"What are you guys up to?"

Mick gasped. "Man, you scared me."

"Don't you know that Mattingale may come at any time?"

"That's what I've been telling this clown."

"Look, it's worth the risk," Howie said as he went back to inspecting the desk. "I'm going to make us famous. All we've got to do is figure out how to get into this drawer."

"You guys should've posted a lookout."

"Hey, that's a good idea," Mick said, standing up. "I'll volunteer for that."

Adam squatted beside Howie. "Just how do you plan to do this?"

"See this?" Howie held up a paper clip that had been bent to form a hook. He inserted it into the keyhole of the desk's drawer. His ear against the wood drawer, he turned his homemade key.

"That's not going to work."

"Shhh," Howie whispered. "I want to hear the lock trip."

"She's coming!" Mick warned as he rushed into the room. He shut the door and made a dash for his classroom seat.

Scrambling to get up, Adam knocked Howie's head against the drawer. Sprawled on the floor, the would-be safe cracker moaned.

"Howie, are you okay?" Mick asked.

"I almost had it opened," he groaned. "I even heard it click."

"I'll click you. You dummy, that was Adam snapping his fingers. Come on, get up and get back here. Mattingale's coming."

As Howie rushed to get to his seat, Adam tried to think of something to tell their teacher about why they were in her classroom. He was just about to ask Mick for some suggestions when they both noticed Howie's ear.

"What happened to your ear?" Mick asked.

Before Howie could respond, Miss Mattingale walked through the door. She sat down at her desk and had just opened her purse when she nearly froze. "What are you three doing here? Shouldn't you be in your home rooms?"

"Sorry we frightened you, Miss Mattingale," Adam said. "Our homeroom teachers excused us because we wanted to discuss with you the recent paper you assigned."

"The three of you would like to discuss the assignment?"

"Yes, ma'am," Mick said, giving Adam a conspiratorial look. "We'd like to, ah, hear your insights on how to tap into our personal creativity."

"I see." Miss Mattingale sounded pleased. "I am not accustomed to this. Students usually are not so sensitive. It is delightful to—" Her eyes widened. "Howard, what in heaven's name is wrong with your ear?"

Howie looked behind him before pointing to himself.

"Yes, you, Howard. Please come up here at once." She waited for him to come to her. "Why, Howard, your ear is bleeding!" she exclaimed, being careful not to touch his ear with her white gloves.

“Oh, I must’ve cut myself shaving this morning.”

“But how would that explain that?” She pointed to his ear.

“Explain what?”

“My poor boy, don’t you realize? You have a long wooden sliver imbedded in your earlobe.”

“A sliver?” Howie’s face turned pale.

“Miss Mattingale,” Adam said. “He may be going into shock. I’d suggest that he go to the nurse’s office immediately.”

“I agree. Howard, go to the nurse’s office now.” Wide-eyed, she continued to stare at his ear. “Do you feel you will require assistance?”

“I can make it on my own.” At the doorway Howie paused, turned and looked at his two friends. “Would you guys please take notes on Miss Mattingale’s suggestions? I wouldn’t want to miss her insights.”

“What a dedicated young man,” Miss Mattingale proclaimed after Howie left. “Well, we shall not disappoint him.”

She made sure that Mick and Adam had notebooks and pencils in hand before passionately lecturing to them for the next twenty minutes. She also made sure that the two of them took copious notes for the sake of “that dear boy, Howard”. At the end of the time, both Mick and Adam had written nearly three pages of notes.

Later that day at lunch, Howie told Adam and Mick that he had asked the school nurse if having had a sliver imbedded in your earlobe would cause a person to lose their hearing.

“What do you guys think?” he asked.

Mick quietly took Howie’s peanut butter sandwich and squeezed it into a ball. “Why don’t you stick that in your ear and see if you can still hear?”

For Adam, the next two days went slowly. When Wednesday finally came, he went about doing the day’s activities in a very deliberate way, being careful not to reveal his anxiety. Howie didn’t notice anything different about him, but he suspected that Mick had questions about him and Logan.

That night when he met Danny Logan and his two friends in the alley behind the liquor store, Adam could smell the whiskey on their breaths.

Chapter 11

Dressed in jeans, black tee shirts, and black leather jackets, Danny and his pals were ready to rumble. "Hey, Adam, my man. Ready to see some ass kickin' tonight?" Danny took a swig from a pint bottle and offered it to him.

"I'll pass."

"Suit yourself. Pete's ready to kick some ass, ain't ya?"

Pete grunted his reply. When Pete quit school at age sixteen, Danny had bragged to Adam, "He's better off with me. Ain't nobody knows the streets better than Danny Logan."

"Johnny's ready, too," Danny said.

"Sure am man." Johnny sounded pumped for action. Although shorter than Pete he had the build of a wrestler.

Adam took note of what Pete held by his side. "What's with the baseball bat?"

"Goin' to play some baseball, man," Danny said. "We got the bat and old Frank's goin' to be the ball."

Adam wanted Frank hurt, but hadn't counted on this. "You'll know him, won't you?"

Danny sneered. "The way ya described his ugly puss, can't miss him."

"You won't need the bat," Adam said, keeping his tone casual. "The three of you should handle him easy."

"We'll handle him any way we want," Danny said. "Got a problem with that?"

Adam noted that Pete held the bat firmly in both hands as though daring anyone to take it from him. "I just thought that—"

"Forget it because we're goin' to have ourselves a little game of baseball tonight." Danny grabbed the bottle from Pete. "Damn! Ya didn't leave me more than a swallow."

Pete shrugged as Danny finished what was left.

Danny pointed to the back of the building next to the alley. "Adam, ya can stand over there. Frank won't see ya there. You'll have a front row seat."

A flood light from the warehouse down the alley gave Adam just enough light to distinguish Johnny and Pete's features. He watched as they disappeared into the shadows on the other side of the empty lot. Before long, a tiny flame appeared, flickered for a few seconds, and vanished. A cigarette passed back and forth between them, its red tip, dancing like a firefly, had a hypnotic effect upon Adam until it dropped to the ground and disappeared.

Danny positioned himself at the front corner of the liquor store next to the empty lot. Ten minutes later, as Frank walked by, Danny stepped directly into his path.

"Watch where you're goin' old man!" Danny shouted.

"What the hell?" Frank stood his ground.

"I said move it. Get your drunken ass outta my way."

"Why ya young punk! Who in hell do ya think you're talkin' to?"

"Shove it, old man."

"Ya little hood, ya want your ass kicked?"

Danny laughed. "By who? Ya?"

"Damn right. Right now. Right here."

Danny slowly backed into the vacant lot, taunting Frank. "Come on. Come on old man if ya think ya can do it."

Frank took the bait. "Damn no good punk!"

"Come over here in the light old man so ya can see what you're swingin' at."

"No good punk! I'll show ya who—"

The blow came from Pete who stepped from the shadows, whacking Frank in the side with the bat. Frank screamed in pain and clutched his ribs. "Home run!" Pete yelled as he handed the bat to Johnny. The next blow struck Frank in the back. He cried in agony as he went down.

"Hey, man!" Johnny yelled. "What do ya know? I hit a home run, too."

Danny strolled over and slipped on brass knuckles. Adam watched as Pete and Johnny held Frank's arms down. Danny straddled him for a moment before plopping down on his chest.

"No, please!" Frank cried.

"Hey, old man, can't let my friends have all the fun." His fist crashed into Frank's nose. Frank's cries turned into moans as Danny hit him again and again.

Adam shut his eyes and clamped his hands over his ears as the beating continued. He was just about to yell *that's enough* when Danny stood up.

"Shit, look at these," Danny said, showing the brass knuckles to Pete. "Damn things are comin' apart."

"They're a piece of junk," Pete said. "Where did ya buy them?"

"Man, I didn't buy them. I made them."

"Ya did. No shit. Let me see those suckers."

Adam listened as they talked about the brass knuckles. The knot in his stomach tightened. His shoulders ached. He felt nauseous.

"Hey, Adam, ya come on out now!" Danny yelled. "He won't recognize ya. Hell, he won't recognize anybody."

Adam pressed the back of his head harder into the brick wall. He didn't want to be there and he didn't want to see Frank. He wanted to run and get as far away from Broadway as he could.

"Come on!" Danny shouted. "We ain't got all night."

Taking a deep breath, Adam moved slowly from out of the shadows to where Frank's body lay.

"Cracked a few ribs," Danny said as he lit a cigarette. "His nose is sure as hell busted, and he ain't goin' to see out of those eyes for awhile."

Unable to speak, Adam felt numb.

"Let's get the hell outta here," Danny said. "I know where we can get another bottle of booze. Ya comin'?" he asked Adam.

Adam shook his head.

"Catch, ya later." Danny took off with Johnny and Pete, their voices fading into the night.

Adam moved back into the shadows. Hidden in his own world, he felt no satisfaction; only a sickening emptiness. He didn't know how long he waited before someone walked by, saw the body, and ran for help. When Adam heard the sirens, he left.

Chapter 12

"Pa, are you sure you've got that straight?" Virg asked as she and Adam sat at the kitchen table. "Wanda didn't say anything about that to me."

"What's the matter? Don't believe?" Paul Kurtz feigned surprise that his own daughter would think his version of why Frank was released a day early from the hospital was anything less than trustworthy. "How come don't believe?"

"I'm sorry, but I just don't."

He peered over his glasses at Adam, hoping for his support but his grandson seemed detached from the conversation.

"Don't look at Butch to help you out on this." She shook her finger at her father. "You got yourself into this now and you've been known to exaggerate."

Paul opened his mouth, but his daughter put up her hand. "Let me finish. You're telling me that Frank was kicked out of the hospital because he had an argument with the doctor. I think you've stretched your exaggeration a little bit too far this time."

"I tell you, I no exaggerate. Frank swore at doctor. I know because Wanda tell me. Maybe she don't tell you everything, eh?" Paul pushed his gray work cap back upon his head and scratched the lone thin tuft of hair at the peak of his forehead. "That damn Frank. You'd think having ass kicked would knock meanness out." His eyes went to Adam. "Don't you think?"

"I don't know, I guess so."

Adam's reticent reply troubled him. As soon as he had entered his daughter's apartment that morning he noticed his grandson's quiet mood. Paul had come to get away from Frank and to work on a pocket watch. One of his drinking buddies sold the watch to him for a pint of whiskey. Adam had just finished washing for school and was buttoning his shirt when he answered the knock on the door. He asked his grandson to stay for a while so they could visit as he worked on the watch. Adam, who seemed reluctant at first, said he would stay for a half hour or so, but anything longer he'd have to hustle to get to school on time. "So if few minutes late," Paul said. "Just tell teacher you spent time with grandfather. They excuse. I write note. Then they know you no lie."

When Virg came home from work fifteen minutes later, she found the two of them sitting at the kitchen table. Her father was working on a pocket watch as Adam looked on. After heating a pot of coffee, she sat at the table with them. No sooner had she sat down than her father told her about Frank and why he had to leave the hospital a day earlier than planned.

"Pa, let's not talk about Frank anymore. Have a donut."

Paul peeked into the brown paper bag his daughter held out to him. "Where you get?"

"From work. They'll go good with your coffee."

Picking up his cup, Paul finished what he had left. He held the cup upside down and smiled at his daughter.

Virg got up to get the coffee pot. She refilled her father's cup and poured a cup for herself. She offered to get her son a glass of milk but he declined. "So tell me again, Pa," she said as she settled in her chair. "What are you doing here so early on a Thursday morning?"

"I tell you already. You no listen? Frank came home from hospital last night." Paul reached in the bag for a donut. "Up already this morning, moaning and groaning." He broke the donut in half, dunked the end of one half into his coffee, and popped it in his mouth, washing it down with coffee. "I decide come here. Is okay?"

"Of course. You know you're always welcomed. It's nice to come home and find my two favorite men here." She offered the bag of donuts to her son, but he declined. "Don't you have to leave for school soon?" she asked.

"I've got time."

"What about Mick?"

"I called and told him I was leaving late this morning. It's no big deal. I'll see him in first hour class."

Paul finished off his donut, downing it with a gulp of coffee. His grandson hadn't seemed himself for nearly a week. He couldn't figure out why Adam wasn't more enthusiastic about

Frank getting what he deserved.

"Pa, do you want another donut?"

"No. Had enough."

"I'll bring the rest to Wanda."

"How's she doing?" Adam asked.

"Oh, she's tired from spending so much time at the hospital this past week. I talked to her on Tuesday evening. She said that Frank was coming home in a couple of days." Virg opened the bag of donuts and took one with chocolate frosting. "This has been such a terrible strain on her. She even broke down and cried. That's not like her."

"She cry?" Paul asked. "Over Frank?"

"Yes. Over Frank."

"Waste."

"Pa, don't talk like that."

"I say what I say. Waste."

Virg shot her father a stern look before turning to her son. "Have you seen her since it happened?"

"No. I was afraid that she might want me to go in to see Frank. I didn't want to do that."

"Good," Paul said.

"Pa, I know you don't like Frank, and I may not like him either, but I just shudder at the thought of what happened to him. It must've been terrible being beaten up and then left in that lot. Who would do such a thing like that?"

"Lots of people," Paul said. "They'd stand in line to do it."

"You're terrible," Virg scolded. "Frank's just lucky someone saw him laying there." She shuddered. "What's this world coming to anyway?"

Paul picked up the pocket watch to examine it with a magnifying glass. It would take a lot of work to repair and clean it. Some would say it was beyond repair. It would be a challenge to fix, but he looked forward to it. He found satisfaction in restoring a watch that others had given up as being useless. "I fix you, don't worry," he said out loud. Scratching the stubble on his chin, he began to chuckle.

"What's so funny?" Virg asked.

"Frank call doctor son'n'bitch. No wonder kicked out day early."

"They didn't kick him out," Virg said. "They released him."

"I know Frank, and I say kicked out."

"No, they decided to let him leave early. They do that sometimes. Wanda told me the nurses were giving Frank a bad time and that's why he got angry. She didn't say anything about him swearing at the doctor."

"Giving him bad time? Ack! Don't take nothing to get Frank mad. Was born mad. Gives everybody bad time."

"Pa, I'm not going to argue with you about Frank's temper, but his injuries were severe enough that he spent a week in the hospital."

"I hope doctor stuck thermometer up his ass." Paul chuckled as he formed a mental image of the doctor using a three-foot long thermometer. His chuckling turned into a coughing spell. "I'm okay," he said after coughing for nearly a minute. His eyes drifted to Adam. "You hope doc did that to Frank?"

"I guess so."

Virg gave her son a look of concern. "Are you feeling okay? You're not coming down with something, are you?"

"I'm just a little tired. Harry's been working me hard for the Thanksgiving Day Sale."

"You tell Harry to stop that if he wants me to fix his eggs the way he likes them," Virg said. "And speaking of Thanksgiving, Wanda would be pleased if you came for dinner. Oscar's coming and I'll get there later after I'm done at work. She really wants to have us there for Frank. It's going to be a coming-home-from-the-hospital celebration party."

"Do I have to?"

"Where would you eat? You know, you've got to eat."

"I thought I'd come down to Andy's and have one of those turkey specials you're always talking about serving."

Although Paul resumed working on the watch, he listened to the conversation. Adam didn't want to go because of Frank, but there seemed to be something more in his grandson's tone of voice, but he wasn't quite sure what.

"That would be nice if you came down to Andy's," Virg said. "But come on Christmas Eve instead. We'll serve the same turkey special then. That way you can stay for our Christmas party. I'd like for you to go to Wanda's. It'd mean a lot to her."

"Okay, okay, but I'm not staying long."

"Just as long as you're there for awhile. You have to understand, Wanda's upset about what happened to Frank. I saw the poor man at the hospital the next day. His face looked terrible. It was hard to tell if it was him."

"Just look at teeth. If big and yellow, then it's Frank," Paul said as he worked at rubbing away the grime encrusted on the inside cover of the watch.

"Frank's lucky he didn't die," Virg said, making the sign of the cross.

"Ack. Frank's lucky to have hard head." When he saw his daughter crossing herself, his own hand automatically rose to do the same, but then stopped. The last time he had crossed himself was a lifetime ago. He was sitting in a hospital room while a priest prayed for the healing of his young wife. She died that very night and as far as Paul was concerned, so did God.

"I wonder if they'll ever catch the ones who did it," Virg said.

"Catch them?" Paul said. "What for? Give medals?"

"Pa, that's no way to talk. I know Frank isn't the best man in the world."

"I agree." Paul resumed cleaning the watch. As part of the grime rubbed off, he discovered an inscription. He picked up his magnifying glass and examined the inside cover. After setting the magnifying glass down, he reached in his back pocket, took out a frayed handkerchief, wetted a portion of it with his tongue, and rubbed the cover. Squinting through his bifocals, he continued to examine the inscription.

Virg set her coffee cup aside. "I need to say this for the sake of Frank. He may not be the best man, but he's a human being and deserves as much consideration as one of those watches you work on. Don't you think?"

"Maybe. Maybe not." Paul continued to examine the watch. "I stick to clocks. Clocks are good. I know them. With Frank, who knows?"

"You'll never change," she replied. "You're just plain old stubborn. I'm not going to sit here and argue with you about Frank. I've some shopping to do for Wanda."

"What shopping?" Paul asked.

"I told her I'd pick up some food for Thanksgiving." Virg stood up. "She doesn't want to leave Frank alone because he's still unsteady on his feet." She got her coat, said good-bye, and left.

To Paul, it seemed like a long time before any words were spoken. His grandson appeared to be content just watching him work. "Inscription on inside cover," he said as he looked through his magnifying glass.

"What does it say?"

"Don't know. Can't make out words yet."

Paul worked on the watch for another five minutes before setting it down, announcing that the joints in his fingers were hurting and he needed another cup of coffee. After pouring himself a cup, he sat down and stretched his arms as he looked toward the windows in the living room.

"Butch. Look. Snowing out." He leaned back and smiled. "Ah, yes. First snowfall. Brings memories." Staring at the feather-like flakes floating past the window, he thought about woodlands, country roads, and a horse-drawn sleigh. Faces of brothers and sisters flashed through his mind.

"Grandpa, what are you thinking about?"

The sound of his grandson's voice whisked Paul from the woodlands back to his daughter's apartment. "How first snowfall make everything clean. I think about people I knew long time ago."

"Too bad things can't stay clean and white."

"Things never stay way you want." Paul picked up the watch and held it in the palm of his hand. He had been able to uncover enough of the letters to make out several words. By the words he had seen, he knew what the inscription said.

"Do you think Frank will ever change?"

Paul looked at his grandson, wondering why there wasn't the usual harsh edge in his voice in mentioning Frank's name. "I answer this way. I find cuckoo clock in alley. Broken. Needs repair. I replace parts. Put back together. I polish. Looks brand new. I give new start in life, but still cuckoo clock."

"I guess you're right. It's just that Wanda deserves a better break in life. I don't care if she does love the guy. It's just not fair."

"Ah, know what you mean. She cuckoo staying with him." Paul felt his grandson's anguish. Taking his glasses off, he rubbed his eyes, and put his glasses back on. He valued their time together. It reminded him of earlier days when they were closer. He very much wanted that again. His drinking was a problem and his grandson was ashamed of it. Paul was also ashamed of it. He loved his grandson, and needed his respect and his love. Being together like this was special, and he was deeply moved by the moment. His thoughts turned to the inscription on the watch.

"Butch. After I fix and clean watch, I want you have it."

"Why are you giving it to me?"

"Because of message inscribed. I know it now. I think you read many times. It be gift. My gift to you." Although Paul smiled, his tone turned solemn. "For times you, ah, walk me home. Maybe inscription is something you remember me by."

"What does it say?"

"Ack, won't tell. When I fix and clean, you'll see. I wait until graduation to give. For now, it my secret."

"But what's so special about it?"

"Reminds me of someone." Paul looked at the snow floating past the living room window. "She die too young."

"Are you talking about grandma?"

He nodded. "Words in watch I knew. Grandma knew. I want now you know. Years pass by, you remember them. Maybe do you good."

"How about you?"

As Paul held the watch, he thought about the kind of life he had led since the death of his wife. His grandson's question was a good one, but he didn't know how to answer it. "For me, years passed by. I'd forgotten about words. Maybe no good to me anymore." He paused. "I think they good for you."

"You're not going to tell me, then?"

"I'm old man and too stubborn." Paul chuckled. "Don't tell mom I say that."

"I won't."

"Good. Now, I show how to fix. I take apart. You watch. Learn about clocks and people. Clocks put together like people. Real people. Not like window dummies at Harry's. First lesson, patience."

Paul carefully unscrewed three tiny screws and took off the back plate as Adam looked on. After removing two other screws, he carefully removed a fly wheel, and spent time studying how it fit with the rest of the pieces. He was about to show Adam the watch's gear train when his grandson glanced at the wall clock.

"I'm sorry but I've got to get to school." Adam slipped his jacket on and picked up his schoolbooks. "I'm going to be late now. Just make sure the door is locked when you leave."

"Don't worry. This take time. I still be here when you get home."

After his grandson left, Paul walked into the living room. He looked out at the falling snow and remembered another time. When it snowed where he grew up, the whole countryside became a blanket of white. One could walk into the fields and forests and be enveloped by the solitude the snow had bestowed upon the earth. As a young lad, he could stand on a small knoll and look out in any direction, taking pleasure that the snow cover was unbroken except for the tracks of deer, jackrabbits, or his own footprints. He especially felt good as he contemplated his own tracks. To him, they were proof that someone had passed this way and that it was he who was that someone. His reminiscing was abruptly brought to an end when a car blared its horn, distracting him. Slushy streets and compacted snow-covered sidewalks would provide no opportunity for anyone to look back at their tracks. As he thought about the journey he had been on since his wife died, he also felt no desire to look back at the tracks he had made.

Chapter 13

The school lunchroom was noisier than usual that Wednesday noon when Adam joined Mick and Howie. He had enjoyed the time with his grandfather that morning. The mystery of the watch's inscription had thankfully gotten his mind off Frank for a while.

"I'm not sure you want to sit down here," Mick warned Adam.

"Hey," Howie protested.

"What's the matter?" Adam asked, amused by the antics of his friends.

"You won't believe this, but he's talking about Mattingale's desk again."

"Now what?"

"He hasn't told me. He wanted to keep me in suspense until you got here." Mick poked Howie in the shoulder. "Come on, now. What's it this time?"

"I've decided that I can't tell you."

"What do you mean, you can't?" Mick said.

Howie took a sandwich out of his lunch bag, inspecting it before taking a bite. "Just that," he mumbled while chewing. "I can't. Once I tell you, though, you're not going to believe it because it's so ingenious."

"So when are you going to tell us?" Mick asked.

"After the holidays. It'll take that long for my contact to get me the stuff I need." Howie set his sandwich down and opened his milk carton. "So what are you guys doing for Thanksgiving?"

Mick leaned back in his chair. "Bunch of relatives are coming over. The whole house will be crowded. You won't be able to move, but it'll be a lot of fun. After that, I'll be going over to Mary's. What about you?"

"Me and my dad are having a quiet meal together. His sister and her husband are coming over afterwards." Howie pause. "I sure wish mom was around. I miss her."

"It's got to be tough," Mick said.

Adam also felt bad for Howie but didn't say anything.

"Guess where I'm going on Thanksgiving, though," Howie said in a more upbeat tone.

"Mattingale's house?" Mick deadpanned. "Ever since you let her look at your earlobe, I think she's got the hots for you."

"Come on, give me a break. This kid's going to Cindy's later on that day. I'll be with her entire family. It's going to be great."

"How about you?" Mick asked Adam.

"Going over to my aunt's for awhile. My mom's working but she's coming later."

"Looking forward to it?" Howie asked.

"Not really. Frank just got home from the hospital. I'm only going because of my aunt."

"I heard about what happened to Frank," Howie said. "That's too bad."

The picture of Frank lying in the parking lot with his face bashed in flashed through Adam's mind.

"How about coming over to my house after you're done there?" Mick asked. "You won't have to worry about anything. You'd be like one of the family."

"Maybe. I have to see how it goes"

For the rest of the lunch hour they talked about what certain relatives did to carry on family traditions. It was mainly Howie who led the conversation. Adam only half listened, his thoughts being on Frank. Although he was sure Frank hadn't seen him that night in the empty lot, he felt uneasy going to Wanda's for Thanksgiving. Frank just might be smart enough to connect him with Danny Logan. The whole thing had been a mistake, and he was angry with himself for not having thought it through. It was too late now and if Frank suspected him in any way, he was the kind of person who would seek revenge.

He could avoid Frank for the time being, but Thanksgiving was only three weeks away.

Chapter 14

Adam woke early on the morning of Thanksgiving. Not wanting to wake Oscar, he slipped on his pants and socks, grabbed his shirt and shoes, and moved through the living room into the kitchen. After washing, he fixed himself a bowl of cereal, and ate while reading the sports section. He had just finished eating when the downstairs entrance door slammed shut. The person coming up trudged slowly, stopping at the landing for a time. The stairs began to creak again as though they were as tired as the person climbing them. Adam went back to looking at the newspaper. He was checking the movie section when the door opened and his mother came in.

"How are you?" he asked, noting that she was home early.

"I'm pooped," she announced, plopping down on a chair. "We were really busy last night. I came home early to get a little sleep before I have to go back."

"What time do you have to go back?"

"Around noon. Bertha called in sick." She stretched her arms and yawned. "I told Andy I'd stay until three."

"What about Thanksgiving dinner?"

"I called Wanda and told her. She wasn't too happy. You know how she gets about me working all the time. Thinks I'm not providing a family life. *You* understand, don't you?"

"Sure." Adam never gave much thought to whether they had a family life. He wasn't sure what a family life was supposed to be like.

"Wanda asked me again if you were going to be there. I told her you were. You're going to, aren't you?"

"Yeah, but I'm not staying long. Not with Frank there."

"I understand," she said, yawning again. "I've got to get some sleep. Wake me around eleven-thirty." She started for the living room, but stopped. "Is Oscar still sleeping?"

"Yeah. When he gets up, I'll tell him to be quiet."

She rested her head against the wall. "Butch, I'd like to stay and talk but I'm exhausted. I just have to go lay down."

Adam got out a deck of cards once he finished with the paper. His mother was already asleep on the couch. He sat down and began playing Solitaire. When his mother taught him the game, she said it was called Solitaire, but she preferred calling it Beat the Devil. Shuffling the cards for a new game, Adam thought about Frank.

"Good morning," Oscar whispered as he came into the kitchen. "By golly, I must've been tired. I didn't even hear you get up or your mother come home." He raked his hand through his thick hair. He had gotten his usual haircut: cut short all the way around, except on top. It looked as though a bowl had been placed on his head and used as a guide. "I'm going to make myself some coffee," he said. "Do you want something?"

"No, but don't make too much noise."

Oscar went into the half-kitchen, got a box of matches from the drawer. He struck one to light the front burner on the stove.

Even though this man had lived with them now for nearly seven years, Adam knew very little about him. Oscar, in his fifties, had worked for the railroad ever since his twenties. He didn't seem to have any immediate family. If he did, he never talked about them. The man never received a personal phone call or any mail other than stuff from the railroad.

Within a few minutes Oscar came back into the kitchen. "Mind if I sit down?"

"Go ahead. I don't care."

"It's going to be a good meal today, by golly." Oscar heaped two teaspoons of sugar into his coffee, tasted it, and then added another teaspoon. "Your Aunt Wanda is a good cook. I can taste her cooking now."

Adam continued to play cards. He preferred to be alone but didn't want to hurt Oscar's feelings. In the past, hurting his feelings wouldn't have bothered Adam, but he couldn't bring himself to do that. Ever since that night Danny and his friends attacked Frank, his feelings had been all mixed up.

"I hear we'll be having sweet potatoes and turkey and all the trimmings," Oscar said as he watched Adam play a red four on a black five. "When I was a kid, we had lutefisk on Thanksgiving.

My mother always served it with butter sauce. Hmmm, that was good. We had turkey, too. By golly, though, that lutefisk was so good."

Adam didn't mind Oscar talking, but his thoughts kept going back to Frank. He felt anxious about going to Wanda's, and he wished now that he had simply said no.

"You played the black seven on a black eight," Oscar said, pointing to the card Adam had just put down.

"Okay, I see it. Thanks."

"My mother, she was a darn good cook," Oscar said. He watched in silence for the next fifteen minutes as Adam played two more games before finally winning. "Butch, you won!" he announced.

Adam got up and put the cards away. "I'm going out for a walk. Wake my mother up by eleven-thirty, will you?"

"What should I tell her if she asks where you are?"

"Tell her not to worry." Adam slipped on his jacket and headed toward the door. "I'll get to Wanda's on time. Okay?"

"Okay…Butch?"

"What?"

"Thanks for letting me watch."

Walking for over a mile up Broadway, Adam tried to sort through how he was going to handle seeing Frank in a few hours. Stopping at a coffee shop, he had a cup of hot chocolate and then spent an hour or so watching some guys play the pinball machine. When he left, he knew he would have to hustle to make it to Wanda's on time. He was thinking about Frank when someone called out to him from behind.

"Hey, my man." Danny Logan came strolling up with a cocky grin on his face. "What's happenin'?"

"Nothing, just killing some time."

Danny took a drag off his cigarette before flipping it toward the street. "How's Frankie doin'? Played any baseball lately?"

Adam's insides tensed. He felt like ripping the smirk off Danny's face and shoving it down his throat. "He's been out of the hospital for a couple of weeks now."

"Is that right? How long was he in?"

"A week."

"No shit. Only a week?" Danny stroked his chin. "Man, I

must be losin' my stuff."

"Look, I've got to be going," Adam said, not wanting to be seen with Danny.

"Give me a second, man."

Adam glanced around. "Let's duck into the doorway and get out of the wind."

The two of them moved into the entrance doorway of a liquor store. Danny lit up another cigarette and took a drag. "Listen, man. Do ya want in on somethin'?"

"What are you talking about?"

"Me and the boys are goin' to be makin' some big money soon. I thought ya might want in on the action."

"You don't need me."

"Hey, Pete and Johnny are okay, but I want someone with some smarts." Danny sounded irritated as though he had expected Adam to jump at the chance of working with him. "So, what do ya say?"

"Count me out." Adam defiantly met Danny's glare. "I've got to go now," he said.

Danny took a drag off his cigarette. "Yeah, ya do that. I'll see ya around."

Adam headed toward home, not caring if he had just gotten on the wrong side of Danny. He hoped Danny got the message and would stay away from him. The walk back to the apartment didn't take long. The nearer he got, however, the more anxious he felt. By the time he knocked on Wanda's door, his neck and back muscles had tightened into knots. Within moments, the door opened.

"You're finally here," Wanda said. "Come on in." After she closed the door, they stood in the living room. "I was just ready to start putting the food on the table. Go sit down."

Adam took off his jacket and tossed it on the couch. "Where am I sitting?"

"Don't worry," Wanda whispered. "You won't have to sit by Frank. I've got a spot for you next to your grandfather."

Along with the traditional Thanksgiving fare, she had baked Frank's favorite pie, banana cream. A small cardboard figure of a pilgrim served as a centerpiece for the table. Adam sat next to his grandfather. Across from them sat Wanda and Oscar. At the head of the table sat Frank.

Frank's face still showed signs of the beating. Although most of the swelling had gone down, his face appeared lopsided. His nose seemed more crooked than normal. His bloodshot eyes, caused by ruptured veins from the beating, would be red for some time. Cracked ribs caused his breathing to be short and shallow.

"Hi," Adam said to Frank, thinking it would be better for Wanda if he didn't completely ignore the man.

"He can't talk," Wanda explained. "It's still too painful. The poor man can barely eat. He won't be able to have any turkey. All he'll get to eat is some mashed potatoes." She glanced over at her husband and smiled. "And, of course, banana cream pie."

"Well, I eat turkey!" Adam's grandfather announced. When the platter was passed, he took two large pieces of white meat and smothered them with gravy. "Too bad you no eat," he said to Frank. After cutting a piece of turkey, Paul held it up on his fork, moving it slowly back and forth before placing it in his mouth. "Delicious. Best I've ever eaten."

Frank tried to say something, but couldn't. He groaned so loudly that both Oscar and Wanda momentarily stopped eating and stared at him.

"Oscar, we're so glad you came," Wanda said, the tenseness in her voice evident. "Tell us more about the trains you work with. It must be interesting work."

Adam ate as he listened to Oscar talk about switching stations, track washouts, and boxcar construction. From the corner of his eye, he was aware that Frank was watching him from the end of the table.

"Juicy turkey," Adam's grandfather said. "Better than last year." He grinned at Frank. "After this, I eat pumpkin pie."

"Don't you want a piece of banana cream pie also?" Wanda asked.

"Why I want that?"

"It's good."

"Ack! Only for monkeys."

An angry groan came from the end of the table. Wanda quickly got up and went to Frank, putting her hand on his shoulder. "Are you okay?"

The lopsided head motioned *no*.

"Do you want to lie down on the couch?"

Yes

As Wanda led Frank into the living room, Paul nudged Adam, and chuckled. "Best time I've had with Frank in long time."

Wanda came back and shook her finger at her father before turning her attention to Adam. "By chance, have you heard anything on the street?"

"What do you mean?" Adam asked, trying to sound casual.

"About what happened to Frank. I sure would like to find out who did it." She motioned toward the couch in the living room. "Just look at that poor man. Whoever did it should be ashamed of themselves, picking on someone his age."

"Frank have any ideas who did it?" Oscar asked as he reached for the snuffbox in his shirt pocket. He hesitated and then put it back.

Wanda smiled. "Go ahead and have a dip. It better than smoking," she said, glancing at her father.

"By, golly, thank you, but I'll wait until I'm done with pie."

"Frank doesn't remember who did it," Wanda said. "Says he was slugged from behind."

Not for a second did Adam believe that Frank couldn't remember. "I'm going now," he announced, once dessert was served.

"No pie?" Wanda asked.

"I'm full." Adam said his good-byes, and walked through the living room to the front door. Frank was stretched out on the couch, his eyes closed.

* * *

When Thanksgiving Day arrived, Frank was frustrated that he still couldn't talk. The remark Wanda's father made about banana cream pie being monkey food made him furious. When he went to lie on the couch, he closed his eyes and listened to the talk in the kitchen. He was sure that Adam was somehow involved that night he was jumped by those street punks. When Adam walked through the living room to leave, Frank had kept his eyes closed. As soon as the kid walked by, he opened them and watched him. *Butchie, sure as hell I'll get even with ya.*

Frank closed his eyes and began to make plans. When the idea came to him as to what he would do, he knew he had found the perfect revenge. The last words he heard before falling asleep were Wanda's.

"Oh, look, Pa, Frank's sleeping like a baby."

Chapter 15

"Danny, you shouldn't eat so fast," Sarah Logan said to her son. "It's not good for you." Her husband, George, looked on as he sipped tea.

"I gotta hurry because I'm meetin' some guys."

"On Thanksgiving?" Sarah asked.

"Yeah, on Thanksgivin'." Danny was seldom home anymore except to eat and sleep (and sometimes not to sleep). He especially didn't like being home when his parents were there. Since being kicked out of school, he managed to get an odd job here and there. Mainly, he had been working at a gas station pumping gas. He had scoffed at his father's offer to get him a job at the hardware store where he worked.

"Who are you meeting?" his father asked.

"Friends." Although his father was just trying to show interest in his life, Danny felt like he was being checked up on. "Ain't nobody ya know."

"How do you know, son? Maybe I might know them from the store. A lot of people come in everyday."

"Your father is well-known and respected by quite a few people on Broadway," his mother said with pride. "Isn't that right, dear?"

"Yes, and I'm proud of that. Why, just the other day a man came in and told the owner he was looking for me. Said that he'd heard that George Logan was a man who knows the business and can be trusted."

"Yeah, right," Danny said, feeling as though he had heard this story a hundred times. "You're really makin' a name for yourself. Bet you're about the most honest hardware salesman around. That's why Ma has to work. That's why we live in this crummy little house. Ya may be popular, but ya sure don't make any money at it."

Shock swept over Sarah Logan's face. "Danny, that's no

way to talk to your father! You should be ashamed of yourself. Your father has—"

"Sarah, leave the boy alone. He has a right to say what he feels."

The three ate in silence for the next few minutes. His mother was the first to speak. "Danny, did you hear about what happened in the parking lot by the liquor store? Some poor man got beaten up."

"Whoever did it should be locked up," his father said. "The police said that they used a club on him. It was a terrible beating."

"Sounds cool."

"Nothing cool about it, young man!" his father replied sharply. "It was a cowardly thing to do."

Danny jerked his head toward his father. "What do ya mean? Maybe it was the old man who had the club. Maybe he picked a fight with someone who was tougher. Streets ain't like a hardware store."

"I won't argue with you on that," his father replied. "But it was terrible the way the man was beaten. Paper said there was evidence it was done by at least two people. They ganged up on him. If you ask me, those who did it need help."

"What do ya mean by that?"

"That those responsible should have professional counseling," his father replied. "Probably see a psychiatrist."

"Ya mean a head shrink? Are ya sayin' the guy who did it is crazy?"

"I'm saying that whoever did it needs help." Danny's father cocked his head. "Son, by the way you're talking, it seems like you know more about this than you're letting on. If you do, you should tell the police."

"You don't know anything about this, do you?" Sarah asked anxiously.

"Me? Naw." Danny leaned back in his chair. "Just the stuff I hear on the streets. Word is whoever did it must be one pretty tough guy."

Sarah shook her head. "I can't agree with you. I don't know how you can think that way. Honestly, there are times I don't understand you at all."

"Sarah," George said. "Have a cup of tea. It'll settle you down." He poured a cup and set it before her.

"Thank you, dear." She took a sip and set the cup down. "All this talk about violence, I just don't like it. I'm sorry I brought it up in the first place. Why don't we talk about something else?" When no one responded, she spoke up. "Christmas is next month. Danny, you still haven't told us what you'd like."

"How about a zip gun?"

"A what?" Sarah shot her husband a puzzled expression.

"Just kiddin'," Danny said, smirking to himself. "Get me some socks or somethin'."

"That's a nice suggestion. Your father and I will talk about it." She turned to her husband. "By the way, we need another string of lights for the tree this year. Do you think you could get some?"

"We're in luck. The store has a sale on them. I'll pick up a new string tomorrow. With my discount, we'll get a good bargain."

Danny rolled his eyes. *Hardware stores, discounts. If I hear any more of this shit, I'm goin' to puke.* He pushed his chair back and stood up. "Gotta go. See ya."

"Already?" his mother asked. "What time will you be back, Danny?"

"Don't know."

"Can't you give me a time?"

"Be back when I get back," Danny snapped. He headed toward the door.

Chapter 16

It was shortly after five on a Saturday afternoon when Adam got off work. Mick had stopped earlier to let him know that he and Howie were going to hang out at Kass' for a while. "Come on over when you're done," he said.

Although tired from working since eight that morning, Adam was more drained by wondering what was going on with Frank. Nearly a month had passed since Thanksgiving, and their paths hadn't crossed. Frank surely suspected that he was involved with the beating in some way. It was just a matter of time before the man would do something to get back at him. Wanda had mentioned that Frank was behaving himself; she even thought he had turned over a new leaf. Adam didn't believe that for one minute.

Adam walked into the drugstore and joined Howie and Mick at the soda fountain.

"I'll be with you in a minute," Kass said from the other end of the counter. He began to whistle as he refilled napkin holders.

"You look a little beat," Mick said as Adam sat next to him. "How are you doing?"

"I'm okay." Adam unsnapped his jacket.

What would Mick and Howie think if they knew I'd planned Frank's beating with Danny Logan? How could I explain that I never expected it to go as far as it did?

* * *

"What were you whistling?" Howie asked Kass as he walked over. "I think I know the tune."

"You should," he replied. "It's *I'm Dreaming of a White Christmas.* But you have to remember, it's the Jewish rendition."

"It sounded good. You could have a whistling career in your future." Howie turned to Mick and Adam. "Don't you guys think so?"

"Sure, anything you say," Mick said.

"How about you, Adam?"

Adam shrugged his shoulders. "If you say so."

"See, Kass, they agree. So, what do you say? Have we got a deal?"

"Afraid not."

"Listen. You could be the Jewish Bing Crosby. I could be your agent."

Kass chuckled. "Ah, Howie, you and your schemes."

"But wouldn't you like to be rich and famous?"

"Why for? I've been operating this drugstore for over twenty-five years now. It provides me with food on the table, a roof over my head, and clothes on my back. I love the neighborhood and the people who live here. So what else do I need?"

"But if you were famous, then everyone would call you Mr. Kass."

"I wouldn't like that. It's too formal."

"I tell you what. When you become a rich and famous whistler, how about if I just call you Herschel?"

"Oh, I see. If you wish to call me by my first name, you are free to do so." Kass leaned on the counter with both elbows, resting his chin in the cradle formed by his hands. "Of course, if we're going by proper first names, then I'd have to call you Howard."

"Okay, okay, you've made your point. How about this? Have you ever considered wrestling? You'd be good at it."

Kass grinned. "You mean because I'm so short and round that they couldn't grab hold of me? I tell you something that you didn't know. I played football in high school."

Mick's eyebrows rose. "You did?"

"Don't act so shocked. Where did you think I got this bald head of mine?" Kass bowed his head as though to pray. "See my head. I blame it on the helmet I wore for three years."

"I didn't know you could go bald that way." Howie motioned for Mick to put his head down so he could see the top of it.

"Get out of here," Mick said, laughing.

"You be careful," Kass teased Mick. "Even with that bushy head of hair, you may end up looking like a monk. Except you'd be a tall Gentile monk. Me, I'm just a short Jewish monk."

"Hey, Kass," Howie said excitedly. "That gives me an idea. Wrestlers always have a ring name like Gorgeous George, or something fancy like that. We could change your name and promote you as the Whistling Jewish Monk. How would you like that?"

"Hello, Kass!" a woman shouted from the front of the store.

"Hello, Mrs. Cutsinger!" Kass yelled back. "She thinks I'm hard of hearing," he explained to the three boys.

When Adam looked, Danny Logan's friend, Johnny, was at the magazine rack. Although paging through a magazine, Johnny seemed to be checking out the store. At one point, their eyes locked. With a slight nod, Johnny acknowledged him. He had never seen Johnny in Kass' before because, according to Danny, it was easier to shoplift at the drugstore three blocks up on Lyndale.

"I'm sorry," Kass said as he turned his attention to Adam. "With all this talk about me and my other careers, I forgot to ask you what you want."

"Cherry Coke."

"Hey, that sounds good," Mick said. "I'll have one, too."

"Coming right up." Kass got a glass from under the counter and held it up to Mick. "This one's on me."

"How come he gets a free one?" Howie protested.

"Because it's my way of honoring him for being named All-Conference, and honorable mention, All-State."

"What's this all about?" Adam asked.

"Didn't he tell you?" Kass replied as he served Mick his drink. "It was in the morning paper, the sports section. It's a fine thing when we have a local boy get that kind of recognition."

"When did this all come about?" Adam asked Mick, feeling disappointed that he hadn't said anything.

"Couple of weeks ago. Coach told me that it was coming. I figured you guys would know sooner or later. I was going to mention it, really I was. Don't get me wrong, I appreciate the honor, but sometimes it gets to be too much. You know what I mean?"

"Forty percent," Howie said. "That's my offer."

"What are you talking about?" Mick asked, looking at Howie as if he had gone crazy.

Howie took a napkin and started scribbling on it. "Now that you're a big-time football star, you're going to need an agent. With your brawn and my brains, we'll make a great team. I might even manage to get your picture on a box of cereal."

Mick grabbed the napkin and wadded it up into a ball. "Just forget this scheme right now. Go back to promoting wrestlers."

Howie started scribbling on another napkin, but kept it out of reach from Mick. "How about thirty-five percent?"

"Not even at one percent."

"Okay, okay." Howie folded the napkin and stuffed it in his shirt pocket.

"How's your dad doing with this?" Adam asked Mick. "I suppose he's pretty excited."

"Yeah, but he wants me to go to a school where the main emphasis is on football. You know my father and football." Mick paused. "Thanks for the Coke, Kass."

"My pleasure." Kass took a towel and wiped off the counter. "Us football players have to watch out for each other."

Howie loudly cleared his throat as he looked at Kass. "Ahem."

"Yes, what do you need?" Kass asked as he put the towel away.

"Do I get a free Coke also?"

Kass chuckled. "You make all-conference, you'll get one, but I didn't see your name in the paper. Who knows though? With you and your forty percent, I should look in the financial section."

"And after all these years of being your best customer, too," Howie said. "You know, *I* could be famous someday. Soon, too. Then you'll see."

"Then Mick charges *you* forty percent, huh?" Kass retorted.

Adam glanced over at the magazine section. Johnny was still there.

"A what?" Kass was asking when Adam's attention came back to the conversation.

"A chocolate Coke," Howie said. "Make it a ten cent one,

and don't be stingy with the chocolate."

After serving Howie his Coke, Kass went to wait on a customer in front of the store.

"What's the latest on Mattingale?" Mick asked Howie.

"Still working on it, but one way or another, I'm getting into her drawers."

No sooner had Howie spoken than Mick started to choke with laughter. Even Adam found himself chuckling. For a moment, Adam thought Mick was going to fall off his stool because he was laughing so hard.

"What's so funny?" Howie asked.

"You. You're going to—" Mick was laughing so hard that he couldn't finish.

"What's with this guy? All-Conference here is going to bust his jockstrap."

"Do you realize what you said?" Adam asked.

"Yeah, I said that All-Conference here is going to—"

"No, no, before that. Think about it."

"Let's see. We were talking about Mattingale. All I said was that I was going to get into her drawers. So what's so funny about—" Howie's eyes grew large. "No way, guys!" he exclaimed. "I was talking about the drawers in her desk."

"Sure you were," Adam said.

"You've always said you go for older women," Mick added, wiping tears of laughter away.

"What's going on here?" Kass asked as he rejoined them. "I go away for a few minutes and—" He stopped and looked at Howie. "You look a little flushed. Are you sick or something? I hope it wasn't that chocolate Coke."

"He's sick all right, but not from the chocolate Coke," Mick said, nudging Adam. "Isn't that right?"

"That's right. Our friend here is love sick."

"I see. Howie, do you want to tell me about it?"

"Look, don't listen to these two," Howie pleaded. "They took an innocent remark and turned it into something—"

"Beautiful," Mick interjected, and then started to laugh again.

"Teenagers." Kass sighed. "The longer I live, the less I understand them." He moved to the other end of the counter and began filling straw containers.

"Guys, I didn't mean it the way it sounded," Howie stammered. "You're not going to say anything at school, are you? I'll never live it down."

"Don't worry, we won't say anything," Mick said. "Remember, we hang around with you and we've got our own reputations to think about."

"You have to admit that you stepped right into that one," Adam said.

"I guess you're right." A thoughtful expression crossed Howie's face. "Can you just imagine me and Mattingale? I wonder what she looked like when she was younger and why she never got married."

"Maybe she's afraid of men," Mick speculated.

"Maybe," Howie said, glancing at the clock. "Look, I got to get going. Are we still on for Christmas Eve?"

"As far as I know," Mick said. "Adam, you're the one with the wheels that night. Are we still going?"

"Yeah, I'll pick you guys up around eight or so. I'll get Howie first and then come get you."

"Great, but won't it be crowded with four in the front seat? You know what I mean, don't you?" Mick nodded toward Howie while mouthing *Mattingale.*

"It might be at that, but they could always have the back seat."

"What are you guys talking about?" Howie asked. "Who else is going?"

"Mattingale," Mick said. "The two of you can have the back seat all to yourselves."

"Then you could find out *all* of her secrets," Adam said.

"Yeah, she might even take off her white gloves for you," Mick quipped.

"That does it," Howie declared. "I'm leaving. As long as I stay here, you two aren't going to let it go. See you guys Christmas Eve."

"He's quite a guy," Mick said as Howie headed for the door. "And he's really a good sport. He can take it as well as dish it out."

Adam nodded his agreement. Their bantering had been like a

release valve for the tenseness he felt about Frank. Now that he and Mick were alone and Kass was occupied with some other customers, it'd be a good time to share his struggles. *But how? And how much?*

"Howie *acted* pretty scared when he thought we were going to tell the guys at school about him and Mattingale's drawers," Adam said.

"Yeah, the big phony." Mick chuckled. "I saw through him right away. He should've tried out for the school play."

"Do you think he ever gets scared for real?"

"Probably."

"How about you? Have you ever been scared?"

"Sure." Mick picked up his glass, took the straw out, and tilted the glass to his mouth until he got some chunks of ice. As he talked, he chewed on the ice, making a crunching sound. "When I was a kid, I went to see this Frankenstein movie. When I got home after the movie, I was so scared that the monster was going to come and get me that I didn't sleep all night."

"Do you ever get scared inside of yourself?"

"What do you mean?"

"Like you thought you knew yourself but then something happens and you're not so sure. You get scared of becoming something you don't want to be. I mean you see things in others that you don't like and you say to yourself that you don't want to end up like that." Adam paused. "Am I making any sense?"

"Sure. It's like going to see Frankenstein and being scared that you're going to end up like him." Mick hunched his shoulders and made a monster face.

"Yeah, something like that," Adam said, offering a tight smile.

"I remember when I first started playing varsity football. There was this kid, a senior, who pulled every dirty trick there was in the game."

"Was that Jason Mueller?" Adam asked.

"You got it. He was a jerk," Mick said. "In practice he always wanted to hurt the other guys. Guess he wanted to prove he was tough. He'd hit you in a way that could cause injuries. Man, he enjoyed it. I had no time for him, not from the first day I met him."

"So what happened?"

"It was the third game of the season. I was playing against a kid from Roosevelt who was trying to gouge me in the eyes all the time. That really made me mad. So the next play I hit him low and hard. The kid went down in agony and lay there screaming. It turned out that I broke his leg. Coach said it was an accident, but I knew what I was doing. In the locker room after the game, Jason comes up to me and says, 'Great hit.' And you know, I felt good about it. Like a dummy, I said 'Thanks.'"

"You don't play that way now."

"That's because after that game I went for a long walk and thought about what I'd done. I felt crummy. Had all these mixed emotions going on and, at first, I wasn't sure why. Then it dawned on me that I could turn out like Jason. I guess I was scared of becoming a jerk myself." Mick paused. "Is that what you're talking about?"

"Yeah, something like that, but it doesn't seem to be as clear-cut as that. I get scared because there are times when I don't seem to know myself. Times when I don't think anybody really knows me."

Mick picked up his glass and shook it until the last pieces of ice slid into his mouth. "Go ahead, man, I'm listening."

"It's like having a little room within you that you keep locked so that no one can come in. The trouble is that you've kept it closed for so long that you, yourself, don't know what's in there. When I try to imagine the room, it feels empty."

"Empty?"

"Yeah, something like that," Adam said, feeling emotionally drained. "I don't know. Maybe I'm crazy or something."

"Hey, you're not crazy."

"Sometimes I don't know. You remembered what happened to Frank?"

"Yeah."

Adam wanted to tell him about how he was involved, but couldn't. "The guy deserved it and yet what happened is just as rotten as Frank himself. Do you know what I mean?"

"You mean that you can't always tell the good guys from the bad guys?"

"Yeah, I guess so."

"You know," Mick said. "I remember this priest we had. Father Hurley. Short guy. Had to stand on a box to see over the pulpit. His sermons were the most boring you could imagine, but there was one where he talked about how in cowboy movies you could always tell the good guys from the bad guys by the different color hats they wore."

As Adam listened, he knew that Mick and his family regularly went to church. For himself, although he believed that there had to be some kind of God, he seldom attended church.

"Father Hurley said that real life isn't like the movies," Mick continued. "He talked about some tree in the Bible that had something to do with it. I didn't get all of that. I must've dozed off, but the point he was making was that we all wear the same colored hats. Only difference is the shade of the color." He shrugged. "At least, that's what I got out of his sermon."

"Do you remember the talk we had about needing someone?" Adam asked.

"Sure. Why?"

"Part of the emptiness is going into that room and finding that you need someone to share it, but there's no one there. That's what scares me."

"Hope I'm not interrupting anything," Kass said as he walked up.

"You're not," Adam said, feeling relieved for the interruption, having shared more than he intended.

"You boys looked like you were having a serious discussion. Anything I can help with?"

"Thanks, but we were just talking about a class paper," Adam quickly said. Out of the corner of his eye, he noticed Mick glance at him.

"You two want another Coke?" Kass asked as he wiped off the counter.

"Not for me," Adam said.

"Me either," Mick added. "I've got to go and do some Christmas shopping. Going to get my mother an embroidered apron that she's been talking about."

"Nice, but get her some perfume, too," Kass suggested. "An apron, no matter how nice, is still for work. Perfume is for play." His eyes twinkled. "So, you're going to spend Christmas at home with your family. That's nice."

"I'll spend some time with them, but then I'm going out with Adam and Howie."

"How about you?" Adam asked Kass.

"Yeah," Mick added. "How're you celebrating Christmas?"

"Boys, you forget I'm Jewish."

"Oh, yeah. I forgot," Mick said. "Sorry."

"Don't worry, it's okay. Sometimes I even forget." Kass scratched the back of his head. "What am I going to do for Christmas? Ever since my wife died, I just have a quiet meal by myself and then I come down to the store here to catch up on a few things."

"What do you do down here?" Adam asked.

"Go over the books and have a glass of wine." Kass looked around, leaned over the counter as far as his belly would allow, and whispered, "I've got a little room in the back. I go in and shut the door. You can't see any light, so nobody will bother me. I go in, have my wine, and relax."

"Sounds good to me," Mick said. "Kass, if I don't see you before, have a nice holiday. I got to go. Hey, Adam, we'll talk about that paper later. Okay?"

Adam nodded, appreciating Mick going along with the lie. He snapped up his jacket. "I'm going, too. See you, Kass. I hope it'll be nice and quiet so you can have your wine in peace."

"I'm sure it will be," Kass replied.

Chapter 17

Danny Logan stood shivering in the doorway of a store, glad that the entryway shielded him from swirls of snow kicked up from occasional gusts of wind. Waiting for Johnny to return from Kass', he'd just lit his second cigarette when he came running up.

"Shit, it took ya long enough," Danny growled. "Freezin' my ass off here."

"Hey, man. Takes time to case it out." Johnny rubbed his hands together. "Man, it's cold. Let me have a drag, will ya?"

Danny flipped him the finger when he reached for the cigarette.

"Come on, it's not my fault," Johnny whined.

"Ya can have one drag." Danny took another pull off his smoke before giving it to Johnny. "So, what did ya find out?"

"Seems easy enough." Johnny took a couple of puffs before giving the cigarette back. "Cash box must be under the front counter."

"Are ya sure?"

"Yeah, pretty sure." Johnny zipped up his jacket nearly to the top. "Saw Kass go up to the register to help the cashier. Some guy gave her a money order or somethin'. She showed it to Kass and he bent down under the counter. Comin' back up, he had bills in his hand." He reached out for the cigarette again but Danny just looked at him. "Don't know how much it was but it was a lot."

"Did he see ya watchin'?"

"Naw, he was too busy." Johnny wiped his nose with his jacket sleeve.

Danny flipped the cigarette away without giving Johnny another drag. It'd piss him off but he didn't care. Served him right for making him wait in the cold. "Shit, this is goin' to be easy."

"How do we get in?"

"Use a crowbar on the back door." Danny took out his cigarettes, shook one out, and offered a smoke to Johnny.

After lighting up, Johnny took a couple of puffs. "Hey, I saw Adam there."

"Oh, yeah. What was he doin'?" Danny asked, annoyed that Adam didn't join up with him.

"Talkin' with some guys sittin' at the soda counter." Johnny took another drag off his cigarette. "They did me a favor."

"How's so?" Danny asked as he and Johnny turned their backs to a sudden gust of wind.

"They were laughin' about somethin'. Don't know what, but it kept the attention of the people on them rather than me." Johnny flicked off the ashes of his cigarette. "Say man, did ya know the new Superman issue is out?"

"Who as hell cares? Didn't send ya to read comic books."

"Don't get out of joint, now." Johnny paused. "Hey, do ya think Adam would say anythin' to Kass?"

"Not if he knows what's good for him."

"Yeah, we could play some baseball with him, too."

"Damn right, and what's more, he wouldn't want Frankie boy to find out that he set him up that night."

"When are we goin' to hit Kass'?" Johnny asked, visibly shivering from the cold. "I'll be seein' Pete later and he'll want to know."

"Next week. Late Wednesday night."

"Wednesday! That's Christmas Eve."

"Hell, I know that. Listen, people will be at home with their families. Fuzz will be drinkin' coffee and eatin' donuts and bitchin' about workin'."

"But Christmas Eve?"

"What the shit? Ya goin' to church or somethin'? Ya goin' stay home and sing Christmas carols with your old man?" He flipped his cigarette at Johnny, hitting him in the chest. "Are ya in or out? Because if you're out, Pete and me can handle it."

"I'm in," Johnny said, wiping ashes off his jacket. "Don't get so pissed, okay?"

"Tell Pete we'll meet that night at eleven."

"Where?"

"Behind Skelly's Liquor Store. And tell him not to worry. Ain't nobody goin' to be at Kass' on Christmas Eve. We'll have the whole place to ourselves."

Chapter 18

Parked outside the aging two-story duplex, his fingers tapping against the steering wheel, Adam banged on the horn of his mother's '54 Buick. "Come on, come on," he muttered, sounding the horn again and looking up at the second floor windows. "Come on, Howie, what's keeping you?" Church music began playing over the car radio as a man announced that the Christmas Eve service was about to be broadcast live from the Cathedral in downtown St. Paul. "It will be an inspirational service for our listening audience," the announcer said.

"Not for me," Adam said, turning the dial. The next station had some woman screeching in a high-pitched voice *Silent night, holy night.* He turned the dial again, but finding nothing to his liking, he turned the radio off. Resting his forehead against the steering wheel, he shut his eyes. The shadowy figures of Danny Logan and his two friends crept into his awareness. Frank's pitiful pleading for help and his cries of pain rang in his ears. Ever since that night, the haunting realization of what he had done fought its way into his consciousness and each time he struggled to push it out.

Just as he was about to honk again, the door to the duplex flew open and Howie dashed out. He got in the car and slammed the door. "Why didn't you just come up? You didn't have to honk. That upsets my father. Remember, he's got that bad heart."

"Why couldn't you have been on time?" Adam snapped, feeling bad as soon as he had said it. "I guess I could've come up but isn't he still mad at me?" he added, in a conciliatory tone.

"What do you mean?"

"You know, for what I wrote in your yearbook last year."

"Yeah, but consider what you wrote."

"All I said was that maybe after graduation we could get an apartment together. It was no big deal. I wrote that in Mick's, too."

"Well, it was a big deal to my father. He thought you were saying that he and I didn't get along, and that's why I should move out."

"I didn't write anything like that," Adam said, hiding his irritation.

"I know, but you know how parents are."

"So, what did you tell him?"

"That you and Mick and I had talked about getting an apartment, but not because of our parents. He was never really mad. He cares about you. Just the other day, he was telling me that he thought you really needed a friend, and not having a father you—"

"Look, I don't feel like sitting here and talking about what your dad thinks of me as if he was a shrink or something."

"Hey, my father wasn't trying—"

"Just drop it, okay?" Adam couldn't understand why things were setting him off, but didn't want to deal with it now. Too many things were happening in his life and he felt as if his emotions were on a roller coaster ride. He started the car. "Look, Howie, I'm just tired tonight. What do you say that we go get Mick now?"

"Okay."

Adam put the car in gear and pulled away from the curb.

Howie settled back and looked out his window. They drove several blocks before he broke the silence. "My father and I were talking about my mother just before you came. When she was alive, we used to get a big Christmas tree every year. The three of us would decorate the house together."

"Sounds nice," Adam said, wondering what it would be like to have a family gathering.

"Mom would cook a big meal and afterwards, we'd sit and listen to Christmas music. I remember her singing. She loved music. When she was healthy, she sang in the church choir." Howie sighed. "She sure hated to give that up when she got sick."

The light at the upcoming intersection turned red. Adam pulled to a stop. While waiting for the light to change, he berated himself for having been such a jerk with Howie. "What happens now with you and your dad?" he asked as the light turned green and he stepped on the gas.

"He cooks a meal and we exchange gifts. He hasn't been well for the past couple of years. I'm worried about him."

Adam wanted to offer sympathy, but didn't know what words to use. If Mick was here, he'd know what to say.

"How about you?" Howie asked. "What did you and your mom do earlier tonight?"

"Nothing much. I went down to Andy's to eat. My mom was going to come home for awhile, but I reminded her that I was going out with you guys."

"What's she going to do?"

"Stay for the party that the boss has for them later on."

"So when do you exchange gifts?"

"We did that earlier." He had gotten socks from Oscar, but hadn't given him anything in return. That it bothered him was a new feeling. "I got her some perfume."

"Do you get together with Wanda and Frank at all?"

Frank's name triggered the inner turmoil and tension of the past couple of months. "Hey, listen. I don't want to talk about all this family stuff."

"Man, you're sure touchy tonight."

"Just leave it alone, okay?" Adam felt angry with himself. Howie was just trying to show interest in his life. For the rest of the way to Mick's house they rode in silence.

Adam parked across the street from their friend's house, still feeling crummy about snapping at Howie. "Go get Mick, will you? I'll wait in the car."

Howie ran up to the house and rang the doorbell. Within moments, the door opened, and sounds of music and laughter flowed out into the night.

While Howie was gone, Adam tried to sort out his feelings. The thing with Danny and Frank gnawed at him. He wanted to share it with his friends, but this wasn't the right time. Within a few minutes Mick came out and ran over to the driver's side, motioning to Adam to roll down the window.

"How you doing, old buddy?" Mick said in a cheerful voice. "Come on in and stay for awhile. Have some food. We've got lots of it."

"I don't think so."

"Brrrr, it's too cold out here without a coat." Mick trotted over to the passenger's side and got in, asking Adam to turn up the heat.

Just after Mick got in, Howie came out of the house and ran up to the car. Mick rolled the window down and Howie poked his head in. "Hey, Adam. Come on in. Man, have they got the food."

"Not hungry."

"Sure you don't want to come in for a few minutes?" Mick asked. "It's all family in there. You've met most of them."

"Listen, guys, I don't feel like it. If you want to, go ahead. It's okay with me. I'll just go for a ride."

"Come on, Howie," Mick said. "Get in before he leaves us. Stay with him. Make sure he doesn't take off while I get my coat. And keep the window seat warm for me."

"Hey, wait a minute," Howie said as Mick shut the door.

"What?"

"Bring me back a turkey sandwich, will you? And a couple of cookies."

"Anything else?"

"Have you got a menu?"

Mick chuckled and ran toward his house.

Waiting for Mick to return, Adam gazed across the street at a house decorated with multi-colored lights strung around each window. A large Christmas wreath adorned with a red bow hung on the door. Underneath the living room bay window sat a manger scene. He turned toward Howie but couldn't look him in the eye. "Hey, ah…"

"Yeah?"

"I'm…ah…sorry about being a jerk earlier."

"No big deal. Forget it. Hey, here comes Mick."

Mick opened the door and motioned for Howie to slide over.

"Why do I always have to sit in the middle?" Howie protested.

"Because Adam's driving and I brought you food."

"That doesn't make any sense."

"Life doesn't always have to make sense." Mick handed him his sandwich and cookies. "So, what have you got lined up for us?" he asked Adam.

Adam started the car. "How about going downtown? When we get there, we'll see what's happening."

"Sounds good to me," Mick said, settling back and unzipping his jacket.

"Me, too."

Mick playfully punched Howie in the arm. "Who's asking you, *Turkey Face*?"

As they pulled away from Mick's house, it began to snow.

"Man, look at those snowflakes now!" Howie exclaimed ten minutes later. "They're as big as parachutes."

During the twenty-minute ride to downtown Minneapolis Adam listened as his friends chatted. Howie excitedly talked about going to Cindy's for Christmas Day dinner. Mick shared that he got Mary a silver necklace for Christmas.

By the time they turned onto Hennepin Avenue the snow was falling heavily.

"Will you look at this?" Howie said as he checked one side of the street and then the other. "It's practically deserted down here."

"First time I've been here when it's been so empty," Adam said.

"Sort of spooky," Howie said. "Where is everyone?"

"Probably at home with their families," Mick interjected. "But look on the bright side."

"Oh, yeah. And what would that be?" Howie asked.

"We won't have any trouble finding a parking space."

Howie scanned the area. "So, what are we going to do? Everything looks closed except for a few eating places and the movie theaters."

"How about a movie?" Adam said, trying to sound enthusiastic. "There's a western at the State that's supposed to be pretty good."

"Sounds okay with me," Howie said.

"Sure, why not?" Mick added.

Adam parked across the street from the theater. Howie and Mick scrambled out and raced to see who would be first to buy their ticket.

By the time Adam got to the ticket booth, both Mick and Howie had purchased their tickets and gone inside. An attractive older lady in her late sixties sat in the ticket booth. He gave her his money. She handed him his ticket without looking up. Adam stood, staring at her while waiting for his change. *What's she doing here on Christmas Eve? Where was her family? Does she even have a family?* After receiving his change, he remained, feeling as though he needed to have his questions answered before moving on. When she looked up and asked if there was anything else, Adam was immediately taken by her sad eyes.

"Anything else?" the woman with the sad eyes asked again.

"No, ma'am." Adam took his change and went in the theater.

Walking into the theater it took several moments before their eyes adjusted to the darkness.

"We're in luck, it's just beginning," Adam said as they stood at the back, his own words sounding hollow to him. As they stood in the back, the scene depressed him. In a theater seating nearly four hundred, only three other people were watching the movie. All three appeared to be men and each sitting in a different part of the theater.

"Let's be sure and sit way behind those guys," Howie whispered. "I don't like the looks of them."

"Sure you don't want to go up and sit with one of them?" Mick whispered.

"Funny guy. I'll take my chances with you two."

The three young men took seats in the back. Adam stared at the screen but wasn't seeing the movie. The dialogue became little more than muffled sounds. Before the movie was half over, he leaned over to his friends. "Let's get out of here," he said. He didn't get any argument.

"Hey man," Howie said as they stepped outside. "It's a winter wonderland out here. Got to be three or four inches at least. Man, it look's nice."

The crisp night air brought a welcome relief to Adam. After Mick and Howie helped him brush the snow off the car, Adam unlocked the doors. Before he got in, he looked back at the ticket booth. The old woman looked up, their eyes met for a moment, and then she looked away.

"Now what?" Howie asked after Adam got in and started up the engine.

"I suppose we could go home," Mick offered, not sounding

like he really wanted to.

"Let's ride around some more," Adam said.

For the next half hour, they stayed around the downtown area. Without anyone suggesting it, Adam drove through some of the residential areas just south of downtown. They drove past homes where Christmas trees stood as brightly lit sentinels in living room windows. He turned down one street where nearly all the houses were elaborately decorated with lights.

"Wow!" Howie exclaimed. "Get a gander at these houses!"

Adam slowed the car as they gazed into the living room windows. At one house, people sat around a table, laughing. At another house, a family gathered around a piano. Adam brought the car to a stop across the street from that house and rolled down his window. He turned off the headlights and let the engine idle. They sat in silence listening to the sounds of Christmas carols coming from the house.

"What time is it?" Howie finally asked.

"Few minutes after midnight," Mick said. "Suppose it's time to go home."

"You're probably right," Howie said. "What do you think, Adam?"

Although Adam heard Howie, his thoughts were still on the old woman sitting in the ticket booth at the theater.

"Hey, Adam. Don't you think it's time to go?"

"Yeah, I guess so."

On the way back to the North Side, they made plans for getting together in the next couple of days. After dropping his friends off, Adam went home, parked the car, and walked up the stairs to his apartment. A small night lamp in the living room provided enough light for him to see. His mother had left it on for him. She was sound asleep, and he was careful not to make any noise. Oscar stirred in his bed but didn't wake up when he went into the bedroom. He undressed and got into bed. The last sound he heard before falling asleep was a police siren, but he was too tired to think about it.

Chapter 19

Enclosed in a glass booth Adam had no way to escape. In any direction, as far as he could see, the landscape was barren. He rubbed his eyes with the heels of his hands, and scanned the surroundings again. Off in the distance, a woman walked slowly toward him. When she reached the booth, she stood facing him, not saying a word. Something about her sad eyes was familiar. Where had he seen those— The old woman in the ticket booth! What is she doing here? What did she want? As if reading his thoughts, she opened her mouth to speak but, just as she did, the booth shook violently and surged upward.

'Stop, stop!' he screamed. 'I need to hear what she's going to say.'

Within moments, though, the glass booth was hurling through space, its prisoner looking back upon a shrinking world. Smaller and smaller the earth became until only a starless void enveloped him. Pounding on his glass coffin, he screamed, but no sound came forth. Without warning, the booth began to rattle and—

Adam awoke in a sweat. He blinked his eyes and looked around. The window above his bed was rattling as a bus passed by on the street below. Exhausted from the dream, he took a deep breath and closed his eyes.

Within moments, he became aware of his mom and Oscar talking. The aroma of fresh brewed coffee floated in with their voices. He thought about getting up but dismissed the idea, not being in the mood for a conversation. Checking his alarm clock, he discovered to his surprise that he had slept until nearly ten, something he hadn't done for a long time.

Sitting up, he peered out the window, his eyes squinting from the bright sunlight reflecting off the snow. Broadway had been plowed. Traffic appeared light. The few cars passing by didn't have any trouble traveling the snow-compacted street. The sidewalk across the way hadn't been shoveled. By the looks of the accumulated snow, it must have snowed a half-a-foot or more.

Lying back down, he thought about his dream. *What was that old woman going to say to me?* Confused about how his life was going, he turned over on his side. He had started his senior year knowing that he wanted to get away from the North Side and the people who lived there. It seemed so clear-cut in his mind, but now he wasn't sure what or who he was running away from.

A change in the inflection of the voices coming from the kitchen caught his attention. Something wasn't right.

"I tell you, Oscar, it's a terrible thing to happen."

Adam jumped out of bed, worried that something had happened to Wanda again. Slipping on a pair of jeans and a sweatshirt, he walked barefoot into the kitchen. Oscar and his mother sat at the table, eating donuts and drinking coffee. Both wore somber expressions.

"What's going on?" Adam asked, taking a seat at the end of the table across from his mother. "What happened?"

"Kass was beaten and robbed last night!" she blurted out, her voice shaking with emotion. "It's just awful. He's such a nice person. Who could've done such a thing? And on Christmas Eve."

Adam sat stunned. "Is…is he okay?"

"We're not sure. All we know is that he's in the hospital."

Kass had been the first person to make Adam and his mother feel welcomed on Broadway. He and Kass had always gotten along over the years. "How did you find out about this?"

"When Oscar went to get the morning paper down at Kass'."

"Yah, by golly, but the place was closed," Oscar said. "I couldn't figure out what was going on. He's always open by nine. I was standing there waiting, thinking that maybe Kass was late. You know with it being Christmas Day and all that. Then this here guy comes up and says to me that the drugstore wasn't going to be open today."

"It was Phil Rizzo," his mother said.

A look of puzzlement flashed across Adam's face. "Who?"

"Phil Rizzo, the detective. He works out of the Fifth Street

Precinct. He comes into Andy's for coffee every now and then."

"So, what did he say?"

"You tell him, Oscar. He talked to you."

"Yah, I will." Oscar looked pleased that he was being asked to talk. He took his Copenhagen from his flannel shirt pocket, opened it, took out a pinch, and stuffed it in his mouth. "This here detective, Rizzo, tells me that the drugstore was robbed some time last night. Whoever done it knocked Kass out. He had to be taken to the hospital. I asked this detective guy if Kass was dead. By golly, I thought he might be. I figured he maybe wasn't saying, but he tells me no and says to me that we can't have rumors like that going around. So he says that old man Kass got cracked on the skull. That he might have a, uh, a concushion."

"Concussion," Adam's mother corrected.

"Yah, that's what he called it. So by golly, he takes out this little notebook and begins asking me questions."

"What kind of questions?" Adam asked.

"Like how well I know Kass. If I thought he'd any enemies and if I'd seen any suspicious characters hanging around the drugstore."

"Butch, you're looking a little pale," his mother said. "Are you hungry? I'll fix you some breakfast."

"I'll get something later." Adam recalled hearing a siren before falling asleep last night. "What time did this all happen?"

"Gee, I don't know. That detective didn't say." Oscar appeared worried as he looked over at Adam's mother. "Maybe I should've asked, huh?"

"Don't worry, you did good," she assured him.

Oscar grinned and got up from his chair. He walked over, got a coffee can from the cupboard underneath the sink, spit into it, and put the can back. Sitting down again, he wiped his mouth with a handkerchief. "First Frank and now, old man Kass. By golly, it just ain't safe anymore. Heck of a world."

"Did that detective say anything else?" Adam asked.

"Nope, can't say he did, but if I find out anything more, I'll tell you, by golly."

"Well, I'm sure I'll find out more," his mother said. "I'm going down to Andy's around eleven to help out with the Christmas Day rush. By then there'll be enough talk among the regulars about what happened."

"Do you think you'll hear anything?" Adam asked.

"Quite a few of the cops come in. They know they better tell me or else they won't get served."

Adam's mother prided herself on knowing more about what was going on around Broadway than most people. Customers liked to sit and have a cup of coffee with her, sharing the latest rumors as to what was happening on the street. More than one cop had gotten leads from her.

"Butch, are you coming down to Andy's later to eat? I've already told Oscar that he should. It's going to be my treat."

"I'm coming, but not until after the noon rush. That place gets too packed for me."

"I know. Too bad we have only so many stools."

"Yah," Oscar said, chuckling. "And if you don't get one, you have to stand and wait."

"And you can get pretty hungry doing that," she said. "You should see it sometimes when it's really crowded. Some of the customers can't wait, so they order their food and eat standing up. The place usually thins out after two. There's plenty of food and I'll make sure we save the juiciest parts of the turkey for the two of you."

"Thanks," Adam said. "But I don't want you going around and introducing me like you usually do."

"But I—"

"Mom, I'm not coming if you're going to do that. You know I just don't like being put on display."

"Okay, okay, I won't." Although she smiled, disappointment could be heard in her voice. "It's just that I'm proud of you and I like to show you off."

"Not today. You can do it some other time, okay?"

"I'll be down around noon," Oscar said.

"That's when we're the busiest. You might not get served right away. Is that okay?"

"Yah, you bet. I've got lots of time. By golly, I'm looking forward to meeting some of the people. Maybe they'll want to hear about that detective guy talking to me."

* * *

When Adam walked into Andy's that afternoon, his mother kept her promise about not showing him off. He glanced around, thankful there weren't many customers. A couple of empty stools were at one end of the counter. Sitting at the one next to the wall, he took off his jacket and draped it over the empty stool next to him.

"I'm so glad you came down," his mother said as she wiped the counter in front of him. "I hope you're hungry. Have the holiday special. I'll give you extra white meat. If you want more, you can have it. Then you can have either apple or pumpkin—"

"Mom, I don't want all of that. I'll just have a hamburger and malt. Bring the other stuff home when you get off work. I'll eat tonight."

"But…okay. I remember when you were younger," she said, setting a glass of water in front of him. "You would come in and watch me play the pinball machine. All you would need would be your burger and chocolate malt…and fries if you were really hungry. Do you remember that?"

Adam nodded. He especially remembered sipping on his malt and eating fries while watching his mother banter back and forth with the customers. The first time he had witnessed the bantering, he thought they were angry at one another because of the things they were saying and their tone of voice. In time, he realized his mother was well liked and respected because the customers knew she could dish it back as much as they dished it to her.

"Butch, do you remember how you would even bring some of your friends? You'd come in and say, 'There's my mom. She makes the best malts on Broadway.' Do you remember that?"

Nodding, he decided not to make an issue of her calling him Butch with other people around.

"Those times seem so long ago now," she mused.

"Mom, I'm getting hungry. How about some food?"

"I'll go right now and fix it."

He watched her put the hamburger patty on the hot grill. The meat sizzled and spattered its juices, causing her to step back. Within a couple of minutes, she flipped the patty over and placed a buttered bun upon it.

"Betty," she called out to the other waitress. "Handle the coffee refills for a few minutes, will you? I've got a special customer to serve." She soon had the metal container filled with ice cream and attached to the malt machine.

Adam shifted nervously as customers stole glances at him.

"I put extra ice cream in," she said, setting the malt glass down in front of him, filled nearly overflowing and topped with whipped cream. She set the metal malt container down, saying that there was more in it.

"Looks good," he said.

"Your burger will be coming right up." She went back to the grill, slid the spatula under the hamburger and, in one motion, placed it on the bun waiting on the plate. After adding a couple of pickles on the plate, she brought it to him. "Anything else?" she asked.

"No, this will be enough. Did you hear anything more about Kass?"

A frown crossed her face. "Not as much as I thought I would." She pointed to his hamburger. "You eat while it's hot."

"I will. Tell me about Kass."

"He'll be in the hospital for a few days, but he'll be okay."

Adam quietly breathed a sigh of relief. "That's good to hear."

"Sure is and we can thank God for it."

He tried to take a sip of his malt using the straw but found he had to use a spoon. His mother stood, watching him eat.

"I told you it was thick," she said with a note of pride.

"It's good," Adam replied, eating a spoonful of the creamy chocolate. "Did you hear anything else?"

"I guess the doctor will let him out only if he promises that he'll stay home for a few days."

"Do you think he will?"

"You know him. If it was possible, he'd never go home. Ever since his wife died, he spends all his time down at that drugstore." Picking up the malt container, she poured the remainder into his glass.

"Do they have any idea who did it?"

"I talked to Lyle; he's one of the cops. He said that they didn't have much to go by, but they think it was kids."

Adam put his hamburger down. "Why kids?"

"Because a bunch of comic books were taken." She glanced around and then lowered her voice. "I shouldn't be telling you this because Lyle said it's part of an ongoing investigation, but all the Superman comic books were taken. Whoever did it broke in through the back door. Lyle thought it was a pretty amateur operation."

An uneasy feeling swept over Adam. "Anything else?"

"Yeah, do you remember Phil, the detective that Oscar talked about this morning?"

Adam nodded as he picked up his hamburger to take another bite. He was hungrier than he thought.

"Anyway, Phil stopped by to have some pie and coffee about an hour ago. Told me that whoever broke in knew exactly where Kass kept the money. The strange part of it is that whoever did it only took cash."

"I'm not sure what you're getting at," Adam replied as he finished his hamburger, washing it down with the rest of his malt.

"According to Phil, they took comic books but left some expensive watches that Kass had on display for Christmas. Phil said that if they'd taken the watches, they probably could've gotten another thirty bucks selling them to a fence."

"Hey, Virg!" one of the customers yelled.

Adam could tell by the white uniform that it was one of the Clover Leaf milkmen who frequented Andy's. The guy was waving and pointing at his coffee cup.

"How about another cup of that slop you call coffee!" the milkman hollered with a grin that revealed a front tooth missing. "You got anymore left or are you using it to kill the rats?"

"Sam, if you wouldn't drink so much of our coffee, maybe you'd keep your teeth."

A mousy-looking man with thinning reddish hair slapped the milkman on the back. "Hell, Sam, Virg got you again. You know better than to try to get one over on her."

"Butch, I'll be right back. I'll fix you another hamburger if you want."

"That's okay, I'm full. I've got to be going."

"Oh, so soon?"

"Yeah. I'll talk to you later. If you hear anything more about Kass, let me know." As he got his jacket on to leave, he heard Sam, the milkman.

"Hey, Virg, who was that you were talking to?"

"My kid, Butch."

"Really? Good-looking kid. You must be pretty proud of him."

Adam didn't wait to hear her answer as he opened the door to leave.

Chapter 20

Wanda was pleased with Frank's progress. According to the doctor, his recovery was quite remarkable considering his age and the extent of his injuries. His broken nose was healing and the scar over his right eye would be partially concealed by his bushy eyebrow once it grew back. Frank had told Wanda that he got "mad as hell" when he discovered that his eyebrow had been shaved off. The doctor had assured him that with plastic surgery the scar would never show, but Frank told him to go to hell. "Had enough of ya damn doctors," he had fumed.

Sitting at the kitchen table with her father, Wanda put Frank's confrontation with the doctor aside. Her husband lay on the couch in the living room. "Do you want another cup of coffee?" she asked her father.

Paul held out his cup. "One more."

As Wanda walked over to the stove, she looked in at Frank. He was too absorbed in a magazine to notice her. She picked up the coffee pot, poured her father another cup, and refilled her own. She thought about asking if Frank wanted coffee. But no. He had been more touchy than usual lately and she didn't want to deal with any of his mood swings right now. Returning the coffee pot to the stove, she sat back down at the table. For the past hour she and her father had been talking about the robbery at the drugstore. Both were upset because Kass had been such a good friend over the years.

Wanda shifted in the chair; her back aching from all the extra care Frank demanded. She had thought about seeing a doctor about her back but with Frank not working, her paycheck barely covered food and rent. "Pa, how's the watch coming?"

"Can't figure out. Had apart twice." Paul took the watch from his pocket and placed it on the table. He scratched the side of his head. "I do everything. Still not work right."

Wanda picked up the watch and held it in her palm, admiring

the intricate scrolled design upon its gold case. “What do you think is wrong with it?”

“Don’t know. Keeps time, but stops.” He sipped his coffee, adjusted his glasses, and took the watch. “I think gear bent. I bend back but still no work. I try again.”

“If anyone can do it, you can. I’m sure Butch will be pleased with it.” Wanda paused, thinking she heard Frank move on the couch. She wondered if he was going to get up, silently wishing he wouldn’t. She was enjoying this time with her father. “How long do you think it will take to repair it?”

“I bend gear more. Then maybe fixed. Now, I take apart. Clean. Polish. Look brand new.” Her father opened the cover and smiled as he examined it.

“What are you looking at?”

“Words inside. You read but no tell Butch, you hear?”

Wanda took the watch and held it at an angle, allowing the light to reflect off it so she could see the inscription. “Let’s see, it says *Cast…*” She read the rest in silence. Her eyes moistened. “Pa, I…”

“I know. I know. Remember, don’t say.”

“I won’t.” Wanda handed the watch back, understanding how important it was for him to give it to his grandson. Her father once said that the hands of a clock can only go forward; they can never go back. Those words took on new meaning now after having read the inscription.

“Babe! Bring me a beer, will ya?”

Paul shook his head. “Lazy son’n’—”

“Pa, don’t,” Wanda pleaded and looked toward the living room. “He’ll hear you. I don’t want to start anything today.”

“Babe!” Frank’s voice growled with impatience. “Get me a goddamn beer!”

“Just a minute.” Wanda put her finger up to her lips and shook her head at her father to remind him once again not to say anything. She slowly got up and went to the refrigerator. When she bent to get a beer from the bottom rack, she felt a sharp pain in her back. “Oooh!”

“What’s matter?” Paul asked, a look of concern in his eyes.

“Nothing,” she replied, afraid that he’d make another remark to Frank about being so lazy. “I just bent the wrong way.”

Frank's supply of beer was in need of replenishing. "Better get some more," she muttered. She didn't like his drinking, but his nature was so much better when he had his beer.

Frank was still stretched out on the couch when she brought the beer. Pillows propped up behind his head. He made no effort at hiding his magazine of scantily dressed women.

She handed him his beer. "Here you go. Anything else?"

"Not now, but later." He held the magazine up and showed her one of the pictures. "Maybe ya can pose like that."

Wanda felt disgusted. She wanted to take all his girlie magazines and throw them in the trash. "I don't know how you can look at such things."

"Open my beer for me, damn it! I can't do it lyin' down." He handed her the bottle and the opener she had brought. "At least ya can be good for somethin'."

She took the bottle, praying he wouldn't see how scared she was. After opening it, she handed it back to him.

Frank took a couple of swigs, belched loudly, and wiped his mouth with the sleeve of his shirt. "What the hell are ya doin' in the kitchen?"

"Just talking to Pa and having some coffee. He's trying to fix a pocket watch so that he can give it to Butch."

"Damn kid." He dismissed her with a grunt and went back to his magazine.

When she sat down at the kitchen table, her father was polishing the watch's case.

"This be graduation present," he announced.

"That's a wonderful idea." She tried to sound cheerful, but was still troubled by the look on Frank's face when she had mentioned Butch's name.

"Good gift, you think?"

"Oh, yes. It'll mean a lot to him. You know, Pa, Butch thinks you're pretty special. He may not always show it, but I know he does."

"He good kid." Her father continued polishing the watch.

"Do you realize that our Butch will be the first one in the family to graduate from high school? That's quite some accomplishment."

"That Butch, he smart kid all right." Paul set the watch aside.

He took a couple of sips of coffee and motioned to Wanda to get him some more. After she filled his cup, he tasted it, and smiled. “Butch take after grandmother. Smart woman.”

Wanda leaned forward to give him her full attention, since her father seldom talked about her mother.

“She have little schooling, but taught self.” Paul was quiet for a moment. “Always read books. Many books. All kinds. Even got me read books.”

“You really loved her, didn’t you, Pa?”

“More than words tell.” He pointed to the watch. “Like this. Two main gears inside. When mesh, movement like music. Your mother and me like two main gears. Together we give perfect time. Yes, I love.”

Wanda embraced her father’s words. Seldom had she heard him speak with such tenderness. “I miss mom, but I know that you really miss her.”

“Yes, I miss. Like watch with missing gear. My life never run same since she die. I know she be proud of our Butch. He—”

“Babe! I need another beer.”

Angry at Frank’s interruption, she nevertheless obeyed. He was still looking at his magazine when she brought him his beer, making sure she had first opened it.

Frank laid his magazine aside. “I heard what he was saying about his dead wife. Too bad she died. Maybe she could’ve saved him from being a drunk.”

Wanda swallowed her fury.

“So Butchie thinks the old man is special, eh?”

“What’s wrong with that?”

“Nothin’, Babe, nothin’.” Frank sneered. “Get the hell out of here now. Go and gab with your Pa some more. Let me finish lookin’ at my pictures.”

As Wanda went back into the kitchen, she had an uneasy feeling about whatever was going through Frank head wasn’t good.

Chapter 21

"Are you sure about that? That's great!" Howie said, excited as he listened to his friend at the other end of the phone. He had been anxiously waiting for this call for several weeks. "When can I get it? Really? Good. I'll call you next week. No, don't call me." He checked to see if his father was still in the next room, and lowered his voice. "You see, I don't want my father to get suspicious. I'm not sure he'd understand. Yeah, I know, take care."

"Who was that?" Howie's father asked as he stopped on his way into the kitchen.

"Oh, ah, that was somebody from school." Howie didn't like lying, but felt justified in doing so. As much as Howie loved his father, he thought he could be old fashioned at times. And this would be *one* of those times if he knew the subject of the telephone conversation. "My friend wanted to know about some homework."

"I see," his father replied and walked into the kitchen. Before long, he came back. "I could use some assistance with supper. You can peel the potatoes."

Howie followed him into the kitchen and sat at the table where several potatoes were laying on a piece of newspaper. His father stood at the sink washing dishes. Picking up the peeler, Howie went to work on a large potato as though carving a piece of wood. "How're you feeling?" he asked.

"Not too bad. Doctor wants me to try out this new medicine for a while. Tastes terrible, but so far it seems to be helping. Only problem is it makes me a little tired," he said, adding with a smile, "but then at my age, everything makes me tired."

Howie was happy to hear him sounding more upbeat. It reminded him of a father who used to laugh and joke all the time. His father, however, had aged since the death of Howie's mother. Although the doctor blamed an inoperable heart valve for his growing health problems, Howie, however, felt that his father's spirit had been crushed when his wife died.

"How's Adam coming along these days?"

"He's doing fine. Why?"

"Haven't seen him for a long time. Say hello to him for me." He paused. "Tell you what. Let's think about inviting him and Mick over for supper some time. It'll do us both some good."

"I'll ask, but they've been pretty busy."

"I understand. As soon as you get down with those potatoes we're going to have some good old fashioned potato and dumpling soup, just like your mother used to make." He cleared his throat. "Ahem, that is, if we have any potatoes left after you get done peeling them."

Howie looked at the potato in his hand. It was half its original size. "Sorry. I guess I got carried away."

"Don't worry, when your mother and I were first married, and she had me peel potatoes, I did the same thing."

* * *

The coming weeks brought a number of changes to everyone. Frank's injuries healed completely and he went back to frequenting the bars. He still, however, wasn't working, claiming that there were no jobs that matched his skills. When Wanda told that to her father, he just scoffed. Kass returned to work within a day of getting out of the hospital. Adam and Mick went to see him and were pleased to find that his experience didn't change his outlook on life. As far as who robbed him, the police still had no suspects.

* * *

It was noon, and Adam and Mick were nearly finished with their lunches when Howie walked over and sat down. Howie looked around the school lunchroom before placing a bulging brown paper bag on the table.

"Looks like you're carrying enough for three lunches," Mick said.

Howie leaned over the table. "This is it," he whispered,

holding the bag with both hands.

"This is what?" Mick whispered back, a humorous twinkle in his eyes.

"What I've been waiting for. It's going to help make us famous."

"Make sense. What are you talking about?"

Adam nudged Mick. "Hey, are you sure you want to know? Look at him. He's got that gleam in his eyes again. Just remember last time."

Howie opened the bag and cautiously looked around the lunchroom again. "Just want to make sure there are no teachers around," he explained. He tilted the open end of the bag toward Mick. "Have a peek."

"So what's the big deal? I see some sandwiches, a bag of potato chips, and…wait a minute! What the heck is that thing at the bottom? It looks like…like some kind of bomb!"

"Shhh," Howie said, glancing around.

Adam leaned forward. "Let me see."

"Do it quickly," Howie said.

"What are you doing with that?" Adam asked, his eyes doubling in size. "Planning to blow up the school or something?"

"Come on, guys," Howie pleaded. "This is the answer to Mattingale's desk."

"What are you going to do?" Adam asked. "Blow it up?"

"No, no, no. What you're looking at is a smoke bomb."

Mick chuckled. "Why can't you just bring her a shiny red apple like a normal kid?"

"Very funny." Howie closed the bag but not before taking out one of his sandwiches. "Don't you see? This is part of the scheme I've been planning. I contacted this friend last month. His dad travels a lot on business."

"So, what are you telling us?" Mick asked. "That his dad's business is bombs?"

"Get serious, now. He's a salesman or something. I told my friend to ask his dad to get me one of these the next time he travels to a state where they sell things like this. I just got it this weekend. It's a little bigger than I planned, but that's okay."

"What are you going to do with it?" Adam asked.

"I figure we'll let it off and—"

"We!" Mick exclaimed. "What's with this *we* business?"

"Hey, give me a chance to explain. We'll set it off. Everybody will think the school's on fire. There'll be mass confusion. During that time we'll slip into Mattingale's room, shimmy the lock, find out the secret of her desk drawer, and be out before anyone is the wiser." Howie leaned back and took a bite of his sandwich, a look of triumphant satisfaction on his face.

"But that thing you got is a bomb," Mike said.

"It's just a smoke bomb." Howie opened the brown sack and took out a bag of potato chips and another sandwich. "There won't be any real damage done." He took a sip from his pint of milk. "We'll miss a class or two. Big Deal. Even the teachers won't mind that."

"Are you sure?" Adam asked.

"Yeah. Look at it this way. We'd be doing them a favor. The principal and the teachers will have a chance to practice their fire drill. The fire department will get some training. I figure that's good community service." Howie offered the bag of potato chips to his friends. Adam waved it off but Mick reached in and took a handful. Howie munched on chips as he talked. "Hey, when you think about it, it'll be good all around. Someday, they may even thank me for it. Besides— Oh, oh. Don't look now, but here comes Mueller!"

The burly gym teacher walked up and stood eyeing the three of them. "I see you're bringing your own lunch now-a-days, Howard. What's the matter, school lunches not nutritious enough for you?"

"No, sir. I mean, yes, sir. I mean you just can't trust the food around here anymore."

Mueller glanced over at Mick and Adam before turning his attention back to Howie. "I'm amazed how innocent you can appear."

"Thank you Mr.—"

"I said, *appear*. You see, I suspect you were involved in that spaghetti fiasco we had this fall, but I can't prove it. Just know, I'll have my eye on you." Mr. Mueller glanced over at Mick and Adam before looking back at their friend. "Enjoy your lunch, Howard. It looks like you brought enough." He gave Howie a nod and walked away.

As soon as the gym teacher was out of hearing range, Mick turned to Howie. "I can't believe this. You've had some harebrain schemes but this takes the cake."

"Keep it down, will you," Howie said. "You want everyone to hear you? You understand, don't you?" he asked Adam.

"I have to agree with Mick on this one. How are you going to pull this off? You got some kind of plan?"

"Sure I do." Howie sounded offended that Adam would suggest such a thing. "I just haven't worked out all the details. Just give me a few days." He looked at his friends with pleading eyes. "Come on, you guys, we've been through a lot together. You're not going to chicken out on this, are you?"

Mick sighed. "I don't know why I listen to you, but what the heck, it's our last year in school."

"Great, I knew you would. I think—"

"Just wait a minute," Mick said. "I'm going along just to protect you from yourself. I've grown attached to you and your father, especially to your father. I made him a promise that I wouldn't let anything happen to you. One thing I ask."

"What's that?"

"You can't keep anything from us. You have to let us know exactly what you're planning."

"I will. I promise." Howie grinned as he made the gesture of crossing his heart. "Man, this is going to be terrific." He looked over at Adam. "You're in on this too, aren't you?"

"I guess I don't have that much choice." Adam reached for Howie's bag of potato chips.

"Great," Howie said. "There's one more thing I'd ask. Can I be the first one to look in Mattingale's drawers?"

* * *

Mr. Mueller looked over at where Howard and his friends were sitting. Both Adam and Mick were laughing so hard that they were about ready to fall off their chairs. Howard, however, sat there without a smile on his face, holding on to his brown paper lunch sack with both hands. "Strange kids," Mueller said out loud to no one in particular. He made a vow to himself to keep an eye on those three in the days ahead.

Chapter 22

Wanda stood at the doorway to the kitchen as she slipped her coat on. Her father sat at the kitchen table drinking coffee. The pocket watch lay in front of him on one of her new dishtowels. “Pa, before I go to work I want to ask you something.”

Paul leaned back in his chair and took a sip of coffee. “So ask.”

“Did you hear Frank and me talking on Christmas?”

“What you mean?”

“Remember we were here in the kitchen and Frank had me bring him a beer? Could you hear us talking in the living room?”

“When he talk, I not listen.” Paul peered over his glasses. “Why you ask?”

“For no special reason.”

Paul gave his daughter a stern look. “You asked. Must be reason. What you getting at?”

“Oh, I…I was just curious about your hearing. Lately, it seems to be getting worse. That’s all.”

Paul did have a hearing problem, and, at times, intentionally tuned Frank out. He didn’t believe her explanation and wondered what she was trying to cover up. Her concern didn’t surprise him since Frank was always shooting his mouth off. It wouldn’t have been the first time Frank had made a nasty remark about him. He cursed Frank for causing her to always be on edge. *That son’n’bitch! If I younger, I teach him lesson.*

“I see you’re working on the watch,” Wanda said, buttoning her coat. “How’s it going?”

“Almost ready. Put new gear in. Works now.” His daughter was purposely shifting the conversation. Talking about the pocket watch was safe. “One more thing do,” he said, holding it up for her to see. “Needs more cleaning. Then ready for Butch.”

“Good. He’ll be pleased.” Wanda picked up her purse and looked around the kitchen. “Tell Frank there’s a new box of cereal over by the toaster."

Let him find himself. I no wait on him.

"One more thing. Frank's sleeping now so try to be quiet, okay? He needs his rest."

"For what? To drink more beer?" Paul shook his head in disgust, feeling bad for his daughter having to put up with such a man. "Ack, he always rests. Lazy."

"Frank's not lazy," she said unconvincingly. "He told me only last night that he's going this afternoon to check out a job over at the warehouse on Fourth Street. If he gets it, he'd celebrate by fixing supper for us tonight." She glanced at the clock above the stove. "I better be going, but let me say this. Maybe he's going to do some changing. We've just got to give him a chance."

Paul didn't believe that Frank was going to look for any job, but didn't want to argue. His daughter would die of starvation if she depended upon Frank to fix a meal. "Radio say bitter cold out. Might get worse. Be careful."

"I will. Don't worry about me."

After she left, Paul poured himself a cup of coffee. He picked up the pocket watch and read the finely engraved inscription. Closing his eyes, his thoughts went back to a warm July summer day when he and his wife, Mary, had a picnic in a park. It was just after they had gotten married. After the picnic, they walked around a small lake and talked about their future. It had been a wonderful day and—

"Ouch! Goddamn it!"

The yell came from the bedroom. Within a few minutes, Frank ambled into the kitchen wearing just his underwear and socks.

"Mornin', Pa."

Frank's unusually friendly tone caught Paul off guard. He wondered what was going on as he watched Frank stretch his hairy arms.

"Shit, I need some coffee," he groaned. "Can I get ya some?"

Paul shook his head, wishing Frank would go back to bed. When Frank walked over to the stove, Paul slipped the watch back into his pocket.

Frank filled his coffee cup. Coming back to the table, he

spilled coffee on the floor. "Goddamn it." He used his stocking foot to wipe the spill before sitting down. "Radio last night said today is supposed to be damn cold. Hell, it even feels cold in here. Hope Wanda dressed warm."

Bullshit. Since when you care about my daughter?

"Ah, shit, warm as piss," Frank said after taking a sip of coffee. After scratching his chest, his hand moved down to his crotch. "Be right back. Gotta take a leak."

After he left, Paul tried to figure out how his daughter ever ended up with someone like Frank. *If only Mary here, she'd know what advice give Wanda.*

Frank grinned as he came back and sat down at the table. "Ah, nothin' like a good piss. Pa, I've been thinkin'. Things haven't always been right with us. Hell, maybe I might have even said some things I shouldn't have."

Paul listened, trying to figure out what had come over Frank. The last time he had acted so friendly was the day he married Wanda.

"Just so there ain't no hard feelin's," Frank said, "let me get somethin'." Getting up from his chair, he headed toward the bedroom. After a while, the closet door banged.

What Frank up to? He trying to change?

Frank came back with a fifth of whiskey. Paul watched with interest as he set the bottle on the table and went to the cupboard. Coming back with two glasses, he sat down and put the larger of the two glasses in front of Paul. Without saying anything, he opened the bottle and sniffed the contents.

Paul's mouth watered as his glass was filled three quarters full.

"Go ahead," Frank urged. "Jack Daniel's. Damn good booze."

Paul stared at the golden nectar, his tongue caressing his lips. His insides craved for the contents of the glass. *How long had it been?*

"Hell, Pa, don't worry," Frank said, pushing Paul's glass closer to him. "I ain't goin' to tell Wanda. This is just between us men."

Paul's hand moved toward the glass. Whatever Frank's ulterior motive wasn't important. Frank wasn't important. What his daughter thought wasn't important. Only the golden nectar sitting in front of him. He picked the glass up and took a couple of healthy swallows. "You have some?"

"Sure as hell am." Frank laughed as he poured some into a glass. "Us men gotta stick together. Pa, there are some things that women just don't understand."

Paul noted that Frank poured himself only half a glass, but that didn't matter. All that mattered to him was how his body welcomed the warmth of the liquid. Raising the glass to his lips for a second time, he drank its contents like water. He set the empty glass down, hoping Frank would pour him another.

"I suppose ya miss your wife a lot."

Paul nodded, his eyes on the bottle of Jack Daniels. Maybe if he stared at it long enough, Frank would get the message. If that didn't work, he'd pick up his glass and make a show of drinking the few remaining drops.

"Her name was Mary, wasn't it?"

Paul nodded, irritated that Frank would even dare speak his wife's name. He didn't say anything for fear that if he did, the golden nectar would be taken away.

"Mary. Hell, that's a nice name. Didn't she die around this time of the year?"

The pain and anguish of the many years without his wife surged through Paul. He didn't care what Frank was up to. He needed the golden nectar. "She die long time ago," he said, briefly glancing up at Frank and then looking down at his empty glass. He picked his glass up and drank the last few drops.

"Jesus, that's too goddamn bad about your wife. Bet Wanda and Virg really miss their ma. Must've been rough raisin' two girls without their ma around." Frank grinned. "Pa, I see your glass is empty. Let me fill it up again."

Paul watched as Frank poured the golden liquid into his glass. It seemed strange to be with Frank, acting as if the two of them were drinking buddies. *Maybe Wanda right. Maybe Frank change.* Paul gulped down half his glass within moments after Frank filled it. He noticed that Frank was only sipping his, but he didn't care because that meant there would be more for him.

Chapter 23

Adam met Wanda in the hallway as he left his apartment. She had just come around the corner from the direction of her apartment.

"Going to work?" he asked.

She nodded.

The two of them talked as they walked down the stairs. He noted that his aunt gripped the railing as she took the stairs slowly. Halfway down, at the landing, she needed to rest. "Just a little tired," she said.

"Hey, that's okay." Adam tried to sound cheerful but was worried about her. Her eyes had sunk so deep into their sockets that it would be only a matter of time before they disappeared entirely.

Leaning against the wall at the landing, she looked at him with a puzzled expression. "Where are you going at this time of the morning? It's too early for school."

"I'm meeting Mick and Howie to talk over some things about school."

"Going down to Andys'?"

"No, the Rainbow Café."

"How come you're not going down to where your mom works? She'd like that, wouldn't she?"

"Yeah, but they don't have booths and it gets crowded at this time of morning."

She shook her finger at him. "You button up your coat. The radio says it's fifteen below and may even get colder."

"Okay," Adam replied, thinking that having one mom was enough. "How's Grandpa?"

"Just fine. He's sitting at the kitchen table tinkering with that pocket watch. He better stay inside today. With his emphysema, this cold weather isn't good for him. Well, I better go or else I'll miss my bus."

Adam followed her out the door. She turned left, and he, right.

Mick was stomping his feet and rubbing his hands together when Adam met him on the corner. “Can you believe this weather?” Mick said. “My feet are frozen. That crazy Howie. Why did he have to pick a day like this to tell us his plan for Mattingale’s desk? Man, it’s cold. I’m surprised they haven’t closed school.”

“Let’s get going,” Adam said. “I’m freezing my buns just standing here.”

“Let’s hustle,” Mick pleaded.

It didn’t take long to run the five blocks to the cafe. When they entered, the aroma of freshly baked pastries welcomed them. Howie sat in a booth near the jukebox.

“Hey, guys!” Howie shouted, waving his hands. “Over here.”

“Look at the silly grin he’s got,” Adam whispered to Mick as they walked to the booth.

“Yeah, I can hardly wait to hear what he’s cooked up this time.”

“You poor souls look cold,” Howie said. Mick slid in with him leaving Adam to take the seat across from them. “Order some of this hot chocolate. It’s great.”

After the waitress took their orders, Mick turned to Howie. “Are you sure you want to go through with this?”

“Of course I do. This is our big chance. Man, I’ve been planning this for a long time. We’re going to make history today.”

“Today?” Adam said. “It’s going to happen today?”

“That’s right.”

“But why today?” Mick asked. “Why can’t we wait until it warms up?”

“Trust me, this weather is perfect.”

“Perfect? For who?” Adam asked. “Eskimos?”

After the waitress brought their hot chocolates, the three were enjoying their drinks when the entrance door opened. Danny Logan and his friend, Johnny, came in. When they walked past, Danny shot a glance toward Adam. Their eyes met briefly, Danny acknowledging him with a slight nod.

Howie waited until Danny and Johnny were well past their booth before speaking. “You want to hear about the plan now?” he asked in a hushed tone.

“Do we have a choice?” Mick asked

“Tell it to Mick,” Adam said. “I’ll be right back.”

“You going to see Danny and Johnny?” Mick asked.

“Yeah.”

“What do you want with those two?” Howie asked. “They’re trouble.”

Adam slid out of the booth. Before he left, he looked at Mick. “Do me a favor. Keep Howie and his plan within the bounds of lunacy.” As he turned to walk away, he felt a tug at his jacket. It was Howie.

“Don’t forget, we’re here if you need us.”

Danny had just lit a cigarette when Adam walked up. “Hey, Johnny, look who’s here. He leaned back and blew a ring of smoke toward the ceiling. “How’re ya doin’ Adam?”

“Okay,” Adam replied curtly.

“Johnny, where’s your manners? Move your ass and make some room for our friend here.”

“Don’t bother.”

“Suit yourself.”

“You made the hit on Kass’, didn’t you?”

Danny glanced at Johnny before looking up at Adam. “So we picked up some loose change. What’s it to ya?”

Adam took a couple of deep breaths to calm himself. “Kass is a friend of mine.”

“What happened to old man Kass just happened.” Danny took a drag off his cigarette. “We didn’t know he was goin’ to be there.”

Adam’s nails dug into his palms. “Who hit him over the head?”

Danny nudged Johnny. “Maybe it was Johnny.” He rolled his cigarette between his fingers. “Maybe me. Hell, maybe it was Pete.” He smirked as he took another drag off his cigarette. “Say, maybe it was Frankie. Ya know Frankie, don’t ya? He’s the guy who got the shit kicked out of him.” Danny passed his cigarette over to Johnny. “Heard he got his ass kicked as a favor to someone. Ya know what I mean?”

"Yeah, I catch your drift." When Frank's name was mentioned, Adam hoped Danny didn't notice that he was taken off guard. If he did, he would take that as weakness.

"If ya think we had anythin' to do with old man Kass, keep your mouth shut and don't be talkin' to the fuzz." Danny flashed a half crooked smile. "Call it repayin' a favor to Danny Logan…or doin' a favor for yourself."

"I won't tell the cops, but just remember one thing."

"What's that, man?"

"We're even now on favors. Stay out of my way."

"Are ya goin' to take that shit from him?" Johnny asked, a sneer on his face.

Before Danny could answer, Adam walked away.

"It's about time you got back," Mick said as Adam sat down. "Everything okay?"

"For now, it is." Adam's insides had twisted into knots. Although wanting to share what was going on, he worried what his two friends might think if they found out about his part in Frank's beating. "Tell me about this plan that's going to make us famous."

"I guarantee you won't believe this." Mick nudged Howie. "You tell him. It's your plan.

Howie took a sip of his hot chocolate. "Okay. Here's the deal. Mattingale goes to get her glass of milk at precisely twelve-o-seven every day and—"

"Wait a minute," Adam said. "How do you know that?"

"I asked him the same question," Mick said.

"I'd like both of you to know that you're not dealing with an amateur. I've timed her habits for the past week and a half. It takes her ten minutes to go down to the lunchroom and return to her classroom. It takes that long because she washes her glass before using it. A rather strange habit, but knowing Mattingale…Anyway, while she's gone, that should give us enough time to sneak into her room. We'll tie a slip knot around the S.O.B. and—"

"The what?" Adam looked at Mick for an answer, but his friend was too busy trying to keep from laughing to be of any help.

"It's a code name," Howie explained. "Smoke Operational

Bomb. S.O.B."

Adam rolled his eyes. "Of course, I should've known that."

"We'll lower the S.O.B. out the window and swing it so it crashes through Mr. Mueller's health class window."

"Through his window? Mick, am I hearing this guy right? We're going to crash it through the window?"

"Hey, it's nice to hear that you're having the same reactions as I did."

"Let me finish," Howie implored. "The window will be an unfortunate casualty of this operation, but remember, at that hour, there'll be no class in session. Mueller will be out of his classroom doing his duties as lunchroom monitor. So you see, nobody will get hurt."

"Hold on," Adam said. "Maybe I'm a little bit slow, but I'm not sure if I'm following all this. Why are we crashing it through the window? If the room's empty, why don't we just go down and put the thing in the room ourselves? Then we don't have to break any windows."

"Crashing it through the window is the ingenuous part," Mick interjected. "I have to give him credit on this."

"Thank you," Howie said. "Naturally, the fire department will arrive and, as stupid as they may be, they'll discover the S.O.B. Instead of it looking like it was an inside job, having it crash through the window will make it look like someone threw it in from the outside."

"Tell him why we won't be suspects," Mick said. "I like that part."

"That's simple. Students aren't allowed outside during lunch and since there are monitors at each entrance to make sure we all stay inside, we then wouldn't be under suspicion."

"Don't forget to tell him about the fuse," Mick added.

"I was just coming to that. The S.O.B. has a two-minute fuse. As it crashes through the window, I'll yank the rope so it pops out of the slipknot. When the fire alarms go off, we'll wait for Mattingale to come out. After she's gone, we'll go in and the desk is ours. Simple and I might add, brilliant."

"How do you plan to get the drawer open?" Adam asked.

"I found this book in the library written by a former burglar who shared secrets about his profession. Terrific book. It was called *Confessions of a Safe Cracker* or something like that." Howie paused for a moment. "I might even do a book report on it for Mattingale. You know, the one due next month. Of course, I'd leave out that particular chapter and—"

"Hey, just go on with how you're going to do it," Adam said.

"Okay, okay. I got this jackknife. All I have to do is slip the blade in between the drawer and the casing and shimmy the lock. Two seconds and it's done. We get an eye full, push the drawer back, and are outside before the fire trucks come. Nobody will know the difference." Howie settled back with a triumphant grin.

Adam looked at Mick. "It sounds so easy, but why do I feel like we are headed for trouble?"

"Hey, trust me," Howie said. "Now, let's get to school. This is going to be one day that we won't forget."

The three young men got up and, after paying the bill, started toward the door. Adam lagged a few steps behind and glanced back at the booth where Danny and Johnny were sitting. He and Danny Logan would cross paths again.

Chapter 24

"Okay, guys. Any questions?" Howie asked as he stood outside Mattingale's classroom.

"None for me," Adam said. He and Mick listened as their friend went over last minute details of the plan shared with them that morning at the Rainbow Café.

"Yeah, I've got one," Mick said, raising his hand.

"What?"

"Is there such a thing as personal insurance for smoke bomb injuries?"

Howie scowled. "Quit clowning around. Class is going to begin any minute. Are you guys coming?"

"Go ahead. We'll be right in," Mick said. After Howie left, he turned to Adam. "When you talked to Danny this morning, it looked like you guys weren't too happy with each other. What's going on?"

Adam hesitated. "It was Logan and his friends who beat up Kass."

"What!"

"They were robbing the place. Kass got in the way."

"What a bunch of lousy creeps! What did you say to Danny?"

"That I didn't like what they did to Kass and that he better stay out of my way."

"Just be careful. Danny's a punk, but he's a guy you don't want to turn your back on. If you ever need help, let me know, okay?"

"I will. We better get going," Adam said as the first bell sounded.

When Adam walked past Howie, he noticed that he was sketching what looked like a floor plan on a piece of notebook paper. When the second bell rang and Miss Mattingale came in, he saw Howie quickly fold the paper and stuff it in his shirt pocket.

Miss Mattingale made some preliminary remarks and then told the class to use the next half hour to work on their assignments. “Do it quietly and wisely,” she instructed.

Adam worked on his theme paper while occasionally glancing over at Howie. “Stop staring at her desk,” he whispered.

“Can’t help it,” Howie whispered back.

“You better or else she’ll get wise.”

“Yeah,” Mick joined in, poking Howie in the back with his finger. “You’ve been eyeballing it ever since we came to class.”

Howie turned his attention toward the blackboard where Mattingale was busy writing the page numbers for tomorrow’s class assignment.

“Let’s see, class, where was I?” Miss Mattingale rubbed the side of her right cheek with a gloved hand. “Oh, yes. Your assigned papers are due in a week and although they have no doubt been challenging, I promise you that these papers will be the high point of your school year. Indeed, I dare say, they may even be the high point of your educational experience thus far. Class, I am so enthralled about reading your papers that I can hardly wait to see them...”

When the bell finally rang ending the class, Adam, like the other students, however, remained seated. Miss Mattingale was still talking, and it was understood by all that class ended only when she dismissed it. Finally, she looked at the clock. “One last thought, class. Remember, the spoken word may be bound by the limits of time, but the written word is timeless. What you will be expressing in the written word will have an ageless quality to it. So please take care as to how you want to preserve your thoughts; how you would like to be remembered by the generations yet to be born.”

As soon as Adam and his friends were in the hallway and away from the other kids, Howie couldn’t contain his excitement. “Just think, in a few hours we’re going to know her secret.”

“Calm down,” Adam said.

“I’ll try. See you guys later. There are a couple of details I have to check on.”

“What do you mean?” Mick asked. “What are you going to do now?”

“Just going to check on the S.O.B. and—”

“Hello, boys.”

“Hello, Mr. Mueller,” Mick said, swallowing hard. “We didn’t see you come up.”

Mueller eyed them suspiciously. “I trust all of you are staying out of trouble?”

“Trouble is the last thing we want to get into,” Howie said. “We were just talking about the exciting opportunity Miss Mattingale has given us. We’re going to become famous.”

Mick cast a quick but reproachful eye toward Howie before speaking up. “What he means is that Miss Mattingale is having us do a theme paper about ourselves. She said that what we write will have a timeless quality to it. That’s what Howie means by having the opportunity of being famous.”

“Pleased to hear that,” Mueller said. “Miss Mattingale must be making quite an impression upon you as she has upon all of us. You’ll have to excuse me but I must see her for a minute.” He turned his attention to Howie. “Before I go, I just want you to realize that I know what S.O.B. stands for.”

Howie gulped. “You do?”

“I most certainly do.” Mueller folded his arms as he gave all of them a stern look. “Why is it that you kids always think teachers are dumb? We weren’t born yesterday.” He pointed his finger at Howie. “I know you’re a senior and that you’ll be graduating in four months, but I want you to know that as long as I’m a teacher here that kind of language will not be tolerated.”

“Language? I’m not sure what you're referring to, Mr. Mueller.”

“Don’t be cute with me, Howard.” Mueller gave Mick and Adam a brusque look that warned them to stay out of it. “And don’t you think your friends are going to help you.” The gym teacher, who wasn’t much taller than Howie, moved so close that his face wasn’t more than six inches from Howie’s nose. “I’m talking about the vulgar language you were just using. And don’t you deny it because I overheard you speaking to your friends here. I don’t want to hear anymore of it. Am I making myself clear?”

"Yes, sir."

"And Howard?"

"Yes?"

"Do you know what they did to kids who used language like that when I was in school?"

"No, sir."

"They washed our mouths out with soap." The gym teacher made it sound like he had just announced a punishment equal to the death penalty.

"Soap?" Howie said, wrinkling his nose.

"Yes, soap." He gave Howie a stern look as he tapped him on the chest with his finger. "Do you understand?"

"I think so," Howie stammered.

"Good. I'll give you a second chance this time, but if I ever catch you swearing again in school, even if it's only using the initials, you'll regret it." Without saying another word he entered Mattingale's room.

"Wonder what he's going to see Mattingale about?" Mick asked

"Who knows?" Howie said. "I always told you teachers are strange. That's why they hang around together in the teacher's lounge. Nobody but their own kind understands them."

"Maybe they're strange, but Mueller almost nailed you," Adam said.

Mick leaned back against the hallway wall. "Yeah. I thought you were dead meat."

A winsome smile crossed Howie's face. "Like I've told you before, I lead a charmed life. I knew all along what Mueller was getting at."

* * *

Mr. Mueller quietly closed the door to Mattingale's classroom. She was at her desk, correcting papers. He stood at the door, making a point of loudly clearing his throat. "Miss Mattingale?"

She looked up, startled. "Oh, Mr. Mueller," she said, regaining her composure. "How may I help you?"

"May I have the pleasure of talking with you over the lunch

period today for a few minutes?"

"Oh, my. This is so unexpected. And what would be the purpose of our meeting?"

Before replying, Mr. Mueller walked up and stood by the side of her desk. "I'd like your opinion concerning three students who have been acting rather strangely."

"But, why me? Surely, there are other teachers who could help you. If need be, you could speak with the principal."

"Yes, I'm sure I could." Mr. Mueller admired her and even felt an attraction toward her. Although older, she certainly could pass for someone his own age. Her grace and elegance appealed to him. "These three are in your class. It's well known that you have the ability to gain an intimate knowledge of students through their writings. That kind of insight would be invaluable to me," he explained.

"Why, thank you, Mr. Mueller. What you say about knowing an individual through his writing is true. May I assume that this will not require the entire lunch period?"

"I can assure you, it won't take more than fifteen minutes of your time. My questions will be brief. I know you treasure your lunch time and I respect that."

"Your request seems reasonable. I shall meet with you." Miss Mattingale smiled. "However, I first must obtain my liquid refreshment from the cafeteria. I will plan to come back a few minutes earlier. Shall we say that we meet at 12:15? Will that be to your suiting?"

"Yes, it will. Thank you." Mr. Mueller turned and walked toward the door. As he opened it, he paused. "Miss Mattingale?"

"Yes?"

"I must say that you look lovely today in that dress. It's very becoming."

She blushed. "Why, Mr. Mueller. Thank you."

Closing the door gently behind him, Mr. Mueller was feeling good about what he had just accomplished. He wasn't only going to get some insights on Howard and his two pals, but also the added bonus of being granted a portion of Miss Mattingale's precious lunch period time. Feeling pleased, he thought about what the other teachers would say when they heard that she agreed to meet with him. He wondered if she would ever agree to have lunch together. Strolling down the hallway, he told himself that this would be a day he would long remember.

Chapter 25

"Okay, this is it!" Howie announced. He, along with Mick and Adam, met at Adam's school locker. He glanced around before turning his attention back to his friends. "It's 11:49. Check your watches."

"I don't wear a watch," Mick said.

"Me either," Adam said.

"Hmmm, that's okay. We'll go by mine. In five minutes I'll go to my locker and get the S.O.B. I'll meet you guys by the boys' bathroom at 12:05. We'll wait around the corner until she leaves and then we move." Howie looked at Adam. "You'll stand guard after Mick and I go in. Now, let me review it once more." He took out a piece of paper that had scribbling on it. "While I tie the bomb and light it, Mick, you'll have to get the window open." Borrowing a pencil from Adam, Howie made a check mark on his paper. "I'll take charge of swinging the S.O.B. so it gains enough momentum to crash through the window." Another check mark. "The whole operation will be done by 12:15 and we'll be out of there by 12:16. That gives us four minutes to spare." As he talked, Howie periodically checked off items on his paper.

Mick chuckled. "You know, after you're done checking off whatever you got on that paper, you're going to have to eat it so there's no evidence."

Howie gave Mick a *get serious* look before continuing. "The fuse is slow burning so by the time the S.O.B. goes off we'll be in the boy's bathroom. Once it goes off, it won't take long for the smoke to get into the hallways."

"What then?" Mick asked.

"After they've clear the school, we'll slip into Mattingale's room, do the desk, and get a look at her secrets. Before anyone's wiser, we'll be out helping the teachers control the panic stricken sophomores."

“Won’t anyone notice we’re missing?” Adam asked.

“Teachers aren’t that smart,” Howie said as he tore the paper into tiny pieces. “Anyway, we’ll still be on lunch break. Remember last year when we had that fire drill? There were kids in the bathrooms who never went outside, and they were never missed.” He handed the pieces of paper to Mick. “Here, get rid of the evidence.”

Mick nodded as he popped a couple pieces of paper in his mouth. Howie and Adam watched in disbelief as he chewed the pieces for several seconds, swallowed and opened his mouth to show that the evidence was gone. “Your turn,” he said as he handed some pieces to Howie.

“Get serious!” Howie checked his watch. “Time to go. See you guys in a few minutes.”

Mick and Adam were waiting by the boy’s bathroom when Howie came running up clutching a brown paper sack containing the smoke bomb. Within minutes, they had positioned themselves just around the corner from Mattingale’s classroom, waiting in silence for her to leave. As Howie had predicted, she came out at precisely the time he had said she would. He flashed an *I told you so grin* and pointed to his watch. After closing her door, Miss Mattingale walked down the hall toward the stairway, but then stopped, turned around, and came back.

“What’s she doing?” Mick whispered.

“Don’t sweat it,” Adam said. “She probably forgot something.”

They watched as she went back into her room. A few minutes passed before the door opened, and Mattingale emerged carrying what looked like a small hand towel. She went down the hall toward the staircase leading to the first floor.

“Okay, this is it,” Howie said. “We’re running two minutes and...ah...thirteen seconds late, but we still have plenty of time. Let’s move out.”

When they got to the classroom, Howie opened the door and peeked in. “It’s empty.” Before going in, he turned to Adam. “Remember, knock twice if you see anyone coming who even looks like a teacher.”

Howie directed Mick toward the windows. “Get that middle window open while I tie the S.O.B. with the twine.” He tied a slipknot as Mick struggled with the window. "Need help?" he asked Mick.

"No, it's...it's coming." The window shot up with a bang. "Wow!" Mick exclaimed.

Howie nearly dropped the smoke bomb. "What's the matter?"

"The air. It's freezing."

"Is that all?" Howie moved over to the window and carefully lowered the smoke bomb as he and Mick watched the wind whip it from side to side.

"Wait!" Mick yelled.

"Why? I'm almost there."

"You didn't light it!"

Howie hauled it up as fast as he could. "Just a little nervous," he explained.

"Your hands are shaking."

"Ca…can't help it. They're like icicles. It's freezing out there."

"It's not too warm in here either. Hurry up!"

Howie stood unmoving, looking at Mick.

"What now?" Mick asked.

"Have you got the matches?"

"Me? You're the one who's supposed to have all the stuff."

"Hold the S.O.B. while I look." He rifled through his pockets. "They got to be here some place," he said.

"Come on, we don't have all day."

"Found them." As Howie went to strike a match, he noticed that the match cover advertised a mail order course in becoming a private investigator. He made a mental note to send for the information. His hands were shaking so much that he had trouble lighting the match.

"Take this thing and give me those matches!" Mick gave Howie the smoke bomb. On the third attempt, he lit one. "Hold that steady so I can light it."

"I'm trying," he said, shivering from the frigid air blowing in through the open window.

"Okay, it's lit," Mick said. "Now, hurry up! Time must be running out."

Howie again lowered the smoke bomb out the window, but

when he tried to swing it out far enough to crash it through the window below, he couldn't do it. "I've got to lean out farther. Hang on to me!" he pleaded as he looked down at the ground two stories below. "And don't let go!"

As Mick hung onto the back of his belt, Howie leaned out as far as he could. His numb hands could barely feel the twine he was holding. Time and time again he swung the smoke bomb out only to have it thud against the window.

"Pull me back in!" Howie yelled, his teeth chattering.

Mick hauled him inside. "Man, your lips are blue!"

"I couldn't get it to break through the window. Let me warm up a little and I'll try—"

The classroom door flew opened and Adam rushed in. "Mattingale's coming up the staircase! She'll be here any minute."

"Oh, man," Mick moaned. "I'll shut the window."

"Wait!" Howie exclaimed. "I've got to pull the bomb up." Within seconds, Howie was holding the bomb in his hands.

Adam's mouth dropped open. "What are you doing? That thing's still lit! Get rid of it!"

"What should I—"

"I don't care. Throw it out the window and let's get out of here."

Adam and Mick rushed out leaving Howie. When he finally appeared in the hallway his hands were empty.

The three of them ran down to the end of the hallway and ducked around the corner. "What did you do with it?" Mick asked.

"I was going to toss it out, but there were people on the sidewalk."

"What did you do with it, then?" Adam asked.

"Tossed it in Mattingale's closet."

"You did what!" Mick exclaimed.

"Shhh," Adam whispered. "Here she comes."

They watched as Mattingale entered her classroom and closed the door behind her.

"If we're lucky, she won't find it," Adam said.

Howie leaned back against the wall, closed his eyes, and took a couple of deep breaths. His eyes suddenly popped open and he began banging his fist against the wall. "Oh, no!"

"Now what?" Mick cried, looking at him as if he had gone crazy.

"The fuse."

"What about it?"

"I can't remember if I put it out."

Adam glanced at Mick and then back at Howie. "You're kidding."

"I was in so much of a hurry to get rid of it, I forgot about the fuse."

"You mean it still could be lit?" Mick peeked around the corner and looked in the direction of Mattingale's room.

"It's no big deal if it goes off." Howie tried to sound optimistic. "When Mattingale sees the smoke, she'll sound the alarm, and then go outside with the others. We're still clear. No one has seen us, have they? The principal will know that it's an inside job but that's no problem for us. There's any number of kids who could be suspects."

"When is it due to go off?" Adam asked.

Howie glanced at his watch. "Any time now. What do you think of this? When Mattingale leaves, why don't we slip in and do the desk? It's going to be mass confusion around here, anyway."

"I think the numbness from your hands has moved up to your head," Mick said.

"We've taken enough chances already," Adam said. "Let's not push our luck."

* * *

After Miss Mattingale entered her classroom, she set her glass of milk down on her desk. Wondering why the room was so chilly, she checked the thermostat. Once satisfied that it was set to the proper temperature, she made a mental note to take up the discrepancy with the school janitor. She sat down at her desk, took a sip of her milk, and began reading a student's paper. Sniffing the air, she detected an unfamiliar odor. Standing up, she scanned the room and saw smoke curling up from under the closet door. Her first concern was for her record player and the classical records stored in the closet. Rushing to the closet she opened the door and was enveloped by thick black smoke.

"Oh, no! Not again!" she cried, and fainted.

* * *

"Shouldn't she have seen the smoke by now?" Adam asked anxiously.

"According to my figures, the thing should've gone off two minutes ago," Howie said. "Maybe the thing fizzled. Hey, if it did, I'm getting my money back. It was supposed to be guaranteed. Might even be a double your money back guarantee."

"Screw your guarantee!" Mick cried as he pointed toward Mattingale's classroom. "Look at the smoke coming out from under her door."

Without saying another word, Mick ran toward Mattingale's room. Howie and Adam were right behind him. When Mick opened her door, the black smoke rushed out into the hallway. Without hesitating for a moment, all three of them entered.

"Open some windows!" Mick shouted. "We got to get this smoke out."

Mick and Adam found their way to the windows and managed to open three of them, the other two refusing to budge.

"Over here by the closet door!" Howie shouted. "Mattingale's here."

The three of them picked their teacher up, carried her out the door and down the hall. Howie and Adam each held a leg while Mick held her under the arms. When they had gotten far enough away, they laid her down.

"She's not dead, is she?" Howie cried.

"No, she's breathing," Adam said.

"Man, was she heavy or am I getting weaker?"

"You're just out of shape, Mick," Adam said.

"How can you two be so calm?" Howie exclaimed. "She needs artificial respiration."

Adam gave Mick a knowing wink before turning to Howie. "It's got to be up to you. I know you can handle it." Without giving Howie a chance to respond, Adam turned to Mick. "Don't you think so?"

"Oh yeah, I see what you mean. I'm afraid if it's not done soon, she may suffer brain damage."

"You do it, okay?" Howie pleaded with Mick.

"Oh, I can't. I'm too nervous."

"So am I," Adam said. "You're the one who's got to do it."

Howie looked like he had just sucked on a lemon. "You mean that mouth-to-mouth stuff?"

Mick placed his hand on Howie's shoulder. "You're going to have to be the one. You start while we go for help."

Adam and Mick rushed away without waiting for any reply. Halfway down the hall, they stopped and looked back at Howie. "Do you think we ought to tell him?" Mick asked.

"No way, he deserves this."

"I agree. That guy has led too charmed of a life. About time he got into some trouble with his crazy schemes."

Adam looked at Howie who was now kneeling beside Miss Mattingale. "Can you imagine the reputation he's going to get on this? He'll never live it down."

Mick chuckled. "This is one time he isn't going to come out smelling like a rose."

"Hurry up, you guys!" Howie yelled as he bent over Mattingale.

Adam poked Mick. "Do you think he's trying to work up the courage to do it?"

"Howie!" Mick yelled. "It all depends on you. You'll be a hero!"

"Guys, hurry up!" Howie yelled back as he hovered over the outstretched body of his English teacher.

***

Howie watched his friends disappear down the staircase. Leaning over Miss Mattingale, he wondered if there was some kind of prayer he should say before starting what he knew he had to do. Just as he was about to begin mouth-to-mouth, Mr. Mueller came running around the corner.

"What's going on here?" he shouted.

"I was just—"

Mueller knelt down and put his ear to her face. "Thank God, she's breathing! Howard, I'll be a S.O.B.! You've saved her life!"

Chapter 26

Mick and Adam crossed the intersection at Lyndale and Broadway on their way home from school. “Only a couple of more blocks to go,” Mick said as they started onto the next block. “I’ll be glad when we get to Kass’.”

“Hope it’s warm there.”

“It better be because I’m freezing.” Mick shaded his eyes as he looked up toward the sun. “How can it be so cold when it’s a sunny day?”

When Adam slipped his gloved hands into the pockets of his jacket, he recalled Howie complaining about how cold his hands got while leaning out of Mattingale’s window yesterday. “Do you think Kass knows about Howie?”

“You mean about him being given credit for saving Mattingale’s life?”

“Yeah.”

“If he hasn’t, he will as soon as Howie sees him. That guy’s been hard to live with ever since he’s become a hero.” Mick clamped his gloved hands over his ears for a few moments. “The way he tells it, he single handily saved the entire school.”

“Man, that was quite a day.”

“Tell me about it. I’ll never forget hearing those sirens.”

“What got me was seeing those firemen come rushing up the stairs in full gear.”

“I know what you mean. I’d liked to have seen Howie’s face when he first saw those guys. Sure glad Mattingale didn’t have to go to the hospital. That would’ve been a bummer.”

“I heard Waite told her to take some time off,” Adam said. “And that Mueller drove her home that day. What gets me is that Howie still came out smelling like a rose. How does that guy do it?”

“Search me.” Mick kicked a chunk of ice, propelling it down the sidewalk like a hockey puck.

The wind shifted and swirling snow assaulted them. Heads bent, they walked into the wind. For a while, they tried walking backwards when the blowing snow became too much. With three quarters of a block to go, they decided to run the rest of the way. The cowbell hanging over the inside door at Kass' clanged loudly announcing their arrival.

"Brrr!" Mick exclaimed, shivering, and quickly shutting the door behind them.

Kass looked up from the front cash register and smiled as his two young friends stomped the snow off their shoes. "Boys, boys, why aren't you wearing galoshes in weather like this?" he scolded.

"We're seniors now," Mick announced proudly. "We don't wear those things anymore. It's not cool."

"What's this cool? I suppose you think you two are cool? This I tell you. By the looks of you two, you're cool all right. Your numbed hands and fingers are cool. Your frozen feet and toes are cool. Your red ears and drippy noses are cool."

"Come on, give us a break," Adam said. "Only sophomores and little kids wear galoshes."

Kass motioned toward the soda fountain. "Go sit down. I'll be right with you and fix you up with some nice steaming hot chocolate."

"Man, that sounds good," Mick said, continuing to rub his hands together. "Maybe I'll just stick my hands into it."

Kass shook his finger at them. "When your mothers come in, I'm going to tell them to buy you boys some galoshes and hats with ear flaps."

"Oh, no," Mick pleaded. "Not the dreaded galoshes and hats with ear flaps. We'll do anything. We'll mop your floor every night. We'll become your slaves. We'll...Adam, what else will we do?"

"Ah, you boys are always joking with me. That's good. It makes me feel young again."

Mick and Adam had no trouble finding a place at the soda fountain since all six stools were unoccupied. Kass went behind the counter to fix the hot chocolates for them.

"Here you are." Kass placed the cups in front of Mick and Adam. "I even gave you an extra shot of whipped cream."

While Mick sipped his hot chocolate, Adam continued to cradle his cup in his hands. The numbness in his fingers slowly subsided as the heat from the cup penetrated. A radio next to the hot fudge dispenser gave the weather report: cold and blustery weather for the next several days with temperatures dipping into the below zero range through the evening and night hours.

Kass turned the radio off. “I’ve heard enough about the weather,” he explained.

“How’ve you been doing since you got out of the hospital?” Mick asked.

Kass set his cup down and tenderly touched the top of his head. “It takes more than a knock on the head to stop me, but I tell you this. I now know how Goliath must’ve felt when David conked him on the head.”

“We’re just glad you’re okay,” Adam said. “Ah…do you have any idea who did it?”

“Afraid not. The back room isn’t well lit. And it happened so fast. Besides, when I got hit on the head I was just waking up from a little nap.” Kass chuckled. “You know, an old man like me needs his rest. I remember opening up my eyes, stretching, and thinking it was time to go home. Then I heard a noise behind me. Before I had a chance to turn around, bam, the lights went out.”

“Ouch! That must’ve hurt,” Mick said.

“Not at the time because it happened so fast. When I woke up in the ambulance on the way to the hospital, I sure had a headache.”

“How’d the police find out?” Adam asked.

“It was just lucky that a woman coming back from Midnight Mass saw the back door ajar. She got suspicious and called the police.”

“Wow!” Mick exclaimed. “It was good she came along.”

“Yes, I know. After I got out of the hospital I called her up and told her that any time she wanted a banana split for the next year, they were on me. I also told her that if she ever visited the Pope, she should tell him he can come for one any time he wants.” Kass shrugged his shoulders and smiled. “It’d be good for business.”

“What are the police saying?” Mick asked.

"I talked to them this morning again. They still have no leads. They tell me that they have a suspect or two, but nothing to connect them to the crime scene."

Adam's neck and back tensed. *What would Kass think if he found out that I knew who robbed him?* "Did they tell you who the suspects are?"

"Oh, no. The police never tell you those things." Kass gestured toward Adam's cup. "Drink up. Get some of that inside you." He picked up Mick's cup. "Looks like you also need some more. I'll give you a refill, and here's a napkin for your mustache."

Mick licked his top lip, wiped his mouth with a napkin, and grinned. "How's that?"

"I think I liked you better with the mustache," Adam said with a forced laugh, hoping it would hide his growing uneasiness.

"A little more whipped cream this time," Mick said to Kass whose back was now turned towards them. "My friend here wants me to grow another mustache."

"I'm really sorry about what happened to you," Adam said as Kass gave Mick his cup.

"Thanks. Appreciate your concern." Kass paused. "Adam, is something troubling you?"

Taken back by Kass' question, Adam had hoped his inner struggles weren't that evident. His instinct was to retreat back into himself. Having opened up a little to Mick had helped. It showed that he could share his feelings without others thinking less of him. He trusted both Mick and Howie, and he knew that Kass was also a person he could trust. "Give me a minute," he said. "I need to think this through. You caught me off guard."

"Sure, no problem." Kass' face and voice reflected concern. "And if you decide you don't want to talk, that's okay with me. Just want you to know that I care."

Adam listened as Kass and Mick talk about the frigid weather, knowing they were waiting for him to say something. "Don't you ever get tired of this place?" he finally asked Kass during a break in the conversation.

"What do you mean? My drugstore?"

Adam shook his head, noting that Mick continued to sip his

drink without looking at him or Kass. "Don't you ever want to get away from the North Side? Look at what happened to you on Christmas Eve. How can you stay on Broadway after that? You could've been killed right here in your own store."

"Yes, that's true, but I wasn't."

"But you could've been. It could even have been someone you know."

"I hadn't thought about it in that way, but you're right."

"That's what I mean about Broadway and the people who live here. You help them out and they shit on you!" Adam stopped, realizing the rising intensity of his own voice. He brushed back a shock of hair that had fallen across his forehead. "Sorry for swearing and getting so worked up."

"Don't worry. Sometimes only certain words can express our feelings." Kass smiled. "*Shit* is a good word. You should hear some of the words used in the Yiddish language. They burst with emotion. You don't even have to know the Yiddish meaning of the word, but just saying it out loud, the feeling comes across." He paused to take a sip of his hot chocolate. "Adam, you may be right about me knowing the person who robbed me. I've been here on Broadway for a long time. The people who I don't know, you could count on one hand. If whoever did it is from here, then chances are very good I do know them. But living here is like a marriage. For better or worse, this is still my home. These are the people I live and work with, and someday will die with."

"But what about those who beat and robbed you?" Adam said, aware that Mick was now watching the two of them. "How can you live and work with them?"

"Yes, there are those who spoil it for me and everybody else. No matter where you go, you'll find those kinds of people. Broadway has no special claim on such people. There are good people here also. Lots of them."

"But what—"

Kass held up his hand. "Wait, let me finish. Since that night a number of people have offered to help me. They've offered anything from giving me a hand here in the drugstore to giving me remedies to prevent headaches. Did you know that your mother was one of the first persons to offer help?"

"She was?" Adam said, surprised since she hadn't said

anything to him about it. "I didn't know that."

"She sent meals over to me the first few days back on the job so I wouldn't have to go out in the cold weather. Not only that, she told the milkmen if they didn't deliver the meals she wouldn't serve them their coffee anymore." Kass chuckled. "When I think of those milkmen in their trucks stopping in front of the drugstore on their way to make deliveries…"

"I also heard something," Mick said, breaking into the conversation. "My father told me that every time the milkmen delivered their meals, they left with their favorite flavor of ice cream cone as a tip."

Kass shrugged. "A small token for their kindness," he replied before turning his attention back to Adam. "It was your mother's doing. She's helped a lot of people over the years. There are many stories about her providing a meal for people down on their luck."

Adam turned to Mick. "Did you know about that?"

"Yeah, I've heard those stories."

"Why wasn't I aware of it?" Adam felt guilty and embarrassed that he didn't know this about his own mother.

Kass reached out and touched him on the arm. "I hope you don't mind me saying this, but ever since school started, it seems like you've had your mind on other things. I don't know what they are, but I think maybe they're not good kind of things."

"How did you know that?" Adam asked, surprised that Kass had picked up on something that he thought he had done a good job of hiding.

"Adam, I've known you for a long time. I've always been aware as to your feelings about Broadway."

"But…" Adam wasn't sure how he felt about having Kass know him so well. *Did Mick and Howie know him better than he thought they did? How about others?* He and Sue had been dating off and on for over a year. If she knew him better than he thought she did, she had never let on either. "But how do you know all that about me?"

"You ask how? Like I said, I've known you for a long time. I remember when your mother took a picture of you when you were only five or six years old. You were standing in front of this very drugstore holding an ice cream cone in one hand and a bottle of Coke in the other. You and Mick and Howie have been coming in here ever since you were wearing galoshes." With his mention of galoshes, Kass smiled and then winked at Mick before turning his attention back to Adam. "How many times have I talked with the three of you as you sat at this very counter? Sometimes it was just two of you. Other times, just one. I listen because I care. As for your mother, I want you to know that she's well thought of around here. She's a kind and sensitive woman. Do you know something else? I think you also have those same qualities."

"So do I," Mick said.

Adam didn't know what to say or how he felt about what he had just been told about himself. Earlier, his body had been tense and rigid. Now, it felt limp and drained.

"You don't have to say anything," Kass said. "Take some time and think about it." He glanced over at Mick. "Right?"

"That's right." Mick tapped Adam on the shoulder. "And remember we're here for you."

The cowbell clanged. "Just a minute," Kass said. "I see I've got some customers coming in who may need my help. I'll be back."

"That guy's great," Mick said as Kass walked away. "Don't you think so?"

"Yeah, and with what happened to him, he still thinks of Broadway as home." Adam felt confused. "I hear what he's saying, but I just find it so hard to accept. It just blows my mind. Do you know what bothers me the most?"

Mick gave him a puzzled look.

"What if I do accept it?"

"What do you mean?"

"I don't know. It's hard to explain. I've always seen this area as someplace to escape from. Since I was a kid, I didn't want to live here. When I leave the area, I never tell people I'm from Broadway. I don't want them to know that. Those feelings have been with me so long that if I don't have them, I won't know myself anymore. If I lose them, I'd feel like I'm losing part of myself. I don't know if I'm making much sense. It doesn't make any sense to me."

"I'm not sure if I understand everything you're saying, but I think you're too hard on yourself," Mick said. "This may sound dumb, but whoever you are is who you are. Whether you were raised by wealthy parents in Edina and lived in a big fancy house, or whether you were raised by a woman who is a waitress and who does her best to make ends meet, it doesn't change you. Do know what Mr. Swingle says?"

"No, I didn't have him for Social Studies."

"He said that our environments shape us, but I don't believe that anyone has to let that determine who they are. Look at Kass. As crummy as Broadway can be, he certainly hasn't been affected by it. If anything, he's made this area a better place to live by being such a good friend to everyone."

"Maybe but he wasn't raised here. He came here by choice. If you want some examples, look at Danny Logan and his two friends. They're on a road that leads nowhere." Adam felt the tension building within him again. "And let's not forget Frank. He was raised here. A purebred homegrown Broadway boy. We should bring him to Swingle's class for show and tell." Adam glanced over at Kass and saw he was still busy with his customer. "Do you remember the night that Frank was beat up?" he asked hesitantly.

"Sure."

"I was there. I set it up and then watched the whole thing." The words came quickly. He wanted to get it out. No more hesitating. No more hiding. "I was standing in the shadows near the back of Skelly's Liquor Store. After Danny and his friends left, I stayed around. Frank was lying in his own blood and I didn't do anything. I told myself he had it coming, that he deserved to get the shit kicked out of him."

"Hey, man. He beat up your aunt. You were just getting back at him."

"I know. That's why I tell myself he deserved it. When it happened, I thought I'd enjoy it."

"And did you?"

"No, I just wanted to puke. He looked so pathetic lying there. I'd thought it would change him, but it hasn't. He's the same old Frank, and he's still as pathetic as ever. I almost feel…"

"Sorry?" Mick said, supplying the word.

Adam nodded. “Yeah, I felt sorry for the guy. Isn't that crazy? What's wrong with me?”

“Nothing. If you would've told me that you got a kick out of seeing Frank lying there, then I would've thought that there was something wrong with you. There's nothing wrong about feeling sorry for the guy, even if he is a jerk.”

“So, you're saying it's okay to feel that way?”

“Yeah, sure. And you're right about Frank being pathetic. So are Danny Logan and his two buddies. They're all the same. When you look at Frank, you're looking at Danny's future. I wonder what Frank sees when he looks at someone like Danny?”

“Frank's too dumb to see anything. He's probably envious of Danny.”

“What do you mean?”

“Danny's young and just starting out while Frank's old. Maybe he wishes he was young again.”

“I never thought about it in that way but you might be right. That doesn't mean that living on Broadway is the problem, does it?”

“That's what I'm struggling with,” Adam admitted, feeling more confused than ever. “I need to find some answers. There are a number of things that I've got to figure out. I think I've got to get away from here to do that.”

“What are you going to do?”

“I don't know exactly. Graduation is a few months away. After that I'll work at Harry's. The first thing I want to do is to save enough money to get out on my own.”

“Sounds okay to me. How about college?”

“That's not in the cards. No money.” Adam gave Mick a half smile. “Working at Harry's doesn't exactly make you rich, and my mother doesn't have the money to...Here comes Kass.”

Mick leaned over and whispered, “I think what Kass said about you taking after your mother is true. You're a pretty caring guy.”

“How come you two didn't tell me about Howie?” Kass asked as he walked up.

Mick and Adam exchanged glances. “What are you talking about?” Mick asked.

“What am I talking about? Do you know that man I was

talking with? That's Mr. Sobinski. His son works for the fire department, Station 8. The one by the school. They had supper together yesterday and his son told him about answering the alarm at the school." Kass raised his hands upward, gesturing toward the heavens. "Thank God, it was just some kind of prank. His son told him about how Howie saved a teacher's life."

"We sort of forgot about that," Adam offered.

"Forgot?" Kass' eyebrows rose. "How can you forget such a thing? So tell me now. This Howie is a hero from what I hear."

The cowbell clanged. "Don't look now," Mick said. "But the hero just blew in."

Howie, wearing a bright red stocking cap pulled down over his ears and halfway down his forehead, looked over at them and waved.

"Hi, guys. Hi, Kass." Howie took off his cap, letting unruly reddish blond hair escape. "Sorry I'm late, but Waite had me in his office for a little talk."

"Waite's the principal, isn't he?" Kass asked.

"That's right," Howie said as he unzipped his jacket.

"What did he want with you?" Mick asked with a sly grin. "Were you a naughty little boy?"

Howie flashed an ingratiating smile. "No, actually he wanted to tell me that some reporter is coming to school tomorrow to interview me and take my picture."

"Why, that's great!" Kass nearly shouted as he looked at Mick and Adam. "Isn't that great?"

"Terrific," Adam said. "Just terrific."

"Couldn't be any better," Mick added.

"You boys don't sound very enthusiastic."

"Don't mind them," Howie said. "They're just overwhelmed with me being a hero."

Mick sighed, shaking his head. "Howie, you're so modest."

"Thanks. Say, I might be able to get your names in the paper. After all, you did go for help." Howie stroked his chin as though in deep thought. "Maybe I might even be able to persuade the photographer to take a picture of you guys. I can't promise, but I'll see what I can do."

"That does it!" Mick exclaimed. "I have to go. My mother's calling me home."

"Wait for me," Adam said. "I think she's also calling me. Nice visiting with you, Kass. Glad you're doing better." As he snapped up his jacket, he nodded to Kass. "And thanks."

"Sure, any time. Old man Kass is always here." He motioned toward Howie. "Aren't you boys going to stay and hear his story? If he's going to tell that reporter everything, you may want to add some things he's forgotten."

Mick chuckled. "I'm sure we couldn't add *anything* to the story that would be helpful."

"Can't argue with that," Adam added, feeling better since he had shared with Mick about his involvement with Danny Logan and Frank. Even though still confused about his feelings concerning Broadway, he was glad he and Kass had talked.

Once outside, Adam and Mick chatted for a few minutes before they both admitted that it was too cold to stand around and talk. Adam said good-bye. "Thanks Mick for being a friend. Lets talk some more. Okay?"

"Sure enough," Mick replied.

As Adam walked the half block back to the apartment, he thought about what Kass and Mick had said, and wondered how he was ever going to sort through his mixed-up feelings. He had a start on sorting through his feelings, but there was still a long ways to go. It would be easier if only Frank and Danny Logan were out of the picture. Maybe he could just avoid them. It was worth a try.

Chapter 27

Shivering from the bitter cold, Adam reached the entrance door to his apartment building. Running up the stairs, taking two at a time, he was barely breathing hard when he opened the door to his apartment seconds later. He walked through the kitchen into the living room. His mother sat on the couch reading a magazine. When she looked up at him, he saw the concern on her face.

"I was worried about you," she said, setting her magazine aside. "You're late and it's so cold outside."

"Mom, you didn't have to worry. Mick and I stopped at Kass' for awhile and warmed up." He plopped down in a cushioned chair and took off his gloves.

"I wish you'd wear a hat," she pleaded. "You're going to freeze your ears off one of these days."

Adam wished she would stop treating him like her little boy. She was always doing that, especially when she was worried.

"How's Kass doing?"

"He's okay." Adam took his shoes off. "We were talking about Howie and what happened at school yesterday."

"Some of the customers down at work were talking about that this morning."

"What were they saying?"

His mother snickered. "I don't mean to laugh but the way they told it, Howie saved the entire school faculty."

"It was only one teacher. Miss Mattingale, the English teacher. She was a little shaken but no big deal." Adam swung around so he was sitting sideways in the chair, his legs dangling over the chair's arm.

His mother laughed. "It's just like all the other stories that float around Broadway. By the time the stories get down to Andy's, they've taken on a life all their own." She slipped off her penny loafers, adjusted her white anklets, and stretched her legs out until her feet rested on one corner of the coffee table. "I'm glad for Howie. He's a nice boy. I'm happy that the two of you are friends." She placed a pillow behind her head. "Did he really rescue Miss Mattingale from a burning classroom and give her mouth-to-mouth?"

"There was no burning classroom…but Howie did save her life," he said, having little choice but to validate the *hero*. He couldn't tell her what really happened without getting him and his two friends in trouble.

"Really!" His mother leaned forward. "Tell me what happened."

"Just a minute." He stood up, took off his jacket, tossed it on one end of the couch and plopped back in the chair, sitting sideways again. He repeated the "official" version going around school. "There was no fire, but Mattingale was overcome from a smoke bomb someone slipped in her closet. Mick and I helped Howie carry her out of her classroom."

"Really? You and Mick were the ones?"

"Yeah, why? Didn't you know that?"

"No, I just heard there were a couple of other students involved, but that they only played a minor role."

A minor role! Adam nearly laughed out loud. It sounded like something Howie would say.

"Howie is such a wonderful, brave boy," she said.

Having finished recounting the rest of the story, Adam walked out into the kitchen and opened the refrigerator. He poured himself a glass of milk and sat at the kitchen table, his thoughts going back to the conversation he had with Kass. *How could Kass think of Broadway as home with what happen to him?* When he went back into the living room, his mother was reading. Picking up a magazine he plopped into the chair.

After a few minutes, his mother looked over at him. "Is something wrong?"

"No. Why?"

"Because you normally spend your time in the bedroom. Don't get me wrong. I like that we're together, but I can't remember the last time the two of us sat reading in the living room."

"I'm warming up my shoes," he said, pointing to his shoes in front of the coal gas heater sitting in the corner.

For the next few minutes the only sounds came from the rattling of the bedroom window and an occasional car horn blaring from the street. After flipping through a few more pages, Adam got up and went back into the kitchen to get a glass of water. Bringing his glass, he stood at the entrance to the living room. His mother looked up, smiled, and resumed looking at her magazine. He went over to the window and looked down upon Broadway. Traffic was lighter than normal. After a while, he sat down and picked up his magazine again. Flipping through the magazine, he gnawed at his lip.

"Something must be wrong," his mother said, laying her magazine aside. "What is it?"

"Did you ever think about moving from this place?"

"I think about getting a back apartment. Then we wouldn't have the traffic noise all the time. I've even thought about moving to the apartment building up on Broadway; the one across from the bakery."

"That's not what I mean. I'm talking about moving out of the area."

"You mean away from Broadway?" When Adam nodded, she was quick to reply. "Yes, I've thought about it, but I wouldn't want to do that."

"Kass said the same thing. Even though he was robbed, he still considers Broadway his home, and he likes the people who live here. I don't understand."

"I can. Most of them are good, hard working people. They're decent and always ready to help if you give them a chance."

Adam was confused as to why no one could see Broadway as he did. *Maybe it's me who isn't seeing clearly. Maybe I'm wrong. Maybe I've always been wrong. Maybe I'm just some kind of coward for wanting to get away from Broadway.* He had a lot of things to sort out and wasn't sure how to do it by himself.

"Perhaps some day you'll understand that growing up here wasn't all that bad," his mother said. "Those who live here are just ordinary people. If you give them a chance, you can learn a lot about life from them."

When the knock at the door came, his mother got up to answer it.

As soon as the door opened, he heard Wanda's voice. "We've got to talk," she said. When she and his mother came into the living room, he could tell by the expression on Wanda's face that something was wrong. *Was Frank threatening her again?*

"Have either of you seen Pa?"

"I haven't," Adam said as he sat up in the chair.

"Neither have I," Virg said anxiously. "Why?"

Wanda sighed. "I found an empty whiskey bottle in the garbage under the sink. You know what that usually means."

"Oh, no!" Virg said. "He promised us he wouldn't."

Wanda slowly eased herself down on the couch. "I know he promised but you know Pa, he's promised before."

"What about Frank?" Virg asked. "Does he know anything?"

"No, he says that Pa was gone before he got up." Wanda shifted on the couch. "My back is bothering me a bit." She sat for a moment before speaking. "I'm angry, but I'm more worried because it's so cold out."

Adam began putting his shoes on. He had no idea where he would look, but the image of his grandfather passed out drunk in some alley flashed through his mind. "I'll go look for him."

"Are you sure?" his mother asked. "What about work?"

"I'll call Harry and tell him I'm not coming in until later."

"No, you go to work," Wanda said forcefully. "He's done this before and he usually shows up. We don't want to also worry about you being out in this weather."

Adam wasn't surprised by Wanda's take-charge attitude. His mother had told him that her sister had assumed responsibility for the household when their mother died. Wanda was only ten at the time. During that time, she had to give her father support as well since he became a broken man when their mother died. Virg had told Adam that she also felt sorry for Wanda because she never got to enjoy her teenage years. "She managed to stay in school until she was sixteen, and then went to work in a bakery," his mother had told him.

"I'll go to work," Adam said. "But you call me if you hear anything."

"We will," his mother promised. "I'm going down to Andy's in a little while. I'll ask about Pa. I'm sure somebody has seen him. A few of his old drinking cronies come in from time to time. They might be able to tell us where to look."

"Good," Wanda said. "I'll stay home just in case he shows up. When he does, I'll let both of you know."

Adam felt uneasy that Frank's name even came up in all of this. Something didn't make sense. "Are you sure Frank doesn't know anything more?" he asked his aunt.

"He says he doesn't. He even offered to help look for Pa."

"Well, let me know if you hear anything. I'm going to work now."

* * *

After Adam left, Virg asked her sister to stay for a cup of coffee. As the coffee perked, she and Wanda sat at the kitchen table.

"Butch would like to move away from Broadway," Virg said.

"He has a right to move out and try to improve himself."

"I don't disagree. I just get the feeling he's embarrassed about living here and that he…"

"That he what?"

"That he's even embarrassed about his family." Virg blinked back tears. "You know, me being just a waitress and…and Pa for being what he is."

"Butch loves you and Pa."

"I know, but I wonder if he moved away…if he'd ever come back to visit or if...if he'll think he's too good for us."

"Do you think he feels that way about me?"

"Oh, I know he doesn't." Virg realized that her sister had been taken back by the possibility that he would think that of her. Not being able to have children of her own, Wanda always thought of Butch as a son. "Butch has a lot of respect for you," she offered. "I hope you know that. The problem is Frank. He doesn't like the man. It's just that he doesn't think Frank deserves you and…and neither do I."

"I know Frank is…"

"Is what?"

"He is what he is, and I'm afraid to be alone. You and Pa are my family, but what happens when Pa dies?"

"You'll still have me."

"But what if you move away or get married. I just don't want to be alone."

"Is that why you stick with Frank?" This was the first time Virg could remember her sister opening up to her like this.

Wanda nodded. "I'm so tired of crying and feeling pain," she confessed. "Tired of trying to be the strong one in the family. All I've ever wanted was to be cared for and loved." She looked at Virg with eyes that seemed as if they had been drained of their life force. "I thought…hoped that Frank would be that person."

Virg reached over and took her sister's hand. Without looking up, Wanda took hold of hers as well.

* * *

It was early evening when the telephone rang. Frank was in the kitchen drinking a bottle of beer and reading the newspaper. He heard Wanda answer the phone in the living room, and listened with interest.

"Yes, Paul Kurtz is my father. What! Oh, no! Will he be all right? Yes. Yes, of course. I'll be down as soon as I can. Thank you. Good-bye."

"What the hell was that all about?"

Wanda came into the kitchen, her face drained of color. "Pa's in the hospital. That was the nurse calling to tell me he was brought in early this afternoon suffering from exposure."

"Well, what do ya know? At least, the old man will have a warm bed to sleep in tonight."

"That's not funny."

Frank's smile didn't leave his face. She was angry with him for his remark, but that didn't bother him.

"Don't suppose you want to go to the hospital with me?"

Frank sneered. "Not in this shitty weather. Just leave him there to sober up."

Wanda looked at him and shook her head. "I don't understand you."

Frank sat silently, grinning, wondering if the old man would lose a few fingers to frostbite. If he did, wasting a whole bottle of Jack Daniel's on him had been worth it. He felt smug that his plan had worked so well. *Goddamn, what do ya know? With one bottle of booze I'm gettin' back at both Butchie and that wiseass drunk.* As he watched Wanda get ready to leave for the hospital, he wondered if the old man would tell Adam where he got the whiskey. The more he thought about it, the more he wanted Adam to know. *Hell, I don't care if Butchie finds out. I want him to. Goddamn it! I want him to know that it was me!*

Chapter 28

The phone call from the hospital had left Wanda shaken. The anger she had felt about her father's resumption of drinking was replaced by a deep seeded fear for his well being. She had good reason to worry since her father's health had been declining over the past couple of years. He would say it was just his age, but she knew it was the result of his years of drinking. His smoking also aggravated his emphysema. In the past year, his bouts of coughing had increased both in frequency and severity. Now that he was in the hospital, she hoped that being there might cause him to change his ways. It was a long shot. Her father didn't trust hospitals because of her mother's death. Whenever anyone mentioned anything to do with hospitals, he would quickly give his opinion.

"Ack. They take you through front door one day on stretcher. Next day you go out back door in wooden box."

Besides worried and upset about her father, she was angry about Frank's refusal to go with her to the hospital. She couldn't understand how he could be so callous. After finding out that he would be of no help, she picked up the phone and dialed her sister's number. It took forever for her sister to answer. When she finally heard Virg's voice, she blurted out the scant details the nurse had told her. "I'll be there in a minute," she said, lowering her voice in response to her sister's question. "No, he's staying home." She glanced at Frank sitting at the kitchen table reading the newspaper and sipping a bottle of beer. "Be sure to let Butch know," she whispered, glancing at Frank again. "I have to go." She hung up without giving Virg any chance to ask further questions. She put her coat on and stepped into the kitchen to say good-bye to Frank.

"Have fun." He held up his bottle of beer as a parting gesture, and then went back to reading the newspaper.

"Don't wait up for me," Wanda said.

"I won't," he replied, adding with a smirk, "unless I'm in the mood."

She left, relieved to be out of Frank's presence. When she got to her sister's, she was glad that Virg already had her coat on when she opened the door. "Good, you're ready," Wanda said. "Let's go."

"I hope Pa's all right."

"I'm sure he is. Did you call Butch?"

"Yes. We're supposed to pick him up at work."

Walking down the first flight of stairs to the outside entrance, Wanda repeated the few details that the nurse had given her on the phone. "I can't tell you anything more than that. That's all I know. The nurse said that he's resting comfortably."

"I'm so scared," Virg admitted, her voice trembling. "I don't like hospitals."

"I know," Wanda replied. Her sister's feelings about hospitals had been strongly influenced by their father's attitude toward them after his wife died in one.

"If anything ever happened to Pa, I…"

"Nothing's going to happen," Wanda said forcefully, wanting to sound confident for her sister's sake. "We just have to believe that he'll be okay."

At the bottom of the stairs, Wanda rested, massaging her back. "Give me a minute."

"You wait here and stay inside," Virg said. "I'll get the car. Give me a few minutes to warm it for you."

Wanda didn't argue. She wouldn't be able to keep up with her sister and the thought of walking nearly a block in such terribly cold weather didn't appeal to her. While waiting, she leaned against the wall of the entryway. Feeling exhausted, she was afraid if she closed her eyes, she would fall asleep. Her thoughts went to Frank and the awful remarks he had made after the telephone call from the hospital. She had felt like telling him off but she would never dare do that. His outbursts and threats had increased in the past couple of months, and she wasn't sure how far he would go the next time he hit her.

It wasn't long before her sister's blue Buick pulled up. Wanda pushed the door open and stepped out onto the sidewalk. Her first thought was of her father. It worried her to think how long he had been out in this frigid weather. She went as quickly to the car as her back would allow, and got in. The warmth blowing from the car's heater felt good.

"You look so tired," Virg said. "Are you okay?"

"Yeah. Let's go get Butch."

After picking up Adam, Wanda went over again what the nurse had told her. When she asked if he had any questions, he said no. He remained so quiet for the fifteen-minute ride to the hospital that she wondered what was going through his mind.

North Memorial Hospital served as a dividing line between the North Side and the suburbs. To the west of the hospital, the street and the area it ran through was known as *Upper Broadway*. This was the beginning of the suburbs. To the east of the hospital where Adam lived, the street was known as *Lower Broadway*. Whenever those who lived on Upper Broadway were asked by friends visiting them from outside the area what the difference was between them and Lower Broadway, they would laugh. "We sip wine and consider ourselves connoisseurs," they would explain with a smile, adding with a sneer, "those on Lower Broadway guzzle beer and are winos."

After being let out at the hospital's entrance, Wanda and Adam waited while Virg parked the car. A few minutes later she rejoined them. Wanda led the way through the lobby to the information desk. The receptionist sat behind a kidney-shaped mahogany desk. They stood waiting for her to look up from whatever she was doing.

"What room is Paul Kurtz in?" Wanda asked impatiently.

The woman acted as if she didn't hear her.

Wanda looked at Virg and Adam, shook her head in disgust, and asked again; this time in a louder, sterner tone of voice.

When the receptionist looked up, she was startled by the tall creature looming in front of her.

"I'm sorry." Her voice was as plastic as her smile. "What was the name again?"

"Paul Kurtz." Wanda put one hand on the corner of the desk to steady herself. Her back was telling her she needed to sit down.

"Would you mind spelling that last name?" the receptionist asked as she glanced at Wanda's hand resting on her desk.

"K-U-R-T-Z." Wanda felt annoyed about having to wait. The woman's condescending attitude didn't help.

"Let's see…Kurtz…Kurtz." The receptionist opened a card file. After finding the card, she pulled it out, taking time to read it.

Wanda frowned. *Did this woman know they were in a hurry?* She was about to say something when the receptionist spoke.

"Oh, yes. I see from the notation on this card, *he's* the one who came in this afternoon." Her smile had become fixed, set in place as if she had used hairspray on it. "Mr. Kurtz is in Ward 7, the fourth floor."

"Ward 7?" Adam said, looking at his mother. "Don't they have room numbers?"

"Ward 7 has a number of beds in it," Wanda explained.

"That's correct," the woman with the plastic smile replied as she glanced at Adam and Virg before turning her attention back to Wanda. "*You* must be familiar with that area," she said in a patronizing tone before turning to Adam. "You see, young man, when our hospital receives certain people as patients who arrive in such a condition that they're, shall I say, unable to provide us with information, we then must make a judgment as to whether they have insurance."

"What are you trying to say?" Virg asked.

"Under the circumstances when he came in, the way he was dressed, and his condition…" She cleared her throat as if she had an unpleasant taste in her mouth. "Well, such cases are sent to Ward 7." The plastic smile again. "Oh, dear, I'm afraid I'm giving you more than you care to know," she tittered, obviously thinking that she had said something humorous. "My husband says that I should be a teacher because I'm always in the habit of wanting to educate people." She returned to her plastic smile. "May I presume all of you are relatives?"

"Why do you ask?" Wanda could barely hold back her anger. She felt like slapping the smile off her face.

"I have to ask," she sniffed. "We can't let too many people in unless they are related to the patient. Hospital rules, you know."

"Yes, ma'am," Virg said. "We understand, but you see, we're his daughters. And this is his grandson."

"I see. Very well, you may all visit then." She sounded as if she was dismissing them. "Do you think you can find the elevators?"

Wanda took a step forward, bent down, and stared her directly in the face. "Listen toots, if we can't find them, we'll look for the signs. Believe it or not, we can read."

The smile melted from the woman's face as Wanda stood her ground. Virg tugged on her coat sleeve but she didn't budge. "Come on, let's go," she said finally.

"That wasn't very nice but I'm sure glad you said it," Virg whispered as they walked away.

"That old biddy had it coming."

They rode in the elevator in silence. Wanda could see the worry in her sister's eyes. Adam looked straight ahead, his eyes fixed on the elevator doors. They got off on the fourth floor, saw the sign for Ward 7, and headed in the direction the arrow pointed. Within a short time, they arrived at double doors labeled *Ward 7*. Walking in, they found themselves in a large rectangular room that had three beds on each side. The beds could be partitioned off from each other by ceiling-to-floor curtains whose tan color was in drab contrast to the off-white color of the walls. Next to each bed stood a nightstand and a chair. Non-descript but colorful prints in wooden frames hung on the wall above the nightstands. A tall man in a white lab coat stood talking to someone in the bed at the far end of the room. The man standing blocked their view of the patient.

"He looks too young to be a doctor," Virg whispered.

"Is that Grandpa he's talking to?" Adam asked.

"Must be," Wanda said. "All the other beds are empty. Let's go see."

As they walked closer, the man in the white coat was writing in a chart as he talked. When he turned to see who was coming, all of them got an unobstructed view of the person lying in bed. "It's Pa," Wanda said, feeling anxious and relieved. When her father saw them coming, he grinned and waved.

Ignoring the man with the chart Wanda was the first to speak. "Pa, are you okay?"

"Yeah, yeah, all right," he replied, sounding weak. "Doc take good care."

"I'm so glad," Virg said

"Hi, Grandpa."

"Ah, Butch. Good to see you."

"Hello, I'm Doctor Jairvus," the man in the white coat said, his voice calm and soothing. Short blond hair and intelligent eyes gave him a wisdom that went beyond his boyish looks. He stood a few inches taller than Wanda. "I assume you're the family of Mr. Kurtz?" he asked.

"Yes. I'm Wanda and this here is my sister, Virginia. We're his daughters, and this is Adam, his grandson."

"Hello," Jairvus said warmly.

"How is he?" Virg asked.

"Your father's doing well, but I think he may have to be with us for a few days. He suffered a moderate to severe case of frostbite around his face and upper extremities. However, he has a more severe case on his lower extremities." Doctor Jairvus turned toward his patient. "It was fortunate, Mr. Kurtz, that you were found so soon."

"Found?" Wanda exclaimed as she glanced at her father, searching for any reaction. He merely raised his eyebrows and shrugged. "What do you mean, Doctor?"

"The officer—"

"Officer!" Virg cried. "You mean a police officer? He's not in some kind of trouble, is he?"

"Oh, no," Jairvus replied calmly as though he talked about these kind of circumstances every day. "It was just that the police got a call about a man lying in an alley. When they went to investigate, they found your father."

"What happened to him?" Virg asked.

"We don't know exactly because he wasn't conscious at the time. The officer recognized the symptoms and brought him here without bothering to call an ambulance. Your father arrived here around mid-afternoon." Jairvus scanned the chart he was holding. "According to our records, he arrived at two forty-five. We would've notified you sooner, but Mr. Kurtz was…ah," he smiled and winked at his patient. "He was taking a nap. I can assure you that your father's in much better condition now than when he was first brought in."

"How long will he be here?" Wanda asked.

"A few days if everything goes well. I want to see if the damaged skin becomes discolored once the circulation is fully restored. Also, the area could become inflamed and some blistering occur. In that case it could be quite painful." Doctor Jairvus glanced at Paul and smiled before resuming his report to Wanda. "In my opinion that won't happen, but if it does, it'd be better if he were here. Besides, your father said he'd give me a few pointers on how to fix an old grandfather's clock I've been working on. Isn't that right, Mr. Kurtz?"

"That's right, Doc. If you know how put clock back together, then you know how put people together."

Jairvus laughed. "Can't argue with you about that. Maybe we should've had that class in medical school." He turned his attention back to Wanda and Virg. "Do either one of you have any further questions?"

"I don't." Virg glanced at her sister. "Do you?"

Wanda shook her head, more interested in asking her father a few questions.

After Doctor Jairvus excused himself, Paul looked at Adam. "Doc not bad. I no like hospitals but Doc, I like. I teach about clocks. He do good." He made an effort to sit up. "Need pillow fixed."

"Let me do that," Virg quickly offered.

Once his pillows were arranged to his liking, Paul tried to take a deep breath but began coughing. Once the raspy sounding cough subsided, he offered a weak smile at his grandson.

"How you been?"

"Okay, but I was worried about you."

"Ack, not worry. Me too stubborn to let anything happen."

"All right, Pa. Tell us what happened," Wanda said, not wanting her father to turn the conversation away from himself.

"What you mean?"

"You know what I mean. I want to know what happened."

Paul started coughing again, a rattling cough that came from deep within his chest.

Wanda glanced at her sister. Virg met her eyes for a moment. Even though they had heard their father cough many times, having it happen in a hospital gave it an ominous dimension for Virg. Turning her attention back to her father, she sat quietly until his coughing subsided. After it had, she repeated her question. "Tell me now, what happened?"

"Nothing happened. Stay out too long. Should know better."

"Something must have happened," Virg said. "The police found you unconscious in an alley."

"When I left you yesterday you were sitting at the table working on the watch," Wanda said.

"So, had few drinks."

"How many?"

"One, two, don't remember. Then, decide go out."

"Why didn't you take your warm coat?" Virg asked.

"Don't know. Forgot."

"You must have had more than a couple of drinks," Wanda said. "Where did you go?"

"Meet friends. Have few more drinks. After that, walk alleys." Paul looked at Adam and smiled. "Look for clocks, but not find. Walk some more and…"

"And what?" Wanda persisted.

"Don't remember," Paul said stubbornly. "Then I here. Wake up. Doc ask questions. Now, you ask questions. Ack, too many questions."

"You could've frozen to death," Virg said. "All the way here I was so worried about you. You know how much I don't like hospitals."

"I know, I know but—" Paul started coughing; harsh and terrible sounding. "Butch," he said in a hoarse whisper, gesturing to the bedside stand. "Look top drawer. Nurse say my stuff there. Make sure."

Adam opened the drawer. "I see a key chain with three, no, four keys, your billfold, two dimes and a nickel, and something wrapped in tissues."

"Ah, good. It there."

"What are you talking about?" Wanda leaned over to investigate.

"Pocket watch," Paul said as he looked at Adam, and smiled.

"I'm glad you didn't lose it," Wanda replied, relieved that he hadn't sold it for a few drinks. The year after her mother died, she had come home from school to fix supper. It was her father's birthday and she wanted to make it special by using her mother's china. When she went to get the china, it was gone. Her father told her that he had sold it the week before to buy groceries. That may have been, but two weeks before that her father had gone on a drinking binge. She suspected that he had spent what little money they had buying drinks for himself and his buddies. The selling of the china was simply to regain the grocery money he had thrown away on whiskey. What made it especially painful was that her mother had told Wanda that the china would be hers some day. It had taken her a long time to forgive her father for that, and it was still a painful memory. She didn't want Adam to have that kind of experience when it came to the watch. "Unwrap it," she said to Adam.

"Yes," Paul said. "Unwrap. See watch."

Adam picked up the package and carefully began to unwrap it. With Wanda and his mother watching, he removed it from three coverings of tissue. "It's nice," he said as he held the watch in the palm of his hand. "Can I open it?" he asked his grandfather.

"No, no. Just look at outside now."

Wanda watched Adam admire the beautiful scroll design on the watch's front and back cover. Her father had done a good job cleaning and polishing it. She was anxious to know what Adam would say when he read the inscription inside. When her father had let her read it, she instantly thought of her mother. The thought expressed by the inscription was something her mother often talked about. Wanda was reminded of one evening in particular when, as a young child, she was allowed to stay up past her bedtime. Her baby sister, Virg, had fallen asleep in their father's lap and had already been carried to bed. At nine years old, Wanda felt grown up sitting at the kitchen table with her parents and sharing a late evening snack with them. It was that evening that her mother spoke those exact words of the watch's inscription to her. It stood out so vividly because her mother asked if she knew what the words meant. When Wanda shook her head, her mother took her hand into hers and explained as Wanda's father listened. *That was such a long time ago*, Wanda thought to herself as she looked on as Adam turned the pocket watch over in his hands.

Adam looked at his grandfather. "It's heavy."

"Oh, yes," Paul said, his voice sounding weaker. "When you put in pocket, you better have belt on pants or—" The coughing came without warning, lasting longer than the previous one. "Damn cough," he whispered when he was finally able to catch his breath.

"Are they giving you something for that?" Virg asked

Paul nodded. "Ack, terrible stuff. No good." He screwed up his face as though he had bitten into a lemon. "Me not take anymore."

"As long as you're here you should do what they tell you," Wanda gently scolded. Her father gave her the look of stubbornness she had seen so many times before. "You want to get better so you get out of here, don't you?"

"If I take medicine they for sure take me out in wooden box."

"Pa, don't talk like that!" Virg said, frowning.

"I only joke. I no take medicine for cough. I no joke about that."

Wanda knew that it was fruitless to argue with him. "I think we should go, he needs his rest," she quietly said as her father's eyes slowly closed and opened again.

Virg nodded and smiled at her father. "You get some sleep."

With some effort, Wanda rose from her chair. "Pa, we're going now. With that cough you could use some rest." She shook her finger at him. "The one good thing about you being here is that you'll not be able to get any of that booze."

Her father offered a weak smile.

"I'll come up to see you tomorrow after school before I go to work," Adam said.

"Okay with boss?" Paul asked.

"Harry won't mind if I come in a little later than usual."

"Good, good," Paul said, his eyes closing. "You come. I look forward. Let Harry dress dummies in window."

"Pa, I'm not sure if I'll come up again," Virg said. "You know me and hospitals. You understand, don't you?"

"Don't worry," Paul said, sounding like he was on the verge of drifting off. "Me home soon."

"We should talk to the doctor about that cough," Virg said to Wanda.

"Ack, cough is cough," Paul mumbled. He was asleep before they could reply.

Chapter 29

When Adam got home from the hospital, he sat down at the desk in the kitchen. His mother, emotionally exhausted, walked into the living room. Adam stared at the phone, thinking about Sue.

It had been nearly three months since they had gone on the triple date with Mick and Howie, and nearly a month since he had last called her. Even though they had lunch period at the same time, he always ate with his friends. Occasionally, he would stop where she was sitting. He didn't talk long because she always had other girls around her. He started to dial her number and then hung up. Drumming his fingers on the desk, he finally picked up the phone and dialed. It rang several times before Sue answered.

"Hi. This is Adam."

"Hello," she replied, her tone friendly and warm. If she was surprised by the call, there was no hint of it in her voice.

"How're things going?"

"Pretty good." She proceeded to tell him about some of her classes and talked about how she was looking forward to graduation. "What about you? You've been very busy lately."

"Yeah, I have. I know I haven't called. No excuse, I guess."

"I'm so glad you did." She paused. "And *why* did you call?"

"Ah…to see if you had some time during lunch tomorrow. Maybe we could get together."

"Oh, I'd like that."

"Okay, I'll see you tomorrow then."

"Wait, don't hang up yet."

Was something going on in her life that he should have asked about? Senior Prom? But that was over four months away.

"Adam, is there anything wrong?"

"No," he stammered. "Why do you ask?"

"Because you sound different. I'm not sure if I can put it into words. You don't sound like yourself."

"A lot has been happening lately. My grandfather's in the hospital," he blurted out.

"Oh, no. I'm sorry to hear that. What happened?"

Adam chewed his lip, feeling as if his emotions would get away from him if he started talking about it. "I really don't want to talk about it now. I'll tell you tomorrow. It's just that I have to think about some things I haven't worked through yet. Is that okay?"

"Sure, I'll look forward to talking to you tomorrow."

After hanging up, Adam was glad he had called Sue. The call allowed himself to feel her caring for him. He got up and walked into the living room. His mother sat in a chair, gazing out the window. Crumpled tissues filled her lap.

"You okay?" he asked.

"I really hated leaving Pa at the hospital," she said, continuing to stare out the window. "You know how much I dread those places. I'm not going to work tonight."

Adam couldn't remember the last time his mother had stayed home from work for any reason.

"Grandpa will be okay," he said, trying to sound reassuring.

"I hope so but things can happen. I was only three years old, but I remember her."

Adam sat down on the couch. "You're talking about your mother, aren't you?"

"Her long brown hair tickled my nose when I sat on her lap. I don't remember what she looked like, but I remember that brown hair. People told me that she was a beautiful woman." She sighed. "One day, she went away. Pa said it was a place where people went when they got sick. He said that people called doctors would make her better. I...I never saw her again."

"You'll see Grandpa again. He's too stubborn to have anything happen. You liked the doctor, didn't you? He seemed to be nice and knew what he was doing. Grandpa liked him."

"You're right," she said with a half smile. "I shouldn't worry. I know that but I do. Can't help it. Guess I'll always feel uncomfortable around doctors and hospitals."

Adam got up, walked over, and looked out the window. A few people scurried along the sidewalks. The orange neon sign across the street was sputtering its message *Hamm's Beer on Tap*.

"If I ever go to the hospital, don't send me flowers."

"What do you want? A box of candy or something?"

"No, I'm serious. I don't want flowers."

Adam felt bad about his attempt of making light of her request. "Why no flowers?"

She shuddered. "Because I don't like them."

"But why?"

"Because in the days when I was a kid, when a person died, they'd have the body in the house instead of a funeral home. We didn't have visitations in those days but it was the same thing."

"I don't like visitations," Adam said. "Why do people do that?"

"I always thought it was strange, myself. Guess people just want to have one last look. When I was a kid, it wasn't called a visitation."

"What was it called?"

"A wake. I'm not sure why." She looked out the window for a moment. "Now that I think about it, it sure is strange to call it that unless they thought the person was going to wake up or something. I don't remember a lot about when my mother died, but I do remember three things. The first was seeing what I thought was a big box in the living room and this woman with long brown hair laying in the box."

Adam looked around their living room and tried to imagine a coffin in it. "That's a little weird, isn't it?"

"Not when I was growing up. It was done all the time. Now-a-days, visitations are held at the funeral home. When my mother died, it was in our living room. To me, the coffin looked like a big box with a lid." She dabbed the corners of her eyes with a tissue. "The second thing I remember is Pa telling me that my mother was sleeping in it. I tell you, I was so scared to go to bed that night, I didn't want to fall asleep. I was afraid somebody would put me in a big wooden box if I did."

"And what was the third thing?"

"That really sticks out in my mind." His mother closed her eyes. "The smell of the flowers. I was in my bed upstairs and I could smell them. The whole house smelled like flowers. When I smell flowers now, I think back to my mother lying in that box. That's why I don't like flowers. When I die, I don't want any flowers. Promise me that."

"You're not going to die for a long time. Don't talk like that."

"Promise me," she persisted.

"Okay, okay, I promise...but you're still not going to die for a long time."

She dabbed her nose with tissues. "Well, I'm sure glad we have that nice Doctor Jairvus taking care of Pa." She leaned forward, took his hand, and squeezed it. "I'm glad that nothing happened to that pocket watch. You know, it's very important for him to give you that watch, especially because of the inscription."

"Do you have any idea what the inscription says?"

She smiled. "Yes, he showed it to me, but made me promise not to say anything. You'll just have to wait until graduation."

"Well, Grandpa's got me curious."

He and his mother fell silent for several moments as they listened to the traffic sounds from the street below. From the next room they could hear Oscar snoring.

"Oscar must've had a tough day at work," she said, looking toward the bedroom. "He was already in bed when we got home. Does his snoring ever keep you up?"

"Not really."

She leaned back in her chair. "Do you recall what we were talking about earlier today?"

"You mean about moving out of here and away from Broadway?"

"Yes. Do you remember that I told you that we live pretty well because of what we now pay for rent, but if we moved out, we'd end up someplace where we couldn't afford to live?"

"Yeah, I remember."

"And do you remember me saying that Oscar gives us money every month?"

Adam nodded.

"Don't you see, then? If it wasn't for Oscar and the money he gives us, we couldn't afford some of the extra things we have now. That's not to say we're well off but we're doing okay. As much as you may dislike Oscar living here, he's a kind man. Sure, he has his faults but so does everybody else. You just have to learn to accept people as they are. Most of them aren't so bad when you get to know them."

Adam didn't reply. So much had happened that day that he needed time to sort through everything.

* * *

Shortly before midnight, a voice came over the paging system at North Memorial Hospital.

"Doctor Jairvus, please call extension 471. Doctor Jairvus, please call extension 471."

"This is Jairvus. What's up? Really? I see. I don't think it's necessary to call his family at this point. Yes, I'll be right up."

Chapter 30

Adam walked up to Mick and Howie. His friends were standing outside of Mattingale's classroom. Mick was looking on as Howie paged through a book. "Hi guys. Are you two doing some last minute studying?"

"Nope, just waiting for you," Mick replied.

"Mick told me about your grandfather," Howie said as he closed his book. "What a bummer. I'm really sorry. How's he doing?"

"Saw him last night. Pretty weak but he's okay, I guess. Going to see him after school. I'll know more then."

Mick tapped him on the shoulder. "Remember, anything I can do to help, let me know."

"That goes for me, too."

"Thanks, guys. I appreciate it."

Howie opened the door to Mattingale's classroom, peeked in, and then closed it again. "Wow! It's a full house. Looks like everybody's here today."

"What do you expect?" Mick asked. "They're excited about Mattingale being back."

"Guess what I heard about her," Howie whispered.

"I can hardly wait," Adam said.

"I have this inside contact in the principal's office. She told me that she overheard Waite talking with another teacher about Mattingale. When Mattingale called Waite to ask for a day off, her voice was filled with emotion and it quivered as she talked."

"So she talks like that all the time," Adam said.

"Wait a minute. Let me finish. Mattingale asked Waite if the school would reimburse her for all the money she'd spent on hair shampoo."

"Shampoo?" Mick said. "What are you talking about?"

"It was because of the S.O.B." Howie paused. "You remember that, don't you?"

Mick rolled his eyes. "If there's one thing I'll remember from my senior year, it will be that thing."

"You've got to admit it was pretty cool, but I've got another idea that's even better. It's so simple that—"

"Not now," Mick said, groaning.

"Come on, don't you guys want to hear about it? It has to do with the upcoming Valentine's Day Dance and—"

"Let's wait, okay?" Mick said. "I'm not quite ready for another one of your schemes."

"That goes double for me," Adam said. "Just tell us what you heard from your source."

"Oh, yeah, I forgot. Guess I got so excited about my new idea. I tell you guys, it's such a great plan that—"

Mick's hand quickly clamped over Howie's mouth. "Now, Howie," he began slowly, "you're not going to say anything more about your latest scheme, right?"

Howie nodded while giving Adam a look that screamed *are you going to stand there and let him do this?*

"When I let you go, you're just going to talk about what your source said. Right?"

Howie nodded again, but his eyes were signaling *I'm going to get you for this.*

"One more thing. No revenge for this or else we'll walk into Mattingale's class with my hand over your mouth."

Howie's eyebrows shot up as he looked at Mick with shocked horror. He immediately nodded in agreement. After being released, Howie worked his jaw back and forth. "Okay, here it is," he said. "Mattingale told Waite she had to buy all this shampoo because she was having a hard time getting rid of the smoke odor in her hair. According to my source, she bought tons of the stuff."

"I can understand that," Mick said. "Her classroom stunk afterwards. I don't know what they did to get the smell out."

"Well, I'm glad she's back," Adam said. "I missed her."

"You're not the only one," Mick said as the warning bell rang. "Did you see the number of signatures on that welcome-back sign? She should be pleased with that."

"Don't forget about that vase with the three red roses."

"What vase?" Howie asked.

"We thought it was from you, lover boy," Mick said. "It was sitting on her desk when we went in after school yesterday to sign the poster. It didn't say who it was from."

"You have got to believe me. I didn't give it to her."

"Yeah, we figured that out," Mick admitted. "The question is who did?"

"Just think of it as another mystery that Howie will have to solve before graduation," Adam said. He opened the door to the classroom. "Let's go in. Mattingale should be coming any minute."

As soon as Miss Mattingale entered the classroom, she immediately took notice of the poster on the blackboard behind her desk. "Oh, dear!" she exclaimed. She stood, examining the poster for a long time before turning to face her students. Visibly moved, she sat down at her desk, dabbing at the corner of her eye with her white-gloved hand.

"Miss Mattingale?" Mick raised his hand to be recognized.

"Yes, Michael."

Mick stood up. "I've been asked on behalf of the class to welcome you back. We're glad that you weren't seriously injured in the...ah....fire. I mean, by the smoke."

"Thank you." Miss Mattingale scanned the room. "I want to thank all of you for this splendid outpouring of love. I shall treasure the poster for my entire life. There is something I wish to say, but that may need to wait." She looked at the clock. "Oh, dear, they should be here any minute."

As if on cue, the door to the classroom opened and in walked Mr. Waite, Mr. Mueller, and another gentleman who didn't appear familiar to anyone other than Miss Mattingale. The man was medium height, slender, and wore a three-piece dark blue suit. He and Miss Mattingale exchanged smiles.

"That guy looks like Albert Einstein with a haircut," Howie whispered to his friends.

Miss Mattingale stood while the three visitors quietly took places near the side blackboard. "Class, I presume all of you know Mr. Mueller, the gymnastics teacher, and Mr. Waite, our school principal." She breathed deeply before going on. "It is an honor to have them both here this morning. Mr. Waite will introduce our special guest."

"Thank you, Miss Mattingale. Good morning, students." Mr. Waite's deep voice could easily be heard throughout the room. "I have the privilege of introducing to you this morning the Superintendent of Schools, Mr. Keil. He has the very special honor of presenting a certificate of appreciation to one of the students in this class." Mr. Waite motioned for his guest to come. "Mr. Keil, the floor is all yours."

"Thank you, Mr. Waite. Good morning, students. Miss Mattingale, it's good to see you back on the job. You're a credit to the teaching profession and North High is fortunate to have you on its staff."

Mattingale blushed. "Thank you, Mr. Keil."

"When Mr. Waite called and suggested that I make this presentation the day you resumed your duties, I thought it was an excellent idea. Besides, what better place to honor the student than in the very classroom that the heroic action took place."

"What's going on?" Mick whispered to Adam.

"You got me."

"Would Howard Jerome Cummins please stand," Mr. Keil said.

Howie stood as the students in the front desks turned around to see him. He acknowledged his classmates' attention with a winsome grin.

"Howard," Mr. Kiel began, "this Certificate of Merit is in recognition of your courageous action on the day of January 13, 1959. It is being presented to you for saving Miss Mattingale's life by taking decisive action in applying mouth-to-mouth resuscitation. It is signed by Mr. Waite and myself." Mr. Kiel motioned to the hero to come forward. "Class, Howard deserves a round of applause as he comes up to receive this certificate of recognition."

Amidst enthusiastic applause, the Superintendent presented the certificate and then shook Howie's hand. "Now, Howard, perhaps you'd like to say a few words in response."

"Thank you, Mr. Keil. I have to say that I can't believe this is happening to me. It's with modest humility that I accept this award." Howie looked at his two friends and was pleased to see Mick smiling. He almost lost his train of thought, however, when Mick mouth the word *Bullshit.* "Of course, I feel as if I can't accept this without giving some credit to my two friends, Mick and Adam. They're sitting back there," he said, pointing in their direction. "They helped me carry Miss Mattingale from the room and then quickly responded to my suggestion that they go for help as I stayed on the scene to," he paused and glanced at Miss Mattingale, "breathe life back into a teacher we all admire and adore."

Even though Howie had more to say, the look on his friend's faces warned him that he had said enough. "In conclusion, I accept this honor and will try to live up to it for the rest of my life. Thank you." He walked back to his seat, sat down, but then stood again. "I forgot. There's one more thing I'd like to say. I'm sure that what I did was something that any student here would've done as well."

"Magnificent, Howard," Miss Mattingale exclaimed, giving him a muffled applause with her gloved hands. "I must say that you have a gift for words."

"You sure do," Adam whispered.

Howie turned and sheepishly smiled at Mick and Adam. "So, maybe I got carried away a little bit."

"Oh, no, Jerome, not you," Mick said.

"Not at all, Jerome," Adam added.

After the visitors left, Miss Mattingale walked around to the front of her desk. "Now, class, if we may contain our excitement for the moment, we shall turn our attention to the papers you have been so hard at work writing."

Chapter 31

When Adam walked into the school lunchroom at noon he wondered if Howie was still carrying around the *Certificate of Merit* he had been awarded that morning. He had seen Mick in the hallway between classes and Mick told him that he had just come from the school library where Howie was proudly displaying it to another teacher.

Adam saw Sue sitting alone at a table in the corner and walked over to her.

"Hi," she said. "Sit down."

"Give me a second. I have to find Howie and Mick to tell them something. I'll be right back." He looked around the lunchroom. "You haven't seen them, have you?"

Sue pointed toward the far end of the lunchroom. "Try that table over there. The one with the crowd standing in front of it."

Adam pushed his way through the dozen or so students standing in front of the table. Howie looked as though he was holding a news conference. When Adam heard the name of the Superintendent of Schools mentioned, Howie had to be talking about what had taken place that morning. Waiting for the "hero" to finish his story, Adam stood and observed, amused that Mick was leaning back in his chair and gazing at the ceiling tiles while Howie jabbered away.

"Hey, there!" Howie yelled at Adam. "Be right with you." He held up his hands to quiet the crowd. "Look everyone. That's all for now. I need to spend some time with my friends here. Come back tomorrow and I'll finish the story."

"What's going on here?" Adam asked once the crowd had dispersed.

"*Jerome* here has gotten himself a following," Mick said.

"I told you not to call me that!"

"Here's the deal then. I won't call you Jerome and you won't bring up the story about Mattingale anymore. Agreed?"

"What if you guys bring it up?"

"Look," Adam said, "I think you can be sure *we're* not going to bring it up."

"What if somebody else brings it up?" Howie argued. "I can't ignore them. They might think I'm stuck-up or something. I mean it would—"

"Okay, okay, you win," Mick said. "Say no more. How can I argue with a hero?"

"If someone else brings it up we can't do anything about that," Adam said. "As long as you don't encourage it."

"What can I do?" Howie lamented. "I agree but I—"

"Howieee!"

Gloria Huddleston, a sophomore, ran toward them; her blond ponytail swaying back and forth.

"Hi, Gloria." Howie gulped, sheepishly glancing at his two friends.

"Howieee. Will you do a favor for me? If I bring you my megaphone, will you autograph it?"

Mick moaned as he looked at Adam. "I'm going to be sick. I can't believe that we helped create this monster."

"Don't pay any attention to these two," Howie said to his latest admirer. He shot Mick a stern glance before turning his attention back to Gloria. "I tell you what. If you meet me after school, you can have my autograph. I'll even show you the certificate I received from the Superintendent of Schools."

"Really!" Gloria shrieked. "I'll be there. See you, Howieee."

As she started to walk away, he called out, "Gloria?"

"Yes?"

"You can bring some of your friends if you'd like."

Howie was still waving good-bye to Gloria when Adam spoke up. "Look, you guys, I can't stay. I have to talk with Sue about something. I just wanted to remind you not to look for me after school. I'm going up to the hospital."

"I hope your grandfather's okay," Mick said.

"That goes for me, too," Howie added.

"Thanks. He'll be okay. I'll see you guys tomorrow."

"Wait," Mick pleaded. "Are you sure you want to leave me alone with Howie? I don't think I can take it." He gestured toward Gloria who was sitting with some other girls several tables away. "He's even got cheerleaders coming after him for his autograph."

"Aw, come on, you're a football player. You can handle it. Why don't you talk about the Valentine Day Dance next month. He can share with you his plans for Mattingale's desk."

Mick groaned.

Howie's eyes lit up. "Mick, just wait until you hear my plan. You'll love it. We just have to make sure the girls have a ride home and then…"

* * *

As Sue watched Adam walk back to her table, she thought about the first time they had met. It was at a party at Mick's house last year. Mick had asked if she would go over and talk to his friend sitting by himself on the couch. He had warned her that Adam was a loner and could be moody, but he thought it'd be good for him to have company. She had known Adam from classes they had together. When she asked her friends about the dark-haired, good-looking boy in fourth period, Social Studies, she was told he seemed stuck-up.

"Have you had any lunch?" she asked as Adam sat down. "You can have some of mine," she offered. "I've got more than enough."

"I'm not very hungry. Maybe later, okay? How're you doing with that upcoming test in chemistry?"

"I still have to review two more chapters," Sue said, confused as to why he asked about school. "Adam, I don't want to talk about any stupid chemistry test. You told me last night that your grandfather was in the hospital. Tell me what happened."

He didn't say anything for several moments. "You know how cold it's been lately? Well, my grandfather was out in that cold without much protection. He got frostbite on his arms and legs, but the doctor thinks he'll be okay. I'm going up to see him after school."

"I'm glad he's okay but you must be worried." Sue reached out and touched him on the arm. "You've never talked much about your grandfather. Are the two of you very close?"

"I guess we are." Adam paused. "Yeah, we're close. More than I realized."

Sue unwrapped a sandwich. Surprised but pleased that he had not brushed aside her questions like usual.

"Look, I'm...ah...I'm having some confused feelings lately," he stammered. "They're sort of crazy. No, I really don't mean crazy. It's just that I don't like having them. They make me feel..."

"Afraid?"

"What makes you ask that?" he asked, sounding startled.

"Don't get angry with me for saying this," she pleaded. "My guess is that you think a person should never be afraid, or have problems, or…care for others." She reached out and touched him again. "Everyone is afraid at times and everybody has problems. It's okay to share them."

Adam didn't respond immediately. For a second, she feared that he was going to jump up and walk away. "I don't know what to think," he blurted out. "Lately, too much has been happening."

"You've kept your feelings bottled up too long and I think you're convinced you don't need anyone to share them with."

Adam's eyes flickered, but he didn't say anything.

"You're a caring person but you just don't know how to show it." Reaching out, she took his hand, feeling hopeful when he took her hand into his. "Perhaps you want to but maybe you're afraid." Looking into his eyes, she sensed a vulnerability she hadn't seen before. "I think there are times when you feel sorry for yourself, or that you feel ashamed of something."

"Well, maybe so," he snapped and pulled his hand away. "Maybe I've got a lot to feel sorry about. Maybe I don't live in a nice home like you, and maybe I don't know what it's like to have both parents." He leaned toward her, his voice sharp. "Maybe you don't know what cockroaches are, or how it feels to pick up your grandfather off the sidewalk because he's fallen down drunk."

"Don't be angry," she said, momentarily stunned. "I didn't mean it that way. There are lots of people who have troubles. You're not the only one." She put her sandwich down. "My father's an alcoholic."

Adam's mouth dropped open. "He is? I…I didn't know that.

You never mentioned that."

"That's right, I didn't tell you. I was afraid to. I wasn't sure what you'd think." She lowered her eyes for a moment. "I felt ashamed. It's not easy to share that sort of thing with just anyone unless you know that person understands and cares."

"I don't know what to say. I'm such a jerk. I'm sorry. I just…"

She reached over and took his hand. "Thank you."

"For what?"

"For saying you're sorry." She squeezed his hand and he squeezed hers in return. "Saying that shows me you have feelings and that you do care."

"So much has happened lately," Adam continued. "All these thoughts and feelings are running through me. I need time to sort them out. And I need…I…I don't know what I need."

"You need people to share them with. I know Mick and Howie care about you. They're good friends."

Adam glanced over to where Mick and Howie were sitting. "Yeah, I know they are."

"I want to be a friend, also. Someone you can share with when you feel like you need to share something."

"I appreciate that. Right now, I guess I just need some time. Got to make some sense out of all of this. I feel like I'm on a roller coaster. I don't know what to think anymore." He drew in a deep breath. "I'm not even sure if I'm making any sense now," he said, adding in a quiet, almost little boy's voice, "Am I?"

"You are. I just want you to know that I appreciate you sharing as much as you did with me right now. It has been more than you've ever done since we've known each other. Tell me. Was it difficult?"

"A little." Adam looked away for a moment. "No, more than a little. I feel drained…and hungry. I think I could use a sandwich now. Would you mind sharing?"

"Of course not," she said, her eyes twinkling with laughter.

"There's something else. You know, next month is the Valentine Day Dance. I know I should've asked you before this but I wonder if—"

"Yes."

"Wow. That was easy. We'll be tripling with Mick and

Howie again."

"Sounds like fun."

"Let's hope by then that Howie will be over the hero bit." Adam looked over to where his two friends were sitting. "Can I tell you what really happened that day?"

"I can hardly wait. Each time I hear the story, it gets to be a little bit more unbelievable. And will you share something else with me?"

"What's that?"

"Will you also tell me about your grandfather? He sounds pretty special."

"He is. Let me tell you how we used to go to the city dump together and look for clocks. He loves clocks…"

Chapter 32

Adam walked home from school, reflecting on the conversation he had earlier that day with Sue. He had only touched upon a portion of what he had been struggling with lately. The sharing felt good at the time, but now he wasn't sure. Even though Sue said how much she appreciated him sharing, he wondered about what she thought about him now. *Stop it. She cares and wants to be a friend. Don't be a dummy. Remember what she said about trusting her.* By the time he walked into Bloomberg's Department Store, he had decided that he would open up even more. *Share my feeling with her about leaving the North Side. Maybe even tell her about Frank.*

Harry Bloomberg was straightening stacks of men's work pants when Adam walked in. As soon as he saw his young helper, Harry's pudgy face broke into a wide grin, and he waved him over.

"Adam, give me a minute to finish with these," he said. "Stand and watch your boss work for awhile. When I'm done, I'll show you the new stuff we got for the Valentine Day Sale. It's terrific."

"Harry, I—"

"Just wait 'til you see the men's boxer shorts. They have these little red hearts all over them. Can you believe that? Little red hearts? What will they think of next?"

"Listen, I need—"

"We'll put some on display in the window." Harry's charcoal-gray eyes danced with amusement. "Maybe you can get your friends to model them. Wouldn't that cause a stir on Broadway. I bet the customers would flock—"

"Harry! My grandfather's in the hospital."

Harry immediately stopped what he was doing. "He's in the hospital?"

"Yeah. I'm going up to see him now. I just stopped to let you know."

"I saw your grandfather only last week. He seemed fine. What happened?"

Adam related the story, leaving out the part about the drinking. "I'm not sure if I'll be in to work afterwards."

"Don't worry about it. You go now. See your grandfather. That's more important. Tell him that Mama and I are sorry that this has happened."

"Thanks, I will."

"Do you need a ride? I'll take you if you do."

"No, I'm going to drive. Thanks, anyway. See you tomorrow."

Although the kitchen light had been left on, no one was there when Adam got home to get the car keys. On the kitchen table were the car keys and a note from his mother.

Butch,

I've been gone all day. Had to keep myself busy. Tell Pa that

I'll see him when he gets home. Hope he understands. He knows

I don't like hospitals. Drive carefully. The car's in the usual spot.

Love,

Mom.

P.S.

Dress warm. The radio says it's going to be cold again. Wear a hat.

Traffic on Broadway was heavier than usual and it took Adam an extra ten minutes to get to the hospital.

"I'm here to see my grandfather," Adam announced to a silver-haired lady sitting behind the mahogany receptionist desk. He wondered what happened to the other receptionist with the plastic smile.

"If you give me his name, I'll look to see what floor he's on," she said in a pleasant tone.

"I know what floor he's on. Just wondering if I have to check in or something?"

She flashed a warm smile. "Oh, no, that's not necessary."

As soon as Adam walked into Ward 7 he sensed something wasn't right. Three of the six beds were occupied, but his grandfather's bed had been stripped of the blanket and sheets. *Did the doctor release him, or did he leave on his own?* Adam could see his grandfather deciding that he had had enough of hospital life. Hearing footsteps behind him, he turned to see a nurse approaching.

"May I help you?" she asked, her voice friendly but formal.

"I'm looking for my grandfather." Adam gestured to the empty bed. "That's his bed. I mean, it was his bed. His things are gone and I don't know where he is."

"You must be referring to Mr. Kurtz. He moved to another floor this morning."

"Why?"

"Your grandfather developed quite a cough in the middle of the night and we thought it'd be best to place him where he could receive additional care."

"Does Doctor...ah, I forgot his name. He was here yesterday. My mom and I talked to him. He was the doctor helping my grandfather."

"You mean, Doctor Jairvus?"

"Yeah. Does he know about this?"

"Oh, yes. The move was done on his orders. Doctor Jairvus told the staff to be sure to take extra good care of him. It had something to do with your grandfather teaching him about clocks. He said that Mr. Kurtz was going to teach him a few things about clocks and people."

"That's sounds like my grandfather. Is he okay? Can I see him?"

"Of course. I need to tell you, however, that he didn't have a good night. His color is a little gray and he's hurting from coughing so much." She offered a reassuring smile. "He'll be just fine, though. I wouldn't worry. Doctor Jairvus is a very good doctor. Your grandfather's on the second floor, wing 2B. I forget his room number, but just stop at the nurses' station on 2B and the staff there will direct you."

Adam got on the elevator and pushed the button for the second floor. Before the doors closed, an orderly got on pushing an elderly woman in a wheelchair. The old woman looked up at

Adam and smiled. "You remind me of my grandson." Adam smiled but didn't reply. When he got off on the second floor, he nodded to her and said good-bye. Just as the elevator doors were closing, she surprised him by blowing him a kiss. As he walked toward the section where his grandfather was, he wondered what it would have been like if his grandmother had lived. That he missed not knowing her was a feeling he had not experienced before.

The nurses on 2B were cordial when he stopped to inquire about his grandfather. He thanked them and headed to 214B, the room they had directed him to. The room was only two doors down from the nurses' station. The door to 214B was partially open. He hesitated before going in. The first bed was empty. His grandfather was in the bed next to the window. With pillows propped up behind his head, he held a Styrofoam cup, using a straw to sip its contents.

"Hi, Grandpa." Adam got closer, taken back by how drawn and tired he appeared.

His grandfather moved the cup a little, letting the straw slip from his lips. "Oh, Butch, good see you," he said, his voice weak, close to a whisper. Even though Adam had been warned, he was bothered by his grandfather's pasty, gray complexion.

"How're you feeling?"

"Cough all night. No good."

"Are you warm enough?" Adam asked, concerned because the covers were only pulled up slightly to above his waist.

"Warm. Cold. Warm now."

Adam motioned toward the empty bed. "At least it looks like you'll have this place to yourself. It's a lot nicer than that other room you were in yesterday."

"This room, hotel."

"They'll spoil you here," Adam said, trying to sound upbeat. "Then you'll want to stay."

"No stay. Nice, but still hospital."

Adam, bothered by how lethargic he acted, needed to find out as much information as he could because he would be asked when he got home. "What does the doctor say about what's going on with you?"

"Don't remember."

His grandfather took a couple sips of water. When he moved, the hospital gown slipped down over one shoulder, exposing a bony frame. Shocked at how frail he looked, Adam wished he would pull the gown back up around his shoulder. Seeing his grandfather's naked frailty proved upsetting. "Grandpa, the doctor must've said something."

"Take tests. Give pills." He handed his cup to Adam to put on the nightstand. "Doc just here. Said he be back and—"

The coughing came without warning. Adam winced at the sound of the deep, rattling cough. He didn't like standing there and doing nothing as he watched his grandfather clutched his chest.

Paul reached for his cup of water.

"Here, let me." His grandfather took a couple of sips and then waved the cup away. Adam set the cup down and then adjusted the gown so it covered his grandfather's bare shoulder.

His grandfather reached over and placed his hand on Adam's hand. Their eyes met, and to Adam, it seemed as if they were looking into each other souls. He never felt as close to this man as he was feeling at this moment. He felt like weeping and joyfully laughing at the same time. How long that moment lasted, he didn't know. Its magical spell was broken only when his grandfather began coughing again.

Adam waited until the coughing subsided. "Grandpa, I should've went out looking for you."

"Not your fault."

"But I should've. I—"

"No, my fault. Shouldn't listen Frank."

"Frank! What are you talking about?"

"Good evening, Mr. Kurtz," Doctor Jairvus said as he walked in. "How are you doing? And you're Adam, his grandson. Right?"

Adam nodded, swallowing hard, hoping that the doctor hadn't heard his outburst.

"Hope I'm not interrupting anything, but I just wanted to check on my patient." Jairvus glanced at Paul before addressing himself to Adam. "I have a personal interest in your grandfather. He's going to improve my medical skills by teaching me all about repairing clocks. Isn't that right, Mr. Kurtz?"

When his grandfather smiled, Adam liked that Doctor Jairvus was taking care of him. “What happened?” he asked the doctor. “When we were here yesterday, he was doing okay. Even you said that.”

“Yes, I know. Unfortunately, during the night, his cough got worse. It got much worse. Isn’t that right, Mr. Kurtz?”

“Yes, cough not good.”

“I agree. Not good at all.” The doctor gestured toward a chair, but Adam declined to sit. “When I examined him further, I discovered that pneumonia had set in. Considering his age, the exposure and resulting frostbite, I thought it’d be best to move him where we could keep a better eye on him. That is especially important considering his past history with emphysema. Our main concern now that his lungs are inflamed is that there’s no infection. It’s going to require a longer hospital stay, however.”

“Butch, he good Doc.”

“Thank you, Mr. Kurtz. I try, but remember, you’ve agreed to teach me about clocks when you’re better. So you see, I do have a vested interest in you.”

“I remember.” He smiled at his grandson. “I think Doc learn fast.”

“Have you talked to my mother about all of this?”

“I tried to call this morning, but there was no answer. Since the situation isn’t critical, I thought I’d try this evening. That’s why I stopped by. It seems like our admission’s records only show the one home phone number. Adam, it’d be helpful before you leave, if you’d stop at the nurses’ desk and give us the home number of your aunt as well. We’d also like to have the work number for your mother, and if you know it, for your aunt.”

“Why the work numbers?” Adam asked, concerned that his grandfather’s condition was worse than what the doctor was saying.

“In case of an emergency,” Jairvus said, his voice, calm and confident. “There’s no need to worry. That information is just standard operating procedure. We do it with all our patients.”

Adam breathed a sigh of relief. “I can give you the home numbers, but I don’t know my aunt’s work number.”

“Just tell her to call in with the number, or give it to us the next time she comes in.”

"I will. Besides the pneumonia, what else?"

"I'm not sure what you mean."

"My mom will want to know everything, and I don't know all the questions I should be asking. Is there anything else I should be telling her?"

"I see. Tell her that we're monitoring his pneumonia and treating it with antibiotics. The problem is his weakened condition brought on by the exposure. As I told your grandfather, the next couple of days are critical. I don't want to sound alarmist, but the family needs to know that pneumonia is something that we take very seriously."

"If it's that serious, is there anything else that has to be done?"

"No, we're doing everything we can. We just have to let those antibiotics work and hope for the natural healing processes of the body to take place. The human body is pretty amazing at healing itself. Medicine can only go so far. I'm confidant, however. Anything else?"

"I don't think so. Thanks."

"And you, Mr. Kurtz, do you have any questions?"

"What kind clock you fix?"

Jairvus laughed. "When you get better, we'll talk about that. I'll leave you two alone now. Nice meeting you again, Adam. Good-bye, Mr. Kurtz. I'll see you later."

Adam waited until the doctor left before he spoke. "Grandpa, what happened that morning with you and Frank?" Anger rose within him as his grandfather recounted the sequel of events. "Why didn't you tell me yesterday about this?"

"Not good time. Mother, Wanda here." He paused. "Butch, don't be angry."

"I'm not angry at you."

"Don't be angry, Frank."

"What do you mean? It's because of Frank that you're here. He shouldn't have let you go out that morning."

"Hear me. I lay here all night. Cough. Think about life. I look at watch." He lifted his hand and pointed toward the nightstand. "Still there?"

Adam opened the drawer. The pocket watch was wrapped in the same tissue that it had been the day before.

"It's still here." He held it up so that his grandfather could see it.

"Good. It remind me. No good be angry, Frank." Wetting his lips with his tongue, he asked for a sip of water before going on. "Frank angry at life. Never change. He leave anger as memory. Butch, don't be angry at life. Let Frank leave anger behind for memory. Not you. You have pocket watch. I—"

Adam watched as his grandfather again clutched his chest. The coughing was harsh and violent. "I'm going to leave now," he said quietly. "You need your rest. Okay?"

"Butch, remember."

As Adam rode the elevator down to the lobby, he thought about the admonition not to be angry with Frank. He felt torn between trying to honor his grandfather's wishes and wanting to get even with Frank. *How could his grandfather be so forgiving of Frank?*

The woman with the plastic smile was sitting at the receptionist desk when Adam walked out through the lobby area. Swirls of ground snow enveloped him as he stepped out into the chilly air. By the time he reached the car, he was shivering. He got in, started the car, and leaned back. As he sat waiting for the car to warm up, he tried to sort out his feelings. Still feeling angry with Frank, he was puzzled why his grandfather wasn't upset at Frank. It wasn't like him, and probably due to his weakened condition. He, however, dismissed that idea. His grandfather might not be well, but his mind was sharp and he knew what he was talking about. It had to be something to do with the watch's inscription. Ever since his grandfather had discovered it, something changed with him. Adam felt like his head was spinning. Turning on the radio, he moved the dial until he found WDGY. He turned up the volume, put the car in gear, and drove home listening to the countdown of the top forty hits.

When he got back to the apartment, his mother was sitting at the kitchen table having coffee with Oscar.

"How's Grandpa?" his mother asked nervously.

"He's developed pneumonia so he's going to have a longer hospital stay."

"Oh, no!" she cried

Adam unsnapped his jacket, sat down at the table, and

reported the move down to the second floor and what Doctor Jairvus had said about him getting better care. "He's close to the nurses' station so they can keep an eye on him." He described how weak his grandfather was from coughing so much, but also tried to be as reassuring as Jairvus had been to him. He didn't say anything about what his grandfather had told him about Frank. "It's the pneumonia that the doctor's concerned about."

"Pneumonia!" Oscar exclaimed. "Phew! That's some nasty stuff, by golly. Sorry to hear about that."

"I had it when I was young," Virg said. "Took me a long time to recover. I had what they called double pneumonia. Did Doctor Jairvus say anything about that?"

"No, but he said not to worry because they got him on antibiotics."

"I hope they work."

"Me too," Oscar said as he yawned.

"You better go to bed," Virg suggested.

"Yah, you bet. I think I better go and try to catch a little snooze."

"Thanks for listening."

"Yah, sure." Oscar yawned. He stood and stretched. "Butch, is it cold out? I got to go to work tonight at eleven."

"It's pretty cold and it's going to get colder."

Oscar picked up his coffee, took one last sip, and headed toward the bedroom.

"What's this about Oscar listening?"

"When I got home, I am so worried about what you might find out, I had to talk to somebody. I thought about calling Wanda, but she wasn't home from work yet. I felt so guilty about not going up to the hospital. Grandpa understood, didn't he?"

"Yeah, he did. Don't worry about it."

"Oh, good. That makes me feel better." She suppressed a yawn. "I asked Oscar to have a cup of coffee with me until you got here. Poor man, he should've gone to bed. He's already worked one shift, but still he said he'd be glad to. Been sitting here for nearly an hour. He helped me a lot just by listening. I am so worried about Pa. If anything should happen to him, I..."

Seeing his mother's tears brought on the same kind of helpless feeling he had when he had been with his grandfather at the hospital. "You need some water or something?"

"Thank you, but no. I'm sorry, but sometimes people have to let go of their emotions."

"That's okay. Don't forget to tell Wanda to let the hospital know her work number."

"I won't. She should be home from work by now. Do you want to come with me?"

"No," Adam said quickly. "I think I'll go down to Harry's or take a walk over to Mick's."

"It's cold out. You should wear a hat."

Adam scowled. "Mom!"

"Okay, I know. It's just that with Pa in the hospital, I wouldn't know what to do if something happened to you."

"Nothing's going to happen."

"Promise?"

"I promise." Adam got up and walked to the door, but then stopped and turned back toward her. "Mom, don't worry too much. Doctor Jairvus seems to be a pretty nice guy. He'll take good care of Grandpa."

"I hope so."

Adam decided to tell Harry that he would be into work tomorrow as soon as he could after school. Crossing the street to Bloomberg's, he saw Harry in the front window changing the clothing on one of the mannequins. His boss was just climbing out of the window when he walked in.

"I'm too old for this." Harry took out a handkerchief from his back pocket and wiped the perspiration off his baldhead. "It's too warm in here but Zelda says she won't work unless the store temperature is comfortable. What's comfortable for her is hot for me. So, enough already about Zelda. How's your grandfather?"

"He's okay. I just stopped by to let you know that I'll be in tomorrow for sure."

"Good. Good. We'll be getting ready for the January Clearance Sale. After that, it's the Valentine Day Sale. Tomorrow, I'll show you those boxer shorts. With the tiny hearts imprinted on them, they'll be a terrific item. Just wait and see."

"Okay, I'll see you then. Don't work too hard."

The street lights had come on by the time Adam left. The evening had brought colder temperatures. Not feeling like walking the five blocks to Mick's house, he headed back to the apartment. Walking past Kass' Drugstore, he glanced in the window and saw Kass behind the fountain. On impulse, he turned back and went in. The cowbell announced his arrival.

"Hello there," Kass said as Adam walked up to the soda fountain. He was just finishing eating a banana split. Kass shrugged and patted his well-endowed stomach as his young customer sat down. "I know, I know. I shouldn't, but they're the best on Broadway."

"Hey, I won't tell anyone. You of all people deserve it."

"You always say the right thing so I don't have to feel too guilty." Kass used a portion of his white apron to wipe his mouth. "Now, what can I get for you?"

"Coke and a bag of potato chips."

Kass gave him a quizzical look. "That's not your supper, is it?"

"Yeah, why?"

"You wait." Kass disappeared into the back room. Within a few minutes, he came out carrying a black lunch bucket. Setting the bucket on the counter in front of Adam, he undid the side snaps, opened it, and pulled out two sandwiches, each wrapped in wax paper.

"Have one of these," Kass ordered, setting one of the sandwiches in front of Adam. "I'll have one also. It's nice to share."

"This is good," Adam mumbled while chewing. "What is it?"

"Kosher corned beef." Kass set his sandwich down and got a glass from under the counter. "Here, let me get you something to drink with it."

While eating, Kass and Adam talked about the cold weather and how Adam was doing in school. At one point, Kass left to wait on a customer. By the time he returned, Adam had finished the sandwich.

"Can I get you dessert?"

"Oh, no, I'm full." Adam sipped his Coke. "Kass, you know how we were talking the other day about you staying on Broadway even though what happened?"

"I remember."

"Can you say more about why you'd want to stay? I think I understand but I need to hear it again."

"Sure. As I told you, this is where my friends are and it's also my home. While I'm here, I try to be nice to people. I try to help them whenever I can. When something bad happens, I try to make the best of it rather than it getting the best of me. Who I am and what I do with what happens in life will be my legacy."

"Your what?"

"Legacy. A legacy is something you leave behind for others."

"You mean like when someone dies and they leave you an inheritance?"

"Something like that, but in my mind it means more than that." Kass wiped his hands on his apron. "When my grandmother died, she left me a sum of money. Not a lot, but enough. The money was my inheritance. That money enabled me to get this drugstore. Everyday when I come to work, I'm reminded of my grandmother. Because of the inheritance, I have this drugstore. But my grandmother left me more than money. She was a very loving and compassionate woman. Always helping others. No one who came to her door hungry went away hungry. She taught me that though there may be bad things that happen in the world, a good deed done in love is more powerful. Her capacity to show love and compassion in the face of whatever life may bring was her legacy to me. It was like her gift to me. If I leave that kind of gift behind, I will die a happy man because my grandmother's legacy will be passed on." He paused. "Am I making any sense?"

"I think so, but not everybody is like your grandmother or you."

"Ah, that's true, but they also will leave their own legacies. Take, for example, those who robbed me. If that's the kind of life they're going to have, then that's what they'll be remembered by. What they did reflects who they are and their moral values or I should say their lack of moral values. The point is that who they are will be the legacies they leave behind. That's what they'll be remembered for."

"That's not much, is it?"

"I agree. And I feel sorry for those who leave that kind of

legacy. What terrible memories to have to live with."

"I think I understand what you're saying, but I've got to do some thinking about it."

"You do that, and if you want to talk again, we'll talk." Kass took a bite of his sandwich. "You know where to find me."

"Thanks for the sandwich and the Coke." Adam left and started toward home. He hadn't taken twenty steps when he noticed a familiar figure headed toward him from the opposite direction. *Frank!*

Chapter 33

Frank immediately recognized Adam. "Son'n'bitch! Ain't this my lucky night." He slipped his hand into his overcoat pocket and wrapped his fingers around an iron bar. One afternoon he had stopped to borrow a couple of bucks from a drinking buddy who worked in a machine shop as a tool and dye maker. While there, he noticed on his friend's workbench an assortment of steel bars. He picked one up. It was just the right size; an inch in diameter and eight or nine inches long. Ever since his beating, he carried it, hoping it would come in handy.

As Adam now approached him, the timing was perfect. Fifteen minutes ago, he had been drinking a beer and watching television. Virg had come over to tell Wanda that the doctor wanted her to call the hospital to give them her work number. After Wanda made the phone call, she and Virg went into the kitchen to talk. If they thought he wasn't paying any attention to their conversation, they were wrong. He heard everything. When Virg told Wanda about the pneumonia, Frank chuckled to himself.

Serves him goddamn right. By the time I got his coat for him so he could go and look for his junk clocks, he was so drunk he didn't notice that I gave him his lightweight jacket.

Frank felt triumphant when Virg said that Butch looked very worried. "I don't blame him," Wanda had replied. "Pa could've died in this weather." Frank took a swig of beer. *Hell, we all have to die some time.*

Adam was now no more than ten feet away from him. "Hey, Butchie!" he yelled. "Where're ya goin' in such a hurry? Got a minute?"

"What do you want?" Adam asked, slowing his pace.

"How's your grandpa? Hear he's in the hospital."

"No thanks to you."

He knows. Frank gripped the iron bar in his pocket, hoping the kid would come at him. No one would fault him. He'd claim he was being assaulted again. The iron bar was for protection. "Ya sound angry, Butchie. What's the matter?"

Adam said nothing. Picking up his pace, he walked briskly passed him.

"Butchie, ya goddamn grandpa doesn't know when to come out of the cold." When Adam stopped, Frank pulled the iron bar from his pocket and held it along side of him. "Come on, Butchie. Come on. I'm ready for ya." For a moment, he thought Adam started to turn. When he walked on, however, Frank was disappointed. "Chicken shit," he muttered, slipping his weapon back into his pocket.

Frank chuckled to himself. Paul must've said something by the look in Butchie's eyes. He figured that the kid had come close to turning around and coming after him. The more he thought about it, however, the more he liked the idea that nothing happened. This way he could play around with him some more, push him to the edge. *And then, we'll see how tough ya are, Butchie.*

The wind blew and swirling snow found its way down Frank's coat collar. "Goddamn, what am I standin' here for? Goin' to freeze my ass off." The B & B Bar was only a couple of blocks away. Within minutes he walked through the door.

"Hi, Frank," the bartender said, as he walked in. "Cold enough for you?"

"Charlie, it's too cold out there even for an Eskimo to piss."

The bartender laughed. "Then tell him to hold it until spring. Radio says a warm front is moving in from the Dakotas late tonight."

"Shit. About time." Frank unbuttoned his overcoat and plopped down on a barstool. "I need somethin' to warm up my insides."

"Usual?"

"Hell, yes." Frank looked around. The place had less than a dozen customers. Two guys and a woman sat at the end of the bar drinking beer and eating peanuts. Cigarette smoke hung above them like low hanging clouds. The jukebox blared some song he didn't recognize and didn't care to. "Damn Country Western shit," he muttered. He eyed the woman sitting with the two guys. She wore a tight-fitting sweater and a short black skirt. She wasn't a looker, but he could forgive her for that since she had a decent enough looking body. *Wonder if she could handle me in bed?*

The bartender brought Frank his bottle of beer. "Want a glass?"

"Charlie, goddamn it, ya always ask me that. Told ya before, only way for a man to drink beer is from the bottle." Frank smirked. "Like suckin' on it. Reminds me of my first wife. Ya know what I mean?"

"Say, there's a guy here who's looking for you." The bartender pointed beyond the jukebox. "Sitting over in the corner booth. Told me he's a friend of yours. Says you guys go back a long ways."

"What's his name?"

"Didn't say and I didn't ask. Said the two of you were in the same outfit in the Marines."

"Yeah? What's he look like?"

"Short guy. Lean. Dark hair. Has a slight limp."

"Goddamn! Gotta be Dale. Where did ya say the son'n'bitch is?"

"Over in the end booth."

Frank grabbed his beer and walked over to the booth. "Jesus, Dale, I still don't know how the hell the Corp let in such a short shit like ya."

"That's because they already had enough big turds like you. How the hell are you, Frank? You're looking good."

"Could be better." Frank looked over at the bar before sitting down. "Hey, Charlie, two more beers."

"I'm not done with this one," Dale protested.

"Hell, neither am I with mine. Ya know us, jarheads. Whether it's beer or women, we gotta have some in reserve."

"How long has it been since we've had a beer together? Six…seven months?"

"Hell, at least that long." Frank didn't have many friends and was glad to see Dale. "If ya didn't have that goddamn night shift, we could be drinkin' buddies again."

"I know but I got three kids now, and the old lady wants a nicer house in a different area. She doesn't like living around here. Says it scares her because it's too rough of a neighborhood." Dale shrugged and swigged his beer. "Anyway, the night shift pays more and in a couple of years we'll have enough to get out."

"Remember our first day in boot camp?" Frank asked.

Dale chuckled. "Sure as hell do. Those drill instructors had me scared shitless."

"Yeah, me too. But hell, they sure got us in shape." Frank guzzled the rest of his beer and took a swig from the second bottle. "Damn, I miss those days. We were young and could kick the shit out of anybody."

"Hey, Frank. I heard about what happened to you in the parking lot."

"Goddamn punks they were. If I hadn't been so drunk, I could've kicked their asses."

"Surprised you didn't. Twenty years ago, you would've and it wouldn't have mattered how drunk you were. How many do you think jumped you?"

"Hell, I don't know," Frank said, hating the thought of getting old. "Think there were three."

"Recognize any?"

"Hell no! Shit, Dale, I told ya I was drunk. Happened too goddamn fast."

Dale looked toward the bar. "Two more beers, here." The bartender brought their beers and went to wait on a customer who had just come in. Dale leaned over and looked Frank straight in his eyes. "I know who they were, at least, one of them."

"Ya do?"

"Yeah. Punk's name is Danny Logan."

Chapter 34

Adam walked up to Mick standing outside of Kass' Drugstore. His friend was looking at the thermometer on the Coca-Cola sign next to the drugstore's large display window. "So, what does it say?" Adam asked.

"Hang on for a minute." Mick cocked his head. "Okay, I got it. It looks like...ah...seventeen degrees. Hey, that's not too shabby considering how cold it was last night."

"Yeah, not bad for the first week in February. Pretty soon, we can kiss winter good-bye."

Mick sucked in a deep breath. "Man, it feels like we could almost have the beginnings of a spring day."

"Suppose it makes you think of college and football practice," Adam said, the two of them crossing the street on their way to school.

Stepping onto the curb, Mick picked up a chunk of snow and threw it at a lamppost. He groaned when he missed it by a foot. "There's not going to be any spring football practices in my life."

"What do you mean? Don't college teams practice in the spring?"

"Sure they do, but not the college I'm attending."

"How come?"

"Because it doesn't even have a football team."

Adam looked to see if Mick was kidding, but there wasn't a hint of a smile on his friend's face. They had talked about whether Mick was going to play college ball only a couple of days ago. At that time, Mick was still wavering as to what to do. "When did you decide this?"

"Last night when I was in bed. I was going to call you but it was after midnight."

"Are you okay with not playing?"

"Before I made up my mind, I was lying there all bummed

out. I couldn't sleep." Mick picked up another chunk of snow and threw it at a light pole about ten feet ahead of them, merely grazing it. "Once I decided, I felt relieved. Trouble then I was so excited that I'd finally made a decision that I couldn't get to sleep."

"What do you think Mary will say?"

"She'll be supportive. I'm going to talk to her today at lunch. That means you're going to have to put up with Howie."

"I'll manage."

Mick stopped in front of the hardware store and pointed to a poster of this past year's football schedule for North High taped to the bottom right-hand corner of the window. The black print of the once shiny poster had faded by the sun. "Look at that! That thing's fading just like my football career."

They stared at the poster in silence before starting for school again. "How's your dad going to react to all of this?" Adam asked.

"I'll soon find out. He took this afternoon off for a dental appointment. Probably be home when I get there after school. I'll tell him then. I'm not looking forward to it, though." Mick picked up another chunk of snow and slung it at a lamppost, barely missing it.

"What do you think he's going to say?"

"Man, I don't know, but he won't be happy. I'm pretty sure he suspects something, but he hasn't mentioned it."

"How can you tell?"

"By how quiet he's been. He and mom give each other these looks whenever one of my brothers asks me if I've decided where I'm playing football next year. Ever since the last game of the season, he can't figure out why I haven't selected a college yet. He's really been on my case the past couple of weeks to check some out."

"Didn't you get a couple of letters from college coaches?"

"Yeah. They wanted to talk to me about playing football on a scholarship. Didn't make any firm offers, though." Mick grabbed a chunk of snow and hurled it at a street sign, missing it by a wide margin. "My father was higher than a kite about those letters. He can't understand why I haven't wanted to contact the coaches."

"What did you tell him?"

"That it's a big decision and I have to take my time. That always settles him down for a few days." Mick picked up another chunk of snow, looked at Adam, and then pointed to a *No Parking* sign attached to a streetlight a good twenty feet away.

"No way," Adam said.

The snow chunk hit the sign dead center. Mick pumped his arm in triumphant.

For the next half block the two of them joked and laughed as they tossed chunks of snow at a variety of targets.

"You should've been over at my house the other night," Mick said, after heaving a chunk of snow at a fire hydrant. "All I heard at the supper table was my father talking about how I'll be the first one in the family to play college football. I almost told him then that I was thinking about not playing."

"Why didn't you?"

"Because my two brothers were there and I knew they wouldn't understand," Mick said in a tone mixed with anger and sadness. "I sure didn't want the three of them on my case."

"Wouldn't your mom understand?"

"I think so, but she'd be afraid to say anything because of my father. He's the boss in the family and makes sure everybody knows it."

"How come your brothers didn't go to college to play ball? Weren't they pretty good?"

Mick laughed. "Those two were stars on the football field, but in the classroom they were goof-offs. What's sad about it is that they really regret blowing their chances. They wouldn't admit to it, but I know them. They would've loved to have played college ball. That's why they're pushing me so hard. They want me to make up for what they missed out on."

"Sounds like they'd get ticked at you for having the chance and not going with it."

"You got it. Last year at some family outing, I was just kidding around with my oldest brother, Joey, about me not going out for college ball. Man, did he get angry. Told me not to joke about it; it was a chance of a lifetime and I better not screw it up."

"Wow!"

"Yeah, wow is right."

"So, what's the name of this college you're going to?"

"Belmont."

"Belmont? That sounds like a school for girls."

Mick scooped up some snow and playfully threatened Adam. He grinned and tossed the snow aside. "Belmont's a small college in Wisconsin that specializes in education. Has a great reputation for turning out some of the best teachers in the Midwest, and believe it or not, I hope to be one of those teachers."

"I suppose then, I'm going to have to call you Mr. Brunner."

Mick laughed. "And if you don't, you'll be sent to the principal's office. Hey, the bakery's in the next block. I'll buy to celebrate my decision."

"Sounds good to me, *Mr. Brunner*."

When they entered the bakery, the warmth coming from the back room ovens rushed over their faces, bringing with it the aroma of freshly baked rolls. The display cases, stocked with glazed donuts, chocolate éclairs, huge cinnamon rolls, and a variety of other delicious pastries, beckoned to their stomachs.

After getting cinnamon rolls, they moved over to the window and ate while looking out at the traffic. Mick continued to share his anxiety about telling his father, confessing that he didn't know how his father would react, but he was expecting the worst.

"How's your grandfather doing?" Mick asked when they left the bakery.

Adam had already shared with Mick that Frank had been involved. "This whole thing has really aged him."

"How old is he anyway?"

"Don't exactly know." His last birthday party had been when he turned sixty-five. *Was that three or four years ago?* After that party, his grandfather announced that he didn't want another one until he was seventy. Adam never understood why. When he had asked his mother about it, all she did was shrug and say that he was like that some times. "He must be sixty-eight or sixty-nine," Adam guessed.

"That's pretty old, especially when you're dealing with

pneumonia."

"I know. The doctor said the older you are, the tougher it is."

"If Frank had something to do with it, you must be pretty ticked off at him. I'd think your grandfather would be too. Aren't you always telling me how he wants to kick Frank's ass?"

"I know, but something's different this time."

"How so?"

"He isn't mad at Frank. Do you know what he said to me? He said that *I* shouldn't be angry with him either."

"Really? He said that?"

"Yeah, can you believe it? I never thought I'd hear something like that coming from him. Not after some of the things I've heard him say about Frank. Maybe something happened to his mind when he was out in the cold for so long. Do you think that's possible?"

"Don't think so. It's got to be something more than that. Maybe he doesn't have the energy to be angry right now. When he gets better, he'll be his normal self and then he'll feel liking kicking Frank's ass again."

"I don't know. He's changed. There's this old pocket watch he got from one of his friends. Cleaning it up, he uncovered an inscription. It has something to do with all this, but I'm not sure. All I know is that there's something different about him."

"What do you mean, different?"

"Can't exactly put it in words, but the thing about not being angry with Frank is an example."

"Sounds like that watch has something to do with it all right." They walked passed a couple of stores before Mick asked, "What does the inscription say?"

"Don't know. He won't tell me. The watch is for my graduation. He says that I have to wait until then."

As they approached the curb, the stoplight flashed to yellow. "Come on!" Mick shouted. "We can make it." They dashed across, reaching the other side just after the light turned red. "You know," Mick said. "What your grandfather told you about not being angry with Frank isn't all that crazy."

"I don't follow you."

"Maybe he was saying what Middleton spent so much time talking about last year in Psychology."

"What was that?"

"She was talking about human emotions." Mick looked at the overcast sky as though he would pull the answers down from the clouds. "Getting angry at someone is natural and that it's okay to have such feelings."

"Glad to know I'm normal, then."

"That remains to be seen," Mick said, making no attempt to hide a grin. "She also said that what we have to be careful of is hanging onto the anger. I think what she was getting at is if we keep the anger and don't let go of it, then we are letting the other person control us."

"Not sure if I follow you."

"I'll use an example from football. There was this sophomore kid who began this past year starting at left guard. He was big and pretty good."

"Was that Lewinski?"

"Yeah, and he had terrific potential. Only problem was he let the opposing teams get him angry. In the line they'd call him names and make cracks about his mother and stuff like that. He'd get so angry by halfway through the first quarter that he played the rest of the game according to his anger rather than his ability. When he let his anger get the best of him, he was lousy. The other team pushed him all over the place. He also caused penalties and he screwed up on blocking assignments. Got so bad that the coach had to move him to second string. Rumor is that he's decided not to go out for football next year."

"So what you're saying is that if you let someone keep you angry all the time, you can't be yourself?"

"Yeah, something like that. Reason you can't be yourself is because you're letting the other guy control you by keeping you angry. Maybe that's what your grandfather meant. If you let Frank keep making you angry all the time, then the guy is controlling you."

The two of them walked for nearly a block before Adam responded. "Let me tell you, I almost lost it."

"What do you mean?"

"Remember that I told you that my grandfather said that he and Frank were drinking whiskey that day he got frostbite?"

Mick nodded.

"The way I figure it, Frank got him drunk on purpose."

"Are you sure?"

"Yeah. I was so mad after seeing my grandfather at the hospital that night that I was ready to punch Frank out the minute I saw him. All I could think of was what he'd done. I knew I had to cool down so I stopped to talk with Kass."

"Good. I bet that helped."

"It did. Kass is a pretty neat guy. By the time I left, I was feeling better. I was still angry, but not as much. He made me think more about what my Grandfather meant about not being angry." Adam shook his head. "But wouldn't you know it, as soon as I left Kass' and headed for home, here comes Frank walking in my direction."

Mick let out a low whistle.

"You got that right. When Frank saw me, he got that stupid grin he always gets. I could see those big yellow teeth of his. Man, I forgot all about what Kass said. I thought that right then, we were going to have it out." Adam stopped and grabbed Mick's arm for a moment. "I tell you, I got ticked off at the guy all over again. Felt like stomping his face into the sidewalk." He paused, his breaths coming hard and fast. "Frank stops me in the middle of the sidewalk and wants to talk. You know, as if we're buddies or something. Starts asking me about how my grandfather is, like he really cares. The jerk! All the time he's talking, I'm looking at those teeth, thinking he should lose a couple more."

"Do you think he suspected that your grandfather said something about him?"

"He didn't have to. I could see it in his eyes. He was trying to bait me, like he wanted me to take a swing. I felt like punching him out, but I didn't."

"Why not?"

"Man, I don't know. When I walked away I thought I was doing pretty good, but then Frank shouted something that got to me."

"What'd he say?"

"That my grandfather was too dumb to know when to come out of the cold." Adam felt a rush of anger as he recalled Frank's words. "When I heard that, I froze in my tracks. Just stood there, knowing that he was back there grinning. Had to keep telling myself what my grandfather said, and what Kass and I talked about. I bit my lip so hard I could taste the blood. Came close to turning around and going after him. Not sure what stopped me."

Mick didn't say a word for several moments. "Hey, buddy."

"Yeah?"

"Your grandfather would be proud of you. I'm not even a relative, and I'm proud of you."

"Thanks," Adam replied, glad to have Mick as a friend. "By the time I got home, though, I was boiling mad. Not sure what I'll do the next time. I just want to avoid the guy."

"You tell me if I sound like a teacher now," Mick said. "Here's my advice. Don't do anything dumb that you'll regret. You don't want to lower yourself to the same level as Frank. That jerk isn't worth it. If you need help, you know Howie and me are there for you."

"I'm understanding that more and more. Can I tell you something else?"

"What?"

"You *are* sounding more and more like a teacher." Adam grinned. "Come on. Let's get going."

They crossed the street and came in sight of North High. Mick announced, "As old Howie would say, 'there's our beloved school.'"

Chapter 35

The hallways of North High that morning were filled with the usual sights and sounds. Lockers slamming. Boys combing their ducktails and primping before pocketsize mirrors attached to the inside of their locker doors. Outbursts of laughter whenever someone dropped their notebook and sent papers flying. Students anxiously working and reworking their combination locks, hoping they wouldn't be late for their next class. Dates being made for the weekend. Teachers checking the bathrooms for cigarette smoke. Class bells ringing. The din was repeated throughout the morning, reaching its peak during lunch period.

Adam and Howie were sitting in the lunchroom when Mick walked up, looking tired. "Hi guys. I'm not staying long. I need to borrow some money to get some milk for Mary and me."

"Sure thing." Howie handed Mick a couple of quarters. "Will this be enough?"

"Great, I'll pay you Monday." Mick turned to walk away.

"Wait a second," Howie said. He tore a page from his notebook. "Adam, quick, tell me. At three percent daily compounded interest, what does that add up to on fifty cents for five days?" He offered Mick a winsome smile. "No, make that four days. He's a friend."

Mick's eyes narrowed. "While you're at it, figure what it'd be on a buck that was borrowed three months ago and written off to bad debts, but being reconsidered now."

"Oh, oh. I forgot about that." Howie crumpled up the paper and tossed it behind him.

"Look guys. I can't stay. See you later. Adam, say hello to your grandfather for me. Tell him I hope he gets better."

"Thanks."

"Can you wait one more second, Mick?" Howie pleaded. "I was going to outline the plans for the St. Valentine's Day

Caper."

"The what?" Mick asked.

"You know, next Saturday night," Howie whispered. He tore out another sheet of paper. "The Valentine Day Dance…Mattingale's desk…the secret."

Mick pointed to Adam. "Tell *him* about it. He's anxious to hear the details of one of your capers." Howie started to protest, but Mick cut him off. "Look, I really have to go and talk to Mary. She's waiting for me."

"Go ahead." Adam gave Mick a nudge. After their friend left, he turned to Howie. "Okay. Let's hear about it."

Howie glanced around, leaned over the table, and spoke in hushed tones. "This is going to be the best. First we drive two cars to the dance, and then we park one a couple blocks away so it..."

* * *

To Mary, Mick looked more tired than he did a couple of nights ago when he had talked to her about the decision he had to make. The two of them had talked many times as to what he should do about playing college ball. She listened, asked questions that helped him clarify his thoughts, and promised support to whatever decision he would make. She had also told him, however, that she felt his education should come first.

"Where's your lunch?" she asked as he sat down.

He placed three pints of milk on the table. "One of these is for you. The other two are my lunch."

"You have to have more than that for lunch," she gently scolded.

"I had a cinnamon roll this morning." Mick paused. "I'm going to attend that teacher's college."

"I thought you would," she said with pride.

"I decided last night." He opened one of the pints of milk and took a couple of swallows.

"It's the right decision. I'm happy for you."

"I doubt if my father will be."

"I'm so sorry," Mary said, angry with his father. From the first time she had met Mick's father, she didn't like him. His father thought God created the world for men and football. Every time she had been at Mick's house, his mother waited on Mick's father for everything. "Do you think there's any chance of him understanding about you wanting to be a teacher?" she asked.

"Being a teacher isn't the problem as long as I play football. I can just hear him now," he said, mocking his father's voice. "'You can always teach, but you won't always be able to play football.' I'm afraid he'll think I'm betraying the family by not playing. Probably disown me."

Mary took hold of his hand. If they hadn't been in the lunchroom, she would have given him a reassuring hug. "He wouldn't do that. I know your father. It'll be hard on him, but I think he'll come around. He'll be proud of you whether you play football or not," she said, trying to sound confident.

Mick gave her a knowing smile. She knew what that meant. Neither one of them knew for sure what his father would do. Mick had told her once that he couldn't remember his father ever expressing how proud he was of him apart from having it be connected with football. "We've always had a pretty decent relationship," Mick said, adding with an anguished look, "I wouldn't want anything to happen to it."

For the rest of the lunch period the two of them talked about future plans and how great that both of them were planning to be teachers. Mary could tell that although Mick was excited about teaching, his decision was bittersweet.

"You'll call me tonight, won't you? I want to know what he says."

Mick opened his second carton of milk. "I will."

* * *

Adam looked for Mick when school let out, but didn't see him. When he asked Howie, he was told that Mick had left.

"He rushed out," Howie said. "Wasn't his normal self today. He's worried about what his dad's going to say."

After Adam got home, he and his mother went up to the hospital. Although his grandfather appeared stronger, the nurse at the desk said that there had been no change in his condition. His grandfather managed a weak smile when he and his mother entered the room. She sat by the bed while Adam stood along side of it.

"Hi, Grandpa."

"Glad see you," he replied, offering a weak half smile.

"Pa, I got so worried when Butch told me about the pneumonia. I'm sorry I haven't been to see you. How are you?"

"Ack, just bad cough. Doctor fix."

"What did he say today?"

"Don't remember."

"You mean you don't want to tell me."

When Adam glanced at his mother, she appeared anxious and upset. He wasn't sure if it was because of his grandfather's stubbornness, or her being in a hospital. She had told him in the car on the way that she was happy to see her father, but didn't know how long she would stay because of the bad memories associated with hospitals.

"I thought I saw Doctor Jairvus coming down the hall just as we came in," Adam said, hoping that she could get her questions answered quickly. "He's probably at the nurses' station."

"Oh, good, I want to talk to him." She kissed her father on the forehead. "I'll be right back. You and Butch talk."

After his mother left, Adam sat down. His grandfather's color looked better and his eyes seemed brighter. "You seem a little stronger today. Are you?"

"A little."

"How did you sleep last night?"

"Sleep some. Cough some. Nurse in. Nurse out."

Adam struggled whether or not he should bring up Frank. "You told me that Frank was home that morning and that the two of you were drinking. Where did you get the whiskey?"

"Frank get whiskey. I drink."

"You mean it was Frank who got it?" Adam felt the anger rising.

"He offer. I take." His grandfather paused. "Remember. No anger."

"But he purposely gave you the whiskey!" Adam cried as he stood up, shoving the chair back. "Frank knew it was freezing out and he didn't stop you from going out. He even let you go out with a light jacket. How could he…I hate him!"

"Butch, no talk hate." He reached out toward him, waiting until his grandson took hold of his hand. "Not good. Anger. Hate. I know, not good."

"Aren't you angry?"

"Anger no good."

When his grandfather tightened his grip on his hand, Adam was amazed at how strong of a grip he had. The two of them fell silent as a siren could be heard in the distance. The wailing grew as the seconds past.

"Butch?"

"Yeah?"

"Promise not fight Frank."

"But what if he does something again?"

"Anger, no good. Promise." His grandfather grimaced as he began coughing. He released his grip as he clutched his chest.

Adam agonized how he could promise something like that, especially how Frank had tried to bait him into a fight. After the coughing stopped, his grandfather's eyes met his, seeking an answer. "I promise," Adam said.

"Good," his grandfather whispered and motioned toward the cup of water on the nightstand. After a sip, he gave it back. "Enough."

"Is there anything I can bring you? Anything you want from home?"

The frail man shook his head. He looked like he was fighting to keep his eyes open.

"Go ahead, Grandpa. Take a nap. I'll just sit here and be quiet. Don't worry about me."

His grandfather smiled, and within a couple of minutes was asleep. Adam sat there, wondering what his mother and the doctor were talking about. He got up and went over to the window. Across the street was a small park. Kids were skating. It brought back the memory of his first skates. His grandfather had bought them with money he had gotten from a clock he had repaired for a friend. Adam watched the kids for a while before going back and sitting down. His grandfather was still asleep. Within a few minutes the door opened and his mother came back.

"Is he asleep?" she asked.

"Yeah." Adam offered her his chair. "Here. Sit down." When his mother sat, he moved to the foot of the bed. "What did the doctor say?" he asked.

"Pretty much the same thing he told you. He emphasized that with Pa's age and history of emphysema, pneumonia isn't good."

"Anything else?"

"Pa told him that he thinks that the insides of the human body must be like the inner workings of a clock. Doctor Jairus said that he made a good analogy about how when one part of the clock isn't working, it affects other parts." Her voice trembled. She blinked back tears. "Sounds like they were getting along pretty good."

Adam stood listening to his grandfather's shallow breathing.

They stayed for another fifteen minutes before his mother decided that they should leave. On the drive home, both were quiet. Adam wondered if he could keep the promise he had made.

Chapter 36

Adam was worried. It was already ten minutes past the time that Mick usually met him on the corner to walk to school. He waited another few minutes before heading out. Howie would be waiting for him. Making up for lost time, he ran the first three blocks and walked the last two. Howie was leaning against a light pole and looking at a book when he came upon him.

"Where's Mick?" Howie asked.

"Don't know." Adam looked back, hoping to see their friend. "Never showed up."

Howie closed his book. "Hmmm. Not a good sign. Wonder how it worked out with his father last night."

"We'll find out first hour when we see him. Come on, we better hustle or we'll be late."

"How's your grandfather?" Howie asked as they started for school.

"He seemed a little better last night."

Howie asked for his grandfather's hospital room number, explaining that his father wanted to send a card.

Touched that Howie's father would do that, Adam told Howie to be sure and thank him. The conversation turned to Mick and his decision not to play football.

"I give Mick a lot of credit for being willing to stand up against his family," Howie said. "He'll be a good teacher, too. I just know it. So will Mary. They'll probably end up getting married and teach at the same school."

"Yeah, and have ten kids," Adam added.

Howie shifted his books from one arm to the other. "You know, it's hard to believe that school's going to be done in four months. Man, it's gone fast. Have you decided what you're going to do after graduation?"

"Haven't given it much thought."

"How about college?"

"Not in the cards."

"How come?"

"Money, mostly. My grades are okay, but not good enough for any kind of scholarship." Adam glanced behind them to see if Mick was coming. "The biggest thing is that I wouldn't know what I'd take if I did go to college. Right now, my life is too messed up. You know what I mean? College wouldn't be a good idea. How about you?"

"You won't laugh if I tell you, will you?"

"Did Mick laugh?"

"He doesn't know yet."

"Go ahead. Tell me. I promise I won't laugh."

"I'm thinking about becoming a P.I."

"A what?"

"A private investigator! A detective! You know, like Humphrey Bogart was in the movie *The Maltese Falcon.*"

Adam tried to swallow a chuckle.

"Come on, you said you wouldn't laugh."

"I'm just trying to picture you as a Humphrey Bogart-like detective. So tell me how this came about?"

"Mattingale."

"You're kidding."

"Well, it wasn't because of her exactly, but her desk. Remember when we did the smoke bomb?"

"How can I forget that?"

"When I went to light it, I noticed that the matchbook cover advertised a correspondence course for becoming a P.I. Can you believe that! Man, right there and then, I decided to send for some information. It hasn't come yet, but I'm anxious to get it and see what it says."

"You know what, Howie? You never cease to amaze me."

They made it to their homerooms before the second bell rang. After the homeroom ended, they hurried to Mattingale's classroom hoping to see Mick. His chair, however, was empty and remained that way when the bell rang to begin the class period.

It wasn't until lunch that Mick finally showed up. Adam and Howie were sitting at the table when Mick walked up to them.

"Hi, guys. Did you miss me?"

“What’s going on?” Adam asked.

“I told my father last night.” Mick’s voice sounded as weary as he looked. “I knew he’d be upset, but man, he really got ticked off. We had this big blow out. My mom was crying. My brothers were yelling at me. It was a mess.”

“Your brothers didn’t understand at all?” Howie asked incredulously.

“Nope.” Mick reached into Howie’s lunch bag and pulled out a sandwich, unwrapped it, and took a bite. “I’d hoped my brothers would understand, but they didn’t. They thought I was betraying the Brunner family football tradition. My father was so mad that he stormed off, saying he didn’t want to talk about it.”

“Sorry you had to go through that,” Adam said.

“Me, too,” Howie added.

“Thanks, guys. I barely slept all night. This morning, my father comes into my room and says let’s go out for breakfast. I think to myself that, hey, maybe he’s changed and can see it my way. We get in the restaurant and the first thing he does is to apologize for blowing up like he did.”

“That’s good,” Adam said.

“Yeah, that’s what I thought. So we order our food and as we’re waiting for it, he starts in on me. He tells me that he understands my problem. I’m sitting there trying to figure out what’s he talking about. Then he says that he’d pay for a tutor during football season.”

“I don’t get it,” Adam said.

“Neither did I. So I ask him, ‘What are you talking about?’ Before he answered, the food came and he tells me that we should eat first. He’s eating and I’m sitting there, staring at him, and not touching my food.”

“Pretty soon, he looks at me and says, ‘What’s the matter? Aren’t you hungry?’ I almost exploded. I asked him what’s this problem I’m supposed to have?”

“And what did he say?” Howie asked.

“That he knows I’m worried that football would take away from my studies in college so that I wouldn’t get the grades I wanted. That’s no problem now, he says, because he decided that he’d pay for a tutor during football season. He even said he thought that one of those college coaches might agree to include that in a football scholarship if I got one. After all that crap, he tells me to eat up."

"What did you tell him?" Howie asked.

"I tried to keep my cool. I explained to him again as plainly as I could that I didn't have any interest in football anymore."

Adam leaned forward. "What did he say to that?"

"Can you believe that he looked at me in a way that I got the feeling that he was trying to figure out if this was really his son talking." Mick picked up his sandwich, looked at it, and put it back down again. "Football's such a big deal in his life that he can't understand why anyone would walk away from it."

Howie opened up his lunch bag and took out a sandwich. "So, what happened after that?"

"On the way driving me to school, he was pretty quiet. I knew he was even angrier with me." Mick looked across the lunchroom. "Guys, I got to go over and talk to Mary now. I called her last night after the blow up, but she doesn't know about this morning."

"Are you going to meet us after school to walk home?" Howie asked.

"No, I'm going to stay after and check some things out with a couple of the teachers. I'll see you guys later."

"Do you think your dad will come around?" Adam asked.

Mick didn't respond. He didn't have to. The look on his face said it all.

* * *

Around the time the three o'clock bell rang at North High, the phone rang at Danny Logan's house.

Danny answered it on the first ring. "Hell, Pete, about time ya called. Told ya to call early afternoon." Danny listened with impatience to Pete's excuses. "Hey, I don't have time to listen to all this shit. My old man may be home any minute. Look, call Johnny and the two of ya meet me Wednesday night in the alley in back of Skelly's Liquor Store. Nine o'clock. Yeah, I got somethin' to show ya guys." When Pete asked what it was, Danny wouldn't tell him. He wanted to see the expression on his and Johnny's faces when they saw it. "Man, I tell ya," Danny bragged, “we’re goin’ to be in business. Listen. Be on time. I don’t want to be out there freezin’ my ass off waitin’ for ya. Catch ya later.”

After Danny hung up, he went to his room and opened his closet door. He reached up behind some boxes and felt to see if the gun was still there. He took it down and held it in his hand. The handle fit into the palm of his hand perfectly, like it was made for him. Having the gun gave him a sense of power. He was standing in front of the mirror holding the gun when he heard the downstairs front door open. He quickly put the gun back, and shut the closet door.

Chapter 37

Late Wednesday afternoon Adam met Mick and Howie at the soda fountain at Kass'. Nearly a week had gone by since Mick had shared with his family his decision not to play football. On the way to school that morning, he told Adam and Howie that his father had hardly spoken a word to him all week.

"Can you believe it?" Mick exclaimed, taking a seat next to Adam. He leaned forward and pointed to Howie sitting on the other side of Adam. "Our friend there is actually treating."

"Do you think we should pinch ourselves? This could be a dream."

"Hey, you two, don't knock my generosity. It's the only way I can get you guys together to finalize Operation Cupid."

"That name has got to go," Adam said. "Can't you think of a better code name than that?"

Mick grinned. "Oh, I don't know, Adam. I like it. It rhymes with stupid."

"Don't push it guys."

"Boys, boys," Kass said, standing behind the counter rinsing out glasses. "What's all this fighting about?"

"They're giving me a hard time because I'm treating them to banana splits," Howie said.

Kass' eyes widened. "You are!"

Howie groaned. "Not you, too?"

"Just kidding. Allow an old man like me to have some fun. Keeps me young. Let me fix you the best banana splits on Broadway." Kass began peeling the bananas; his back turned to the boys.

Mick placed his elbow on the counter and rested his chin in the palm of his hand as he looked over at Howie. "Okay, let's hear the plan."

Howie put his finger up to his lips, mouthed *shhh*, and then pointed to Kass.

"Don't worry, Howie," Kass said without turning around. "I'll let you boys talk as soon as I'm done with these."

"How…how did you know?" Howie stammered, his mouth dropping open.

"I could tell you that I've eyes in the back of my head, but I'll just remind you that this wall in front of me is one big mirror. And Howie?"

"Yeah?"

"Change the code name or everybody will know it's going to take place this Saturday at the school dance."

Mick snickered. "Man, has he got you pegged."

"But how did he—"

"Think about it," Adam said. "What comes to mind when you hear the word, Cupid?"

"Besides, stupid," Mick pointed out.

"Oh, man," Howie moaned. "It's a dead give-a-way, isn't it?"

"It sure is," Kass said. "All I've been hearing from the kids the past couple of days is who's taking who to the big Valentine Day Dance this Saturday at the school. Change the code name," he advised as he topped the banana splits with whipped cream.

"But to what?" Howie looked to Mick and Adam for help.

Kass placed the first of his creations in front of Howie. "Why not, Operation Banana Split? There are three different kinds of ice cream and three of you. One of you can be chocolate, one vanilla, and the other strawberry. Each of you can have a code name."

"Hey, I like that," Howie said as Kass gave Mick and Adam their splits. He picked up his spoon and gestured toward Kass. "How would you like to be part of this operation? You could have the code name Top Banana."

Kass laughed. "I don't think so." He gave each of them napkins and a glass of water. "You boys eat. I'm going up front and leave you alone."

"He's a neat guy," Mick said, looking over at Howie as Kass walked away. "Go ahead, now. Let's hear this plan."

"Just a minute," Howie mumbled after shoveling a spoonful of ice cream and banana into his mouth. "Okay, I'm ready. Now, listen up. This Saturday we're going to have to take two cars.

My dad said I can use the car. And Mick, you're still getting your dad's car, aren't you?"

"A couple of months ago my father promised that I could use the car, but now, I don't know." Mick paused. "Heck, don't worry about it. He's always been good on his word. Yeah, I'll be driving."

"Good. Here's how it goes then. You and Mary, Adam and Sue, will follow me and Cindy. I'll park a couple blocks away from school over on Girard."

"Why there?" Adam asked.

Howie smiled slyly. "Quite a few people park their cars on that street so one more won't be that noticeable. After we park, we'll get in with you guys and then drive to the dance. So far, so good." He gulped down a couple more spoonfuls of ice cream. "Mick, after the dance, Mary will drive your car to her house. She'll take Sue and Cindy home first."

Mick gave both Adam and Howie a puzzled look. "Where are we going to be?"

"The furnace room," Adam said dryly.

"What furnace room?"

"Ask him."

"What's this about a furnace room?"

Howie held up his hand to signal to wait until he was done with the spoonful of ice cream he had just put in his mouth. He picked up the cherry, showed it to his friends, popped it in his mouth, and chewed it slowly. When finished, he grinned at Mick. "The furnace room is where we're going to hide until the dance clears out."

"We're going to hide in the furnace room?"

"Hey! It's the perfect place. The teachers will be checking the hallways and the bathrooms. They'll never think to look there."

Mick wrinkled his nose. "How long are we going to be stuck in there?"

"Don't worry. The dance is over at eleven. We'll only have to be there for an hour or so. By then, the teachers and chaperones would've gone home. Shortly after midnight we'll come out, go up to Mattingale's room, do the desk drawer, and be out of there in a flash. We'll go to my car, drive to Mary's house, and get your car."

"How do I explain being out that late?" Mick asked. "I got enough troubles at home already."

"Easy. We'll just tell our parents that we're staying overnight at each other's houses."

"Whose house am I suppose to be staying at?"

"You tell your parents you're staying with me. Adam will tell his mom that he's staying at your house."

"But what if they find out?"

"They won't," Howie said confidently. "Trust me. They're parents."

Mick gave Adam a bewildering look. "So the three of us just walk out of the dance and leave the girls by themselves? Won't that look suspicious?"

Adam shrugged. "Howie's the mastermind of this thing. I'll let him answer."

"Don't worry about that, I've worked that out."

"Yeah? So tell me."

Howie nudged Adam. "Come on, don't be modest. You know the plan. Why don't you tell him?"

Adam cleared his throat. "According to *his* plan, we'll go out as couples. The guy will go to the furnace room while the girl goes out to the car and waits for the others. We'll do it at five minute intervals. Right, Howie?"

"You've got it!" Howie's eyebrows rose. "See, Mick. It's perfect. What can go wrong?"

Mick and Adam exchanged questioning looks. Howie sat with a smug smile plastered on his face while his friends finished their banana splits. At one point, Adam noticed Howie scribbling something on a napkin, and stuffing the napkin in his jacket pocket.

After Mick and Adam finished eating, the conversation turned toward Mick. He told them that he and Mary had a good talk last night, and he was feeling better about his decision even though his father's attitude hadn't changed.

After a while, Kass rejoined them. "I see you boys are finished."

"They were terrific," Howie said.

"Good, I'm glad you liked them. Can I get you boys

anything else?"

Adam shook his head. "I'm full."

"So am I," Mick said.

"What about you?"

Howie's face lit up like a neon sign. "I got this scheme to make you a million dollars," he said, barely able to contain his excitement.

Kass looked at Mick and Adam, but both shrugged their shoulders. "Okay. So tell me. How am I going to get so rich?"

Howie pulled out the napkin he had stuffed in his pocket and smoothed it out in front of him on the counter. "I've got it all figured out. All you have to do is put up a sign advertising your banana splits." He gestured toward the wall in back of Kass, drawing an imaginary sign in the air. "Buy one at full price. Buy the second at half price."

Kass glanced back at the imaginary sign. "And I suppose you'd be the first customer?"

Mick and Adam looked at one another, smiled, and got up to leave.

"Where are you guys going?" Howie asked.

"We've already heard enough of your schemes for today," Mick said. "See you, Kass."

"Watch yourself, Kass," Adam warned, nodding toward Howie.

"I'll do that. You two have a good evening."

As Mick and Adam opened the door to go out, Adam looked back and saw a grinning Kass watching Howie scribbling on another napkin.

* * *

It was ten minutes after nine that Wednesday evening when Danny Logan looked at his watch. "Shit, where are those guys?" Placing his hand on the side of his leather jacket, he felt the gun tucked in his pants, pressing against his body. He smiled, thinking about how cool it would be to point it at somebody and see the fear in their eyes when Pete and Johnny walked up.

"I told ya guys, nine!" he snarled, tired of them always being late. He liked for people to be on time; it was a matter of respect.

When people showed up late, he took it personally. “Next time, I’m not waitin’.”

“It was his fault,” Johnny whined as he pointed at Pete.

“Ah, hell,” Pete said, giving Johnny a dirty look. “It ain’t my fault. My old man and I got into it. He wasn’t goin’ to let me out of the house.”

“What did ya tell him?” Danny asked.

“Told him I’m goin’. He don’t care, anyway. Just wants to put on a tough man act.”

“What have ya got to show us?” Johnny asked.

Danny unzipped his jacket. Tucked in his belt on his right side was the gun.

“Man, is that real?” Pete asked.

“Shit, yes,” Danny said. He couldn’t believe that Pete could be so stupid at times. “What do ya think it is, a cap gun?”

“Is it loaded?” Johnny asked.

“It will be.”

Pete reached out. “Can I hold it?”

Danny slapped Pete’s hand away. “I can’t be takin’ it out around here,” he snarled as he zipped up his jacket.

Johnny pulled out a pack of smokes and offered one to Danny. “What are ya goin’ to do with it?”

“Ya know that grocery store on fifth and Colfax?”

“Ya mean, Kelly’s?” Pete asked as he gave Johnny a nervous glance.

“Yeah. We’re goin’ to pay Kelly’s a visit.”

“What!” Pete exclaimed.

“Ya chicken shit or somethin’?” Johnny said. “We did Kass’, didn’t we?”

“Don’t call me chicken shit.” Pete glared at his accuser. “Yeah, we did Kass’, but we didn’t know he was there.” He looked at Danny. “Ain’t goin’ to be the same thing at Kelly’s. Goin’ to be someone workin’, and there’ll be customers.”

“Hey, man, don’t sweat it.” Danny patted the bulge in his jacket. “Got the equalizer right here. Nobody’s goin’to mess with us. Pete, ya get your old man’s car. You’re the driver. Johnny and me will go in before it closes.”

“What time is that?” Johnny asked.

“Eleven.” Danny shot Pete a smirk. He needed Pete with

them because he had the wheels. "If we're lucky, there won't be any customers then. If there is, we'll just wait until they leave, and if they don't leave, we'll handle it." He tapped Johnny on the chest. "Get yourself a ski mask to cover up that ugly puss of yours. We'll go in, get the money, and split. Simple as that."

"I'm bringin' Mickey Mantle," Johnny said.

"We've got this now." Danny pointed to the bulge in his jacket. "Why do ya want to bring that for?"

"Man, to hit a home run with the clerk. Then we don't have to worry about him followin' us."

Danny nodded. "Hey, that's good. Like that. Go ahead and bring it."

"When are we goin' to do this?" Pete asked.

"This Saturday."

"That's when the school's havin' their Valentine Dance," Pete said.

"That gives me an idea," Danny said. "Johnny, after ya do the clerk, we'll tape a Valentine to his forehead. Wouldn't that be cool?"

"Yeah, man, let's do it."

"Okay," Danny said. "Let's split for now. Catch you later."

Chapter 38

Frank was sitting on the couch with his feet up on the coffee table when Wanda came home from work. Watching a television game show, he was just finishing his third beer. A half full bag of potato chips sat in his lap. That morning he had walked four blocks over to the warehouse on Washington Avenue. Wanda had told him that there were job openings and thought that he might like to go and apply. Since he didn't have anything else to do that morning, he decided to check it out. After he got there, he found out that there was one job available and that it was his for the asking. The job required loading and unloading trucks and he would have to start at six in the morning.

"Take your job and shove it," he had told the guy. "I ain't gettin' up with the goddamn birds to work on any damn trucks." For the rest of the day, he felt angry with Wanda for having sent him on a wild goose chase.

"About time, ya got here," Frank complained. "I'm goddamn hungry."

"Frank, I just got home. I'll fix you something as soon as I can." She slipped her coat off. "Did you check on that job?"

"Hell, went over there but there was nothin' for me. Guy said he'd let me know if anythin' came up."

"That's too bad. Did you look through the paper for any other jobs?" When Frank didn't respond, she went into the kitchen. Within a short time, she stepped back into the living room. "Did you hear what I asked? About whether—"

"For Christ's sake, get off my back!"

"I'm sorry, but you haven't worked for nearly three months now," she said timidly. "We're barely making it with my take-home pay, and if it wasn't for the overtime I put in every week, we'd be losing ground."

"Goddamn it!" Frank glared at what he had come to regard as one of the homeliest women he had ever seen. He thought about getting up and slapping her, but held back. If he belted her now, she probably wouldn't make supper. "Ya blamin' me now?" he snarled.

"No, dear, I know you try hard."

"Ya damn right I do. Now, get me some food."

"After I get your supper, I'm going up to see Pa. The doctor said if he continues to make progress, he might come home next week. Won't that be nice?"

"Yeah. Terrific. Why the hell do ya have to go up? Why can't your sister go?"

"She went last night and tonight she has to go into work early because someone is sick."

"Let Butchie go."

"He's going to a school dance. You know, it's hard to believe that Butch is going to be graduating from high school in a few months. He's such a good kid and works so hard. I think—"

"Goddamn it! Butchie this. Butchie that. I suppose he works hard and I don't. That's what ya think, don't ya?"

"I didn't say that. I only—"

"Just get me my supper and let me watch my program in peace. Make yourself useful and get me a beer." He tossed the bag of potatoes chips on the coffee table. "Must have been drunk when I married her," he muttered.

* * *

The Valentine Day Dance was to be held in the school lunchroom. The janitors had spent that afternoon folding the lunchroom tables and storing them. While the tables were being taken down, a committee of teachers and students went to work. The walls were decorated with blue-eyed, rosy-cheeked cupids, red hearts with arrows stuck through them, and an assortment of Valentine Day cards. Red and white crepe paper twisted together draped from one fluorescent light fixture to another, casting a pinkish glow to the room. Round card tables were brought in and covered with red tablecloths. Serving tables were against one wall. On the tables sat two large glass punch bowls containing the head cook's special recipe for fruit punch. A teacher had been assigned to guard the punch bowls to make sure that the only thing that was added was ice. Heart-shaped cookies decorated with red-hot candies sat on trays next to the punch. The music for the evening was made possible through the record collections of several of the students, and had been approved by a specially appointed committee who pre-selected the music to be played.

Howie's plan was also being played out. He and Cindy had driven to the dance in one car while the others followed in Mick's car. After parking his car, Howie and his date got into Mick's car. He went over the plan again. Mick and Adam listened as the girls asked questions. Mary expressed her concern about Mattingale's desk being harmed, and was told that the drawer wouldn't be pried open. "If you did, that'd be property damage," she warned. Howie assured her that he could open the drawer without so much as scratching it. Sue wondered how the guys would get into the furnace room. "Isn't it locked?" she asked. "No," Howie said. "I checked on it Wednesday, and the lock is broken." According to operation 'Banana Split', Howie and Cindy would be the first ones to leave the dance; then Adam and Sue, and finally, Mick and Mary.

"Remember, we'll leave at five minute intervals," Howie said.

During the evening the three couples danced and talked. Adam shared that his grandfather seemed to be doing better. Mick talked about the college he was planning to attend, and only briefly alluded to how his family was reacting. Mary felt terrible about the reaction of Mick's family, but was pleased that he was going into teaching. Howie kidded the two of them about both being teachers, saying he wondered what kind of secrets they will have locked in their desk drawers. Sue talked about getting a job and perhaps attending a secretarial school in the fall. Cindy expressed how glad she was to have gotten to know Howie's friends, and wished that she wasn't at a different school. Howie asked everybody to speculate as to what they might find in Mattingale's desk. When asked what he thought he exclaimed, "Burglary tools!"

Mary shot him a skeptical look. "What are you talking about?"

Howie glanced around at the others before turning his attention back to Mary. "Mattingale could be a cat burglar. You know, someone who slips into houses at night."

Mary giggled. "That's crazy. How did you even come up with such a far-fetched idea like that?"

"It's easy for him," Mick said. "That's how his mind operates."

Adam spoke up. "Yeah. He comes up with screwy ideas all the time. He never has any normal ones."

Howie was undaunted by his friends' remarks. "Don't listen to these two, they're just jealous." He leaned closer to Mary and whispered, "Don't you know that being a cat burglar could explain why she wears those gloves all the time." He held his hands in front of him, palms up. "Mattingale probably dipped the ends of her fingers into acid so she wouldn't leave finger prints. She wears those white gloves to cover up the scars."

"Mattingale wouldn't have to dip her fingers into acid if she wore gloves," Adam pointed out.

"You'll have to excuse Howie," Mick explained. "He's just learning how to be a detective."

"I didn't know you were thinking about that," Cindy said. "Tell me about it."

For the next half hour Howie enthusiastically shared his dream of becoming a private investigator as Mick and Adam took turns going for punch and cookies. At one point, both of them got up to go. When the girls asked why they didn't want to stay and listen, Mick said that they had heard the story enough times already. Later on, more dancing followed and the evening slipped away as the three couples enjoyed each other's company.

"It's ten thirty," Howie announced. "Time for Cindy and me to leave. Remember, Adam, give us five minutes before you and Sue leave."

"See you in the car," Cindy said to the two other girls.

After Howie and Cindy had been gone for a couple of minutes, Adam turned to Mick. "This sounds stupid, but I don't know where the door is to the furnace room. I forgot to ask Howie."

"I don't know where it is either. I was going to ask you."

"Oh, no!" Mary said. "What are you guys going to do?"

"Let me think." Mick gazed in the direction of the dance floor. "Okay, I got it. We'll go to the athletic equipment storage room. Okay, Adam?"

"I guess so. At least, I know where that is, but isn't that door locked?"

"Yeah, but during football season I was given a key to open it for the team every day before practice." Mick dug in his pocket and took out his keys. He held up the key chain and pointed to a small silver key. "I just forgot to turn it in, that's all."

"Great, you go first then. Just leave it open for me."

"What is Howie going to think when you two don't show up?" Mary asked.

"He'll go on with the plan by himself," Mick said. "We'll just have to hope that he sticks to the schedule, and then we'll meet him in Mattingale's room."

Sue giggled. "I'm sorry, I don't mean to laugh." She giggled again. "Oh, yes I do. This is hilarious."

"Well, it's time," Mick announced. "Mary, you explain to Cindy what's happening when you get out to the car. We'll see you in a little bit," he said to Adam. "I'll leave the door open for you."

* * *

Cindy and Mary were waiting in the car when Sue opened the passenger's door and got in the front seat with them. "I hope everything goes well for the guys."

"Do you think Howie will be okay?" Cindy asked with some anxiety.

"Oh, sure," Mary said. "He's pretty resourceful."

"I can hardly wait until tomorrow to find out what happened," Sue said. "Adam said he'd call me."

Mary started the car, looked behind her, and pulled out from the curb. They hadn't gone very far when she asked Sue a question that had been on her mind. "How's Adam seemed to you lately? It seems like he's changed to me." She paused, wanting to make sure she was accurately describing what she was feeling. "Like he's opened up a little more," she explained.

"I know what you mean. He's been sharing with me more than he has ever before."

"I noticed he's more talkative," Cindy said. "The first time we met, I wasn't sure what to think. He was so quiet and moody."

"Talk about being moody," Mary interjected. "Ever since Mick told his family about not playing football, he has been up and down. Yesterday, he even snapped at me. That's not like him, and he apologized afterwards."

"You and Mick are pretty serious, aren't you?" Sue asked.

The car slowed to a stop for a red light. Mary looked at her passengers and smiled. "Oh, yes. We've even talked about getting married."

"Married!" Sue exclaimed. "That's wonderful!"

Mary smiled. "Wait a minute. That's a ways off. For now, we both agreed that it'd be after we finish college."

"But it's still exciting," Cindy said. "You two are such a nice couple."

"Thank you, I think we are, too." Pulling away from the stoplight, Mary glanced over at Sue. "Tell us more about you and Adam."

Chapter 39

Mick and Adam sat on the floor in the L-shaped equipment room, using the storage lockers as a backrest. They positioned themselves around the corner of the L, away from the two windows looking out into the boy's locker room. The locker room lights, shining through the two windows, provided enough illumination to distinguish each other's features. Neither knew why the lights in the locker room were on. They had thought about turning them off, but didn't want to do anything that might look suspicious.

"What time is it?" Adam asked.

"A few minutes past eleven thirty."

"Is that all? Feels like we've been sitting here for hours. My butt's sore. Wonder what Howie is doing right now?"

Mick stretched out his long legs. "Probably trying to figure out what happened to us."

Adam leaned his head against the metal locker. He poked Mick with his elbow.

"Yeah?"

"How're you doing? You know, you and your dad?"

"Okay. He hasn't said anything further about it. Of course, he hasn't said much at all to me. Giving me the silent treatment as if I don't exist."

"Do you think he'll ever understand?"

"Who knows?" Mick stretched his arms. "I think he'll come around eventually. I mean, he'll talk to me. At least, I hope so. He believes in education and all that stuff, but football has always been number one." He handed Adam his watch. "Keep track of the time, will you? I want to take a little nap."

* * *

The noises in the boiler room got on Howie's nerves. Pacing

back and forth, he considered possible reasons why Mick and Adam never showed up. When neither showed, he considered going back to the lunchroom, but it wasn't worth the risk. If he had to accomplish this mission by himself, he would do so.

* * *

Adam grabbed Mick's shoulder and shook him. "Wake up! Five after twelve. Time to go."

Mick groaned as he stood up. "Too many football injuries. Old body's just not what it used to be."

Adam led the way. After leaving the equipment room, they moved through the locker area to the door leading out into the hallway. Adam opened the door a crack and peeked out. "Looks clear," he whispered, opening the door and stepping into the darkened hallway.

Mick closed the door behind him. "It sure seems different at night," he said, scanning the hallway. "I never realized it could be so spooky."

The two moved down the hallway, past the library, the science lab, and the administrative offices until they got to the stairway leading up to the second floor. Creeping up the stairs, they were careful to be as quiet as possible.

Mick stopped halfway up. "Hold it!"

"What's the matter?"

"I thought I heard something."

"Maybe it was Howie. What do you think it was?"

"Don't know. Maybe the old school moaning and creaking."

They climbed the rest of the stairs, took a right, and tiptoed down the hallway to Mattingale's classroom. Mick turned the knob and slipped in with Adam right behind him. No sooner had he closed the door when Mick stopped in his tracks. "What the—"

Adam couldn't believe his eyes. Howie was curled in a ball, sleeping on the spot where Mattingale's desk normally sat. The desk was nowhere in sight.

Chapter 40

At the same time Adam left the dance to join Mick in the equipment room, Danny Logan and his two friends drove up in front of Kelly's Market after circling the block twice. The first time, Danny recognized kids from North High going in, and decided to wait until they left. They were waiting now to be sure that there weren't any customers in the store.

"Back up the car some, will ya," Danny snarled, afraid it would look suspicious if they were parked in front of the entrance.

Pete threw the car in reverse and backed up ten to fifteen feet. "How's this?"

"That's cool. Keep the motor runnin' and when ya see us come out, pull up. As soon we get our asses in, get us the hell out of here."

"Ya and Johnny get to have all the fun," Pete whined. "Why do I have to drive?"

"Hey, man, cool it," Danny said, angry with Pete for being such a crybaby. "Next time Johnny will drive and ya come with me, okay?"

"Okay," Pete said, sounding pacified.

Danny turned toward the back seat and tossed Johnny a red ski mask. "Take that. Put it on. When we go through the door, pull it over your face."

"Hey, Danny," Johnny said.

"Yeah?"

"Can I have the other one?"

"What's wrong with the one I gave ya?"

"Don't like the color. Rather have the black one."

Danny wondered if Johnny should handle the car and have Pete come with him. He thought about making the switch, but changed his mind. He wasn't sure if Johnny could be trusted to handle the driving. *Dumb shit probably stall the engine*. "What the hell difference does the color make?" he snapped.

"Don't like red."

"Shit, give me the red one and hurry up." Danny threw the black ski mask at him. "We ain't got all night."

"Ain't mad at me, are ya?"

"Just get it done!" Danny felt like jumping in the back seat and knocking the shit out of Johnny with his own baseball bat.

Danny and Johnny got out of the car, walked up to the entrance door and opened it, pulling their ski masks down over their faces. They were in luck. No customers. They quickly moved to the counter where the clerk, a blond-haired man in his twenties, was busy straightening up a candy bar display.

"Is it that cold out?" the clerk asked, looking up, giving no hint he knew what was happening.

Pulling out the gun, Danny pointed it at the clerk's chest. "Ya goin' to be cold meat if ya don't fork over the dough in the register."

The man's smile faded as he first looked at the person pointing the gun and then at the other holding a baseball bat. "Hey, now. I'll…I'll do whatever you want." He punched a key on the cash register and the drawer opened. "I'm getting the money."

"Get the stuff under the drawer also," Danny ordered, thrilled with the power the gun gave him. Cold fear in the eyes of the clerk excited him. "Hurry the hell up!" he shouted. Cold sweat ran down Danny's forehead and the sides of his face. *Damn ski mask's messin' up my hair.* With a free hand he felt his pocket to see if he had his comb. "Put all of it in a bag!" he yelled, wondering if he could scare the guy enough so that he'd piss his pants.

"Hey, man," Johnny said. "Remember Mickey Mantle."

Danny nodded. "Hurry up! Ain't goin' tell ya a second time." He chuckled as the clerk's hand shook as he pulled out the money and stuffed it into a brown paper bag.

"That's...that's all of it," the young man said, his eyes riveted on the gun pointed at him. "I swear it is."

"Damn better be," Danny growled. "Leave the bag on the counter and move your ass out here."

The clerk, his face drained of color, slowly moved from

behind the counter and stood before Danny and Johnny. "What are you guys going to do?"

Danny enjoyed hearing the fear in his voice. While he kept the gun pointed at him, Johnny swung the bat. The clerk saw it coming and jumped aside. "Goddamn it, stand still!" Johnny screamed.

The clerk lunged for the baseball bat.

Whether the clerk's sudden movement startled him in pulling the trigger or the excitement of the moment, Danny didn't know nor care. The gun fired and the clerk went down holding his chest. Lying on the floor moaning, the clerk's shirt with the Kelly's Market emblem embroidered above the pocket became soaked with blood. Momentarily stunned, Danny stood staring at the crumpled body.

"Come on, man!" Johnny screamed. "Let's get the hell out of here!"

Danny grabbed the bag of money. "Wait a minute." He took out the Valentine Day card he had brought and tossed it on the floor next to his victim. Running out to the waiting car, Danny felt so excited that he almost pissed his pants.

Next to the wounded clerk lay a heart shaped card with the words *Hugs and Kisses* inscribed on it.

Chapter 41

It had been a tiring weekend for Adam. On Sunday, with only four hours sleep, he worked six hours at Bloomberg's. Harry had asked him to come in, needing help to set up for the *After Valentine Day Sale*. On Sunday afternoon, Adam and his mother went to the hospital. His grandfather, weak from coughing during the night, dozed off and on. They left after fifteen minutes.

Doctor Jairvus had briefly spoken to them in the hallway. "There's been some improvement in his condition. Takes time for the antibiotics to work. We can be optimistic, but it needs to be a cautious optimism."

On the way home from the hospital she asked Adam, "Don't you think Grandpa has aged?"

"I didn't notice," Adam replied, afraid to say that he thought his grandfather looked terrible, and further upsetting her.

Physically and emotionally exhausted by Sunday evening, Adam had gone to bed shortly after eight, relieved to have the bedroom to himself since Oscar had been called into work. The last thing he remembered was lying down on the bed. Awakening the next morning, he felt more rested than he had for weeks. After dressing, washing, and having breakfast, he picked up his schoolbooks, and left to meet Mick at the corner. The day, bright and full of sunshine, invigorated him. Although the unseasonably warm temperatures of last week had ended, it was still reasonably mild as far as he was concerned. When Mick walked up, Adam was checking Kass' window display.

"See anything interesting?"

"Naw, just looking. Since Harry's got me doing window displays, I like to see what other stores do."

"Hey, maybe you'll end up being a window designer and work for Dayton's downtown."

"I doubt that. Come on. Let's get going. Today's the day we

find out what happened to Mattingale's desk. I've been curious about that all weekend."

"Me too. This whole thing has got me puzzled."

They crossed the street and walked by the movie theater, briefly stopping to check the movie posters.

"Did you go up to the hospital yesterday?" Mick asked as they continued on their way.

"Yeah, my mom and I went."

"How's your grandfather doing?"

"Doctor says he's holding his own, but I don't know. He looked pretty tired, and he didn't talk much."

"Probably worn out," Mick said. "My mother said that what he's going through is really tough on the body."

"How does she know that?"

"She read up on it years ago. A cousin got a severe case of frostbite in Korea. When she found out about him, she wanted to know as much about it as she could."

"What happened? I mean, is he still living?"

"Oh, sure, he's doing fine. Mom told me to tell you that your grandfather's in her thoughts and prayers. She said to remember, that at his age, it just takes longer to heal. She thinks he'll be okay."

Walking at a brisk pace, Adam and Mick crossed the street and onto the next block. Going past the bakery, they paused for a moment and then walked on, making a pact to stop tomorrow for a cinnamon roll.

"Have you talked to Howie?" Adam asked.

"We talked last night on the phone."

"Has he come up with any answers about what happened to Mattingale's desk?"

"Nope, he's just as stumped as we are. Get this. He says that when he walked in and found it missing, he couldn't believe it. At first, he thought he'd gone into the wrong room. He went back into the hallway to check the number on the door. What a clown. We should've left him sleeping there. Good old Howie; we can always count on him for something."

Adam pointed up ahead. "Speaking of you-know-who. Here he comes."

Their friend was a half a block away. Seeing them, he waved

frantically. Instead of waiting, he trotted toward them. "Hi guys," he said upon reaching them.

"Hey, have you come up with any ideas about Mattingale's desk?" Mick asked.

"Yeah," Adam said. "Give us your best shot."

"I've got this theory about who took it. Couldn't sleep last night. Tossed and turned until about midnight, and then it came to me. I'm pretty sure who did it."

"This I have to hear," Mick said.

"Come on, tell us," Adam said. "Who took it?"

"Sophomores."

"Sophomores!" Mick exclaimed. "What did you do? Fall out of bed last night and hit your head?"

"Nooo! I tell you, it had to be sophomores."

For the rest of the way to school, he expounded his idea that there were sophomores who were out to make a name for their class so they could out-do the seniors. "All we have to do is corner one of the sophomores during lunch period and make him talk, and if the kid doesn't come clean, we'd threaten to tie him up and keep him in one of our lockers until graduation."

Mick and Adam were still chuckling about Howie's kidnapping scheme when they entered the school building.

To Adam's surprise, Mattingale's desk was in its usual spot when they walked into her classroom. "Look at that," he said. "What's going on here?"

"Wow!" Howie shot a look at Adam and Mick. "That's her desk, isn't it? It is, isn't it?"

"I'm pretty sure it's hers," Mick replied. "But it looks brand new."

"It's those sophomores," Howie whispered. "They're playing with our minds."

Mick poked Howie in the arm. "When it comes to you, they don't have much to play with."

The bell rang before Howie could respond, and he and his two friends hustled to the back of the room and sat down. Before long, Miss Mattingale walked in accompanied by Mr. Waite, the school principal. When their English teacher saw the desk, she let out an audible gasp. "Oh, Mr. Waite, it's beautiful. I can hardly believe it's the same desk."

"I'm asking again," Adam whispered. "What's going on here?"

Mick smiled and replied just loud enough to make sure both Adam and Howie heard,

"Don't you know? It's the sophomores. Waite's probably in cahoots with them."

"Class, we are fortunate and quite honored to have Mr. Waite with us this morning," Miss Mattingale announced in a voice exuding excitement. "As you know, this is the second time this year our esteemed principal has visited our classroom. We welcome you, Mr. Waite."

"Thank you, Miss Mattingale." Mr. Waite paused until she moved off to one side. "I just wanted to take a few moments to share with your students how the rest of the teachers at North High decided to demonstrate their support of you."

Miss Mattingale smiled. "Thank you," she replied, holding her gloved hands in front of her as if she was praying.

Mr. Waite acknowledged her with a slight bow before addressing the class. "We wanted to recognize, as well as honor, Miss Mattingale's willingness to resume her teaching. As all of you students must realize, it was especially courageous of her to walk back into this classroom in light of the unfortunate incident that occurred last month. If it were not for one of your loyal students…" Mr. Waite paused, looked at Miss Mattingale, and then toward the back of the classroom. "Howard."

"Yes, sir?"

"Please stand up for a moment."

When Howie stood up, Adam looked over at Mick and whispered, "Here we go again."

"If it were not for Howard Cummins, we might not be having this moment to honor Miss Mattingale. Thank you, Howard. You may sit down now."

"As I was about to say," Mr. Waite continued. "Although Miss Mattingale's desk wasn't physically damaged in any way, it did retain a certain odor that was a constant reminder of that dreadful day. So, because of the affection that all of us have for your teacher, the faculty here at North High took up a collection to pay for her desk to be refurbished. Since we didn't want her to go even a day without her beloved desk, it was picked up last

Friday afternoon, and delivered early this morning." Mr. Waite walked over to her desk, ran his hand across one corner, and sniffed. "If I might say so myself, they did a wonderful job. It's another testimony of the teamwork we have here and shows…"

While Mr. Waite continued with his speech, Mick passed a note to Adam. Adam read it and passed it on to Howie. The note read *So much for the sophomore conspirators!* After Howie read the note, he crumpled it, and tossed it back at Mick.

* * *

Doctor Jairvus was feeling refreshed after the weekend. He and his wife had dined out on Friday, and afterwards, went to a movie. The evening away from the hospital with no interruptions was only part of his Valentine Day weekend gift to her. The next day he had to work, but for Sunday he managed to switch with another doctor and was able to have the entire day off. The time off was even more special because he hadn't been called in for any emergencies on Sunday night. For him, it had been an extraordinarily relaxing weekend. Now, on Monday, he was eager to begin making his rounds. He was just finishing writing in a patient's chart when a nurse approached him.

"Doctor Jairvus, do you have time to see the patient in 214B?" she asked, her voice revealing a note of anxiousness. "He's not doing very well."

"You mean, Mr. Kurtz?"

"I'm afraid so."

"I'll be right there."

Chapter 42

In fifth period Social Studies class a student came in and handed Mrs. Blackwell, the teacher, a note. She read it, looked over at Adam, and motioned for him to come up front.

"You're to go to the office," she said quietly.

"Why?"

"The note doesn't say, but since class is almost over take your books."

Adam's mother was sitting in a chair when he walked into the office. She immediately got up and went to him.

"Oh, Butch!" she cried, her voice shaky. "Grandpa's not doing well."

A jolt of electricity shot through him. "What happened?"

"He's had a relapse. Doctor Jairvus called and started to tell me all the details, but I told him I wanted to talk to him in person."

"I want to see Grandpa," Adam said.

"Good. That's why I'm here. I thought you would. I called Wanda. She'll take a taxi and meet us there."

Doctor Jairvus was at the nurses' station talking with Wanda when Adam and his mother hurriedly walked up. "Doctor, how's my father?" Virg asked nervously.

"He's holding his own," Doctor Jairvus replied gently. "The pneumonia has worsened. His lungs are congested. He's been running a temperature for the past twelve hours, fluctuating between 100 and 101 degrees. Now, that's not excessively high. At his age, however, it does cause us some concern."

Virg wrung her hands.

"Anything else we should be concerned about?" Wanda asked.

"Yes, he's eating very little solid foods. But he's taking in enough liquids for now. If that intake decreases, though, we'll have to put him on an IV."

"You mean…" Virg could barely say the words. "Put…put tubes in him?"

"It would only be one tube and that would be in his forearm. It's a common hospital procedure and not the least bit painful."

"Mom, it'll be okay," Adam said. "Grandpa's tough."

"There's one other thing," Jairvus cautioned. "Your father's heart isn't all that strong and with everything that he's been through, we're most concerned about that."

"Is he going to be okay?" she asked as she glanced from Wanda to Adam.

"As I told your sister, we're doing all we can. Your father's body is just plain run down."

"Can I see him?" Adam asked.

"Certainly. In fact, he's been talking to me about you. Seems you two have had some great times looking for discarded clocks."

"Butch, go," Wanda urged.

"Tell him we'll come in soon," Virg said, and turned back to Doctor Jairvus. "This is all coming so fast. I need to ask a few more questions."

"That's fine. I'll try to answer them the best I can, and then I'd like to ask some questions about his medical history. I'm afraid we don't have a very complete health history on him. That's why I called you."

* * *

Paul didn't notice when his grandson opened the door and walked into his room. It was only when Adam came and stood by the side of his bed that he slowly turned his head toward his visitor. Not wearing his glasses, it took him a few moments to focus. When he realized that it was his grandson, he managed a weak smile. His dry throat caused his voice to sound raspy. It took so much energy even to whisper.

"Butch, glad you here. Get chair. Sit."

Adam got a chair from the corner and moved it along side the bed. "How are you doing, Grandpa?"

"Good. Not good."

"What do you mean?"

"Me, not good. Good, you here." Squinting, he looked toward the nightstand. "Get glasses. I see better."

Adam picked up the glasses and put them on his grandfather. "There, is that better?"

He nodded and looked at Adam, studying his face. "Butch, you worried? What wrong?"

"I'm worried about you. You've got to get better."

"Ack. Don't worry."

"I don't want anything to happen to you," Adam said, his voice unsteady.

Paul tried to take a deep breath but couldn't. His chest hurt from the constant coughing; it felt as though a heavy weight lay upon it. He motioned toward the water glass sitting on the nightstand. After a few sips, he waved it away, swallowing several times before speaking. "Butch, sometimes clock runs down."

"Grandpa, I wish I could do something."

With much effort, Paul raised his hand toward his grandson. Adam quickly reached out to grasp it. As Paul lay there, he closed his eyes and thought back to the times when the two of them would walk to the city dump together. Adam would hold his hand whenever they crossed the street. Such a tiny hand it was. "Butch, you got big, strong hand like man. Good."

"They're not as strong as yours."

"Remember walks together?"

"It seems like a long time ago."

"Yes. Long time." Paul took some deep breaths. "You soon graduate high school. I proud."

"I want you there at my graduation."

"Butch, I want be there." He squeezed Adam's hand. "I want be there," he repeated. The two of them shared a few moments in silence. Still holding onto his grandson's hand, he asked about Adam's mother and Wanda.

"They're talking to Doctor Jairvus."

"He good man," Paul said slowly, barely getting the last word out.

"Grandpa, why don't you just close your eyes and rest until they come."

"Yes, I do that."

* * *

When Wanda and Virg entered the room, they found Adam sitting by the bed, his hand being grasped by their father's. The scene brought tears to Adam's mother as Wanda reached over and put her arm around her. They walked quietly over to the bed, whispered hello to Adam, and then stood silently watching their father. After a while, Paul opened his eyes when he began to cough. When the coughing spell ceased, he looked up and smiled. They visited for only a short time before his eyes began to close. Within moments, he was asleep. Before they left, both of the daughters kissed their father on the forehead.

Adam, the last to leave the room, glanced back at his grandfather before he closed the door. On the drive home he sat in the back seat, closed his eyes, and thought back to the walks he and his grandfather used to take.

Chapter 43

While Adam waited for Mick at the corner of Kass', he thought about the troubling dream he had during the night. In the dream his grandfather had tubes sticking out of his arms and legs. Whenever he coughed, a tube popped out. As soon as one popped out, a nurse rushed in and replaced it with not one, but two new ones. Adam sat next to the bed witnessing the whole thing. Every time the nurse entered, his grandfather would look at him with eyes filled with fear. He would cry out, "Butch! Help me!" Adam, however, couldn't budge from the chair.

"Good morning."

The voice startled Adam. "Hi, Kass," he stammered, feeling embarrassed. "I didn't see you come up."

"I could understand why," Kass replied with a grin. "You looked like you were in deep thought. Maybe a girl, eh?"

"Maybe."

"Waiting for Mick?"

"Yeah." Adam watched as Kass reached in his coat pocket and pulled out a key ring holding a half dozen or more keys. "I didn't think the drugstore opened this early," he said.

"It doesn't, but I have to go over some inventory." Kass inserted his key and opened the door.

"It's cold out this morning. Want to come in and wait?"

"No, thanks. Mick will be here any minute."

"Sure enough. Say hello to him for me."

Within a few minutes Mick showed, and they began their trek to school.

"Where were you yesterday after school?" Mick asked.

"My mom picked me up. We went up to the hospital."

"How's your grandfather doing?"

"He didn't look that good. When I was with him I..." he took a deep breath, exhaling it slowly, determined to keep his emotions under control. "I got this feeling that he doesn't think he's going to make it."

"Why do you say that?"

"You know how he's always talking about clocks and comparing them with people? One of the last things he told me was how clocks can run down."

"Oh, man. What did your mom say about that?"

"I didn't tell her. She was shook up enough."

They stopped at the corner and waited for the light to change. "You know," Adam said. "In the past couple of years there have been times when I didn't like my grandfather. I was angry with him for being a wino. Didn't want anybody to know we were related."

"And now?" Mick asked. The light turned and the two of them started crossing the street.

"If anyone would say anything against him now, I'd deck him." Adam raked his hand through his hair. "All of it gets pretty mixed up."

"In what way?"

"I thought I was angry with him because he embarrassed me, but I think I was angrier for what he was doing to himself." Adam glanced up at some white puffy clouds, and thought about how much simpler life would be if he were a cloud floating around. "Then there's Frank and the promise my grandfather had me make about him. Man, what am I going to do? If something happens to my grandfather, I'd want to…"

The two of them walked in silence for some time before Mick spoke. "It seems to me that the promise you made is the most important thing to hang on to. Your grandfather had good reason for you to make it."

"Yeah, I suppose. He didn't want me to do anything that I'll regret. He knows how I feel about Frank. Probably thinks that I'd do something stupid and end up in jail or something."

"If you go to jail, I'll think of some way to spring you."

"Gee, thanks," Adam said appreciating Mick's attempt to lighten the conversation. "That's just what I need; another one of Howie's schemes."

"Hey, I just thought of something. It sounds like your grandfather has a reason for not wanting you to do anything to Frank."

"And what's that?"

"Maybe he's thinking that if Frank wants to be the way he is, let him. But your grandfather doesn't want you to be that way. It's like playing football. There were a lot of guys on the other teams who played dirty. Everybody knew who they were. Our coach knew."

"So, what did he say?"

"The only thing he said to us is don't play football on their level. He told us that if they want to play dirty, that's what they'll be remembered for. That doesn't mean you have to play dirty…unless that's what you want to be remembered for also."

"That sounds good, but Frank pushes me to the edge."

"So stay clear of the guy."

"I'm doing everything I can to avoid him."

"That's good." Mick gestured ahead. "Here comes Howie."

"How's your grandfather?" Howie asked as soon as he reached them.

Adam repeated what he had shared with Mick, appreciating Howie's words of support and his offer to help in any way.

"You know," Howie said. "Too many bad things have been happening around here lately. Did you hear about that guy who got shot during a robbery?"

Adam glanced at Mick. By the shocked expression on his face, he apparently hadn't heard of it either.

"Some guys robbed that grocery store over on Fifth and Colfax. They walked in, took the cash, and shot the clerk."

"When did all this happen?" Adam asked.

"Last Saturday. And get this. Whoever did it left a valentine as a calling card."

"How do you know about the card?" Adam asked.

"I got sources."

"You've got what?" Mick asked.

"Okay, so it was on the five o'clock news the next night. The police have reason to believe that at least three people were involved. Two were in the store with ski masks on. They think a third person drove a get-away car."

"How's the clerk doing?" Mick asked.

"He's going to recover, but it'll be a long hospital stay. There's one thing that's puzzling."

"What's that?"

"According to what the clerk told the police, one of the robbers had a gun but the other had a baseball bat."

"What did he have?" Adam asked, trying to keep his voice calm.

"A baseball bat."

For the rest of the way to school, Adam mainly listened as his friends talked about the robbery. He had noticed Mick glance at him when the baseball bat was mentioned, no doubt connecting it with Danny Logan and his friends using one on Frank.

"I'm going up to the hospital after school," Adam said as they walked up to the front door of North High. "Sue's going with me."

"She is, huh?" Mick nudged Howie. "Sounds pretty serious, don't you think?"

"Sure does. Adam? Is she walking you home from school, or are you walking her?"

"Neither wise guy. We're meeting at Kass' and then going. If that's okay with you guys."

Mick grinned. "As long as you'll walk us home every now and then."

"And buy us Cokes," Howie added.

"Get out of here," Adam said, laughing. "I'll see you guys later." After his friends left, he thought about the clerk who had been shot. Should he tell the police? If he did, though, Danny might tell them the circumstances surrounding Frank's beating.

Chapter 44

Sue's mother had given her a ride to meet Adam at the drugstore that afternoon, arriving shortly before four o'clock. Getting out of the car Sue saw Adam inside the drugstore, looking out the window at her. When their eyes met, he smiled. By the time she had shut the door, he had come out to meet her.

"Hello," she said.

"Hi, I hope you don't mind, but I have to make a quick trip over to where I work. Have to check on my schedule for the weekend. It's just up the block. It won't take long."

"That's okay. I'll wait in the drugstore."

"Sure. I'll introduce you to Kass. He's been looking forward to meeting you. You'll like him."

The two of them went in and walked back to the soda fountain. Kass was talking to an elderly gentleman who was just finishing a dish of ice cream. Kass glanced up at them and smiled. "I'll be right with you."

After she and Adam sat on the two end stools, she asked about his grandfather. Adam had just finished filling her in when Kass approached them.

"And who is this nice young lady you have with you?"

"This is Sue."

Kass reached for Sue's extended hand and shook it, holding it with both of his hands. "Oh, yes. He's told me about you. The two of you went to the Valentine Day Dance together. It's my pleasure meeting you."

"Thank you, Mr. Kass, I—"

"Please, just call me Kass like everyone else."

"Thank you...Kass. I've looked forward to coming here. You have such a nice place. It doesn't seem like a drugstore. It's so homey."

"Adam, I'm going to like her. She's already charmed me into giving her a free Coke as a first time patron."

"Take good care of her, will you. I'm going over to Harry's for a few minutes. Be right back."

"That's a mighty fine young man you're dating," Kass said after Adam left. He placed her drink on the counter.

"Thank you. How long have you known Adam?"

"Oh, my. I remember when he and his mother first came to live on Broadway. Let me see, that had to be thirteen, fourteen years ago."

"What was he like then?" she asked, hoping to get a few more insights into Adam.

"Such a shy, quiet little boy. He'd come into the drugstore and buy comic books, and was always so polite. I remember his mother taking a picture of him when he was around six or seven. He was standing right out there on the corner in front of my drugstore with an ice cream cone in one hand and a bottle of Coke in the other. He looked so content. Like he had everything he ever wanted right there and then."

"He's still quiet and shy, isn't he?"

"Oh, yes."

Sue sipped her Coke. "He also seems to have a hard time expressing his feelings."

"Oooh, I see you know him well. That's good. He needs someone like you. And being his girlfriend, I'm sure you've noticed that he needs someone to share himself."

Sue felt her cheeks blush at the word *girlfriend.* "He seems to want to reach out more, but I don't think he quite knows how all the time."

"I know what you mean, and like I said, you'll be good for him."

"Thank you." Sue felt like she had found a friend in Kass. "But what makes you think that?"

"For one thing, I've been around for a long time and I'm a pretty good judge of people. You're the kind of person who someone would be comfortable with sharing things. And secondly, you're the first girl he ever brought in here."

"I hope I can be of some help to Adam," she replied, blushing again. "I care about him."

"I can tell that, and that's good."

They talked for a while about her plans after graduation. She shared that she planned to go to business school and become a court stenographer. She was telling him how she and Adam first met when the cowbell clanged over the entrance door.

"Here comes that special guy now," Kass whispered.

"Didn't mean to be gone so long," Adam said as he sat next to Sue. "I hope you two have been getting to know each other."

"Yes, we have. She's a nice girl and I'd like to see her around more often."

"Thank you," Sue said, giving a sideward glance to Adam. "I'd like that also."

"You two must have of gotten along pretty good," Adam said, glancing at the two of them.

"Kass is easy to get along with. We share the same interests."

"That we do." Kass got a glass from underneath the counter and placed it in front of Adam.

"How about something to drink?"

"Thanks, but I'm anxious to get up to the hospital. I'll take a rain check."

"Tell your grandfather that he's in my thoughts. Now, remember, if there is anything I can do for him, let me know."

"Thanks, I will."

"Kass, it's really been nice meeting you," Sue said, buttoning her coat.

"It's been all my pleasure," Kass replied as he bowed.

On the drive to the hospital Sue listened as Adam talked about his grandfather. Once, when she made the comment that he and his grandfather must be very close, his voice cracked when he replied that he was closer to his grandfather than he had realized.

They parked the car, walked through the hospital's main lobby, past the information desk. When Adam pointed out the receptionist with the plastic smile, Sue took an instant disliking to her, agreeing that she appeared snooty. They rode the elevator in silence as they listened to two women talk about the critical condition of a friend who had been involved in a car accident that morning. When Sue glanced over at Adam, he was chewing on his lip.

"You're going to like Doctor Jairvus," Adam said as they got off the elevator and headed in the direction of the nurses' station.

"Can I help you?" One of the nurses asked as they walked up.

"I'm looking for Doctor Jairvus. He's taking care of my grandfather."

The nurse smiled. "And what's your grandfather's name?"

"Paul Kurtz."

"Oh, yes, Mr. Kurtz," she replied, sounding like she was referring to an old friend. "The doctor is involved in a conference right now but he did see Mr. Kurtz this morning. I'll tell him you're looking for him when he comes back."

"Thank you. Do you know how my grandfather is doing?"

"He's had a rough past twenty-four hours, but appears to be doing a little better. I was just in there. He's resting comfortably, but you may find him quite sleepy." The nurse offered a warm smile. "I wouldn't be alarmed about his drowsiness. It's a side effect of the medication he's on."

As Adam and Sue walked to the room, she thought about how much she liked the sound of Adam saying, "Can *we* go in to see him." She was glad to be there and hoped that his grandfather liked her.

Adam's grandfather was lying on his side facing the door, his eyes closed. Sue went with Adam as he walked up to the side of the bed. She reached over and took hold of Adam's hand.

"Hello, Grandpa."

Paul opened his eyes, focused them, and managed a smile. "Butch," he whispered.

Although Adam had told her that he would be called Butch, hearing it was a surprise.

"Grandpa, this is Sue. She's the girl I've been dating. I wanted her to meet you."

"Hello, I'm sorry you're sick. Adam has told me so much about you. I feel like I know you already."

"Grandpa, I told her how you like to fix clocks, and that you can take a clock apart and put it back together blindfolded. And that you're going to teach the doctor how to repair his clock."

Sue, touched by the closeness she sensed between Adam and his grandfather, felt bad for Adam and how he must be feeling as she strained to listened to his grandfather speak in a voice that barely could be heard.

"Doctor, good. I teach. He learn fast. He..." Paul's eyes slowly closed, opened, and then closed again.

She squeezed his hand. "At least, he seems to be breathing easy," she whispered. "He doesn't appear to be in any pain."

"Yeah. I'm thankful for that. Do you mind if we stay for awhile?"

"Of course not."

Although his grandfather had dozed off, Adam and Sue stayed for nearly an hour. His grandfather slept most of the time. The couple of times he opened his eyes, he managed a smile and once even whispered, "Butch" before slipping back to sleep. When they left, Adam told Sue that he wanted to check at the nurses' station to see if Doctor Jairvus was around.

"I'm sorry," the nurse said. "He was called to do emergency surgery. I'm afraid he won't be finished with that for another hour. Don't worry, though, your grandfather's in no immediate danger. If his condition should worsen, the hospital will be in touch with the family."

"Thank you. And tell my grandfather when he wakes up that I'll be back to see him tomorrow after school."

Chapter 45

Danny Logan lit a cigarette to keep warm. "Shit, it's cold," he muttered while hurrying to Johnny's house. He hated having to walk places. The sound of snow crunching under his feet only reminded him that some day he'd live any place where it was warm and never had any snow. He had wanted a car, but his parents said they couldn't afford to buy him one. With no money saved, the little money he made working part-time at a gas station went fast. The cash he got from Kass' on Christmas Eve was gone in a week.

Johnny lived in a run-down, two-story white-framed house that needed painting. Between the house and the garage was a black 1949 Ford that hadn't run in years. Johnny's old man put the car there to overhaul the engine but never got around to it.

Stepping onto the porch, Danny knocked on a door showing slivers of light coming through from the inside.

"Hey, man, come on in," Johnny said as he opened the door. "Pete's already here. He's out in the kitchen."

Johnny led Danny through a drafty living room into the kitchen where dishes were piled high in the sink. A faint odor of garbage floated past his nose. By the refrigerator a stack of newspapers spilled onto the floor. He sat on a vinyl-covered chair, the soft white stuffing sticking out from a rip on the seat.

"What are ya drinkin'?" Danny asked as Pete raised a glass to his lips.

Pete looked at him and flashed a crooked smile. "Some damn good stuff," he slurred. He raised his glass toward Danny, tilting it in a salute, spilling some of its contents on the floor.

"So, what is it?" Danny asked again.

"Coke and tequila," Johnny answered for Pete. "I found where my old man was hidin' the bottle. Want some?"

"Yeah, man!" Danny watched Johnny pour the tequila into a glass, filling the glass about a quarter full, and then filling the rest of it with Coke. “What’s your old man goin’ to say when he finds some of his booze gone?”

“Who cares?”

Danny laughed. “He’ll kick your ass.”

“Hell, he will,” Johnny snarled, adding bitterly, “Better not even try.” He stared at the bottle he held before looking back at Danny. “Shit, he’ll never find out. All I have to do is this.” He went over to the sink, turned the water on, and held the bottle under the faucet for a couple of seconds. “Whatever I take out, I replace. He’ll never know.”

“Won’t he taste the difference?”

“Not him.” Johnny turned the water off. “He’s too drunk when he finally gets around to this stuff. Doesn’t even like it.”

“No shit.” Danny took a sip of his drink. “How come?”

Johnny laughed. “Says it burns his insides. Calls it Mexican fire water.”

Danny took another sip of his drink, but still couldn’t taste the tequila. He didn’t know if he was supposed to. He thought about asking but Johnny or Pete might laugh at him for not knowing. “Where’re your parents now?”

“Out shoppin’. My old man got a few extra bucks workin’ overtime. Goin’ to be a big spender and buy somethin’ for my little brat of a sister.”

“How about ya? Don’t ya get anythin’?”

“Shit, he asked me if I wanted anythin’. Told him to take his money and shove it. So, he’s pissed at me now. They won’t be home for a couple of hours.”

“How about your sister?” Having met his sister before, Danny agreed that she was a little brat.

“Told the snothead to get out of the house because I had somebody comin’ over. She went over to a friend’s.”

“Hey, man,” Pete broke in, raising his glass in a toast to Danny. “That was cool the way ya put down that clerk. Even was in the paper. Callin’ us the Valentine Day Bandits.”

“The way ya two came runnin’ out,” Pete said. “I didn’t know what was goin’ on.”

“Yeah, man,” Johnny said. “Excitin’ as hell. Almost pissed my pants.”

“I gotta take a leak now.” Pete got up, and then plopped back down. "Hell, I'll piss later."

Johnny sat at the table with Danny, turning a chair around and straddling it. "How did it feel to do that guy?"

"Man, I was pumped."

Johnny poured more Coke and tequila into his nearly empty glass. "Too bad we didn't make too much on it."

"Twenty bucks a piece ain't bad." Danny didn't like any suggestion that what he did wasn't worth much. "Hell, that's just a warm up. We're goin' big time."

"What do ya mean?" Pete asked.

"We're goin' to hit Skelly's Liquor Store. That's where the big money is."

"But that's right on Broadway."

"No shit. Don't ya think I know that?" Danny snapped.

"Man, I didn't mean nothin'. Was only—"

"Forget it. I'll case the place out and plan the hit. Don't worry about it. Just leave it to Danny Logan."

"Let's have some more of that Mexican fire water," Johnny said.

Danny watched Johnny pour the drinks. *It had felt good to put that clerk down. Might even feel better to put someone down permanently.*

Chapter 46

"Butch! Wake up!"

Adam awoke with a start, aware of his mother sitting on his bed and that it was still dark outside. "What's wrong?" he mumbled.

"Grandpa died!" His mother's voice trembled with emotion.

"No…no!" he cried, the news hitting him like a bolt of lightning. "When?"

"An hour ago."

"What happen?"

"I don't know. The hospital called Wanda. She called me at work. We're going down to see Pa before they…Oh, Butch, this is so hard. I just can't believe it." She wiped the tears running down her cheeks.

Adam wasn't sure what to do or say, having never seen his mother so distraught. Wanting to be strong for her, he fought back his own feelings.

"You'll come down with us, won't you?"

"Yeah, sure." Adam's mind raced. *Was he in pain…who was with him when…did he call out for me before he…?* "Let me get dressed."

His mother reached over and brushed his hair to one side. "I'll wait in the living room."

Sitting on the edge of his bed, the words *Grandpa died* echoed through his head. He buried his face in his hands and thought about visiting him earlier that evening. *I should have stayed longer. Maybe he would've woken up later and we would've talked. Maybe he would've shown Sue the watch. Maybe...* He looked toward the living room, hoping that his mother would come in and announce that Doctor Jairvus just called and said the hospital had made a mistake; that his grandfather wasn't dead. He got up and grabbed a pair of pants and a shirt. As he dressed, he bumped into Oscar's bed.

"Is that you, Butch?" Oscar mumbled.

"Sorry, didn't mean to wake you."

"That's okay. What's going on?"

"I'm going down to the hospital with mom." Adam fought back tears. "Grandpa died."

"Golly, no." Oscar sat up. "What happened?"

"Don't know. We'll tell you about it when we get home. Go back to sleep." Adam opened the dresser drawer, took out a pair of socks, and sat down on his bed to put his socks and shoes on.

"I'll miss him by golly. Your grandpa was a good man."

His mother sat by the window in the living room. Upon seeing him come in, she got up, put her arms around him, and hugged him. Adam put his arms around her and stood listening to her sobbing, feeling her body convulse with emotion. It felt strange holding his mother like this. It had always been the other way around. As a kid, he had witnessed a dog hit by a car as the animal tried to run across Broadway. When he had come up to the apartment sobbing, his mother had held him tightly in her arms. Now, as he stood holding her, he felt tears rolling down his cheeks.

"I'm sorry," his mother sniffled as she lifted her head from his shoulder. "I'm getting your shirt all wet."

"That's okay." He looked toward the windows, not wanting her to see his tears.

She gave him a final hug and went back to her chair to get a tissue. "Will you drive? I don't think I can."

"Sure, no problem."

"I'll go get Wanda while you get the car." She opened her purse, dug through it, and handed him the keys. "It's parked around the corner on Third Street. We'll meet you in front."

"Okay. Give me about ten minutes." Adam went back to his room to get a sweater. He slipped it on, wondering how Wanda was doing. No sooner had the image of her flashed through his mind than another image came; big yellow teeth behind a sneering grin. He slammed his fist into the wall.

"Good golly, what was that?" Oscar mumbled.

"Butch, are you okay?" his mother yelled, appearing at the bedroom entrance and looked in.

"I just dropped something." Adam's hand throbbed with

pain. The knuckles felt tender but he didn't think they were bleeding. He had punched a hole in the wall. He would explain tomorrow, not tonight. When he walked into the living room, he tried to keep his voice steady, wanting to hide his anger. "Mom? Frank's not coming, is he?" He didn't want the guy anywhere near his grandfather's body.

His mother shook her head. "He told Wanda that he didn't want to come."

Doctor Jairvus was at the nurses' station when they arrived. "I'm sorry, there was nothing we could do," he said, his voice sounding weary

"What happened?" Virg asked, her lower lip trembling.

"His heart just gave out, but I can assure you that he died peacefully and didn't have to struggle. The nurse went in at eleven forty-five to check on him. Your father was resting comfortably then. Shortly after midnight, she checked on him again. He wasn't breathing, and she couldn't get a pulse. They paged me. After a preliminary check, I knew there was nothing more we could do."

"What time was that?" Wanda asked.

"Twelve-ten. The official cause of death is cardiac failure. That will be listed on the death certificate." Jairvus paused. "Adam, knowing your grandfather, he probably would say that his mainspring just got tired and stopped."

Adam blinked back tears as he nodded that he understood.

Jairvus answered the questions Virg and Wanda had, and when they had no more, he again expressed his sympathy.

"Thank you, Doctor," Wanda said. "You did all you could."

"I only wish we could've done more."

"Can we see him now?" Virg asked.

"Certainly. We put his glasses on him. He looks more like himself that way."

"Thank you," Virg said, her voice cracking with emotion.

"Are there papers to be signed?" Wanda asked.

"You can do all that afterwards. There's no rush. When you're ready, the nurses will help you with all the necessary forms." Jairvus cleared his throat. "They'll also contact whatever funeral home you decide on."

Wanda nodded. "We'll talk about it and let them know."

Jairvus turned to Adam. "After you have spent some time with your grandfather, I'd like to talk to you. He gave me something a couple of days ago and wanted me to personally give it to you if anything happened to him."

Adam could only nod, afraid if he tried to speak, words would get stuck in his throat. He was still wondering what Doctor Jairvus was talking about as he walked to his grandfather's room.

When they opened the door and stepped in, Virg froze. She began sobbing as soon as she saw her father. Adam swallowed hard, staring at his grandfather lying motionless.

Wanda reached out and put her arm around his sister. "Come on, it's okay. Pa's at peace. He looks like he's asleep, doesn't he?"

"But I want him to wake up!" Virg cried.

"I do, too," Wanda replied, her own voice cracking. "Let's go tell him we love him."

Adam walked up with them. His eyes stung and he blinked away tears. He couldn't believe that his grandfather was dead. He wanted him to wake up and say, "Ah Butch, good you here."

"Hello, Grandpa," Adam whispered. "I'm here."

"Oh, Pa," Virg sobbed. She bent down and kissed him while stroking the side of his face. "I love you, Pa. I love you."

"He loved you, too," Wanda said.

Adam saw tears rolling down Wanda's face. Tears formed in his eyes, but he fought them back, afraid they wouldn't stop once started. He needed to be strong for his mother. *Grandpa would want that.*

"Do you need a tissue?" Wanda held out the box for her sister.

"Thanks." Virg wiped her eyes and then blew her nose. Still sniffling, she turned to Adam. "Do you need one?" After he shook his head, she put her arm around him. "How're you doing?"

"Okay," he said, not about to tell her that he felt numb.

"We need to talk about what funeral home we want," Wanda said to her sister. "They're going to want to know."

Virg motioned to the other side of the room. "Let's go sit over there. I don't want to be talking about it in front of Pa," she whispered as though her father might overhear.

Wanda turned to Adam. "Do you want to sit down with us?"

"You can help us decide," his mother said.

"No, you do it." He didn't want to talk about funeral homes or coffins or flowers or anything like that. "I just want to stay here for a minute and then I'm going to see Doctor Jairvus."

Standing alone at the bedside, the voices of his mother and Wanda became muffled background noises. He and grandfather were alone together. His face was less lined and younger appearing. He looked peaceful, like he was asleep. Impulsively, Adam reached out and touched his grandfather's hand. It felt cool to the touch. He thought about how his hands had repaired discarded clocks. He remembered how it felt when he held his grandfather's hand as they crossed the street. His grandfather's hands were strong and firm, and yet, they could so gently handle the delicate inner workings of a clock. An overwhelming sadness enveloped him as he realized that no longer would he walk hand-in-hand with his grandfather. He had no idea how long he stood there. If need be, he would stand watch until his grandfather would say, *Go now, Butch. It time.* He closed his eyes and longed to hear his grandfather's voice again.

"Pa looks peaceful, doesn't he?" Virg said to Wanda as they came and stood next to Adam.

"Yes, he does."

"And he's with Ma, now, isn't he?"

"The two of them are together. Pa always loved her."

"I'm going to see Doctor Jairvus now," Adam said.

"Go ahead," his mother said. "We'll be here for awhile."

Adam opened the door to leave and looked back at his mother and Wanda standing by his grandfather's bed. Those three were the only family he had and now one was gone. An overwhelming sadness welled up within him as he realized how he had missed out on so many opportunities in the past several years with his grandfather. He quietly closed the door and went to find Doctor Jairvus.

"Hello," Doctor Jairvus said as Adam walked up to the nurses' station. He put his chart down and spoke to the nurse. Adam didn't understand what he was telling her because of the medical jargon. When Doctor Jairvus finished, he turned to

Adam. "Come with me into the family conference room. We'll have some privacy there."

Adam followed him into a nicely decorated room with a small couch, a couple of cushioned chairs, and an end table with a lamp sitting on it. A floor lamp in the corner gave the room a soft warm glow. A painting of a sunset over a peaceful lake hung on the wall. The room felt comfortable and restful. Adam sat in one chair as Doctor Jairvus pulled the other chair closer to him.

"I'm pleased we can spend this time together," Jairvus said. "Your grandfather was a remarkable man. I'm only sorry that I didn't have the chance to know him longer."

"Thanks, I know what you mean." Adam kept his eyes fixed on the end of his chair's armrest, running his fingers back and forth over its soft velvet material.

"He was going to give me some instructions in repairing clocks when he got better," Doctor Jairvus' said, his tone continuing to be warm and friendly. "However, we did manage to have a number of talks. He thought the world of you. It was obvious to all of us that he was quite proud to have you as a grandson."

Adam continued to rub the fabric of the chair.

"There were two things your grandfather wanted me to do. I have to confess that I normally don't get so involved in the personal lives of my patients. Your grandfather, however, was a unique individual and I might add, quite persuasive." Doctor Jairvus smiled. "He was also stubborn enough not to take no for an answer."

Adam smiled in return.

"The first thing he requested was for me to give you this." He reached into his coat pocket and took out a small package, wrapped in gold foil, and decorated with a red bow. "It's your graduation present. He told me that you knew what it was, but that you didn't know the inscription."

Adam bit his lip to hold back the tears. "The pocket watch," he said quietly.

"Yes, and he told me that you weren't to open it until just before you graduated. He said you could wear it on the day of your graduation." Jairvus smiled again. "He even got me to wrap it for him. He said if I was going to be his apprentice in restoring clocks, I'd have to start with small projects. Can you keep a secret?" he whispered.

Adam nodded.

"Your grandfather approved of my wrapping technique. The last time I felt so in need of approval was when I was a medical intern twenty years ago and wanted the approval of my superior. Your grandfather's approval was that important to me."

Upon hearing Jairvus' words Adam realized that he had also felt the same way about his grandfather. The first time he had gone with looking for clocks at the city dump, Adam had found one and ran to show it to him. "Perfect," his grandfather had proclaimed. With that one word, Adam had felt like a king.

"The other request he made is one that frankly I'm not sure I understand. The way he said it, however, he knew that you'd know."

Adam gave the doctor a puzzled look.

"He told me to tell you to remember the promise." Jairvus waited for a moment. "Do you know what he meant by that?"

Adam rubbed the knuckles of his right hand. It had felt good smashing his fist into that wall, but now he felt guilty, as if he had broken the promise he had made to his grandfather.

Realizing that Jairvus was waiting for a reply, he nodded.

"I thought you might. I've now fulfilled the two requests made by your grandfather, and I feel better."

"My grandfather liked you."

"I liked him also. I surely did."

Chapter 47

The funeral for Paul Kurtz was held on a late Friday afternoon at the Anderson Funeral Parlor. The funeral home, located a block off Broadway on Lyndale Avenue, had served the area for close to forty years. It had been rumored to have been one of the finest homes in the area before it was converted to its present use. The bronze casket was placed in what was called the Sunrise Room. Around the casket stood a half-dozen flower arrangements in addition to the one the family had gotten.

Adam, dressed in a dark suit that was also to be his graduation suit, looked around the room as he stood with his mother and Wanda. Some forty people were present. Kass was there. So was Adam's boss, Harry. Howie and Cindy were sitting in one corner of the room talking with Mick and Mary. Sue had told Adam that she was planning to come. He recognized a number of the regular customers from Andy's. Wanda had told him that some people from her workplace were there as well. Frank stood in the corner talking to some people Adam didn't recognize. Every now and then, Frank would glance over at him. He felt angry with Frank, but was determined to live up to the promise he had made to his grandfather.

After shaking the hand of some woman who worked with Wanda, Adam turned to his mother. "I'm going over to be with my friends."

"But there are people still coming in that I'd like you to meet."

"I can meet them later."

"Virg, let him go," Wanda said. "He wants to be with his friends."

Adam felt relieved to get away, tired of meeting people he didn't know and having to listen as they talked about how good his grandfather looked in the suit he was wearing. His grandfather didn't like suits, preferring work pants and flannel shirt.

"I'm sorry about your grandfather," Mary said as Adam came over to the group.

"Thanks." Adam moved a chair over and sat down to complete the small circle.

"How're you doing, buddy?" Mick asked.

"Hanging in there." Adam looked toward the entryway as a group of people came in and headed toward his mother and Wanda.

"Who are they?" Howie asked.

"Not sure. Many of these people I recognize but I really don't know them."

"My father would've come, but he wasn't feeling well," Howie said.

"Tell him the family appreciated the flowers he sent," Adam said, noting the worried look on Howie's face when he mentioned that his father was sick.

"Here comes Sue," Cindy said.

As soon as Adam saw Sue, he went to meet her. "Hi. Glad you could come."

"I wanted to be here with you," she said, her eyes reflecting a deep sadness. "I'm so sorry."

"Thank you. That means a lot. Would you like to go up and see him?"

"I'd like that."

They walked up to the casket and stood before it. Her hand found his. "I wish I would've gotten to know him. From what you've told me, he was a pretty special man."

"Yeah, he was. I think—"

"Hello, Butchie. Too bad about your grandpa."

Adam stiffened.

"Whose your friend?" Frank asked.

Adam was about to walk away when Sue replied. "I'm Sue. A friend from school."

Frank's eyes crawled over her. "And a might pretty one at that."

"Come on, Sue, let's go back to the others," Adam quietly said. As they walked away, he felt the anger rising within him. He could sense Frank's eyes boring into his back. *Remember the promise...Remember the promise...*

"Who was that?" Sue asked. "He's creepy."

"That was Frank. He's married to my aunt. I'll tell you about him later." Adam took a deep breath. "I'll tell you the whole story and you'll understand why I had to walk away."

Ten minutes before the service was to begin, Adam was called over by his mother. The funeral director wanted to have a final word with the family. Adam listened as the tall lean man wearing a dark blue suit explained that he would lead the family to the front row to be seated. He then asked if the family would prefer not to view the closing of the casket. Virg looked at Wanda and said she wanted to if that was okay with her. Wanda replied she had no problem with it. Adam wasn't sure, but decided to go along with his mom and Wanda. He had never been to a funeral before so he didn't know what to expect.

The seating arrangement would be Adam, his mother, Wanda, and Frank. Adam had asked his mother to talk with the funeral director about the seating arrangement, and to tell him that he wanted to sit as far away from Frank as he could. He also asked if Sue could sit with him. "Of course, she can," his mother had answered.

The family along with Sue was led up front. Adam sat down and stared at the casket in front of him. The organ played softly as he watched two men dressed in dark suits walk up and pause before the casket. They tucked in the draping cloth and slowly closed the lid. Adam stared straight ahead as he heard his mother sobbing quietly. It wasn't long before tears rolled down his cheeks. When Sue reached over, took his hand in hers, and squeezed, he squeezed in return.

The service was conducted by a Catholic priest. After the service, Adam, Howie and Mick, served as pallbearers. Wanda had told Adam that Frank would be willing to do it but his back had been hurting and he didn't think he should do any lifting. "Good," Adam had replied. "I don't want him touching Grandpa's coffin." Wanda reached out and hugged him. When she did, she whispered in his ear, "I understand."

The drive to the cemetery took less than twenty minutes. After the casket was placed on the rollers over the grave, Adam stepped back and stood by Sue. Once the brief graveside service concluded, Wanda went up and took a flower from the funeral spray on the casket. When Adam's mother went up to do the same, she began sobbing and had to be led away by her sister.

Sue told Adam that she would ride back with Mick and Mary. He told her that he really appreciated her being there and that he would call her later. When he got back to the car, he stared out the window at the casket sitting on the stand. "Good-bye, Grandpa," he whispered. As the car drove away, he put his head back and closed his eyes.

Chapter 48

Nearly a month had passed since the funeral and Adam was having a difficult time accepting that his grandfather was gone. Every night in bed, he would hold the package containing the pocket watch and reflect on the times he and his grandfather had spent together. Sometimes, he would turn on his side and lay the package between him and the window, letting the streetlights from Broadway illuminate its foil wrapping. Always within reach, the package sat on the shelf behind his bed. Having it near was a way of feeling his grandfather's presence. If he woke in the middle of the night, he would reach behind him and touch it before going back to sleep.

"Do you want me to keep it for you?" his mother asked him the day after the funeral. "Then you won't be tempted to open it before graduation."

"No, it's not a problem," he had replied.

As the days and weeks went by, however, he realized that his mother knew him better than he thought. The temptation to open it grew because of his desire to hold the pocket watch his grandfather's hands had so lovingly cared for and touched. He longed to wind its stem; to put the watch to his ear and listen to the ticking as though it embodied his grandfather's spirit. Most of all, he was anxious to read the watch's inscription. He knew that the inscription had meant so much to his grandfather, and he was curious to find out why his grandfather thought it so important to share with him. *And what does this have to do with me promising not to be angry with Frank? Grandpa, you're trying to teach me a lesson about life, aren't you? But what?*

Just two days after Adam had told his mother that she needn't worry about him being tempted, he had gone into the bedroom and sat on his bed debating whether to open the package. The only thing that prevented him was knowing that he would later regret not honoring his grandfather's wishes. *I can wait, Grandpa. Graduation is less than three months away.*

"I'm going to school now," Adam said, having finished his breakfast. His mother sat in the living room, sipping her morning cup of coffee, and gazing out the window. An unopened magazine lay in her lap.

"Mom?" Adam waited for a response. Gazing out the window, she acted as if she didn't hear him. For weeks after the funeral, she had been preoccupied. Only in the past couple of days had she seemed to be getting back to normal. With both of her parents now dead, she said she felt like an orphan. He was taken back by the thought. Everybody at school had parents. Most had both their parents. A few, like Howie, only had one parent. He had never thought about adults not having parents and he couldn't imagine what it must be like for them not to have any around. "Mom!" he called out again. "I'm going to school now."

"Okay, I'll see you later," she said, her voice lacking its usual energy and pep.

"Mom, you okay?"

"Yeah, I just miss Grandpa. I can't believe he's gone."

"I feel the same way." Adam put his books on a chair. Mick would wait for him if he was a few minutes late.

"When I was looking out the window just now, there was this little boy walking with, I don't know, his father, I guess. They looked like they were laughing and having lots of fun." She stared at the cup she held in her lap. "Reminded me when I was a little girl and Pa used to take me by my arms and swing me around in a circle. We laughed and laughed because we both got so dizzy." She paused. "Funny, the things that brings back memories."

"I know what you mean. Every time I look at a clock I think of Grandpa."

"He'd like that." She glanced at her watch. "You better go now or Mick will wonder where you are. I'll be okay."

Adam picked up his books. "I'll see you after school." He turned to leave when he heard his mother call his name.

"I'm just thankful that this past month things have been okay and nothing else has happened." Her eyes searched his. "Do you understand what I'm talking about?"

"You're talking about Frank. Don't worry, nothing's going to happen."

"Promise?"

"I promise."

"See you tonight," she said.

Going down the stairs, Adam wondered if his mother would have had him promise if she had known it was Frank who had gotten her father drunk that day. Why he didn't tell her, he wasn't sure. Maybe because she was upset enough.

That there had been no confrontations between him and Frank since his grandfather's death gave him a sense of relief. Of course, he hadn't seen Frank since the day of the funeral and the promise hadn't been put to the test. He was just thankful that the days had been routine and predictable. He went to school every day; did homework and took tests; ate lunch at the same time; talked and joked around with Mick and Howie; worked at Harry's every evening and on Saturdays; and stopped every so often to talk with Kass. The weather had predictability about it as well. They had gotten the usual snowfall in the early part of March, and then the weather turned mild and the snow began to disappear. Just before the State High School Basketball Tournament in mid-March, winter came forth with one final burst of energy. With April a few weeks away, the weather turned mild again and the snow turned to slush. Soon all traces of winter would be gone and spring would make its predictable arrival.

The one area in his life that hadn't been predictable was his growing relationship with Sue. In the past, they had dated once every couple of months. Since that day she came to the hospital with him to see his grandfather, he wanted to share more of himself with her. They had had three dates in the past month. He had also called her on a weekly basis and spent part of his lunch hour with her from time to time. The more he shared with her, the easier it became for him to do so. He even told her about Frank and how he had beaten Wanda. Sue had called Frank a horrible man and told Adam to be careful.

"For once I beat you here," Mick said as Adam met him at the corner. "Everything okay?"

"I was just talking with my mom. My grandfather's death

has really been hard on her," Adam replied as they crossed the street to the next block. "That's tough. How're you doing with it?"

"Sometimes, great. Other times…Man, I don't know. Just doesn't seem real that he's gone. Hard to believe it's been a month already."

For the next couple of blocks the two of them continued to talk about Adam's grandfather. Adam appreciated the opportunity to express his feelings. One of the things he would miss after graduation was the daily walks to school with his friends.

"How about you?" Adam asked. "What's it like at your house?"

"A little better. My mother saw to it that my father at least talks to me."

"So, he still doesn't understand why you don't want to play football?"

"Nope."

"That's too bad."

"That the breaks," Mick said with a touch of sadness. He pointed ahead. "There's Howie waiting for us."

"Hi, guys," Howie greeted them as they walked up. "We've got some serious thinking to do."

"About what?" Mick asked. "That chemistry final Ross is threatening us with?"

"Forget that. Don't you realize that it's going to be the first of April in a few weeks?"

"So, what does that mean?" Adam asked. "Are you planning to play an April Fool's joke on the teachers or something?"

"No, no, no! This is far more serious. It's Mattingale's desk! Before you know it, we'll be graduating and her secret will be left to the next class to unlock. We can't allow that to happen. As the graduating class of 1959, we've a sacred obligation to fulfill. It's our destiny."

Mick gave Howie a mock salute. "I'll sign up," he said solemnly. "You're full of it, but you sound serious."

"I am!"

"Serious or full of it?" Adam asked.

"Or seriously full of it?" Mick added.

"Very funny, guys. I tell you, this kid is serious."

"What have you got planned now?" Adam asked as they stopped at the corner and waited for the light to change.

"That's the problem. I don't have one single idea."

Mick grabbed Adam by the arm. "Hey, this is serious."

"I see what you mean. He looks lost for ideas."

"Maybe, he's just lost," Mick said.

"Come on, guys, quit horsing around. We need to come up with something." The light turned green and the three of them walked across. It wasn't until they stepped onto the next block that

Howie continued. "What do you say we think about it in the next couple of days?"

"Sure," Mick said.

"Yeah, why not?" Adam added.

Howie flashed a winsome grin. "And while you're thinking about Mattingale's desk, let's think about an April fool's joke to pull on the principal. I'd love to get Waite on something before I leave North."

"I wouldn't push your luck." Mick said. "Mattingale's desk is enough for us to think about."

Even though Howie tried to argue that an April fool's joke would be a classy way to go into the final two months of their senior year, Mick and Adam remained unconvinced. By the time they got to school, Howie had resumed talking about Mattingale's desk.

Miss Mattingale stood in front of her desk and smiled at her students as Howie slipped into his chair. The second bell hadn't rung yet and students were quietly chatting amongst themselves. As soon as Howie sat, he joined in the conversation with Mick and Adam. They were talking about their triple date for the senior prom when Adam whispered that Mattingale was coming toward them. Howie turned just in time to see that she had stopped at his desk.

"Howard, I would like to see you after class for a few minutes."

"Me?"

"Yes, Howard, you," she replied, bestowing a smile upon him. "Now, if you'll excuse me, it's time to begin class."

As Miss Mattingale walked to her desk, Howie glanced back at his two friends and shrugged.

"Class, may I have your attention." Miss Mattingale sternly eyed a couple of students in the back who were still talking. Once the room quieted, she continued. "We have less than six weeks of class before your term papers are due and we begin preparing for the final examinations. It's truly hard to believe that this school year is coming to an end. What a momentous year it has been. So much has happened."

"You can say that again," Adam muttered.

"One of the absolutely thrilling moments of this year for me was having my desk refinished." With obvious pride, Miss Mattingale looked lovingly at her desk. "There is only one other event of this year that would be the equal of that. Could anyone guess what that event might be?" She paused. When no one ventured an answer, she continued. "It was that day when I walked in and discovered notes from students and fellow teachers welcoming me back after that unfortunate incident."

"Hey," Mick whispered to Adam but loud enough for Howie to hear as well. "I thought it would be when she got mouth-to-mouth by you-know-who."

"Very funny."

Mattingale looked in Howie's direction. "Howard? What do you think is *very funny?*"

"Oh, ah…I was just making a comment about your desk. It's funny that such an important item in your life was, ah....refinished. Funny, not ha-ha funny, but…ah, funny it being so coincidental. You know, it was *very funny* that it happened that way."

"Why, Howard, that is precisely the point I was about to make." Miss Mattingale cleared her throat. "I perhaps, however, would not have used your choice of descriptive words, but I agree with you." She turned her attention to the rest of her class. "It's true that there is a relationship between what I teach and my desk per se. A desk is symbolic of the source from which many great works of writing have had their birth." With a theatrical sweep of her hand, she gestured toward the desk. "This desk, any desk, is a symbol of the written word. Sitting at it, one with pen and paper in hand creates that which will be passed on to future generations."

For the next thirty minutes Miss Mattingale talked about the great writers of history as she showed photographs of their desks.

When the bell rang ending the hour, Mick tapped Howie on the back. "Don't forget your date with the teacher now."

Adam got up from his desk. "Too bad, that you don't have a nice shiny apple to give her."

"*I do*, but I'm eating it myself."

Chapter 49

Mick and Adam were in the lunchroom waiting for Howie, speculating why Mattingale wanted to see him. Howie showed up with a sheepish grin on his face and sat down across the table from them.

"What did she want?" Adam asked Howie.

"Bet she wanted his body," Mick said. "Isn't that right? Come on lover-boy, tell us all the lurid details."

"Not much to tell." Howie opened his lunch bag and took out a sandwich. He sniffed the air. "School lunch smells good today. What are they serving?"

"Spaghetti," Adam said.

Mick shook his finger at Howie. "Don't you dare."

"What are you talking about?"

"Don't give me that innocent crap. You know what I mean. This is the first time they've served spaghetti since you set off that riot. Just don't get any wild ideas. I want to eat my lunch in peace."

"You don't have to worry. I've reformed."

Mick rolled his eyes.

"Come on," Adam said. "Tell us about Mattingale."

"Not much to tell." Howie took a bite of his sandwich, chewed, and washed it down with a couple gulps of milk. "All she wanted was to ask me if I had time to talk with her in a couple of weeks."

"Are you kidding?" Mick exclaimed.

"No, she said she didn't have time today."

Adam gave him a puzzled look. "Why two weeks?"

"Didn't tell me. Said she'd let me know when we'll meet in her classroom after school."

"Wonder what she wants?" Adam said.

"Maybe she wants to elope with him," Mick said. "You know, once you've been given mouth-to-mouth by *Howard* here, you become his love slave."

"All right, enough of that." Howie glanced around as though worried somebody might be listening. "Who knows why she wants to talk. Teachers think differently than normal people." He reached into his lunch bag and took out a Twinkie. "You guys got any ideas about her desk yet?"

Mick moaned. "Howie! You gave us that assignment only this morning. Give us a break."

"Hey, can I help it if I'm anxious?" Howie reached over and took Mick's notebook. He flipped through it until he found some blank pages and tore one out over Mick's protest.

"Why don't we do some brain storming and come up with some ideas?" he asked, handing the notebook back. Mick grabbed the notebook from a grinning Howie and hit him over the head with it.

"You two clowns are going to have to do it yourselves," Adam said, seeing Sue walk into the lunchroom. "I'm going over and talk with Sue for awhile."

"Take me with you," Mick pleaded as he started to get up.

"Sit down," Howie ordered, pulling Mick down.

"Howie, why don't you share your Twinkie with Mick?"

"Yeah, my brain will work better then."

"No way!" Howie snatched his Twinkle to shield it from Mick who was leaning over, trying to grab it.

"Have fun you two, I'm leaving."

* * *

Sue was pleased when she saw Adam walking over to her. In the past month, she had gotten to know him better than in all the previous time they had been dating. His grandfather's death had been hard on him, but had proven to be a pivotal point in her and Adam's relationship. Where as before, Adam had kept his thoughts and feelings to himself, he had now begun to open up and share more. The walls that she had seen in his eyes that had kept her out were slowly, but surely, coming down. It had been a struggle for him. He, himself, admitted that sharing his feelings was a new experience.

"Hi," Adam said, sitting down across the table from her. He

set his lunch bag down and opened up a carton of milk.

"I was hoping you'd come over. I wanted—" Sue looked across the lunchroom in the direction that Adam had just come from. "I think Mick's trying to get your attention."

Adam turned to look. A grinning Mick was standing up and pointing to something he had in his hand.

"What's that he's holding?" Sue asked.

"I think it's part of a Twinkie. Don't mind them. They're nuts."

"They're fun." Sue giggled as she glanced over at them. It looked like Howie was trying to take the Twinkie from Mick. "They've been good for you, haven't they?"

"Yeah, I don't know where I'd be if it hadn't been for those guys." Adam opened his lunch bag, took out a sandwich, and sat staring at it.

"What wrong?" Sue asked.

Adam hesitated. "This morning my mom and I were talking about my grandfather again. We were sharing some memories. He's been on my mind so much since…I just want to tell you again how much I appreciated you being there with me at the hospital and then...later at the funeral."

She reached over and placed her hand upon his. "I wanted to be with you. I'm glad you asked me."

Glancing around, he took her hand, and gently squeezed it before releasing it. "So am I."

Aware that Adam had a difficult time showing affection in public, she was pleased that even that was changing. She leaned toward him. "I heard so many wonderful stories about your grandfather from the people who were at the funeral. He was really a kind and caring man."

"It's funny, I think I always knew that deep down inside, but for the past couple of years I had forgotten it. Hate to say this, but all I could think of was that he was one of the winos on Broadway. I don't want to have that kind of memory of him."

"You don't have to. Your Aunt Wanda shared with me her memories of him playing the violin for your grandmother. One night he played for hours. Even though your aunt said she was only a little girl, the music was so beautiful that tears came to her eyes."

"Really, I never heard that story."

"She said that she'd forgotten about it until one of his old friends mentioned how your grandfather once played a violin for him. He was visiting this man's house and saw a violin lying on the table. He picked it up and just began playing."

Adam leaned back in his chair. "Oh, man. I wonder how many things there are about him that I don't know."

When Sue shifted in her chair, she felt her foot move up against what she thought was the table leg. And then the "table leg" pressed against her foot. "Just remember all the things you have of him that you can feel good about," she said, continuing to press her foot against his. "Like how he compared clocks to people. The things you told me about him and his love affair with clocks were wonderful. I especially liked how your grandfather and that doctor in the hospital…what was his name again?"

"Doctor Jairvus."

"I liked how he and your grandfather hit it off. That was so nice when he told you how much he thought of your grandfather."

"My grandfather taught me more about life than anyone else. I'm only beginning to realize that now. I thought he was only talking about clocks and stuff like that, but now I understand how much it was about people."

"And just think, he left you a pocket watch to remember him by. I think that's so neat. I wonder what the inscription says. Would…would you ever show me the inscription?"

Adam pressed his foot against hers again. "At the beginning of this year, I probably wouldn't have shared it with anybody."

"And now?"

"Now, I want to share it with you."

"I'd like that very much." She impulsively reached over and took his hand before realizing that Adam might feel embarrassed. Just as she was going to take her hand away, she felt his hand take hers and hold it tight.

"We're going to have to wait for a couple of months to find out what the inscription says," he said, still holding onto her hand.

"That's okay. I'm glad you're keeping your promise. Your

grandfather would be proud."

"It's been easy so far. I haven't even seen the guy. Frank's probably forgotten all about me."

"I hope so." A chill ran down her spine. "I'd be afraid of him."

"Don't worry, nothing's going to happen."

* * *

It was early evening when Danny Logan and his two friends met in a park a couple of blocks away from North High School. Pete and Johnny sat on a picnic table while Danny stood, leaning up against a tree.

"I tell ya," Pete said as he watched Danny light up a cigarette. "We'll leave an Easter egg as our callin' card. That'll be cool."

"Yeah," Johnny said as he nodded toward Pete and then looked at Danny. "Didn't ya read what the paper said about us leavin' that valentine with that clerk?"

Pete took a drag off his cigarette. "What do ya think?" he asked, offering Johnny a drag.

"Maybe one of those plastic eggs with the jelly beans inside or maybe a real one."

"Real one would be cool," Johnny said. "We could decorate it and write our own message on it."

"Listen, ya dumb shits, we ain't goin' to worry about that now. The liquor store ain't going to be as easy. I'll case it out next week. Pete, you're drivin'. Johnny's goin' in with me." Danny took a drag off of his cigarette and flicked it away. "Man, we're goin' to score big this time."

Chapter 50

Spirited energy charged the hallways at North High that second week in April. Seasoned teachers attributed the student's exuberance to the spring-like weather. Mr. Nichols, a Biology teacher in his twentieth year, explained to his peers as they sat in the teacher's lounge, "The snow's nearly gone, the robins are back, the trees are budding, and these kids smell it. They're like bear cubs coming out of hibernation." Mrs. Taylor, the Algebra teacher, nodded in agreement. "And don't forget, the senior prom is only five weeks away and everybody is buzzing about that."

In addition to the anticipation of the senior prom, the school yearbooks were scheduled to arrive in two weeks. Excitement would only crescendo as students began the ritual of racing around and signing yearbooks while giddily reading what others had written in theirs. Then there would be the senior party, sponsored and chaperoned by the school (not to mention the numerous other *non-chaperoned* parties). All of these things normally would have been very exciting for Howie if he could have focused upon them. What distracted him had been Mattingale's indication that she wished to speak to him. Over two weeks had gone by since she had initially mentioned it, and he had almost given up. That changed, however, when she approached him at the end of class one day.

"Howard, I would like to see you before you leave."

"Okay, Miss Mattingale." Howie turned to Mick and Adam. "See you guys at lunch, okay?"

"Should we start without you if you're not there?" Mick asked with a devilish twinkle in his eyes.

Adam patted Howie on the back. "Yeah, just in case you're detained by something unexpected."

"I'll be there, don't worry about it," Howie said through clenched teeth.

Mattingale waited until Adam and Mick left before speaking. "Would you have time today to come in to see me after school?"

Howie's heart skipped a beat. "Sure."

"Splendid. Shall we say 3:15 here in my classroom?"

***

During lunch, Howie kept pointing at the clock. "Do you think that's right? Maybe we should have the janitor check it. That second hand's going around too slow."

"Relax, you'll see Mattingale soon enough," Mick said.

"I know…I know, but I'm anxious to find out what she wants to see me about. It's been driving me nuts. I can't think of anything else."

"Don't sweat it," Adam said. "Maybe she wants to see you about some paper you've written."

"Or, maybe she's been noticing you nodding off to sleep the past couple of days," Mick added.

"Hey! I'm entitled. I'm a senior."

"Whatever it is, you'll find out soon enough." Adam reached into his lunch bag and pulled out a package of cookies. "Guys want one? My mom brought them home from work this morning. They're chocolate chip."

"Thanks, man." Howie snatched a couple, picked up his milk carton and shook it. "Got to get some more milk. Guard my lunch, will you?"

Mick grabbed Howie's lunch bag and placed it by his. "If you're not back in five minutes, we'll feed it to the sophomores."

"That's a good idea," Adam said. "I've seen some of them. They look pretty scrawny."

Howie glared at Adam. "Yeah, and they're going to stay that way. Mick, keep an eye on him so he doesn't get any weird ideas about my food, okay? I'll be right back."

"That Howie's all right," Adam said after their friend left.

"Yeah, he's a good guy." Mick reached for another cookie. "Man, these are great. Tell your mom to send cookies anytime she wants."

"What's the latest with you and your dad?"

"He still isn't talking to me very much, but he's not as ticked off."

"How do you know that?"

"Overheard him and my brothers talking about me the other night. They were in the kitchen. They thought I was still up in my room."

"What were they saying?"

"Don't know exactly. Didn't hang around, but from what I heard, I got the sense that my father was defending me."

"Really! In what way?"

"About my right to make a choice." Mick shrugged. "At least, that's what it sounded like."

"That's something, isn't it?"

"Yeah, I know, but it makes me feel guilty. Man, I just hated to disappoint him."

"He'll get over it."

"I don't know. When it comes to football, it's pretty serious business with him. When he coached me as a kid, he never let up. It wasn't fun."

"When you and Mary get hitched and have kids, you can coach them and that'll be fun."

"Me coaching, huh? Hey, that's a good idea."

"You know a lot about football, so it'd be easy, wouldn't it?"

"Not sure how easy it'd be, but I think I could do it."

"Whatever school you're teaching at, you could help with coaching the football team. Man, you could even be the coach. Wouldn't your dad like that? Think about it."

Mick's eyes lit up. "That might be a good way to keep up the football tradition and keep my father happy. I'm going to check into that. Thanks for the idea."

"Just trying to repay you for all you've done for me this year."

"It's been one heck of a year, hasn't it?"

"Sure has. I'm glad it's almost over."

"What's almost over?" Howie asked as he came back, carrying two pints of milk.

"The time we gave you to get your butt back here," Mick said. He grabbed for one of Howie's pints of milk, but Howie back away. Mick pointed to a table across the way from them. "We're just ready to give your lunch to one of those skinny sophomores. They could use some milk, also," he said, making a sudden lunge for the milk again.

"Oh, no, you don't." Howie shielded the milk with his body. "I need to have this to keep up my energy."

"Energy for what?" Mick asked.

"For my meeting with Mattingale." Howie sat down and grabbed his lunch bag from Mick, checking its contents.

"Hey, Adam. Look at that. He doesn't trust us."

"Pass me a couple more of those cookies, will you?" Howie asked.

***

Howie had no trouble maintaining his energy level for the rest of the afternoon. It was exactly fifteen minutes after three when he walked into Miss Mattingale's classroom.

She glanced at the clock. "Howard, you're so punctual. I admire that quality in an individual. I wish more students would follow your example."

"I always try to be on time. It's something my father taught me."

"Very good for him." Mattingale motioned to the chair next to her desk. "You may sit while we talk. How is your father?" she asked after he sat down. "I understand he's been ill."

"He tries to take it easy whenever he can," he said, wondering how she knew about his father. "It's his heart. He's on medication and has to watch what he does."

"Please tell him that he's in my thoughts and prayers."

"I will. Thanks."

"Now, I imagine you're wondering why I wished to speak to you?"

"Yes, ma'am."

"Do you remember the day of that terrible incident and how you came to my rescue?"

Howie panicked, wondering if she had found out it was him who put the smoke bomb in her closet. He wiped his sweaty palms on his pants. "Who can forget that?" he asked, managing a weak smile.

"I must say that it was not only an unforgettable experience for me, but also a traumatic one. The guilty party will have to live with what they did for the rest of their lives. Don't you agree?"

He found it hard to speak. When the words finally came, they popped out as if they had been stuck in his throat. "Yes, ma'am."

"Are you okay, Howard?"

"Yes, I just...ah, had something stuck in my throat." *She knows! Maybe she'll go easy on me if I confess.*

"That it was a terrifying experience, I cannot deny."

When Miss Mattingale leaned toward him, Howie thought for a moment she would point an accusing finger at him and scream, "*You* did it!" He shifted uneasily on the chair and prepared himself.

"But, Howard, it wasn't my first experience."

Howie's mouth dropped open. "I…I don't understand."

"Of course you don't. That's why I asked to speak to you. I owe you my life and have made the decision to tell you a story that I haven't told anyone for many years. I'm sharing it because when one's life is given back to them by another, there is a special bond formed." She paused and smiled. "Do you understand what I'm telling you?"

"I…I think so."

"There is something in my desk drawer that I would like to show you. It will take a minute to get my key and open it."

Howie watched as Miss Mattingale opened her purse, took out her keys, and inserted one into the lock. As the drawer slowly open, he forgot about any confession he was going to make.

Chapter 51

Before Wanda went to work on Tuesday morning, she left a note on the kitchen table suggesting to Frank that he should look at the help want ads in the paper.

Frank,

I circled some job openings that you might want to check on today.

Wanda.

She purposely didn't sign it *love, Wanda*. It was her way of showing that she was upset with him for not having worked for nearly a year. He wouldn't notice her act of defiance, but that didn't matter.

* * *

When Frank finally decided to crawl out of bed, it was mid-morning. He strolled into the kitchen, grabbed a beer from the refrigerator, and sat down to read the comic section of the newspaper. When he saw Wanda's note, he picked it up and read it. "Goddamn it," he muttered, crumpling the note and throwing it on the floor. *Who does she think she is tellin' me what to do?* He guzzled his beer, belched, and stretched his arms as he looked around the kitchen. The crumbled note caught his attention. *Shit, ever since her wino father died, she's been on my case about one goddamn thing or another.* The more he thought about the note, the angrier he got. He scratched his throat and decided he needed another beer. After getting his beer, he slammed the refrigerator door. *Son'n'bitch, she makes me mad.* He grabbed the comics, sauntered into the living room, and plopped on the couch, spilling beer on the armrest. *If she thinks I'm goin' to run my ass all over lookin' for a job she's goddamn nuts.*

* * *

About the time Wanda was writing the note to Frank, Adam and Mick were meeting Howie on the way to school. The warm morning sun melted the snow, leaving streams of water running along the curbing gutters. Finally, the weariness of winter was being washed away with the freshness of spring.

"Come on, tell us every detail of your rendezvous with Mattingale yesterday," Adam said.

"Yeah, I could hardly sleep last night thinking about it," Mick added.

"What's to tell? It's was no big deal."

"What do you mean no big deal?" Mick cried. "What did she want?"

"Oh, she…ah, wanted to go over that last paper I turned in," Howie said, still trying to sort through his feelings about what he had seen in her desk drawer and the incredible story she had shared with him.

"Wait a minute!" Adam said. "The class turned those papers in a week ago. Something isn't jiving here. Didn't she tell you a couple of weeks ago that she wanted to talk to you?"

"Yeah, come clean," Mick said. "What are you hiding?"

"Nothing," Howie shot back. "Like what I told you. She wanted to see me about a paper I turned in a month ago. Since we were meeting, she decided to also talk about this last paper."

"Are you sure that's all?" Mick asked.

"What else would there be?"

"I was hoping for some juicy stories, but I guess not."

"Did you get a good look at her desk again?" Adam asked.

"Sure did."

"And did you come up with any ideas about unlocking that drawer?" Mick asked. "You do remember that you wanted to solve that mystery before graduation?"

"Yeah…but I don't have any new ideas yet."

"Well, don't worry," Mick said. "We still have plenty of time to come up with something."

* * *

By late morning Frank had finished off the last of the beer. He cursed Wanda for not having more in the house. He checked his wallet. Two bucks. *Goddamn it! That won't buy piss.* He rummaged around in the kitchen cupboard until finding a tin tea bag container. It held Wanda's money for emergencies. Opening it, he found fourteen dollars and some change. He took ten dollars and was replacing the cover when he paused, opened it again, and took the rest of the money. He placed the empty can back where he had found it. *Hell, serves her right. Besides, this is a goddamn emergency*. On the way to the liquor store he made a spur-of-the-moment decision to stop at the B & B Bar to have a beer. When he walked in, there were only a couple of customers sitting at the bar.

Frank took a seat at the far end of the bar. "Hey, Charlie," he said to the bartender. "I thought ya only worked nights."

"I usually do but Larry's sick and I'm filling in for him." Charlie wiped the counter in front of him. "What will you have?"

"Gimme a beer, and Charlie, don't ask if I want it in a goddamn glass. I'm not in a mood for any shit today."

Charlie placed the bottle in front of him. "What's the matter? Got problems?"

"I ain't got any, but the goddamn woman I'm married to is goin' to have some if she doesn't quit chewin' on my ass."

"I know what you mean. My first wife was ragging on me all the time about one thing or another. She didn't want me working nights. Thought I was cheating on her."

Frank took a couple swigs of his beer. "What did ya do?"

"Got rid of her." Charlie chuckled as he wiped the counter again. "And then I married the woman I was playing around with."

Frank laughed. "I'll be goddamn."

"Hell, it didn't last more than a year." Charlie leaned over the counter and whispered, "Now, I just play around and I don't have to answer to anyone."

"And ya shouldn't have to, goddamn it." Frank drank the last of his beer and ordered another. "A man isn't worth shit if he doesn't goddamn stand up for himself."

"You're right on that." Charlie paused. "You're really pissed, aren't you?"

"Damn right and tonight I'm goin' to show her who's boss."

Frank stayed at the bar for most of the afternoon drinking beer and talking with Charlie. The two of them talked about how men should stick together and not give in to what they considered to be the "goddamn unreasonable demands of women."

"Hell," Frank said, laughing, "women need to be slapped around every now and then just to keep them in line."

"You're right on that. They expect it, don't they?"

"Goddamn right they do, Charlie. Goddamn right."

* * *

Wanda was tired. Her back ached from working at a job where she had to stand all day. The bus ride home was long as usual, and the bus was crowded with noisy passengers whose chattering reminded her of the clattering of the machines at the potato chip factory. The only available seat on the bus was near the back, and she could smell the bus fumes the entire ride home. When she got off at her stop, she was wearier than she was when she first got on. Climbing the stairs, she had to stop midway at the landing to catch her breath. She hoped that Frank had a good day because if he had, there might be the possibility of him having had prepared supper. She trudged up the remaining steps and slowly walked to the back apartment. As soon as she opened the door, she saw Frank on the couch. When he looked at her with his nostrils flaring, she knew immediately he had been drinking.

"Hello, how did the day go," she asked, being careful of what she said and how she said it.

"How the hell was it supposed to go?"

Wanda walked into the kitchen, took off her coat, and laid it over a chair. She noticed a crumbled up piece of paper on the floor but was too tired to pick it up.

Frank followed her into the kitchen. "I suppose ya thought ya were pretty damn smart leavin' that note this mornin'? Who the hell are ya to boss me around?"

"What are you talking about? I was just suggesting you look at those jobs."

"Suggested, hell. Ya think I'm a no good bum, don't ya?"

"No, I was just trying to be helpful." She backed away to get distance between the two of them. "Please, Frank, don't shout. The neighbors will hear."

"I don't give a goddamn about the neighbors. And who the hell are ya to tell me to shut up?"

"I wasn't—"

"Goddamn, ya better not, either."

She turned and walked over to the sink, thinking she would wash the dirty dishes. As she turned on the water, she heard him come up behind her.

"Who the hell do ya think ya are, turnin' your back on me and walkin' away?" he screamed. "What's the matter, don't ya want to look at your husband? Think you're too goddamn good for me?"

Wanda turned around. "I wasn't—Frank, no!"

Chapter 52

Adam's mother was sitting at the table when he came home from school on Wednesday afternoon. With legs crossed, her left foot shook in agitation.

"What's wrong?" he asked.

"Frank beat up Wanda!"

"Oh, no!" Adam tossed his schoolbooks on the table, his muscles tightening as old emotions stormed to the surface. "When?"

"Last night." Virg uncrossed her legs, only to cross them again. "She'd just gotten home from work. He'd been drinking and was mad about who knows what." She uncrossed her legs and began tapping the floor with her foot. "You know how he gets when he drinks."

"How are you doing?"

"I'm so angry I could kill Frank! If that man ever shows his face to me, so help me, God, I'll get a gun and shoot him. I don't care if they put me in jail. I'll shoot him dead!"

"Mom, take it easy." Adam had never known her to threaten violence toward anyone. He pulled out a chair and sat down. "Is Wanda okay?"

"It's worse than last time." Virg took a tissue from her pocket and blew her nose. "Her face looks terrible. I'm surprised that she doesn't have a broken jaw."

"How did you find out? Did she call you or something?"

"Yes, just after you left for school. At first, I didn't know who it was because her voice sounded so different and she was barely able to talk." Getting up, she went over to the cupboard, popped three aspirins in her mouth and washed them down with water. Standing at the sink, she leaned against it, holding the empty glass. "I'm so worried about her. I wanted to call a doctor but she said no. She's stubborn just like Pa. Thank God she got some sleep this afternoon."

"So, she didn't go to work?"

"Oh, no! Not with those bruises on her face."

"Is it that bad?"

"That's not the half of it. She could barely get out of bed this morning because of her sore ribs. Frank kicked her when she was on the floor."

Adam ran his hand back through his hair. All the old feelings and inner conflicts about Frank screamed to break loose. Closing his eyes, he concentrated on the promise he had made to his grandfather.

"Butch, do you want an aspirin?"

"No, I'm okay. Where's Frank now?"

"Don't know. He's not at the apartment. I've been checking every half hour or so. I don't want him anywhere near her."

"Hope this convinces her to throw the jerk out."

"That's what I told her to do." Virg sat back down at the table. "I told her to take all his clothes and throw them out in the hallway and bolt the door. She should even change the locks."

"What did she say to that?"

Virg massaged her forehead. "I don't know what's wrong with her. All she could talk about was how worried she was about him leaving. With everything he's done, she still doesn't want him to go. Can you believe that?"

"I'd say good riddance if we never saw him again. I hope he leaves."

"I hope so too, but you have to understand her. She's never had very good luck with men. When Frank came into her life, she felt fortunate because she thinks she's not attractive."

"What has that got to do with it?"

"She says that if Frank left, she'd be alone and she's always been afraid of that." Virg picked up her cup and walked over to the stove. After getting coffee, she came back and stood by the refrigerator. "I'm so angry, I can't see straight."

"Why don't you sit down?"

"I can't. I'm too upset." She leaned against the refrigerator. "I asked her, 'Why do you stay with a man who treats you like that?' Do you know what she said? That she'd rather be in a bad relationship than in no relationship at all. I tried to talk some sense into her but she wouldn't listen. She's already talking about being partly to blame for what happened."

"That's stupid."

"I know, but she's blaming herself for nagging Frank about getting a job."

"That doesn't make sense. She gets beat up and she blames herself? I don't understand her."

"Neither do I and she's my sister. I better go over and fix her some soup. What are you going to do now?"

"Go down and see Kass."

"That's a good idea. Are you going to talk to him about this?"

"Don't know. Maybe. Is that okay?"

"Of course it is."

"Mom? You're not going to do anything, are you? I mean, if you see Frank?"

"Don't worry, I'm not going to shoot him if that's what you mean. I may be angry with the man, but I'm not foolish. Besides, I don't have a gun," she added, giving him a half smile.

* * *

"Be right with you, Adam," Kass hollered when the young man plopped down on a stool. By the look on Adam's face he sensed something was wrong. "Judy, keep an eye on things will you?" he told the woman working at the register. "You look like you have a problem, my boy," Kass said, walking up to Adam. "Anything wrong?"

"Kass, this is my senior year and I always heard it's supposed to be something to look back on to remember. But man, I just want to forget about it."

"Want to talk about it?"

"It's about my Aunt Wanda."

"Oh, yes. Nice woman. I've known her for quite some time."

"She's married to this guy named Frank. Do you know him?"

"I'm afraid I do."

Adam glanced around and lowered his voice. "He beat her up last night."

"Oh, that's terrible."

"And it wasn't the first time."

"Frank's one of the few people that I dislike. I remember him as a young man and I didn't like him then, either."

"What was he like then?"

"Same as now, always acting tough and being a bully. I thought the service might change him, but he came out worse than he went in. When he and your aunt got married, I just shook my head."

"I don't know what to do, Kass. I have all these mixed feelings."

"Like what?"

"When it comes to Frank, you don't want to know. They're not very nice." Adam wet his lips. "Can I have a glass of water?"

"Sure, how about a Coke? We'll each have one." Kass got two glasses, put ice cubes in each one, and filled them. "Tell me, what would your grandfather advise you to do if he was here?"

"I know what he would've said a year ago. He would've told me to kick Frank's ass." Adam bit his lip. "Sorry, but that's what he would've said."

Kass smiled. "No need to apologize. Don't forget that I also knew your grandfather. On more than one occasion, I heard him use some rather colorful language when it came to Frank."

"Yeah, but his attitude changed after he found an old pocket watch."

"It did? Why do you think?"

"It had to do with an inscription he discovered in it."

"What did it say?"

"Won't know until I open it when I graduate. It was his graduation present to me."

"Well, whatever it says, it must've been important enough to change him."

"I know. He still didn't like Frank, but he told me not to let the anger get the best of me; that Frank wasn't worth it." Adam shared the entire story about the watch, including how his grandfather had even gotten Doctor Jairvus involved and about the promise.

"So now you feel caught between wanting to keep this promise you made and getting revenge on Frank."

"You said it."

"That's quite a story. It doesn't surprise me about your grandfather. I don't know what could be engraved in that watch, but, it must've been very important to him."

"You knew him. Do you have any idea what the inscription might be?"

"No, but I knew your grandfather to be a gentle man and very wise about life. He once told me that God must've been a clock maker. When I asked him how he came to that conclusion, he said because all the laws of nature work together like clockwork and that each part of creation depends upon another part, like the inner workings of a clock."

"Ever since my grandfather died, people have shared stories about him with me. I'm finding out things about him that I didn't know."

"That's good. Such things keep his memory alive. Those stories and who he was is his inheritance to you."

He gave Kass a puzzled look. "I thought inheritance was money and stuff like that."

"Yes, most people usually think of inheritance in that way. In that sense, the pocket watch will be your inheritance from your grandfather. Those stories and the kind of man your grandfather was is also your legacy."

"I never thought of it that way before. Do you think that has anything to do with him asking me to make that promise?"

"Yes, I think so. Your grandfather realized that anger isn't a very good inheritance to leave to anyone. Whatever that inscription says, it could've reminded him of that in some way. Perhaps, that's why he tried to change his attitude toward Frank and not let anger control him. He didn't want you to think of him only in that way. Does this make any sense?"

Adam nodded.

"You know, I think Frank's angry. Angry with himself for who he is, but he doesn't realize it. That's why he takes it out on the world and unfortunately, your aunt. Now understand, I don't say that to make excuses for his actions."

"But I can't let Frank continue beating her up. One of these days he's going to kill her."

"Of course, you can't let him continue. It's your aunt, however, who has to put a stop to it. She needs to say enough is enough and realize that she can have a life without him."

"I don't know if she can do that."

"If she can't do it on her own, then maybe she needs a little help."

"What do you mean?"

"Have your mother talk to some of her police officer friends. Tell her to find one who is willing to talk to Frank in an unofficial capacity. Perhaps the threat of jail will stop him."

"That's a good idea. Thanks. I'll talk to her about it."

Kass nodded approvingly. "In the meantime, I'll give some more thought to what else can be done, but remember that in terms of acting upon your anger toward Frank, I agree with your grandfather. Frank's not worth it. You don't want to dishonor your grandfather's memory in that way."

"I'm trying, but it's not easy."

"Nothing worthwhile in life is easy."

When Adam left the drugstore, he was anxious to get home and talk to his mother about what Kass had suggested. It wasn't the entire answer, but it was something. It would make his mother feel as if she was doing something to help. He thought what she would tell her cop friends. *His name is Frank. I want you to talk some sense into him about leaving my sister alone, even if you have to break his arm to do so.*

Walking home, Adam was feeling pretty good until he saw the red lightening bolt insignia on the back of the black leather jacket. Danny Logan was looking into the window of Skelly's Liquor Store. Adam hoped he could walk by without being noticed, but Danny turned around.

"Hey, man, how ya doin'?"

"Okay. You waiting for someone to buy you a pint or something?"

"Shit no. Just hangin' out."

* * *

Frank stood on the other side of the street watching Adam and Danny. *Butchie's up to his tricks again. Talkin' to Danny Logan. Well, I know all about that punk. So ya two must be plannin' to get old Frank again, eh? Well, goddamn it, this time,*

I'm ready. I'll deal with Danny and then with ya, Butchie boy.

Chapter 53

Adam stirred his cup of hot chocolate. He and Mick had left for school a half hour earlier that morning and now were sitting in a booth at the Rainbow café waiting for Howie. "Do you have any idea why he wanted to meet so early?"

"Not really," Mick said. "He hasn't been acting like his normal self."

"Yeah, I know. Man, he's been so quiet."

"Maybe this has something to do with his dad not feeling well."

"Last week he said that his dad was doing better. Hey, here he comes now."

"He sure looks glum," Mick said. "I haven't heard him joke around for nearly a week. You'd think he's got the weight of the whole world on his shoulders."

Howie slid in next to Adam. Almost immediately, the waitress came over to take his order.

"So what's up, Howie?" Mick asked after the waitress left.

"I've got to get something off my chest."

"This sounds like a confession," Mick said. "Are you sure you don't need a priest? Maybe Father Adam here can help you."

"Either me or Father Mick."

"Come on, you two. I don't feel like joking around. This is serious. It's Mattingale's desk. I know what's in that locked drawer."

"How did you find that out?" Mick asked.

The waitress brought Howie's hot chocolate. He waited until she left, but still lowered his voice. "She unlocked the drawer and showed me. Then she took one of her gloves off and—"

"Wait a minute." Mick leaned over the table toward Howie. "She took off her gloves? Miss Mattingale? Our English teacher? She took off those white gloves?"

"Just one of them," Howie said. "Remember when she asked

me to meet her after school?"

"Didn't you say she wanted to see you about some paper?" Adam asked.

"I know I said that, but it had nothing to do with any class assignment. I didn't want to lie to you guys, honest. Man, you two are my best friends. I didn't say anything at the time because I was confused. I had to think through some things. You've got to believe me."

"Hey, buddy, that's okay," Mick said. "We believe you. Don't we, Adam?"

"Sure we do. Come on. Tell us the rest of it."

"We talked about my dad and stuff like that. Then she started talking about, you know…*that* day."

"You mean the smoke bomb?" Adam asked.

"Yeah. For a minute I thought she knew it was me and was going to nail me. Man, I was scared. Then she told me how much she appreciated me saving her life and all that. I was feeling sort of guilty about that so I was just about to come clean."

"You didn't, did you?" Mick asked, his eyes widening.

"No, just then she gets a key out of her purse and unlocks that top right-hand drawer. I couldn't believe it. She unlocks it and as she pulls it out, I see a plastic bag with some stuff in it."

"What kind of stuff?" Adam asked.

"A silver cross on a chain, some other kind of jewelry, and a letter."

"Do you want anything else?" the waitress asked as she stopped while walking by with the coffee pot. All three shook their heads, and then waited impatiently for her to write out and leave the check.

"Okay, what about the letter?" Adam asked once the waitress went to another booth.

"I don't know. She never read it, but she told me that it was the only letter her sister had ever written her."

"Her sister?" Mick glanced at Adam and then looked back at Howie. "Mattingale's got a sister?"

"Yeah, a younger sister. There was something like three years difference between the two of them. Her sister had written the letter a week before she died."

A wave of sadness hit Adam. Hearing about the death of

Mattingale's sister brought memories of his grandfather's death. "How did she die?" he asked.

"There was a fire in their house one night. Mattingale was about twelve or thirteen at the time. She woke up and ran to her sister's room. The smoke and flames were terrible." Howie leaned his head back and closed his eyes for a moment. "She managed to pull her sister out of the burning room. The sister was badly burned and only lived a week."

"Oh, man!" Mick muttered.

Howie took a deep breath. "The cross and other jewelry belonged to her sister. Mattingale keeps them in that drawer along with the letter. The stuff's in a sealed bag. During lunch every day she takes it out and reads the letter. At first, I thought it was sort of spooky until she explained that it was her way of feeling close to her sister."

"Man, that's some sad stuff," Adam said.

"But why the white gloves?" Mick asked.

"When she rescued her sister, she burned her hands so bad that they are scarred. She took one of her gloves off and showed me her hand. It didn't look that bad to me, but you know her and how fussy she is when things aren't right."

"I'm glad we didn't open that desk drawer," Mick said. "I would've felt like a jerk."

"Can you imagine how I would've felt?" Howie said. "After all, it was my stupid idea. I feel bad enough about that smoke bomb after what she told me."

"What do you mean?" Mick asked.

"She said that everybody thought she'd been overcome by smoke that day. But the reason she fainted was seeing and smelling the smoke brought back all the bad memories. She called it a flashback or something like that."

The three young men sat without saying anything for a while. Mick and Adam finished drinking their hot chocolates. Howie barely touched his drink.

"You've got to promise not to tell anyone about this ever," Howie said.

"Don't worry, we won't say a word," Adam said.

Mick agreed. "You can count on that."

* * *

In class that morning, Miss Mattingale talked on how the recorded word has been so important throughout history. "Whether it is the history of the Roman Empire, or the thoughts of one friend as expressed to another in a letter, the written word is the diary of civilization. Throughout this year we have…"

As Adam thought about the letter in Mattingale's desk drawer, he noted that Howie listened with renewed interest in what she had to say.

At lunch, Howie hardly touched his food. When Mick suggested that they think of something they could do during graduation ceremonies as a way to be remembered by future classes, he showed little interest. When asked if he had any ideas, he shook his head.

When Adam got home from school that day, Oscar was sitting at the kitchen table having coffee and a roll. "Do you want one?" he asked. "They're fresh, by golly."

"No, but thanks anyway. I've got to go to work."

"How's your Aunt Wanda doing?"

"As long as Frank leaves her alone, she'll be okay."

"That Frank, he's nothing but trouble. I don't like him. By golly, I didn't even say hello to him when I saw him."

Adam's interest peaked. "When did you see him?"

"About an hour ago when I went to the bakery. He was going into the B & B Bar. When he waved, I pretended I didn't see him."

"Good for you. I'm going now. See you later."

On the way to work, Adam decided that he would stop to see Wanda during his supper break that evening. As far as Frank being at the apartment, he wasn't concerned, figuring that he would be at the bar most of the evening.

The time at work went quickly for Adam. He kept busy stocking shelves and changing the window display. When he had asked for some extra time for supper, Harry told him that it would be no problem. "Don't worry," he said as he pointed to the mannequins in the window. "The dummies will still be here when you get back. They're not going anyplace. Neither am I."

Adam left work and headed for home. Within minutes, he

was knocking on the door to Wanda's apartment.

"Who is it?" she called out.

"Adam."

"Come on in."

She was lying on the couch. Light from two small lamps gave the living room a restful atmosphere. Relaxing, soothing music was coming from the radio out in the kitchen.

"I'm just resting a little before I do the supper dishes. Sit down. Frank's out running some errands."

"How are you doing?"

"Okay. Just a little tired."

"He got you good, didn't he?"

"Butch, I know you're angry with Frank, but don't start anything with him. Please, I ask you not to. He told me that it won't happen again and that he's sorry."

"He's never been sorry for anything," Adam said, fighting to control his anger. "How can you let him beat you up like that and then take him back? I don't understand."

"Maybe when you get older, you'll understand." She winced when she shifted her body. "You're going to be graduating soon. That'll be a happy day for you. You'll get a job. Someday you'll get married and then you'll probably move away from the area."

"I'm not planning to get married."

Wanda smiled. "How many times I've heard people say that. You'll get married. I know you will. When you do and you move away, there's no guarantee what your mother will do."

"I thought you two were going to live together in a house someday."

"I know she's always talked about us doing that, but I don't think that'll happen. Pa's gone now. I've no one but Frank. I know what he's like, but I don't want to face life alone."

"You'll always have my mom," Adam said. "And even if I do move away, I'll always be there for you."

Her face softened. "You don't know how much it pleases me to hear you say that."

"How long are you going to put up with Frank?" Adam blurted out. "When do you say enough is enough? You living alone isn't good, but isn't it better than living each day not knowing whether Frank is going to beat you up?"

Several long moments passed before she replied. "Hearing you talk like that makes me realize you're not that little boy anymore I first saw getting off a Greyhound bus."

"That was a long time ago."

"I know, and you've grown up so fast. Like Pa would say, 'That Butch, he's a man now.'" She smiled. "You're more mature than I ever was at your age. You're going to be wise for your years just like your grandfather." Moving slowly and deliberately, she sat up. "What you're saying about living life not knowing when the next time Frank…I guess I never wanted to look at it that way."

"Do you love him?"

She waited for a long time before answering. "I used to and I think I still do, but not in the same way. So much has changed this past year. I'm so tired."

Adam stayed for another fifteen minutes. They talked mainly about his upcoming graduation. Wanda shared how proud she was of him, adding that his grandfather would be also. "He's probably looking down upon you right now and smiling."

"I hope so." Adam got up to leave.

"I know so," Wanda replied and then added, "I'll think about what you said, okay?"

"Sure, okay," he replied, not convinced that she meant it.

* * *

Frank ordered another beer. For nearly six hours he had been sitting in the B & B Bar talking with Charlie, the bartender. Every now and then, he would get up and play a game of pool, or take a piss break. "Goddamn," Frank bragged, "ya should've seen how I smooth talked her into not kickin' me out."

"What did you do? Buy her flowers or something?" Charlie asked as he wiped the counter.

"Ya nuts? Hell, I just promised that I wouldn't slap her around anymore."

"And she bought it?"

"Ya goddamn right she did." Frank picked up his bottle of beer and tipped it toward the bartender. "Charlie, this one's for the road."

"You'll be home before nine tonight."

"Yeah, that should make my old lady pleased. She'll think I've turned over a new leaf or some goddamn thing like that."

"Ah, women, they like it when we keep them guessing. That way they'll think we're mysterious."

Frank laughed. "Charlie, you're full of shit."

"And you're full of beer. Hey, it's dark out now. Do you think you'll find your way home? Maybe, you want a flashlight or something?"

"Get the hell out of here," Frank said, pretending he was going to throw the bottle at him.

"I'm going. I'm going."

Frank finished his beer. "See ya tomorrow night, Charlie," he yelled as he headed for the door.

The mild night air felt invigorating to Frank. When he walked passed Andy's Dinner, he looked in the window at a short, balding man playing the pinball machine. After crossing the street, he glanced in the window at Kass' Drug Store and saw Kass at the soda fountain talking with a couple of kids. All three were laughing and appearing to be having a good time.

Frank knew that he would soon be walking by the empty lot next to Skelly's Liquor Store. No matter how many times he had passed by it, it still stirred up angry feelings about that night he was beaten. As he approached, he noticed someone in a leather jacket walk into the parking lot. Frank blinked a couple of times to make sure it was the person he thought it was. Ever since his friend, Dale, had told him that it was Danny Logan who gave him his beating, he had made it a point to find out who he was. When he found out that Danny's father worked at the hardware store, the rest was easy. Asking around, he was told where the Logans lived. He spent an entire afternoon one day watching the house until Danny came out. Frank had followed him from a distance. When Danny stopped to have a cigarette, Frank slipped into a doorway of a store and watched. He felt as if he was on one of his reconnaissance missions he used to have in the service. Frank remembered what his lieutenant was fond of saying. *Study your enemy. Get to know him.*

"Hey, stupid!" Frank called out.

Danny Logan instinctively looked around to see who was

yelling. As soon as he saw who it was, he stopped and grinned. He let Frank walk up to within ten feet of him as he stood waiting, his thumbs hooked in his jacket pockets. "Well, if it ain't the old man, Frankie. That's your name, ain't it?"

"And you're the goddamn punk who jumped me with some of your friends."

"Hey, man, ya got me wrong. It wasn't me. Ya must've been dreamin' in your old age."

"It was ya, goddamn it!" Adrenaline surged through his body.

"So, what do ya want old man? More of the same?"

"I don't see any of your friends around. Not so tough now, are ya?"

"Tough enough to take ya on old man."

"So do it."

"Hey, man, not here." Danny gestured toward the back of the parking lot. "Step into my office. More private back there. Or maybe you're too scared of the dark, Frankie. Maybe you're afraid the bogeyman will be back there."

Frank followed Danny as he walked further into the lot. Within moments they had moved into the almost exact spot where Frank had been beaten. They weren't more than five feet apart now.

"Hey, old man, remember what happened here? Me and a couple of my friends played some baseball."

Frank saw Danny reach inside his jacket. *Go ahead punk. Pull out your switchblade. I've got somethin' for ya*. Reaching into his coat pocket, Frank took out the iron bar. "What do ya say I play a little goddamn baseball with this?"

Danny glanced at the iron bar and sneered. "Hey, Frankie, that night was only the minor league. Tonight's goin' to be the big league."

"What the hell?" Frank cried as soon as he saw the gun Danny was pointing at him.

"Well, Frankie, ya got your thing and I got mine. We're goin' to have some fun." He gestured toward the ground. "On your knees and start begging for—"

Frank lunged. In the fracas, the iron bar dropped onto the ground, but he didn't care. He tried to twist Danny's wrist to make him drop the gun. They tussled back and forth, nearly falling down. Frank's sheer bulk was in his favor though, and he slammed Danny into the brick wall of the liquor store. Danny held onto the gun, but Frank's anger drove him like a madman. He was winning and he knew it. The second time he slammed Danny into the wall, the gun went off.

Chapter 54

Frank felt Danny's body go limp. He stepped back in horror as Danny staggered back against the wall of the liquor store. With one hand gripping his stomach, Danny's other hand tried to grab hold of the brick wall behind him. Frank watched as Danny slid slowly to the ground, finding it curious how he ended up - sitting, leaning up against the wall with his legs sprawled out in front of him.

Frank's tongue slid across his lips. He tried to swallow but couldn't. *Jesus, I wish I had a beer.* For one insane moment, he thought about going back to B & B's. Danny's moan brought him back to reality. After glancing around to make sure nobody was in sight, he checked Danny to see where the kid had been shot. When he pulled Danny's jacket open, his hand touched something warm and sticky. Jerking his hand back, he instinctively wiped the blood on his pants. "Goddamn belly wound." He knew from his training in the military that that was the worst kind of wound to have; it required immediate attention. Danny moaned again as his head moved to one side. Frank strained to hear his words, but heard nothing other than the sounds of traffic coming from Broadway.

It was only when Frank stood up that he realized he had the gun in his hand. He couldn't remember how he got it. The whole struggle had happened so fast. His first impulse was to toss the gun away. His mind raced as to what he should do. Danny moaned again; not as loud this time. Frank knew he shouldn't stay and he wasn't about to go for help. *Hell, nobody would believe me. They'd accuse me of shootin' the kid.* "Goddamn it, it was self defense," he muttered. He put the gun in his coat pocket and went around to the back of the liquor store to the alley. All he could think of was getting home without being seen.

Coming out of the alley onto a side street, Frank headed back toward Broadway. He walked quickly to the entrance of the apartment building, climbed the stairs to the first floor, and hurried to the back apartment. Closing the door quietly behind him, he stood in the dark trying to catch his breath. Beads of sweat ran down his temples. His head pounded. His hands trembled. He needed a beer and a smoke. Feeling his way through the living room, he nearly stumbled over a chair.

Without turning on the kitchen light, he inched his way to the refrigerator. After getting a bottle of beer, he rummaged through a drawer until he found the opener, and sat down at the kitchen table. Opening the bottle, he guzzled half of it, and then fumbled around for his cigarettes. He lit a cigarette and took a couple of deep drags. Quickly finishing the rest of his beer, he went to the refrigerator for a second. Sitting in the dark, he replayed in his mind the events of the past half hour.

Damn punk deserved it. Who does he think he is pullin' a gun on me? Frank took a couple swallows of beer. *How the hell did Danny happen to be there when I walked by?* He raised the bottle to his mouth and then set it down again. His mind went back to the night he slapped Wanda around. He had seen Danny and Adam the next afternoon talking in front of that same liquor store. *Goddamn! Butchie must've set me up again. Son'n'bitch, he and Danny Logan planned it just like the last time.* Frank took a couple drags off his cigarette, inhaling deeply. *What do ya know, Butchie? It didn't turn out the way ya planned it.* Feeling the weight of the gun in his coat pocket, he was glad he had kept it.

* * *

Danny's body wasn't discovered until the early hours of the next morning. A cab driver found the body when he pulled into the parking lot to have a cup of coffee and a donut. The cabby, visibly shaken by what he had come upon, told the police that at first he thought the kid was sleeping.

"I sat there eating my donut and drinking my coffee looking at this kid. Figured he was sleeping one off. I see a lot of that stuff in the early morning. I finished my donut and pretty soon started feeling sorry for the kid. Figured his parents must be worried. I got kids. I know what it's like. So I get out and go over. I say, 'Hey, kid! Wake up!' Figured I'd give him the rest of my coffee. And if he's decent with me, maybe give him a ride home if it ain't too far away. I take a good look, and Jesus, I see all this blood. Figured he'd been knifed. Didn't know he'd been shot. You better believe, I busted my butt to get to the nearest phone and called you guys."

The medical examiner ruled that Danny had bled to death from a gunshot to his lower right abdomen. He estimated the time of death to be shortly after midnight. The police immediately ruled it a homicide but had no clues, no weapons, and no witnesses. What hadn't been made known in the paper, however, was the eight-inch iron bar they had found.

Danny Logan's funeral was held the following Monday. Besides his parents and some relatives, two of his former teachers came. Pete and Johnny were there. Danny's mother was so overcome with grief that when they closed the casket, she ran up to it, crying out, "No! No!"

* * *

Adam sat at the soda fountain talking with Kass the day after Danny Logan was buried. "I didn't like the guy, but I never would've expected something like this."

"I know what you mean," Kass said. "Such a tragic way to die. And so young. Just imagine how terrible it must be for his parents. Think of what they have to live with the rest of their lives." He paused. "Has your mother heard anything about the investigation?"

"Not much other than what she read in the newspaper." Adam thought about mentioning the iron bar the police had found next to Danny's body. His mother, however, asked him to keep it to himself because the detective made her promise not to tell anyone. "If the word gets out about that bar they'll never tell me anything anymore," his mother had told him. Adam promised her that he would keep it to himself. "One of the detectives told my mom that they are really stumped. They have no suspects and no witnesses have come forth."

"I heard that the police were talking to a couple of kids that Danny hung around with, but nothing came of it," Kass said.

The cowbell clanged. Mick and Howie came in. Kass smiled warmly to welcome them as they sat down next to Adam.

"Hello, boys, do you want a Coke?"

"Sounds good," Mick said.

"And how about you, Howie?"

"Sure," Howie responded quietly.

"You and Kass solving all the problems of the world?" Mick asked Adam.

"We were talking about Danny Logan."

"Oh, yeah. Everyone at school was talking about it."

Kass served Mick his Coke. "I knew Danny as a youngster. I could see he was headed in the wrong direction then. A couple of times I caught him taking candy bars and other things from the store. Finally, I had to tell him he was no longer welcomed here."

"Did you ever try to talk to him?" Mick asked.

"Oh, sure, but I got nowhere. He always thought he had all the answers."

"I heard you went to his funeral."

"Yes, I wanted to pay my respects and give support to his parents. He was a troubled boy, but he didn't deserve to die."

* * *

Frank aimed the gun at the host of the afternoon television game show. "Bang! I got ya, ya son'n'bitch." He had been steadily drinking ever since Danny's death. His mood swings were increasingly becoming worse, and his seething anger grew whenever Wanda would mention Adam and his upcoming graduation.

Chapter 55

Wanda always thought of herself as the big sister that Virg could lean on in times of trouble. "Wanda's the strong one in the family," their father always said of his oldest daughter. "She's just like her mother."

Having a deep inner strength was something that Wanda took pride in. It was also her way of keeping her mother close to her. Though she had never shared it with anyone, she always privately believed that her fortitude had been passed onto her through her mother. By being strong, Wanda felt she was paying homage to her mother's memory. But lately, she wasn't feeling very strong. She felt exhausted by the energy spent in dealing with Frank and his frequent mood swings. He frightened her, but she was more fearful of failing to live up to her mother's legacy. If she was going to keep that alive, she instinctively knew that she now needed to lean on her sister.

On Monday evening, after Frank had left the apartment, Wanda picked up the phone and dialed her sister's number. Although sure Frank would spend the evening at the bar, she kept glancing toward the door and listening, worried that he might return unexpectedly. If he found her on the phone, she knew he would demand to know who she was talking to and what they were discussing. If he were in a good mood, he would yell for a while and then let it go. If he wasn't, he would relentlessly interrogate her while making wild accusations. One night he had accused her of plotting against him. When she said she didn't understand what he was talking about, he had slapped her a couple of times. "Ya damn well know what I'm gettin' at." Just as she became terrified that she was going to receive a severe beating, he abruptly quit and decided to watch television. A few nights later, he came close to slapping her again when he came home early, walking in on her talking on the phone. She tried to explain that she was talking to a woman co-worker about a problem at work. "Don't give me that shit," he yelled as he grabbed the phone from her and slammed it down on the receiver. For the next half hour he screamed and raved at her, accusing her of seeing other men and calling her a whore. Less than an hour later he began sweet-talking her, telling her he wanted to make love. Although she was emotionally spent and in physical pain because of her back, she dared not refuse. She knew it was more of a demand than a request.

Now, as she stood at the phone waiting for Virg to answer, she thought about how repulsed she had felt when Frank made love to her that night. His breath smelled of beer and cigarettes. His unshaven face nearly rubbed her skin off. When she had moaned because of the severe pains in her back, Frank had assumed something different. "I guess ya needed me tonight," he had bragged after it was over. As she waited for her sister to answer the phone, her body shuddered as she tried to erase the awful memories of that night.

"I've got to come over and talk to you," Wanda hurriedly said as soon as Virg answered. "Are you going to be home for awhile?"

"Sure. Are you okay?"

"We'll talk when I get there." After hanging up, she wrote a note to Frank explaining that she had to borrow some coffee from her sister and that she would be back in a few minutes. If Frank came home in the meantime and questioned why it took so long, she would explain that Virg wanted to talk about Pa.

As soon as Wanda knocked on her sister's door, Virg opened it. "Come on in. I've been waiting for you."

"I need to talk to you," Wanda said after her sister had shut the door. "Could we sit at the kitchen table?" She took a deep breath. "Is anybody else home?"

"No, Butch is at work and Oscar went out. You look tired. Would you like a cup of coffee?"

"I can't stay long, but that sounds good."

"Okay, just a second." Virg got a couple of cups from the cupboard.

"I don't know what's gotten into Frank lately," Wanda said, wondering if her voice betrayed the depth of her emotional exhaustion and frayed nerves. In the past, she would have tried to hide such things from her sister. Now, she didn't care, and in truth, wanted her to know what she was feeling. "He scares me," she said, realizing she was admitting it to herself as well. "The other night we were in the living room. Frank was on the couch. I was in my chair, reading. He was watching some murder mystery on television. During the commercial he looked over at me and says, 'Cops are too dumb to solve anythin'.' Then he grins and says, 'I bet I could kill ya and get away with it.'"

"That's scary!" Virg cried, her face reflecting her shock. "Shouldn't you tell the police?"

"I don't know." The thought of getting the police involved terrified her because if they came and did nothing to Frank, she knew that he would see to it that she paid. "When I told him that he was frightening me, he laughed and said that he was only joking."

"You don't joke about that," Virg said angrily.

"I don't think he was joking either, but I was afraid to say anything more. I thought I knew him but I'm not sure anymore. Something's happened to change him."

"Do you have any idea what?"

"I wish I did."

"I know he's been drinking more, hasn't he?" Virg said.

"How do you know that?"

"This guy, his name is Charlie. He's a bartender down at B & B's. It's the bar that Frank goes to all the time."

"Frank's talked about him. He doesn't sound like someone I'd like."

"Believe me, you wouldn't. He's a first class jerk. Acts like he's God's gift to women. He came in the other night for a sandwich. Frank must have told him that you and I were sisters. After I served him his coffee, he mentioned that he and Frank are becoming good buddies."

"I wish Frank wouldn't hang around people like him. Is this Charlie married?"

"He was at one time. I just put two and two together and figured that since Charlie said he was seeing Frank a lot, that Frank must be drinking more."

"It seems like that's all he does."

"Where does he get the money?"

"He's taken all the spare money I'd saved," she said, breaking eye contact. "I can't trust him anymore."

"I never trusted him in the first place. Do you need some money?"

"No," Wanda said, deeply moved that her sister had offered. "I've managed to put a little aside."

"I hope you put it in a safe place."

"He won't find it this time." Wanda managed to smile even though the aching in her back had increased. "I've got a new hiding place."

"That's got to be terrible. Having to hide your money and living in fear."

"He's so moody. I've got to watch everything I say. It's just so tense around the apartment all the time." She told of Frank's reaction whenever she's on the telephone. "I don't know how much more of this I can take."

"Why don't you move in with us for awhile?"

"Oh, I couldn't do that! I'd be afraid of what he'd do. He'd blame you and Butch. Moving out wouldn't work. I'd be worried about the two of you then."

"I tell you what," Virg said, revealing an element of strength in her voice that Wanda found comforting. "I'll check in on you every night just to see that you're okay." When Wanda started to protest, Virg told her to listen for a moment before saying no. "I'll make up some reason for stopping. Even if he gets suspicious, he'll know that I'm aware that something's going on. Maybe then, he won't try anything."

Although Wanda was worried about her sister's plan, she was too tired to offer any further arguments. It felt good to have someone looking after her. She thought back to the years she and Frank had been married, and tried to think of a single occasion where she felt that he really cared about her. When she realized she couldn't name one time, she felt like crying. She looked at her sister and spoke her name. Virg looked at her with such compassion that Wanda could barely speak above a whisper. "I'm afraid I made a big mistake letting Frank come back this time."

Chapter 56

For the next two evenings, Virg stopped at her sister's apartment before going to work. The first night she used the excuse that she was returning a magazine. Frank sat watching television and drinking beer, glancing over at them every now and then until they left the room to go into the kitchen to have a cup of coffee. The next evening when Virg dropped in, he glared at her from the couch.

"What the hell are ya doin'?" he asked sarcastically.

"What do you mean?" Virg said, not being intimidated by Frank's tone.

"What I goddamn mean is that you're checkin' up on me!" He looked over at Wanda who was sitting passively, her eyes downcast. "What the hell has she been tellin' ya?"

"Nothing." Virg kept her voice calm as her heart pounded against her chest.

With nostrils flaring and big-yellowed teeth, Frank looked like an angry, ugly horse. "Don't give me that shit! I don't goddamn believe ya. Ya think I'm goin' to slap her around some more, don't ya? So what if I do? It's none of your goddamn business."

"You better not touch her if you know what's good for you!" Virg warned.

For a moment, Frank looked like he was going to get up from the couch. If he came after her, she wasn't sure what she would do. If he did come, he would know he had been in a fight.

"Get the hell outta my house!" he yelled.

"I'm going. But if you ever lay another hand on my sister, I swear to God, you'll regret it!"

"What are ya goin' to do? Get Butchie after me? That damn no good son'n—"

"Don't you ever refer to my son in that way!" she cried, her heart pounding. "He's a better man than you'll ever be!"

Fury erupted in Frank's eyes, but he didn't move or utter a word.

Virg turned to leave, but stopped. "Don't you forget, I'm on to you. Touch my sister again and so help me God, I'll talk to my cop friends. They'll know what to do with you." Having said her piece, she walked out.

Once out in the hallway, she took a deep breath. On the way back to her apartment, an overwhelming sense of satisfaction came upon her as she recalled when Frank swallowed his cocky grin as soon as she had mentioned the police.

* * *

Before Adam left for school on Thursday morning, his mother asked if he would check on Wanda.

"I'd go myself, but I have to work over the supper hour at Andy's tonight."

"Won't Frank be home?"

"You don't have to worry about him being there. It's Thursday and Wanda says he always goes down to the bar for happy hour."

On their walk to school that morning, Adam reminded Mick and Howie that the three of them were getting together that evening to study for the chemistry test. "We can study at my place. We'll have the whole place to ourselves."

"Are you going to have any food for us?" Howie asked. "I study better that way."

"You'll have food," Adam replied, glad that Howie seemed to be getting back to his normal self. Both he and Mick had been so worried that they asked Kass to talk to him. When they told Howie about Kass' offer to talk, he was reluctant and a little angry, but he agreed. The next day he went to see him. Whatever Kass said, it worked. A couple of days later, Howie cracked a couple of jokes on the way to school. He even mentioned that since time was running out before graduation, they needed to come up with something to be remembered for by future classes. Mick was so happy about Howie's "recovery", that he gave him a bear hug.

* * *

Frank had been drinking steadily since ten that Thursday morning. By early afternoon, there was only one bottle of beer left in the refrigerator. He went to the cupboard and took down the tin can where Wanda kept the money. He found it full of tea bags. "Goddamn ya, Wanda!" He threw the can on the floor, scattering the tea bags.

Angrily, he began going through the cupboards like a madman, tossing things on the floor. He opened cereal boxes and dumped the contents out, thinking that she could have hidden the money in them. With each shelf he emptied, he angrily repeated his litany of fury. Ever since Virg had threatened him about talking to the police, Wanda had acted more boldly. Last night, she had really gotten him angry when he asked her to make him a sandwich. She told him that she had already made him supper earlier and that she was too tired to do anything more. He was mad enough to clobber her, but didn't. *Maybe I lost yesterday, but I sure as hell ain't goin' to lose today*. He was determined to find the money.

After leaving the kitchen in shambles, he went into the bedroom and began pulling out drawers and dumping their contents on the floor. He went into the closet and tore open the pockets of any of her clothes that were potential hiding places. When he had exhausted the number of places where she could have hidden the money, he stomped back into the living room, turned on the television, and plopped down on the couch. He hadn't found the money, but now had the gun with him. He tucked it between the cushions of the couch and waited.

* * *

"I thought you weren't coming until later," Adam said as he opened the door and found Mick standing next to Howie. Mick just smiled and shrugged.

Howie stepped in ahead of Mick. "He wasn't, but he said he didn't think there would be any food left." Howie's face expressed a mock dismay. "Can you imagine that? It's like he doesn't trust me."

Adam closed the door and walked into the kitchen after them. "I don't think we have to worry about food. My mom bought tons of it. There's lunchmeat in the refrigerator. We can make sandwiches when we're hungry. We have pop and potato chips, and all kinds of other snacks."

"Where are we studying?" Howie asked.

"Kitchen table."

Mick put his books on the table, pulled a chair out, and sat down. "Come on, Howie, sit your butt down. This should be a perfect place for you to study. You'll be closer to the frig." He slapped Howie on the back. "I'm sure glad you're back to your normal self. That stuff about Mattingale's desk was weighing on you on pretty heavy, wasn't it?"

"Yeah, it's still on my mind, but I guess I've got to be myself. Glad you guys told me to talk to Kass. He helped a lot."

For the next couple of hours, the three young men studied, traded wisecracks and talked about their girlfriends.

"What time is it?" Howie asked, "I'm ready for those sandwiches."

"Time for a break, anyway," Adam said, leaning back in his chair. He checked the clock. "Guys, I've got to go check on my aunt pretty soon. Don't let me forget."

"How's she been doing?" Howie asked as he made his sandwich.

"Okay, so far. My mom says that Frank's left her alone, but I don't know."

"What do you mean?" Mick asked.

"I guess he's been acting pretty weird lately." Adam reached for the lunchmeat and slapped a couple pieces between two slices of bread. "My mom thinks it's because he's drinking more."

Mick grabbed a handful of potato chips and passed the bag to Adam. "He likes his sauce, eh?"

"Yeah, he does. He goes to the bar every night."

"That's not good."

"I know. What do you say that we talk about something else?"

"Like what?" Howie asked.

"Like next week. Kass wants us to come down for a pregraduation celebration."

For the next half hour they managed only to get through half of the review questions in the first of the three chapters. Howie complained that at the rate they were going, it was going to take all night. They were in the middle of speculating how long of a test they thought Mr. Breck was going to give when they heard a muffled bang.

"What was that?" Mick asked.

"Maybe it was a car backfiring," Howie suggested.

"Maybe but it didn't come from the street," Adam said. "I better go check on my aunt just in case."

"We'll go with you."

The three of them walked back to Wanda's apartment. Adam knocked on the door but there was no response. He knocked again. "It's Adam. Is everything okay?"

"Butch, don't come in! He's got a gun!"

"Goddamn it! Shut up!"

"Shit, that's Frank," Adam muttered.

"Come on in, Butchie. The door ain't locked."

"I'm going in," Adam said, not wanting his friends or Frank to know how scared he was.

"I'll go with you," Mick said.

"Me, too."

"No, Howie, you go call the police." Adam waited until Howie turned the corner of the hallway before trying the door. His hands sweated and his heart pounded as he opened the door.

Frank sat on the couch holding a gun. Wanda was huddled on the chair to the left of him, terror written across her face. A few feet away from Wanda sat the television set, the screen shattered.

"Never did like that goddamn television program." Frank pointed the gun at the television and then back at the two boys standing just inside the room. "Hi, Butchie," he said, his voice sounding hollow. "And who the hell are ya?" he asked as he pointed the gun at the young man standing next to Adam.

"Adam's friend, Mick."

"Why in hell did ya bring him along, Butchie?" Frank sneered. "What's the matter, can't ya handle an old man like me alone?"

Adam tried to swallowed but couldn't. Wanda appeared paralyzed with fear. "I'm not here for any trouble. Just let me take her home with me."

Frank looked at Wanda and then scratched the back of his head with the barrel of the gun. "Hell, why should I? This is her home-goddamn-sweet home. Ya want to stay here, don't ya?" he asked her. When she didn't respond, Frank yelled, "Don't ya, goddamn it? Answer me!"

"Yes," Wanda replied, her voice barely above a whisper.

"See, Butchie. She doesn't want to go with ya." Frank pointed the gun to the entrance leading into the kitchen. "Ya two stand over there. And shut the goddamn door. Ya born in a barn or somethin'?"

Adam closed the door. Rushing Frank would be risky. He had to be distracted if there would be any chance of getting the gun away from him.

Frank glared at Adam. "Ya know ya always treated me like horseshit. Like I wasn't good enough for ya."

"I never—"

"Goddamn it. Don't lie to me!"

Adam could see that Mick was scared but there was something more. In the brief moment that Mick returned his look and their eyes met, he sensed that Mick was also trying to figure out what to do.

"Don't try anythin'," Frank snarled at Mick. "I saw ya lookin' at Butchie. I don't know ya so I sure as hell wouldn't like shootin' ya, but goddamn it, I will if ya try anythin'!"

"I won't."

"Goddamn right, ya won't! What do ya two think? I'm goddamn stupid or somethin'?" Frank waited for a response. "I know what the two of ya are thinkin'. Ya'd love to jump me and beat the shit out of me, wouldn't ya? Ya think I can't handle ya two, don't ya? If I handled a punk like Danny Logan, I sure as hell can handle ya."

Adam's adrenalin surged. "What's that about Danny?"

When Frank grinned, the light from the corner lamp reflected his stained yellow teeth.

How much time went by, Adam had no way of telling, but hoped the police would come soon. His legs felt wobbly and he wished he could sit down, but he didn't dare move.

Wanda finally broke the silence. “Please let them go,” she pleaded. “I’ll stay with you, Frank. I promise.”

“Always protectin’ the kid, ain’t ya? Butchie always came first in your life. Maybe…maybe I wasn’t good enough for ya. Maybe I ain’t good enough for anybody. Maybe I…” Frank stared at the gun he was holding. When he looked back up at them, his voice sounded unemotional and calm. “Maybe this is the answer.”

Adam’s fingernails dug into the palm of his hands as he watched Frank put the gun up to his mouth.

“Bang!” Frank yelled.

Wanda screamed.

Adam found himself recoiling and shutting his eyes momentarily like he used to do as a kid at parades when the soldiers fired their rifles.

Frank roared with laugher. He pointed the gun toward Adam and Mick. “If I go, we all go. How’s that for a graduation present, Butchie?”

“Frank,” Wanda pleaded as she started to get up.

“Goddamn it! Sit down!” Frank turned toward Wanda, and in that moment, the door flew open. Three police officers came barging in. One of them lunged at Frank and grabbed the hand holding the gun while the two others pointed their weapons at him.

“Drop it!” one of the officers shouted. “Drop it now!”

As soon as Frank dropped the gun, one of the other two officers was upon him as the third kept his gun trained on him. As Adam and Mick watched, the officers cuffed him without a struggle. “You’re under arrest.”

Frank looked stunned. “What did—”

“Shut up! When we want you to talk, we’ll tell you. I don’t want to hear nothing coming from that big trap of yours. Do you understand?”

Frank started to open his mouth again but stopped. While glaring at Adam, he nodded his head in compliance.

One of the officers asked Howie to come in. Howie told Adam and Mick that he and two other police officers had been out in the hallway. He said that he was down the hallway, but was close enough to hear most of everything going on. After the police took the statements of Wanda and of the three young men, they took Frank and left. Adam asked his friends if they could find his mother and tell her what happened. “Try down where she works. I’ll stay here until she comes.”

“Come on, Howie, let’s go,” Mick said.

After they left, Wanda and Adam decided to sit in the kitchen. “How’re you doing?” Adam asked after they sat down at the table.

“I’m still shaking. I was so scared.” She started to cry.

“I was scared, too,” he said, not sure how to comfort her.

They talked quietly about whether she was going to stay in her apartment tonight. He told her that she could sleep at their place, but she said no. When she said she would rather stay in her own apartment, he asked if she wanted him to stay with her.

“That’s nice, but I’ll be okay here.”

“You’re not going to let Frank back, are you?”

“No.”

As soon as Virg arrived, she rushed over to Wanda. The two of them hugged and both started crying. After a few minutes, they sat down at the table. Virg said she would make a pot of coffee.

Adam glanced over at Howie and Mick who were standing quietly off to one side, “Mom, we’re going back to the apartment. We still got some studying to do.”

“Okay, we can talk later. Mick and Howie told me what happened.” She smiled at her son’s friends. “Thank you so much.”

Both nodded in acknowledgment.

“See you later,” Adam said as he and his friends left.

“Wow!” Howie exclaimed as he sat down at the table in Adam’s apartment. “What a night! Those cops were standing outside the door just waiting for the right moment to come in.”

“You mean, they overheard everything that was said?” Adam asked, thinking about Frank’s mention of Danny Logan.

“That’s right.”

For the next hour the three of them talked about what happened. Finally, during a lull in the conversation, Howie looked at the unopened chemistry books in front of them. “You know, we should've asked one of those cops to write a note explaining to our teacher why we didn't study."

"The last thing I want to think about is chemistry," Mick said. "I don't know about you guys, but I'm exhausted. I'm going home and call Mary to let her know what happened."

"Yeah, I've had it too," Adam said, feeling a strong need to share what happened with Sue. As soon as his friends left, he planned to call Sue.

"Is there anything to eat?" Howie asked. "I'm hungry."

Chapter 57

On a cloudless, early June afternoon Adam drove out to the cemetery. He brought the package containing the pocket watch with him. Graduation was in two days and he was anxious to find out what the inscription read. His mother had asked if he wanted company but he declined, saying it was something he needed to do alone.

With the car windows down, he enjoyed the breeze swirling about the car's interior. Every so often, he would glance over at the small, brightly wrapped package sitting next to him. Driving over the bridge crossing the Mississippi River, he thought about his grandfather. Adam wasn't sure what he would feel when he stood at his grave. Stopped at a light, he picked up the package and held it for a moment, looking forward to sharing the opening of it with his grandfather. When he had made the decision months ago to open the package at his grandfather's grave, it seemed so long to wait. But now, in another twenty minutes, all the waiting would come to an end.

As Adam drove up to the cemetery's entrance and passed the massive wrought iron gates, he was struck by two emotions that were at odds with each other. One was a sense of peace brought on by the serenity of the grounds; he was happy that his grandfather was in such a restful place. The second emotion was a deep sense of sadness that his grandfather wouldn't be able to come home with him when he left.

He drove slowly by elaborately sculptured granite monuments with the names of the dead chiseled upon them. How family and friends must have wanted their loved ones to be remembered for all of eternity. Throughout the cemetery huge oak trees stood watch over the dead.

He looked for the civil war cannon that his mother had told him would be at a point in the road where the road divided, going in different directions. He was to keep to the right. "It's not too far from the canon," his mother told him. "Maybe a couple of blocks. You'll know it when you get there. Two gigantic oak trees are on the other side of the road."

Adam hadn't been out to the cemetery since the funeral. Parking the car across from the oak trees, he took the package and walked to where he thought his grandfather was buried remembering that the grave was near a tall evergreen. Up ahead, he saw a couple of evergreens. He walked toward the larger one.

Upon finding his grandfather's grave, he set upright a small bouquet of fresh daisies in a plastic green container that had fallen over. *Who are they from?*

"Hello, Grandpa. It's Butch. I've come…" Adam glanced around to make sure he was alone. "Grandpa, I've come to open your graduation present. I thought you'd like it if I opened it here with you." He didn't know if he should expect to hear his grandfather's voice, but needed to express his feelings out loud. He had heard about people talking to loved ones while visiting their graves. He always thought that strange. That is, until now. Now, it seemed perfectly natural.

"I don't know why I haven't been out before this, Grandpa. I'm sorry. I guess I just couldn't bring myself to do it." He chewed on his lower lip. "I miss you," he said softly. "I wish you could be at my graduation." He wiped the corner of his eyes and cleared his throat. "Grandpa, this past year really has been something, hasn't it? So much has happened since you…" He swallowed hard, took a couple of deep breaths, and began again; this time in a whisper. "So much has happened since you died. Grandpa, I hope you're happy and that you're with Grandma. I never knew her, but I know you loved her a lot." A car on the gravel road distracted him. He waited, listening, wondering if it would stop. While waiting, he studied the bronze marker. *Paul M. Kurtz. 1890 - 1959.* The engraving of a grandfather's clock in one corner of the marker had been his idea. When the sound of the car's wheels crunching the gravel grew fainter, he breathed a sigh of relief.

"Grandpa, you'll be glad to know that Wanda has decided that she's had enough of Frank. She's doing a lot better, too. With him out of the picture, she's had a chance to think clearer. Mom says she's going to be talking to a lawyer about a divorce."

Pausing, he wondered if it was necessary to tell the whole story. He figured that his grandfather somehow knew what had happened in the apartment with Frank and the gun. "I suppose you also know that the police charged Frank in the death of Danny Logan. They came back with a search warrant and found a pair of Frank's pants stuffed in a corner of his closet with Danny's blood on them."

The sound of a plane overhead caught his attention. It was off in the horizon. He watched until it grew smaller and smaller. When it finally disappeared from sight, he reached into his pocket and took out the package.

"Do you see how nicely your gift is wrapped? Doctor Jairvus did a great job. He's a nice man and he liked you." Adam looked around, making sure he was still alone in that section of the cemetery. Some people stood in another section, but were too far away to see what he was about to do. "Well, Grandpa, I'm going to open it now."

Tearing off the paper, he uncovered a rich emerald colored felt case. After stuffing the wrapping paper in his pocket, he opened the case. The pocket watch looked elegant lying inside the case's red felt interior. A gold chain matching the color of the watch was attached to the watch's stem. He didn't remember seeing the chain before. "Look at this, Grandpa. I bet it's from Doctor Jairvus." Adam put the case in his shirt pocket, and pressed the watch's side hinge. The cover popped open, and he, positioning it to catch the lettering at just the right angle, had to squint to read the inscription. The stylized letters, though worn, were readable.

Cast your bread upon the waters.

He read the words out loud and then read them again. He stood for a long time, studying the inscription, reading it out loud several times. "Grandpa, I don't understand. What does this mean? Why is this so important?"

Adam remained at the grave for another fifteen minutes hoping that the answer to the inscription's meaning would come. During that time he wound the watch's stem. "See, it works," he said, holding the face of the watch toward the grave marker. "The second hand is moving. And I didn't..." He blinked back tears. Clearing his throat, he took a deep breath. "I didn't overwind it like you taught me never to do." For the next few minutes, his thoughts went back to when he and his grandfather took walks together. He closed his eyes, imagining him and his grandfather walking hand-in-hand. Before saying good-bye, he promised he'd be back again to visit, and soon. "I'll be wearing this watch during graduation on Thursday and I'll be thinking of you."

Adam stopped a couple of times and looked back at his grandfather's grave. Once in the car, he put the key in the ignition, but sat there not wanting to leave. Looking at the inscription again, he felt frustrated that he didn't know what it meant. He looked toward the spot where the green container of daisies stood by his grandfather's marker. "I'll see you, Grandpa," he whispered as he started the car. Glad he had come, driving out the cemetery gates, he wished he knew what the inscription meant.

He would stop at Kass', hoping that Kass might have an idea what the inscription meant. He looked forward to being with Sue that evening. She knew that he was going out to the cemetery this afternoon. When he had asked if she would like to come also, she said she was honored, but felt that it was something he should do alone. As he thought about it now, she was right.

After parking on the side street, he walked the half block to the drugstore. As soon as he was in the store, he saw a banner taped to the wall-length mirror behind the soda fountain.

Congratulations: Mick - Adam - Howie.

He walked over, sat down on a stool, and waited for Kass to finish with a customer. "Adam, I'll be there in a minute," Kass said. "Make yourself comfortable."

It was nearly five minutes before Kass was able to come over, taking his place behind the soda fountain. "Sorry, but that was Mrs. Schmitz and she always has lots of questions about her ailments."

Adam pointed to the banner. "That's great. Thanks."

Kass' eyes sparkled with joy. "It's not every day that I have three friends graduate from high school." He looked back at the neatly stenciled lettering. "I did that myself last night." He paused to admire his work for a moment before turning back to Adam. "Do you want anything while we're waiting for Mick and

Howie?"

"No, thanks." Adam took out the watch. "Can I share something with you?"

"Of course, what are friends for? But just a minute."

Adam watched Kass go to the front cash register and have a brief conversation with his assistant. Kass then walk over to the other clerk who was straightening out magazines in the rack by the front window. With both, he had pointed toward Adam. When he came back, he explained, "I told them they're to handle the customers. I'm not to be disturbed because I've a friend who wants to talk with me. So tell me, what's on your mind?"

He shared with Kass about driving out to the cemetery, unwrapping the package containing the pocket watch, and reading the inscription. "The trouble is I don't understand what it means."

"May I ask what it says?"

"I was hoping you would." Adam reached out to hand the pocket watch to Kass.

"Wait," Kass said, holding up his hand. Adam looked on as Kass wiped his hands on a towel before taking the watch. He handled it with care as he popped the lid open and squinted at the inscription. Reaching under the counter, he got a pair of eyeglasses.

"I never knew you wore glasses."

Kass chuckled. "Shhh. It'll be our secret." He slipped the glasses on and examined the inscription for a very long time. Adam was just about to say something when Kass spoke. "Oh, yes, now, I understand. Knowing your grandfather, this makes sense."

"Do you know what it means, then?" Adam felt a rush of hope surge through him.

"The words are from the Book of Writings."

"From what?"

"Just a minute." Kass handed him the watch. "I'll be right back." He went to the back room. Within a couple of minutes, he reappeared holding a black hardbound book. Before setting the book down, he took a towel from behind him and wiped off the counter. When he opened the book, he opened it from the back and began paging toward the front.

"You look like you're going through that backwards," Adam said.

"Hebrew books are read differently. Writing goes from right to left. This is the Tanach. In a sense, you might call it the Jewish bible. It contains the first five books of what Christians call the Old Testament."

Adam nodded. He hadn't attended church very often. The only thing he knew about the Bible was that the first book of the Bible was Genesis. As far as the other four books that Kass was talking about, he had no idea what they might be, but he trusted that what Kass was saying was true.

"In the Tanach, those five books are referred to as the Torah," Kass explained. "After that, comes the Prophets, and then comes what is referred to as the Book of Writings." He pointed to the pocket watch Adam was holding. "The inscription in that watch comes from the Book of Writings. Of course, in what you call the Old Testament, it is ascribed to Ecclesiastes."

"If you say so. I've never heard of it before."

"Not many people have. I thought I knew the entire verse but I wanted to check to make sure. Give me a second to find it." Adam watched as Kass turned several pages, stopped, and then moved his finger to the center of the page. "Ah, here it is. Should I read it in Hebrew, or should I translate it for you in English?" he asked with a twinkle in his eyes.

"English."

"I though so. It says, 'Cast your bread upon the waters, for you will find it after many days.'"

Adam sat for several moments in silence. "I'm sorry, but I still don't get it."

"Let me try and explain." Kass stroked his chin. "I don't know the exact Christian interpretation of this, but I think the traditional Jewish understanding is quite similar. These words are saying that when you practice charity, you will receive a reward from that which you practiced. Throw bread upon the water and it will always come back to you. In other words, you will benefit from what you sow. If you practice kindness and good will, you'll receive kindness and good will in return."

Adam thought about the promise his grandfather asked him to make concerning Frank. "Does that mean then that if you, ah, cast or throw anger upon the water, anger will come back to you?"

"Yes, you could say that."

"So, when my grandfather found the inscription in the watch, he must've been reminded of that. He must've known what those words meant."

"I know he did. Did he talk much about the Bible?"

"I don't remember him doing it."

"Well, your grandfather may have seldom talked about it, but he certainly knew his bible. I can vouch for that. He and I had a conversation many years ago about some of the terrible things that had happened in the world during our lifetimes. We had a spirited debate about how God could allow such bad things to happen if God is supposed to be loving and just."

"What side did my grandfather take?"

Kass closed the book and moved it to one side. "I'm afraid that, at the time, he spoke against God as a loving God." He was quiet for a moment and then spoke with a gentle tenderness. "It was evident that he had some painful experiences in his life. I tell you, though, I was very impressed with his biblical knowledge. So I suspect, when he found that pocket watch, and it so happened to have that particular inscription, he may have felt that God was touching him upon the shoulder."

"I know it changed him. It was important to him not to let my anger with Frank get the best of me."

"Your grandfather was right. He didn't want you to be known for your anger, and I suspect he, himself, tried to change because he realized how *his* anger was coming out. I'm sure he didn't want to be remembered for being just an angry old man."

"Is what we're talking about something like what we were talking about before? What we leave behind for others? Is casting your bread upon the waters like leaving a legacy?"

"Oh, yes, we all leave legacies behind. I believe your grandfather wanted to make sure you didn't cast anger upon life and leave that behind as your legacy. Look at Danny Logan and Frank. Those poor souls were a generation apart but so much alike. What they cast upon the waters came back to them. It killed Danny and put Frank in jail."

The cowbell clanged. Howie's excited voice rang through

the store.

"Wow!" Howie pointed to the banner behind the soda fountain. "Will you look at that!" he exclaimed as he and Mick sat next to Adam. He studied the banner for a moment. "Hey, how come my name is last?"

Kass chuckled. "Why, we always save the best for last."

"Finally I'm being recognized." He gave a thumbs-up to Kass and turned to Mick and Adam. "Hey, guys, I been meaning to talk to you about something. Kass, you can be in on this, too."

Kass bowed. "I feel honored."

"What's on your mind?" Adam asked.

"Look, we got two days before we graduate. This will be our last chance to be remembered at good old North High. So I got this plan for the graduation ceremony." Howie glanced at the three of them. "Now, the ceremony is still being planned for outdoors, right?"

"Right, and the weather is supposed to be great," Mick said.

"Good. With what I got in mind, all we need is a gas model air plane and some kite string."

Mick laughed. "What kind of hair brain scheme are you thinking of now?"

"I think he's trying to cast his bread upon the waters," Adam said. "Isn't that right, Kass?"

Mick and Howie gave each other a puzzled look as Kass nodded in agreement.

Visit
Second
Wind
Publishing

19942866R00191

Made in the USA
Charleston, SC
19 June 2013